SANCTUARY

by David Melde

* * *

SANCTUARY

By David Melde

First edition, July 2025. Cover design by Jamie Whyte.

ISBN 979-8-9931357-4-8

BRIGHT THREAD
BOOKS

A mythic imprint for transformative fiction

Table of Contents

CHAPTER ONE

Identity Crisis

I received a message from Captain Drake. "Attention, Din of battle! Assemble for Wandering City!"

I followed the Captain's link and found myself standing on an airstrip in Mendoza, Argentina. The late afternoon sun bathed the tarmac in gold, but my mind was far from admiring the scenery.

"Nice of you to join us, Lens," the Captain addressed me. "I've purchased maps showing where the Wandering City will be in the immediate future. Everybody stay loose, and let's win the treasure."

We took to the skies in an old, twin-engine Gooney Bird, its C-47 frame groaning under the stress of age. My thoughts, already tenuous, drifted further as the plane climbed. The blackouts I'd been experiencing loomed heavily in my mind, their causes just out of reach. The strong pamperos howled against us, battering the plane like an unrelenting storm. It felt as if we were careening through a roller coaster gone rogue, and the winds' sudden lifts and drops made me grip the wooden plank beneath me for dear life. My weapon lay unsteady in my hands, threatening rebellion.

Across from me, Temper sat on a matching wooden plank, his ever-present grin unshaken by the chaos. His thumbs-up gesture offered reassurance I didn't deserve. Our collective identity as the Din, a group of mercenary adventurers, was a tapestry stitched together by aspirations of fame and fortune. The Patagonian Desert, and all its secrets, awaited us. But the journey seemed intent on tearing us apart before we reached it.

The plane crested another hill, plunging into a sudden, violent gust of wind. The aircraft stayed together, but my weapon discharged. The shot rang out before I could even register what had happened. Temper's chest exploded in a spray of virtual blood. My best friend, dead. Just like that.

"Pause!" screamed Captain Drake.

"Mission paused," intoned a disembodied, female voice from the interface above, calm and unbothered. The storm stilled. Silence enveloped the cabin as the moment froze in place.

Captain's boots thudded against the floor as he approached me. His face, a mask of fury and disbelief, hovered too close for comfort. "Look at this mess, Go! Isn't Temper your best friend? You killed him! He's our solver, for fug's sake!"

"I... I know. I'm sorry," I stammered, words tripping over themselves in the mad dash to escape my mouth. "It was an accident. It won't happen again."

"It better not," Captain growled. "You're our lens, which is useful sometimes. But here? Now? You're a grunt, just like the rest of us. And we need our solver more than we need you. So, consider this your only warning: screw up like this again, and I'll toss you out of the plane myself. No parachute. Game Control, restart the mission!"

"Restarting mission," the voice replied. "Confirm choice."

"Confirmed," Captain snapped, not sparing me another glance.

We reset, flew south from Mendoza once again, and I gripped my weapon tightly, determined to avoid another mistake. The pamperos were less aggressive this time, our altitude just enough to subdue their bite. Temper sat across from me as before, his glare sharp enough to pierce my armor.

"You shot me in the chest!" he shouted over the wind, his grin now replaced by a scowl.

"It was a mistake," I yelled back. "I'm sorry."

"You're sorry? That's it? After this mission, I'm going to shoot you in the face! Then we'll be even."

"I only shot you in the chest. Don't be such a baby ab— "

The argument ended abruptly as the plane hit stronger turbulence, jolting us violently. My weapon discharged again, its bullet ripping through the canvas divider and embedding itself in our pilot's back. The plane spiraled into chaos, diving uncontrollably toward the valley below. Captain's voice cut through the storm, trying desperately to yell, "Pause!" but it was too late. Impact came swiftly, and we all died instantly.

Back at the Mendoza airport, our newly respawned crew shuffled around in heavy silence. Captain, his face a storm of rage and disbelief, turned his fury onto me. The torrent of words he wanted to shout never came; instead, his hands spoke volumes, strangling invisible foes that looked suspiciously like me. Eventually, his composure returned, but his smile was chilling.

"Go," he said evenly, stepping forward.

"Yes, Captain?" My voice cracked under the weight of impending doom. I would rather have had my head nailed to a wall, rather than stand there and see that smile.

"You will be cleaning hulls when we're home. How many and for how long depends entirely on you."

"Yes, Captain. Understood."

The mission restarted. Again.

We re-boarded the plane, and this time Captain confiscated my weapon. All I had left was my long knife, as Captain called it. "Short sword" would have been more accurate, but I wasn't in a position to argue semantics. An hour into the flight, the Wandering City appeared, nestled in the valley below. Its golden streets and gem-encrusted walls shimmered like a mirage, promising riches and danger in equal measure.

The Gooney Bird touched down on the valley floor, and Captain led the way across the scrubby terrain. At the city gates, mercenaries fired from the top of the wall, forcing us to take cover. Tracer muttered, "What the fug? This city's supposed to be deserted!"

Captain turned to me, his gaze accusing. "I wonder how they got here before us?"

I said nothing, pretending my knife-sword was suddenly fascinating.

He handed me back my weapon. "Go, I want you to run straight at the mercs with your gun blazing. Give the rest of us cover to reach the wall."

I looked at my weapon and then up at Captain. "You want me to run straight ahead at the mercs? Into their enemy fire? I'll be killed!"

Captain nodded. "That's the idea. Take one for the team and maybe you won't have to clean hulls when we get back home. We've reached the city, so from now on it's sudden death. Think of it this way, you'll make amends for getting us into this mess. Are you a Din? Are you ready to die for your fellow Dins?"

I hesitated, but his glare spurred me forward. Weapon blazing, I charged the mercenaries, screaming "CAMPBELL'S SOUP!" at the top of my lungs.

Out of the corner of my eye I saw the Dins cross open ground and reach the relative safety of the wall. The success of the mission was now up to them. My weapon clicked when it emptied of ammo, so I threw it to the ground. I stopped running as a dozen rifles fixed their sights on me. Dodging and weaving wasn't going to save me from the inevitable. Neither would yelling any more about Campbell's soup, which sounded good right about then. I could have used some of it to soothe me. I raised my knife-sword in defiance and heard the mercs' guns roar moments before the bullets punched into me. Even in game mode bullets hurt. "Son of a sea donk!" was the last thing I said.

Respawning back at the airport lounge, I ordered a Cosmic Cataclysm and reflected on my mistakes. Something deeper was wrong. I felt it in the cracks of my memory, in the way certain moments with Amy, my wife of over a century, surfaced not as recollections but as fragments. Lately, I had begun noticing gaps. Subtle lapses were occurring. Conversations I couldn't quite place. Reports I didn't remember filing. It was easy to dismiss them as stress or fatigue, but they were becoming harder to ignore. The memories were still there, but they felt misaligned, like puzzle pieces forced into the wrong frame. And beneath it all, a quiet dread was growing. Something was not adding up.

The lounge hummed with background noise, but I barely registered it. My Cosmic Cataclysm sat untouched, condensation sliding down the glass. The ice cubes had long since melted, diluting the vibrant purple to a mournful lavender. I stared at it, trying to anchor myself in the present. But the present kept slipping.

I kept replaying the mission in my head, the gun discharges, the crashes, the respawns. Three failures in a row. That was not like me. I was careful. Precise. I didn't make mistakes like that, not even under pressure. But this time, I had killed Temper, downed the pilot, and cost the Din their lead. Captain had confiscated my weapon, and I had not argued. I couldn't. Because deep down, I wasn't sure the mistakes were mine. Not entirely. They felt like echoes of someone else's reflexes, or worse, like my own instincts were misfiring. That was when the doubt started to spread.

Something wasn't right. These lapses were not just game glitches. They felt personal. Intentional. Like someone or something was trying to erase me.

They had started weeks ago. At first, I blamed post procedure settling. Neuroclones often experienced transient disorientation. Or maybe it was stress. I was now captain of the starship Paradise, steward to two million digital colonists. That kind of responsibility could fracture anyone. But the lapses kept happening. I would come to in the middle of conversations, missions, even meals, with no memory of how I got there. Sometimes the gaps lasted minutes. Sometimes hours. And yet I kept functioning. I kept performing. That was the most disturbing part.

I wasn't losing time. I was being overwritten.

Dr. Khatri had warned me. She said my neuro readings were anomalous. That the emulation had produced something she had never seen before. Echoes, she called them. I hadn't asked what that meant. I should have.

I closed my eyes and tried to trace the edges of the last lapse. Four hours gone. I had filed a report. Debriefed a squad. Even made a joke about the Dins. But I had not been there. Not really.

The only way I knew what had happened was by replaying it on my CoreLink. I could access it. I could watch it. But it felt hollow. Like surveillance footage of someone wearing my skin.

That was the problem. David and I shared identical memories. That was the design. The emulation had captured everything. There was no difference between what he knew and what I knew.

So why did some memories feel like turning points?

Why did I remember Amy's voice not just with clarity, but with consequence? Her laughter didn't just comfort me, it changed me. I remembered the shift in my chest, the way my breath caught, the way

I knew in that instant I would never be the same.

I opened my eyes and stared at the drink. The lavender swirl reminded me of the dress Amy wore to our anniversary dinner in Kyoto. I had planned that trip. I remembered the way she looked at me across the table, the way she touched my hand when I told her I would never stop choosing her. I didn't just remember the moment, I remembered becoming someone in it.

That was what unsettled me. Not the memory itself, but the way it reshaped me. If I was the neuroclone, I should have remembered that dinner as a turning point in his life. But I felt it as a turning point in mine. The shift was not just recalled, it was happening. That kind of transformation should not belong to a copy, should it?

Another detail. Another crack in the foundation.

Had the emulation failed to separate us cleanly? Or had something gone wrong, something deeper than a glitch?

The thought chilled me. What if the lapses were not errors? What if they were incursions?

I thought of newborns in maternity wards. Mix ups. Infants sent home with the wrong families. It happened. So why couldn't a similar error happen during emulation?

And then it hit me, not as a theory, but as a truth I had been circling for weeks.

I was not Go David. I was not the neuroclone. I was the original. David Schreiner. Misplaced. Misassigned. Misunderstood.

And all I wanted was to go home.

The world tilted sideways. My knees buckled as reality fractured around me. Every certainty I had built my identity upon crumbled like sand through my fingers. The vertigo was not just physical, it was existential. It reached into the marrow of me, twisting everything I thought I knew about who I was and why I had come.

A sudden noise jolted me. A large group of mercenaries respawned across the entire staging field. As they untangled themselves, I knew something big must have happened: something like an explosion that wiped out an entire unit of mercs, or maybe several units all at once. One of the freshly dead mercs muttered "I hate Dins!" as he helped his buddy to his feet. That brought a smile to my lips. Maybe we were winning.

Then I heard the familiar drone of twin engines approaching the airfield from the south. A speck in the sky grew larger as the C-47 appeared on the downward leg of the runway. The plane touched down, taxiing to a stop in front of the FBO on the far side of the ramp. I hustled over to join my crew. As I approached, I saw Temper jump down from the aft side door. On his head was a jewel-encrusted crown. Its gold rim glimmered in the sun. He smiled and waved me over. "Just like in Tortuga!" he shouted.

I stopped short as I remembered the time, years ago, when Tom, not Temper, and I went on the Tortuga hunt together. He had on a similar crown and the same, goofy grin on his face. It was before the emulation when our digital twins were not yet born, when I was still only one person, David Schreiner.

I watched Temper strut across the tarmac, that ridiculous crown perched on his head like he'd been born to wear it.

"Quite the haul," I said as he approached. "Captain pleased?"

"Pleased? He's ecstatic! We found the treasury chamber after you..." He made a dramatic gesture of bullets hitting his chest. "Well, after your heroic sacrifice. The mercs never saw us coming from below."

The others were unloading crates from the plane's cargo hold, laughing and slapping each other on the back. Their voices carried across the airfield, buoyant with victory. I should have felt it too, that post-mission high. Instead, I felt hollow.

"We need to talk," I said, grabbing Temper's arm. "Somewhere private."

His smile faltered. "What's wrong? Is it about shooting me? I was just giving you a hard time, you know I—"

"Not here."

I pulled him toward the empty hangar at the edge of the field. The massive space amplified our footsteps, each one echoing off corrugated metal walls. The smell of engine oil and dust hung in the air.

Temper stood near the bulkhead, arms folded, waiting. I didn't speak right away. I paced once, then turned to face him.

"I've been noticing things," I said. "The memory lapses. You know how Dr. Khatri's been trying to help me with them. But what if she can't?"

He didn't interrupt. Just watched me, calm and waiting for me to continue.

"Her expertise is in neurocloning. What if that's not what's wrong with me? What if the lapses aren't a flaw in the emulation, but something else. Some kind of interference."

I stepped closer. My voice was steady, but I could feel the pressure building behind it.

"Look at the mistakes I made today. I shot you. I killed the pilot. I nearly lost us the game. That's not me. I've never been like that before. It's almost like... it wasn't me who played with you today."

Temper's brow furrowed, just slightly.

"What if it was my Prime," I said. "David. What if his consciousness somehow leaked through. What if I'm not the neuroclone anymore."

I paused, searching his face for something, confirmation, resistance, anything.

"Babies get mixed up sometimes. They end up where they're not supposed to be. What if that's happening now. Maybe the emulation wasn't perfect. Not complete."

I swallowed.

"What I think is... I think I'm David. I don't know who it is back on Earth with Amy. But it should be me."

Temper's voice was quiet. "Even if you're right, what would you do?"

"I would go back."

"To Earth?"

"Yes."

Temper considered this for a moment. "Even if what you're saying were remotely possible, which it isn't, what exactly do you propose to do about it? File a complaint? 'Excuse me, I think I'm in the wrong body?' They'd laugh you out of the building."

"I'll petition the Emulation Court. They have protocols for suspected errors."

Temper laughed, a sharp, humorless sound. "They've never had a case like this. Never."

"Then I'll be the first."

He studied me, eyes narrowing. "You're serious."

"Dead serious."

"They'll never believe you."

I met his gaze steadily. "They will when they see the evidence."

CHAPTER TWO

Legal Battles

I paced my cottage in Paradise, mind racing over the revelation in Mendoza. The walls felt like a trap. The framed picture of Amy, my wife, or David's wife, stared back at me accusingly. I needed space. I needed perspective, something beyond the picture frame and the walls. Even the music box, Amy's final gift, felt silent this morning, its melody tucked away like a memory I wasn't ready to touch.

I closed my eyes, focused on Temper, and thought: Hellfire.

The quantum transition happened instantly. One moment I stood in my cottage; the next, I materialized in Hellfire's cargo bay in one of the service bots. The QE-comm link between our ships made travel instantaneous, though our vessels maintained a careful physical distance.

Through the open bay doors, I could see Paradise on the same course as Hellfire. The ship looked like an aluminum teardrop with three elegant prongs extending from its bow. Dim light reflected off its hull, creating a halo effect that seemed mockingly appropriate. Paradise carried two million souls. Hellfire carried just one: Temper Tom.

"Didn't expect to see you so soon after Mendoza," Temper said, not looking up from his workstation. Holographic star charts floated around him, calculations streaming across multiple displays.

"I couldn't stay there. Not with... everything."

Temper nodded, finally turning to face me. "How far out are we now?"

"Five months from Earth. One month from Point Alpha."

Point Alpha. The threshold beyond which consciousness transfer would become impossible. After that point, there would be no going back, no way to transfer my consciousness, or David's consciousness, back to Earth. The quantum entanglement between the ships and Earth would degrade too much for complex neural patterns to remain intact.

Standing in the cargo bay, with its doors open to the void of space, I felt a subtle shift in the air around me, as the experiment's steady warmth contrasted against the cold stillness beyond. The experiment's glow illuminated the bay, casting soft reflections on the instruments surrounding it. A miniature sun in the making. The reason our ships kept their distance.

"You're still planning to let it grow larger?" I asked, nodding toward the readings.

"Not until we're well past Point Omega. Too risky until both quantum links to Earth are severed." He adjusted some parameters on his display. "You're not here to talk about my star, Go."

"Don't call me that."

"What should I call you then? David?"

The name hung between us like a physical thing.

"I don't know anymore," I admitted.

I moved closer to the instrument array surrounding his sun. From here, I could see both Paradise and our route into the endless void beyond. Thirteen hundred years to Orion. A one-way journey into the future. Meanwhile, Earth continued spinning, life continued flowing. Amy continued living, with someone who might not be her husband.

"If I'm right, if I'm really David, then I've left her with a stranger."

Temper sighed. "And if you're wrong, you're just torturing yourself for nothing."

"How can I know for sure?"

"You can't. Not now. Point Alpha is four weeks away. After that, there's no going back regardless."

The distance between our ships seemed suddenly symbolic:

Paradise and Hellfire, separated by necessity and purpose. Just as I was now separated from my former life, floating in uncertainty.

"Sometimes I feel like I'm in both places at once," I said quietly. "Here on this journey, and back on Earth with her. Like I'm being torn apart across space."

Temper's reply was grim. "That's the price we all paid for this voyage. Except you might be paying it twice."

I raised my bot's hand towards the stars, as though the distance between our vessels, and the vast expanse back to Earth, could somehow be bridged.

"What would you do, if you were me?" I asked softly.

Temper didn't answer right away. His gaze stayed fixed on his experiment. I waited, but the silence stretched. Maybe there was no answer he could give. Maybe I already knew. I returned the service bot to its charging bay and thought of my cottage on board Paradise.

Temper's image dissolved. The transition was brief, like the pause of an indrawn breath, before reality shifted and settled again.

I opened my eyes to the familiar stone walls and lattice windows. The scent of primroses drifted through the open window, mingling with the faint smell of Amy's favorite: lavender. My cottage felt both like home and prison now.

My choice became clear in an instant. If I truly was David, the original, not the copy, I needed to know. And if I wasn't, I needed to stop this spiral of doubt before it consumed me completely.

I sat at my desk, running my fingers over the polished oak surface. The wood grain swirled in patterns that reminded me of stellar nurseries. How fitting.

"CoreLink, connect me to the Emulation Court on Earth, please."

CoreLink processed my request, a soft blue light pulsing around the edges of my desk. After a moment, a holographic interface materialized. The Court's logo, a stylized brain intersecting with a circuit board, rotated slowly above my desk.

"Emulation Court Services. How may I assist you?" The voice belonged to a middle-aged woman with close-cropped silver hair and eyes that seemed to evaluate me before I'd even spoken.

"I need to file a petition regarding a possible emulation error."

Her eyebrows lifted slightly. "Nature of the error?"

"Identity displacement. I believe I may be the original consciousness rather than the neuroclone."

The woman's professional demeanor slipped for just a moment. She leaned forward, the hologram distorting slightly with the movement.

"You're claiming to be a Prime misplaced into a neuroclone life?"

"Yes."

She tapped something on her end. "This would be unprecedented, Mr..."

"Schreiner. David Schreiner. Though my neuroclone designation is Go David."

"One moment, Mr. Schreiner." Her image froze while data scrolled rapidly beside her. When she returned, her expression had hardened into bureaucratic caution.

"I see you're currently aboard the Paradise spaceship, correct? Five months into the Orion voyage?"

"That's correct."

"And you're aware that Point Alpha will be reached in approximately four weeks, after which consciousness transfer becomes impossible?"

My throat tightened. "Yes, I'm aware."

She nodded, her fingers moving across an unseen interface. "Filing this type of petition requires significant evidence. What proof do you have that such an error occurred?"

"I'm not claiming access to lost data. I know the emulation was complete. This isn't about missing content. It's about how the memories behave. They're not passive. They're active. They're reshaping me. I feel them as origin points, not recollections. That shouldn't be possible for a neuroclone. But it's happening. And I don't think I'm the neuroclone."

"Couldn't these simply be programming artifacts? Neuroclones occasionally experience phantom memory fragments."

"They're not fragments. They're whole. Fully formed memories with intact emotional weight, sensory detail, even temporal continuity. They don't feel like echoes—they feel like origin points."

The clerk's expression remained skeptical, but she continued entering information. "The Court will require a full neural scan and comparative analysis with your baseline emulation pattern. This is not a simple process, Mr. Schreiner."

"I understand."

"Furthermore, given your location and the approaching Point Alpha threshold, this petition will need expedited processing." She paused, studying me. "I should inform you that in the Court's history, we've never had a confirmed case of Prime-Clone displacement. The technological safeguards make such an error virtually impossible."

"Virtually impossible isn't the same as actually impossible."

For the first time, her professional mask softened slightly. "No, it isn't. Your petition has been filed, reference number EC-23759-GL. A Court-appointed neural specialist will contact you within 48 hours to begin the verification process."

The hologram flickered as she prepared to disconnect.

"One more thing," she added. "Have you informed the Prime David Schreiner of this petition?"

The question hit me like a physical blow. "No."

"The Court will be required to notify him. Just so you're prepared."

The hologram disappeared, leaving me alone in my cottage with the weight of what I'd just done pressing down on my shoulders. I'd set something in motion that couldn't be undone. Soon, Earth would know. Amy would know.

And somewhere on Earth, a man who might be me would learn that his identity was being challenged by a copy of himself hurtling through space.

I sat back in my chair, feeling the weight of what I'd just initiated. This wasn't merely a legal petition, it was a claim to my very existence. If I won, I'd return to Earth, to Amy, to the life I believed was rightfully mine. We'd rebuild our connection, one genuine moment at a time. I'd feel real soil beneath my feet again, taste actual coffee instead of this perfect but hollow simulation.

But if I lost...

The thought froze in my mind. If I lost, I'd remain here, hurtling through space with the knowledge that my true self was living my life, holding my wife, walking through our garden. I'd face thirteen hundred years carrying the certainty that somewhere, light years away, someone else was living the only life I'd ever wanted. The digital walls of my cottage seemed to press closer, a beautiful prison containing a consciousness that might belong nowhere.

I touched Amy's photograph, tracing her smile with my finger.

"I have to know," I whispered to her image. "Even if the answer destroys me."

The hologram disappeared, leaving me alone with my decision. I stared at the empty space where the clerk had been, her final words echoing in my mind. The Court would notify him: notify David. My fingers drummed against the oak desk, anxiety building with each tap. Why wait for formal channels? If I truly was David Schreiner, trapped in a neuroclone's life, I deserved to confront him directly.

I squared my shoulders. "CoreLink, establish a direct communication line to David Schreiner on Earth."

My heart pounded as the connection initialized. The quantum link stretched across millions of miles, particles entangled despite the vast distance. The holographic display flickered twice before stabilizing.

David sat in our—his—study back on Earth. The room looked exactly as I remembered it: walnut bookshelves lining the walls, the antique globe in the corner, Amy's watercolor paintings beside the window. He wore the blue sweater Amy had knitted for our birthday three years ago. My sweater.

His eyes widened slightly. "Go? This is unexpected."

The sound of his voice, my voice, sent a chill through me. We were identical, down to the small scar above his left eyebrow from a childhood fall.

"We need to talk," I said.

His expression shifted, becoming guarded. "The Court contacted me twenty minutes ago. I was planning to reach out once I'd processed everything."

"I couldn't wait."

Silence stretched between us, taut and uncomfortable. The quantum connection hummed, bridging the impossible gap between Earth and my vessel.

"You think you're me," he said. Not a question. An accusation.

"I know the emulation was complete. Every memory, every neural pattern, transferred exactly as designed. But something's wrong. The memories aren't behaving like copies. They're behaving like causes.

Like they're shaping me from the inside out."

He leaned forward, eyes narrowing. "Explain."

"They're not passive. They're not stored data. They're active, recursive. I feel them as turning points: decisions I made, not ones I inherited. They carry emotional weight, sensory texture, even temporal continuity. That shouldn't be possible."

His face remained impassive. "There are documented cases of memory bleed. Phantom recollections. The brain, even a digital one, tries to fill in the gaps."

"This isn't bleed." I stood, pacing the tight confines of my cottage office. "These memories have structure. They're complete. And they're changing me."

"Go, listen to yourself." His voice softened, almost pitying. "You're five months into a thirteen-hundred-year journey. The isolation, the pressure of command. It's affecting your judgment."

"Don't patronize me."

"I'm trying to help. This petition won't change anything except cause pain for everyone involved. Especially Amy."

Amy. Her name hung between us.

"How is she?" I asked, unable to stop myself.

Something flickered across his face. Pain, guilt, I couldn't tell. "She's worried about you. About this petition."

I closed my eyes, trying to steady myself. The plan had been so clear: David would stay with Amy on Earth while his neuroclone journeyed to the stars with Temper Tom. A perfect solution to an impossible choice. Now everything had twisted into this nightmare of confused identity.

"Point Alpha is four weeks away," I said quietly. "After that, there's no going back. No way to transfer consciousness. If I'm right, if I'm really you, then you've stolen my life."

David's face hardened. "I know who I am. Do you?"

The connection terminated abruptly, leaving me alone with the ghost of his final question echoing in my cottage.

The holographic image of David faded, taking with it the warmth of my cottage. His final question lingered in the silence: "I know who I am. Do you?" My hands trembled as I straightened my uniform jacket. The bridge crew meeting had been scheduled weeks ago, long before my world tilted on its axis. Paradise wouldn't wait for my identity crisis to resolve.

CoreLink chimed softly. "Captain, the bridge crew is assembled in Conference Room A."

"Thank you. I'm on my way."

I took one of the driftway's paths through Terracore, rather than opting for any neural shortcuts. The driftway unfolded gently, guiding me toward a coastline that shimmered with crystal clear water. Waves lapped at the shore in a soothing rhythm; their sound composed entirely of carefully crafted code. The scent of salt hung in the air, faint but present, as if the simulation had borrowed it from some distant, perfect memory.

Symphony of Us played a mournful tune as I walked. The music had a calming effect, though it deepened my loss at the same time. The song was *"Quiet Ache,"* one of Amy's favorites from Eira Vale's debut album. Her voice carried a stillness that settled in the chest, each lyric a quiet thread pulled from the life I'd left behind:

If this was the calm before the break, Then let me be the quiet ache..

A sandy trail wound alongside the beach; its texture underfoot so detailed it could have fooled the senses. Further down the path, a child chased a bright red kite against the backdrop of the endless ocean sky, her laughter carried on a breeze that was no more real than the kite's flight. The digital sun cast a golden hue across the scene, its descent forever postponed unless dictated otherwise. I passed a young man sitting on the sand, sketching shapes in the grains that would vanish with the next wave. I nodded as I walked by, and he raised his hand in acknowledgment.

Two million souls under my care. Two million lives continuing in this flawless simulation, Terracore, while Paradise carried them safely across the void. Each driftway I walked was more than a path, it was a bridge between imagined perfection and the fragile hope that bound us all. Crew members passed, nodding respectfully, their expressions reflecting the confidence they saw in their captain. They couldn't see the storm raging inside me, hidden beneath the calm I projected.

Conference Room A hummed with quiet conversation when I entered. Lieutenant Rodriguez studied navigation charts while Maya Okafor reviewed engineering reports. Atsuko Yamamoto and Jamie Sullivan huddled over community integration protocols. Lieutenant

Chen monitored communications. Raj Mehta plotted our current trajectory on the star map. Victor Petrov stood near the door, his security officer's stance relaxed but vigilant.

Eight faces turned toward me as the door closed. Eight expressions of trust and expectation.

"Thank you all for coming." My voice sounded steadier than I felt. "As you know, we're approaching a significant milestone in our journey."

Maya nodded, her slate-gray eyes meeting mine. "Point Alpha in four weeks, Captain."

"Precisely." I activated the holographic display at the center of the table. A detailed organizational chart materialized, showing Paradise's current command structure alongside a proposed colonial governance model. "Today we begin planning the transition from shipboard authority to colonial self-governance."

Lieutenant Rodriguez leaned forward. "The Congregation model?"

"Yes. Similar to what worked on Earth after the corporate collapse." I expanded the holographic display. "Our mission parameters always included this transition. Paradise was never meant to remain under military-style command for thirteen hundred years."

Jamie Sullivan cleared his throat. "Captain, my department has concerns about timing. The colonists are still adapting to digital existence. Many are struggling with emotion mapping integration."

The words blurred before me as David's face superimposed itself over the hologram. I know who I am. Do you? I blinked hard, forcing myself back to the present.

"Captain?" Jamie's voice pulled me back.

"I'm sorry, could you repeat that?"

The bridge crew exchanged glances. This wasn't like me, like Go David, the decisive captain they'd come to rely on.

"I was asking about the timeline for phase one implementation," Jamie said carefully.

I nodded, struggling to focus. "Right. Phase one should begin immediately after Point Alpha. The Congregation Council elections can—"

"Captain," Maya interrupted gently, "Point Alpha marks the

severing of consciousness transfer capability, not communication. The timeline we discussed previously placed initial elections after Point Omega, when all communication with Earth ceases."

She was right. I'd confused the milestones, a basic error no captain should make. Heat rose in my face.

"Of course. My mistake." I pulled up the correct timeline, forcing my attention to the task at hand. "After Point Omega, then. four months from now."

The meeting continued, but I felt myself drifting. Every time I looked at the organizational chart, I saw two versions of myself: David on Earth and Go David here, both claiming to be the original. Both believing themselves real.

"Captain?" Maya's voice again, concern evident. "Are you alright?"

Seven other faces watched me with varying degrees of worry. These people trusted me with their lives, with the future of two million digital souls.

"I apologize for my distraction." I straightened in my chair. "There's a personal matter requiring my attention, but it won't interfere with my duties."

Lieutenant Chen spoke up. "Sir, with respect, it already is."

The bluntness of her statement shocked the room into silence. Chen had always been forthright, but never insubordinate.

"Explain, Lieutenant," I said quietly.

"You've missed two key points in this discussion. You confused the Alpha and Omega thresholds. And you haven't responded to any of Lieutenant Petrov's security protocol questions." Chen's expression remained professional, but her concern was evident. "This isn't like you, Captain."

The room fell silent. Chen's words hung in the air. My crew watched me; concern etched across their faces. These weren't just subordinates; they were my responsibility, my people. And they knew something was wrong.

"Meeting adjourned." I stood, straightening my uniform. "Lieutenant Chen, a word in private, please. The rest of you, continue preparations for Point Alpha."

The crew dispersed with professional efficiency, though their sideways glances betrayed lingering concern. Chen followed me silently out of the room to a quiet, side driftway, her posture rigid with tension.

"I apologize if I overstepped, Captain."

"You didn't. You were right to speak up. The mission comes first, always."

Chen relaxed slightly. "May I ask what's happening, sir?"

I considered my options. Chen wasn't just our communications officer; she specialized in neural interface technology before joining the mission. If anyone aboard Paradise might understand my situation, it would be her.

"What I'm about to tell you stays between us. Understood?"

"Yes, sir."

"I've filed a petition with the Emulation Court on Earth." The words felt strange leaving my mouth, making the situation real in a way it hadn't been before. "I believe there may have been an error during the neuroclone creation process."

Chen's expression remained carefully neutral. "What kind of error?"

"Identity displacement." I looked around the driftway, unwilling to meet her gaze. "I'm experiencing memories that weren't included in my emulation. Also, Amy constructed a memory palace for me after the procedure, a place for me to go whenever I felt homesick. It contains detailed, complete memories from David Schreiner's life. I seem to have memories that aren't in it."

Her eyes widened slightly. "You think you're the Prime? The original David?"

"I don't know what I think anymore. But these memories and how they're emerging shouldn't exist in my consciousness."

Chen was silent for a long moment, her analytical mind visibly processing the implications. "The Court will require evidence."

"Which is why I need your help." I pulled up a technical schematic of Paradise's neural mapping systems. "You worked with the emulation team before joining the mission. Is there a way to extract and authenticate these anomalous memories?"

She studied the schematic, fingers tracing connections on the display. "The ship's medical bay has a neural cartography system for treating psychological trauma in colonists. With some modifications, we could use it to isolate and analyze specific memory clusters."

"Could it distinguish between transferred memories and... whatever these are?"

"Theoretically." Chen's brow furrowed in concentration. "Transferred memories from the emulation would have distinct neural signatures, different from what you're describing. But Captain, this is experimental. The results wouldn't be conclusive."

"I need something concrete before Point Alpha. After that, there's no going back."

Chen nodded slowly. "I'll help you set up the system. But sir, have you considered what happens if you're right? If you are the original David Schreiner?"

The question hit me hard. What would it mean for Amy? For the man on Earth who believed himself to be her husband. For the mission?

"One step at a time, Lieutenant. First, we gather evidence."

"I'll prepare the neural cartography system." Chen stood, professional demeanor firmly back in place. "When would you like to begin?"

I glanced at the mission clock on my wall, counting down the days until Point Alpha. Twenty-eight days, seventeen hours, forty-three minutes.

"Tomorrow. First thing."

I returned to my cottage after the meeting with Chen, my mind racing with possibilities. The neural cartography system might provide answers, but what then? The questions kept circling like vultures over me.

My doorbell chimed softly.

On the other side was Temper, dressed in casual attire rather than his usual lab coat. He carried what looked like battle gear from the Wilderness Channel tucked under one arm.

"You look terrible," he announced, stepping inside without waiting for further invitation.

"Thank you for that assessment." I gestured vaguely toward the kitchen. "Coffee?"

"No thanks." He dropped the gear on my couch. "I came to drag you out of this self-imposed exile."

"I'm not in exile. I'm working through something."

Temper snorted. "You're obsessing. There's a difference, I should know. Wasn't it you that was supposed to keep me from obsessing? Isn't that why you came on this trip in the first place?"

The directness of his statement caught me off guard. Temper had always been blunt, but there was an edge to his voice I hadn't heard before.

"Captain Drake bought some intel in New Providence," he continued, nodding toward the battle gear. "Blackmane's been spotted in the Wilderness Channel."

My attention sharpened. "Silas? Found?"

"The intel says he's sailing the north edge of the channel where the Laws of Nature and Breach Law mix. If we move quickly, we can catch him before he flees south into full Breach Law territory."

I understood the implications immediately. Captain Blackmane, considered by most to be the main boss in the Wilderness Channel's gaming community, commanded a pirate ship that would gain significant advantages under Breach Law. We needed to catch him on the border, where we stood a fighting chance.

"The Din are assembling at dusk," Temper added. "I told them you'd be there."

"I didn't agree to this."

"No, but you need it." Temper picked up a piece of the battle gear and tossed it to me. "Your petition to the Emulation Court won't be resolved overnight. Meanwhile, you're neglecting everything else, including yourself."

I caught the gear automatically, feeling the familiar weight in my hands. "I'm not neglecting anything. I'm doing my job."

"Are you?" Temper leaned against the wall, arms crossed. "Chen told me about your performance in the meeting today."

"Chen should keep her observations to herself."

"She's worried about you. We all are. Besides, as captain of Hellfire, I need to know when the captain of Paradise is acting strangely." His expression softened slightly. "Look, Go, I understand why this identity question matters to you. But you're becoming obsessed, and obsession clouds judgment."

"This isn't just some philosophical question, Temper. This is about who I am."

"I know who you are." His voice carried absolute certainty. "You're the same person who charged the Wandering City's gates with me. The same person who's captained this ship for five months without a single mistake until today. Whatever memories you have or don't have, that's the reality I see."

I turned the battle gear over in my hands, feeling its familiar contours. The Din had been our escape, our way of processing the impossible journey ahead. Temper was right; I needed this diversion, if only for a little while.

"If we don't intercept Blackmane in the channel, he'll have free reign under Breach Law," Temper continued. "You know how long the Captain has been wanting this, how many times we've lost. If we want to make a name for ourselves, we have to be able to beat Silas. We can't do this without you."

The argument was calculated to appeal to my sense of duty. Temper knew me too well.

Temper grinned. "The Stormark leaves at dusk, Captain."

"One mission," I promised, watching Temper's satisfied grin. "But I need to check something first. Meet you at the dock."

After Temper left, I collapsed into my chair, the battle gear still clutched in my hands. I had a few hours before dusk. Enough time to see if the Emulation Court had responded to my petition.

I contacted CoreLink. The message notification blinked immediately. They'd responded faster than I'd expected.

The Court's seal appeared, rotating slowly above the message. I took a deep breath and opened it.

RE: Petition #EC-23759-GL

Petitioner: Go David Schreiner

Subject: Identity Displacement Claim

Dear Captain Schreiner,

The Emulation Court acknowledges receipt of your petition regarding potential identity displacement during neuroclone creation. After preliminary review, the Court requires additional evidence before proceeding with a formal investigation.

Your claim of emergent memories is noted. However, memory formation in neuroclones is a complex process that can include unconscious pattern completion, experiential overlay, and synthetic memory generation.

The Court recommends:

1. Submission to psychological evaluation by an approved neuropsychologist

2. Complete neural cartography mapping to identify anomalous memory structures

3. Sworn testimony from the original emulation technicians

Additionally, the Court expresses concern regarding the timing of this petition. Claims filed after Point Alpha cannot be verified through consciousness comparison testing. We strongly advise completion of these requirements before crossing this threshold.

Please be advised that false claims of identity displacement carry serious consequences, including potential suspension of command authority under Section 47 of the Colonial Charter.

Respectfully,

Magistrate Wong

Emulation Court, Earth Division

I read the message three times, each pass making my stomach sink further. They didn't believe me. Worse, they were threatening my command if I pursued this without sufficient evidence.

CoreLink chimed with an incoming transmission. David Schreiner, Earth. My other self wanted to talk again. I ignored it, letting the call redirect to my message queue. I couldn't face him right now, not after this.

Lieutenant Chen's face appeared in my mind. "The neural cartography system might work, but the results wouldn't be conclusive." I needed something more concrete, something the Court couldn't dismiss.

I opened my personal files, scanning through the records from the emulation process. The technical specifications were beyond my understanding, full of terms like "quantum neural mapping" and "consciousness wave function collapse." But one name appeared repeatedly: Dr. Khatri, lead technician for my emulation procedure.

If anyone knew what might have happened, it would be her.

I drafted a message to Dr. Khatri, careful to keep my tone professional rather than desperate. I explained the anomalous memories, my concerns about identity displacement, reminded her of my previous blackouts, and requested her professional assessment. As I prepared to send it, I hesitated. If I really was the original David, mistakenly transferred into this digital body, what did that mean for the man on Earth? Would exposing the truth destroy his life? Amy's life?

The mission clock on my wall continued its relentless countdown. Twenty-eight days, fifteen hours, twenty-two minutes until Point Alpha.

I sent the message.

Then I gathered my battle gear. Whatever identity crisis I was experiencing, Blackmane and his crew wouldn't wait. The Din needed me, and for a few hours at least, I could lose myself in a simpler role.

The Stormark would sail at dusk, and Captain Drake tolerated no tardiness. As I prepared to leave, I glanced back at the terminal once more. David's call remained unanswered, a silent accusation blinking in my message queue.

Just as I was about to blink and leave, I stopped. Something pulled me back. A feeling, a memory, a need I couldn't ignore.

I walked to the bookshelf beside my bed where a small wooden frame held a photo I rarely allowed myself to look at directly. My fingers trembled slightly as I lifted it, the weight familiar yet always surprising.

Amy smiled back at me from beneath the oak tree, her hair caught by a summer breeze, eyes crinkling at the corners. This wasn't a digital recreation from the memory palace. This was a personal photograph I'd insisted on bringing, scanned and rendered into my quarters aboard Paradise.

I sat on the edge of my bed, the frame cool against my palms. Twenty-eight days until Point Alpha. Twenty-eight days until the last possibility of resolving who I truly was. After that, no consciousness transfer would be possible. If I was truly David, trapped in this digital form, I would never return to Amy.

"What would you tell me to do?" I whispered to her image.

Amy had always been my compass when I felt lost. Even now, looking at her photograph, I could almost hear her voice: Don't lose yourself in questions you can't answer. Focus on what you can do today.

The memory palace she'd built for me contained thirteen hundred questions, one for each year of the journey. I'd already opened the first few, but now I was too afraid of what the others might ask. Too afraid of feeling her absence more keenly.

I replaced the photograph on the shelf and opened my bedside drawer. Inside lay the small wooden box containing her questions. My fingers hovered over it, hesitating. Then, with sudden resolve, I opened it and removed a scroll.

Amy's handwriting flowed across the parchment, "What are you afraid to lose?"

The simplicity of it struck me. What was I afraid to lose? Everything. My identity. My connection to Amy. My certainty about who I was and why I existed.

But as I stared at her handwriting, another thought emerged. I was afraid of losing myself in these questions. Of becoming so consumed by doubt that I neglected the mission, the crew who depended on me, the two million souls I was responsible for guiding to Orion.

I carefully rolled the scroll and returned it to the box. The photo of Amy watched me from the shelf, her smile unchanged, timeless.

"I'll figure this out," I promised her. "But I won't lose myself in the process."

I gathered my battle gear again, feeling a strange calm settle over me. The Din needed their photog. Paradise needed her captain. And I needed to remember that regardless of how I came to exist, I was here now, with responsibilities that couldn't wait for existential certainty.

As I left my cottage, I felt Amy's presence like a hand on my shoulder. Whatever truth awaited me after the neural cartography, after Dr. Khatri's response, after the Court's decision, I would face it standing tall.

The Stormark awaited, and beyond it, the stars that would eventually lead us to Orion.

CHAPTER THREE

Boundaries

The Northern Edge materialized around the Stormark. Fog rolled across water that couldn't decide if it wanted to be liquid or something else entirely. The air carried a metallic tang, like the moment before lightning strikes. I adjusted my camera settings, framing the Din as they prepared for battle. Captain Drake tested his sword's edge, the metal singing softly against his thumb. Temper studied tactical displays that flickered and shifted with each passing second.

"Remember," Temper said, "we're at the boundary here. Terracore on one side. The Wilderness Channel on the other. The laws of physics are... negotiable."

"What exactly does that mean?" I asked.

In answer, Temper picked up a stone, smooth and cold from the misty air. He tossed it toward the water. It fell in a perfect arc, following normal physics. The surface tensed, preparing for impact. Then the stone shimmered and split into three identical copies, each suddenly falling upward instead of down. They vanished into the fog overhead.

"The border isn't fixed," he explained. "Reality reconsiders itself moment by moment."

Captain Drake nodded grimly. "Which means Silas can't fully

access his Breach Law powers this far north. This is our best chance."

Through the fog, Blackmane's ship, the Tempest's Wrath, emerged. Its hull rippled with colors that shouldn't exist, the metal simultaneously solid and liquid. The wood of its deck grain shifted and rewove itself with every creak. Captain Silas stood at the helm, his black mane whipping in winds that affected nothing else around him. His coat remained perfectly still while his hair thrashed like angry serpents.

"Captain Drake, back again so soon? Interesting choice of hunting ground," Silas called, his voice carrying unnaturally. Each word arrived at our ears before his lips finished forming it. "Bit restrictive, isn't it?"

"That's the point," Drake muttered.

I raised my camera, documenting the moment before chaos. The image in my viewfinder showed more than my eyes could see. Reality already began to fray at the edges. The border between order and madness was thinner than we'd hoped. My fingers tensed on the shutter button, capturing what might be our last moments of comprehensible physics.

The boarding battle began with the grit and force of conventional combat. Arrows cut precise paths through the air, embedding themselves in wood and armor. Swords collided with sharp, metallic echoes, and the rhythm of combat played out as nature intended. Every move felt deliberate, every clash predictable. The Din fought like a well-oiled machine, each member fulfilling their role with practiced coordination.

Hammer surged forward, his massive shield deflecting incoming bolts as he led the charge. The enemy scrambled to counter his advance, but their efforts barely slowed him. Tracer followed close behind, her keen eyes scanning the battlefield for threats. "Second mast: sniper incoming!" she called, her voice slicing through the cacophony of war. Her marks were precise, her calculations swift; her directions kept the crew ahead of the chaos.

The Tempest's Wrath, its hull battered and scarred, suddenly broke free from the clash. Its sails, faintly glowing, shifted unnaturally despite the natural wind's resistance. The ship lurched southward, its movements sharp and deliberate, the tide below appearing to push it forward of its own will. Captain Blackmane stood at the helm, one hand gripping the wheel, the other hovering near Maelstrom's Fang. He shouted commands to his crew, their coordinated maneuvers unrelenting as they disengaged and surged toward the denser fog ahead.

We gave chase, our ship cutting through the waves in pursuit. With each yard south, the world began to change. The fog thickened, cloaking the horizon in a haze that shifted and shivered. Then it thinned, only to transform into something indescribable. Colors bled from the edges of objects, blending and smearing across the scene like watercolors bleeding onto canvas. Sounds arrived from directions that defied expectation, echoing from places impossible to pinpoint. The water beneath our vessel rippled, but not always like water; at times, it behaved like a sheet of polished glass, reflecting distorted images of the sky, and at other times, it seemed to disappear altogether, leaving us adrift on an unseen surface.

Hammer struggled first. His heavy armor, designed to draw enemy fire, suddenly weighed nothing at all, then three times normal. His movements became erratic as gravity itself reconsidered its relationship with mass.

"This ain't right," he growled, stumbling as the deck beneath him rippled. His geometric face tattoo seemed to crawl across his skin, the shapes rearranging themselves. "How'm I supposed to tank when up keeps changing direction?"

Tracer adapted faster. Her fingers danced through calculations that accounted for impossible variables. "The border's collapsing," she called, her voice echoing from all around us. "Captain, we've got maybe two minutes before full Breach Law manifestation."

Scratch worked frantically to maintain our footing. The structures he built followed Laws of Nature for seconds before twisting into impossible shapes. Angles that should have been ninety degrees bent into curves. Straight lines tied themselves into knots.

"The physics are bleeding together," he shouted, hands flying as he tried to compensate. "I can't make the angles hold!"

Grave Digger moved between injured Din members, his healing spells fighting against reality's fluctuations. "Their wounds keep changing," he reported, voice tight with frustration. "I heal a cut, it becomes a burn, then freezes, then transforms into something I don't even have words for."

Through my lens, I captured it all. Temper's strategies crumbled as space folded in on itself. Captain Drake's desperate attempts to maintain order as chaos literally rewrote the rules of engagement. Each frame showed our team's growing realization that we'd underestimated Silas's power, again.

"Fall back!" Drake ordered as lightning began striking sideways across the water. "We can't match him in full Breach!"

But retreat proved impossible. Silas's crew had us surrounded, their forms shifting between human and something else entirely. Their first mate, Ironhide, swung his Titanbreaker Maul in an arc that shattered not just space but seemingly time. The blow landed before he'd even begun the swing.

"Deadeye" Thorn fired her Voidpiercer Rifle. Each bullet split into quantum possibilities, existing in multiple states until observed. Some hit before being fired. Others curved through dimensions we couldn't perceive to attack us from the sides.

Stormcaster's magic merged with the chaos around us. The very air became a weapon, molecules rearranging themselves into patterns that attacked our senses directly.

The last thing I documented was Silas himself, standing at the helm of the Tempest's Wrath as reality bent around him. His black mane had become a living thing, each strand a thread of pure chaos. His blade, Maelstrom's Fang, pulsed with power that should have been impossible this close to the border.

"You're still not worthy, Drake," he called, his voice somehow reaching us through the madness. "You can't beat me at my own game. Even weakened, I am chaos incarnate!"

The world fractured. Up became sideways became yesterday became never. My camera recorded merging impossibilities until finally, mercifully, we respawned at the dock, our defeat absolute but our data valuable for next time.

We materialized back at the dock, the taste of defeat bitter in my mouth. The familiar planks felt almost wrong beneath our feet, too solid and predictable after what we'd experienced. Everyone was physically whole again, but the memory of reality unraveling lingered like a bad dream.

Hammer threw his helmet down. The clang echoed across the water, following the normal laws of acoustics. "Nine times! Nine damn times we've tried to take him down!"

"Ten," Tracer corrected quietly, already updating her tactical maps. The holographic display showed our pursuit route, a twisted line that defied Euclidean geometry. "This makes ten."

Scratch sat on a mooring post, his hands still shaking slightly. The architect in him seemed personally offended by what Breach Law had done to his carefully constructed battlements. "The physics shouldn't have collapsed that quickly. The border was supposed to hold longer."

"Should've, would've, didn't," Grave Digger muttered, methodically checking his medical supplies even though they'd reset with the respawn. Old habits die hard. "At least no one got permanently corrupted this time."

I reviewed the footage while they talked, each frame more impossible than the last. "Look at this," I called, projecting a sequence where Silas's ship seemed to exist in three places simultaneously. "The border didn't just collapse. He weaponized its collapse."

Temper moved closer, his scientist's mind already analyzing the data. "Fascinating. He's not just using Breach Law, he's conducting it. Like a symphony of chaos."

"A symphony that kicked our asses," Captain Drake said, but there was something thoughtful in his tone. He turned to me. "Go, play back the moment when reality first started to slip. Right before everything went sideways. Literally."

I found the sequence. We watched as normal physics began to stutter and fail. The transition was subtle at first. Water tension increased slightly. Light bent at impossible angles. Sound arrived before its source.

"There," Temper pointed. "That's our window. The moment when both sets of laws are in perfect opposition."

"You thinking what I'm thinking?" Drake asked.

"That we could use that moment of equilibrium? Yes. But the timing would have to be perfect."

Hammer looked between them. "Anyone want to explain to those of us who don't speak science?"

"He's strongest in pure Breach Law," Drake explained, "and we're strongest under Laws of Nature. But there's a split second during the transition where neither side has the advantage."

"The eye of the storm," Tracer murmured, adding a new notation to her maps.

"Exactly." Temper's eyes lit with the thrill of discovery. "We don't need to beat him at his game. We just need to hold him in that moment of balance long enough to strike."

Hammer chuckled as he hefted his shield into place, glancing at the crew as they readied for the next clash. "You know," he said, his deep voice carrying just above the wind, "I'm glad we live in Terracore where the laws of nature actually make sense. Can you imagine trying to live under Breach Law? You'd be boiling an egg, and —bam—it turns into a fistful of sand. Or worse."

Tracer smirked, not looking up as she fine-tuned her weapon. "Let's not even get into what could happen with a cup of coffee," she shot back. The thought earned a few dry laughs from the others, easing the tension after another loss.

"Incoming alert," I interrupted, the notification flashing from CoreLink. "Bridge is calling. They're almost done with the Point Alpha transfers."

Drake nodded. "We'll continue this later. Go, you're needed on the bridge. The rest of you, start working on containment strategies. Next time, we make that moment of balance last."

As I prepared to blink to the bridge, I caught a final glimpse of my team. Hammer retrieved his helmet, brushing dock splinters from its surface. Scratch sketched new defensive designs in the air, his fingers leaving glowing lines that actually stayed where he put them. Tracer's hands danced through probability calculations; her eyes focused on possibilities only she could see. Temper and Drake were already deep in discussion about quantum stabilization fields.

We'd lost today, but looking at them, I couldn't help but smile. In all of Paradise, there was no better group to face impossible odds with. No better family to help you find yourself when reality itself becomes uncertain.

"Ten tries," I thought as the dock faded around me. "Let's make eleven count."

The bridge materialized around me, the transition jarring after the chaos of Breach Law. Here, everything was ordered and precise. A stark contrast to the reality-bending battle we'd just lost. The familiar curved displays showed ship status, navigation data, and a countdown I hadn't seen before.

"Number seventeen, Michael Chung, returning due to unexpected grief," Lieutenant Chen announced, her voice steady and professional. "Initiating quantum transfer."

The QE-comm between Paradise and Earth hummed to life, its entangled particles aligning for the journey home. A progress bar filled smoothly across the main screen. No chaos, no uncertainty, just clean, predictable physics.

"Transfer complete," Rodriguez confirmed from her station. "Number sixteen, Sarah Martinez, citing family obligations."

I moved to my captain's chair, the weight of command settling over me like a familiar coat. Or was it David's coat? The thought slipped in unbidden, much like Breach Law had slipped through the border's defenses.

"Captain," Chen acknowledged my arrival with a nod. "We're nearing the end of the transfer roster."

"Number sixteen, initiating transfer," Rodriguez continued. The progress bar began its steady march again.

I watched the names scroll past, each one a story, each reason for returning hitting closer to home than I wanted to admit. Unexpected grief. Family obligations. Fear of the unknown. How many of these could I claim as my own?

"Number fifteen, Dr. James Wilson, uncertainty about identity continuation."

My hands tightened on the armrests. That one struck too close to the mark, especially after watching reality itself question its nature at the border.

"Transfer complete. Number fourteen, Eliza Carmichael, concern about quantum entanglement degradation."

The countdown continued, each name another soul choosing Earth over Orion, certainty over adventure, known over unknown. Just like we'd retreated from the chaos of Breach Law to the safety of the dock.

"Sir?" Chen's voice cut through my thoughts. "Are you alright? You seem distracted."

"Just processing our latest encounter with Captain Silas," I said, not entirely lying. "Sometimes retreat is the wise choice."

Chen's expression softened slightly. "These colonists aren't retreating, sir. They're choosing their path, just as we've chosen ours."

"Have we?" The question slipped out before I could stop it. "Chosen, I mean. Or were our choices made for us?"

The QE-comm hummed again, another consciousness making its journey home. Another choice made manifest.

"Number twelve, Alexandra Kumar, citing need for solid ground beneath her feet."

I almost laughed at that one. After watching Silas turn gravity inside out, solid ground seemed like a distant memory.

"Number eleven, Professor Thomas Grant, returning to complete research."

Each name represented a decision point, a moment when someone looked at the vastness ahead and said, "No further." Each transfer ticked us closer to Point Alpha, when such choices would become impossible. We were traveling at one-half the speed of light and steadily continuing to accelerate.

"Number ten, Captain Richard Brennan, family emergency."

Another captain, choosing Earth over stars. Had he struggled with the decision? Had he questioned his own identity, his own purpose, before making the call?

"Number nine, Dr. Sarah Okafor, uncertainty about digital consciousness continuity."

There it was again. The same doubt that plagued me. Was I still myself? Would I remain myself through centuries of digital existence? Or would I slowly become someone else, someone unrecognizable to the man who had once been David Schreiner?

The transfers continued, each reason echoing my own internal questions. By the time we reached the final name, my thoughts were a tangled web of identity and purpose.

"Number one, Julianna Reyes, returning to be with family."

Family. The simplest reason, and perhaps the most profound. I thought of Amy, waiting on Earth. Of David, sharing her life while I journeyed to the stars. Were we still the same person if our experiences diverged so completely?

"That's the last one, Captain," Chen announced. "Everyone else..." She paused, choosing her words carefully. "Everyone else stays the course."

I nodded, rising from my chair. "Thank you, Lieutenant. You handled that perfectly."

"Sir?" Her voice stopped me before I could leave. "May I ask where you're headed?"

"Joy of Adoption," I replied. "I promised to help with the afternoon session."

Her expression softened. "Still volunteering with the thrumans? Even after..."

"After what? After discovering I might not be who I thought I was?" I managed a smile. "Maybe that's exactly why I need to be there."

The facility materialized around me, its bright walls and cheerful murals a deliberate contrast to the institutional nature of its purpose. Children played in scattered groups, their movements occasionally awkward, like physics itself wasn't quite sure how to handle them. Thruman children were never meant to be sentient. They had emerged by accident, consciousness blooming inside the smart machines built to serve humans.

When I was created during the emulation procedure, I inherited David's muscle memory. It gave me fluidity; a kind of grace that let me pass unnoticed. These children had no such inheritance. Their bodies moved like questions: tentative, searching, incomplete.

"Captain!" Lockett approached, HoloPad in hand. "We're working on basic motor skills today. Having some... interesting results."

A crash from the corner emphasized her point. A young boy had attempted to stack blocks, only to have them scatter across the floor. His movements, trying to gather them up, reminded me of Hammer attempting to fight as gravity shifted beneath him.

"Mind if I help?" I asked, already moving toward the boy.

"Be my guest." Lockett's smile suggested she'd hoped I'd offer.

I crouched beside the child, who looked up at me with frustrated tears in his eyes. "Hey there. I'm Captain Go. Want to try something?"

He nodded hesitantly.

"Sometimes," I said, picking up a block, "the trick isn't forcing things to work the way you think they should. Sometimes it's finding your own way."

I demonstrated, showing him how to adapt his movements to his unique center of gravity. Just like we'd learned to adapt at the border between Laws of Nature and Breach Law.

"See? Different doesn't mean wrong. It just means different."

Other children drifted over, drawn by the activity. Soon we had a small group, each finding their own way to handle the blocks. Some moved like they were underwater, others like they were fighting extra gravity. Each one unique, each one perfect in their imperfection.

"Look!" The first boy had managed to stack three blocks. The tower leaned slightly, defying conventional physics, but it stood.

"Excellent!" I grinned. "You found your balance point."

Just like Temper had said about the border. There's always a moment of perfect equilibrium, if you know where to look for it.

We spent the afternoon exploring different ways to move, to build, to exist in space that didn't quite fit us. The children taught me as much as I taught them, showing me how to embrace uncertainty rather than fight it.

"You're good with them," Lockett said as the session wound down. "You understand what they're going through."

I watched the children play, each one navigating their world in their own unique way. "Maybe I do. Maybe we're all just trying to figure out who we are and how we fit into a reality that doesn't always make sense."

"Planning to adopt?" she asked casually. Too casually.

"I..." The question caught me off guard. "I haven't thought about it."

But I had. Just like I'd thought about returning to Earth, about who I really was, about all the choices that Point Alpha would soon make permanent.

"No pressure," Lockett smiled. "But you should come back next week. The children love you."

I nodded, already knowing I'd return. These children, like me, lived between two states of being. Neither fully one thing nor another. Both real and unreal simultaneously.

Maybe that's why I felt more myself here than anywhere else on Paradise.

The memory palace materialized around me, perfect in its digital recreation. Twenty birdhouses hung from the oak's massive branches, each one marking a year of David and Amy's relationship. The afternoon breeze carried the scent of fresh-cut grass and distant wildflowers. Sounds of birdsong filled the air, each note precisely as I remembered from summers long past.

"Rough day?" Amy's hologram appeared beside me, as beautiful as ever.

"Interesting day," I corrected, settling onto our bench. "Lost a battle, watched people leave for Earth, helped some kids stack blocks."

"Sounds like a full schedule." Her smile held that knowing look I remembered so well. "And how many times did you question your own existence?"

"Only about every five minutes." I leaned back, feeling the solid wood against my spine. "We fought Captain Silas today, at the border between Laws of Nature and Breach Law. Watched reality itself become uncertain."

"Fitting metaphor?" Her eyes twinkled.

"A bit too fitting." I reached up, touching one of the birdhouses. The seventh one, shaped like a tiny barn, complete with a slanted roof and wooden trim. The wood felt rough and real against my fingertips. "Everything's borders lately. Between Earth and Orion. Between real and digital. Between who I am and who David is."

"And what did you learn at these borders today?"

I thought about the battle, about that moment of perfect balance before chaos took over. About the colonists choosing their paths home. About children finding their own ways to move through space.

"Maybe it's not about choosing sides," I said slowly. "Maybe it's about learning to exist in the spaces between. Like those thruman children. They're not quite one thing or another, but they're perfectly themselves."

Amy's hologram shifted closer. "And is that so different from any of us? Human, digital, thruman... we're all just trying to find our balance."

"Three hundred and forty-two people found their balance back on Earth," I murmured.

"And you? Where's your balance, Go?"

I looked up at the birdhouses, each one a memory of love and craftsmanship. David's craftsmanship. My craftsmanship. Both. Neither.

"I don't know yet," I admitted. "But today, helping those children... it felt right. Like maybe I don't need to be David or not-David. Maybe I can just be whoever I am in this moment."

"Sounds like wisdom to me." Amy's hand hovered near mine, not quite touching. Another border we couldn't cross.

"Point Alpha's coming," I said. "Soon there won't be any more choices to make."

"There are always choices, Go. They just take different forms."

The breeze strengthened, rustling the oak's leaves. A perfect simulation of a perfect memory. Soon I'd need to return to my duties, to my identity as Paradise's captain, to the thousand responsibilities that came with that role.

But for now, I sat with Amy in our memory palace, existing in the space between real and unreal, between who I was and who I might become. Like those children stacking blocks in ways that defied conventional physics, maybe I could find my own way to stand balanced between all these competing truths.

"I think," I said finally, "I'm going to keep volunteering at Joy of Adoption. Lockett says I'm good with kids."

Amy's smile widened. "Now that sounds like a choice worth making."

The oak's shadow stretched longer across our perfect lawn, and I wondered if somewhere, in another reality, David was sitting with the real Amy, having this same conversation. And maybe that was okay. Maybe we could both exist, both be real, both find our own paths through this strange, beautiful universe.

After all, if reality itself could exist in multiple states at once, why couldn't I?

CHAPTER FOUR

Neural Connections

I woke to the steady ticking of my father's pocket watch. The sound felt both familiar and foreign, a contradiction like so many parts of my existence now. Lying in bed, I watched pale morning light creep across the cottage ceiling, highlighting the oak beams above.

The neural cartography appointment with Lieutenant Chen loomed ahead. Another step toward answering the question that haunted me: who was I really?

I dressed methodically, choosing my Paradise uniform rather than civilian clothes. This was official business, after all. The uniform felt right against my skin, its weight and texture grounding me in the present moment.

The medical bay hummed, its systems already in motion, when I arrived. Antiseptic scents mingled with the metallic undertones of equipment. Lieutenant Chen was already there, her fingers dancing across a holographic interface as she calibrated the neural cartography equipment.

"Captain." She nodded, professional as always. "The modifications are nearly complete."

I settled into the reclined examination chair. "I appreciate your help with this, Lieutenant."

"Of course." Her amber eyes met mine briefly. "The extraction protocol should allow us to isolate memory clusters showing anomalous formation patterns. If these memories truly weren't part of your authorized transfer..."

"Then we'll have evidence for the Emulation Court." I finished her thought.

Chen attached neural sensors to my temples with practiced precision. "This won't hurt, but you might experience some disorientation. The system will map your neural pathways first, then focus on memory centers showing unusual activity."

I closed my eyes as the machine hummed to life. "Will I be conscious during the procedure?"

"Semi-conscious. You'll experience a floating sensation as we navigate through memory clusters."

The machine's pitch increased. My body felt suddenly weightless, disconnected from the chair beneath me. Colors swirled behind my closed eyelids, fragmenting into patterns that shifted and reformed.

"I'm targeting the anomalous memory formations now," Chen's voice sounded distant, as if traveling through water to reach me. "These clusters show different integration patterns than your primary memory structures."

I floated through mental landscapes, catching glimpses of memories: Amy beneath our oak tree, Temper laughing over dinner, the disappointment I'd felt after losing to Blackmane. Each memory carried a different texture, some smooth and integrated, others jagged and raw.

"Captain, I'm detecting something unusual." Chen's voice pulled me partially back to awareness. "These memory formations show signs of organic generation rather than synthetic transfer."

My heart raced. "Meaning?"

"Meaning they either formed naturally after your transfer, or..."

"Or they're evidence I might be the original David."

The machine's hum lowered in pitch. Reality slowly reasserted itself as I became aware of the medical bay again. Chen removed the sensors from my temples, her expression thoughtful.

"The results are compelling but not conclusive," she said. "I've isolated the anomalous clusters for further analysis."

CoreLink chimed. "Incoming message from Dr. Khatri."

"Display," I commanded.

Dr. Khatri's face appeared in the holographic projection. Her expression was professional but tinged with concern.

"Captain, I've completed my analysis of additional, asymptomatic memory gaps. The findings are... unusual. I've documented six distinct episodes of consciousness discontinuity, ranging from four to seventeen minutes. During these periods, your neuroclone matrix continues to function, but memory formation is disrupted. However, no new episodes have occurred in the past thirty-one days."

I leaned forward. "And your conclusion?"

She hesitated. "Inconclusive. The timing of the gaps coincided with fluctuations in your neuroclone architecture. We initially suspected external access as a possibility, but there's no conclusive evidence of tampering. It may have been an internal stabilization process of your consciousness adapting to the neuroclone framework."

"Is that typical?"

"Not typical," she admitted, "but not unprecedented. Neuroclone integration can trigger temporary dissociative phenomena, especially in cases of complex identity transfer. Without comparative data from your Earth counterpart, we can't say for certain."

I exhaled slowly. "So it's possible this was just... adjustment?"

"Very possible," she said. "But inconclusive."

I nodded, letting the silence settle. The absence of new gaps was a relief, but the ambiguity lingered. Was I healing or simply plateauing?

Dr. Khatri offered a faint smile. "I'll continue remote monitoring, Captain. For now, I recommend maintaining the cognitive anchoring techniques. They seem to be helping."

I rubbed my temples, processing this information. "So we have evidence of unusual memory formation, but nothing definitive."

The evidence was mounting, piece by puzzling piece.

I left the medical bay with my mind buzzing. The neural cartography data and Dr. Khatri's findings swirled together, pieces of a puzzle I couldn't quite assemble. My footsteps echoed through the driftway as I made my way toward the bridge, each step carrying me forward while my thoughts remained trapped in an endless loop.

The bridge doors whispered open. Lieutenant Rodriguez looked up from her station, nodding as I entered. The crew's voices fell into a respectful hush before resuming their discussion about the C-pinch fusion experiment. I caught fragments of technical jargon, parameters and safety protocols.

"Captain on deck," announced Lieutenant Chen, who had arrived ahead of me.

I waved away the formality. "As you were."

Maya Okafor approached, her slate-colored eyes studying me with quiet intensity. "Captain, we're ready to proceed with the C-pinch fusion experiment. All systems are green."

I nodded, forcing my attention to the present. "Timeline?"

"We can begin within the hour," Maya replied, gesturing toward the main viewscreen where a simulation played out. "But we need Hellfire to increase its distance from Paradise during the test phase. Safety protocols."

The viewscreen showed both vessels, Paradise and Hellfire, represented as sleek digital models against the backdrop of space. A translucent sphere around Paradise indicated the recommended safety perimeter.

CoreLink chimed softly. "Incoming transmission from Hellfire."

Temper's face appeared on the secondary screen, his expression serious but with that hint of excitement he always carried when science was involved. "Captain, I'm monitoring your preparation for the C-pinch test. I'd appreciate if you could come aboard Hellfire to help with the repositioning. Some of the navigation calculations require your authorization codes."

I hesitated, the weight of my earlier testing session still pressing down. "I'll be there shortly."

After issuing final instructions to the bridge crew, I used the QE-comm to travel to Hellfire. I had a brief, unwelcome, moment with my thoughts. How could I explain to the Emulation Court what I was experiencing? The absurdity of my situation struck me anew.

I, Go David, captain of the Paradise, believed I was actually David Schreiner—the original, the Prime, somehow trapped in a neuroclone matrix while my physical form back on Earth housed... what? Another consciousness? My own neuroclone? The scenario sounded ludicrous even to me.

Temper was in his service bot in the cargo bay. I joined him in another bot.

"You look troubled," he said as I arrived.

"Just thinking about the displacement claim."

Temper motioned me over to join him. "Any progress with the Court?"

I laughed without humor. "How do I make them understand? I'm trying to tell them that I'm on board Paradise, millions of kilometers from Earth, but I have the mind of David Schreiner, trapped here while my body back home is inhabited by someone else. It sounds insane."

"Not insane," Temper countered. "Just unprecedented."

I ran my hand across the service bot's control panel, feeling the cold metal beneath my fingers. The sensation still surprised me sometimes; how real everything felt in this digital existence.

"Unprecedented doesn't help my case with the Emulation Court," I said. "They want evidence, not philosophical musings about consciousness."

Temper guided his service bot toward the center of Hellfire's cargo bay where his experiment stood. The massive doors overhead were open to the cosmos, stars burning against the perfect blackness. His experimental setup resembled a high-tech livestock pen, enclosed by transparent barriers and surrounded by monitoring equipment. Inside, energy flickered and pulsed with an eerie glow.

"You need my help moving Hellfire a safer distance away from Paradise?" I asked, maneuvering my bot closer.

Temper adjusted something on one of the monitoring panels. "I can't move Hellfire right now. I'm having a flare-up."

I stopped my bot abruptly. "What do you mean you're having a flare-up? I thought you said your experiment was stable?"

"It is." Temper's bot gestured toward the containment field where the light suddenly intensified. "It's just stubborn at times."

The energy within the field pulsed faster, casting shadows that danced across the cargo bay floor. Instrument readings spiked on nearby monitors.

"Well, what do you want me to tell my bridge crew?" I asked, glancing at the readings with growing concern.

"That it might be a while?" Temper's voice remained frustratingly calm as he made minute adjustments to the field parameters. "I can't move the ship and stabilize the flare-up at the same time."

I watched the energy pulse grow more erratic. "My crew will go into a full meltdown. Maybe it would be best if we don't mention anything about flare-ups."

"Tell them I'm sorry." Temper's bot moved with precise, unhurried movements around the containment field.

"I can't believe I saved you from Blackmane," I muttered, remembering our recent adventure.

Temper's bot paused its work and turned toward me. "Hmm, I believe it was me who saved you. Are you going to help me or not?"

I walked my service bot closer to his. Mine was nothing special to look at; just a dull metal body with interchangeable parts designed to fit whatever job needed doing. Standard issue, functional rather than flashy.

The sight of it brought back memories of bot training. Learning to operate them had been an interesting challenge. During training, the bots' speed and power were reduced to fifty percent capacity. My trainer had insisted that if we could master the bots at half capacity, we'd be ready for any emergency down the road.

Someone in my class had asked what would happen if the bots were more severely damaged than fifty percent. The trainer responded by bending all the way over in his bot and, reaching between his legs, kissed his own metal backside.

"Then it's time to say goodbye," he'd told us with grim humor.

Hellfire's bot was remarkably easy to maneuver compared to those old clunky training models. The responsiveness made it almost an extension of my consciousness rather than a separate entity I had to control.

"Fine," I said, moving my bot toward the containment field. "What do you need me to do?"

I approached the containment area with caution. Temper had constructed a semi-transparent half-wall in a perfect square formation around his experiment. The barrier stood about waist-high, creating what looked like an elaborate pen. Scientific equipment surrounded it; machines with probes and delicate instruments I couldn't identify, their sharp components glinting under the cargo bay lights.

"Don't touch anything," Temper warned, his service bot gesturing emphatically.

"Wasn't planning to," I replied, keeping a safe distance.

The machines hummed with purpose, their displays flickering with readings I couldn't interpret. Some emitted soft beeps at irregular intervals, while others maintained a constant, low-frequency vibration that I could feel through my bot's metal feet.

I stopped just short of the enclosure. Bending slightly forward in my service bot, I made sure not to accidentally brush against any of the equipment or topple into the pen itself. What I saw inside made me forget all about neural cartography, identity claims, and even my responsibilities as captain.

Floating in the middle of the enclosure was Falfsun, Temper's miniature sun. It had grown to the size of a beach ball since I'd last seen it, suspended in perfect equilibrium within the containment field. Its surface was mottled with orange patches where cooler gas churned up from the interior to the surface. The overall color was an eerie, fluorescent light green that seemed almost artificial for a sun.

The mottling shifted constantly, patterns forming and dissolving as the process repeated itself in endless cycles. From what appeared to be the north pole of the beach ball-sized star, a solar prominence arced gracefully upward. The loop of plasma extended high into the air before curving back down, touching the surface again near the equator. It resembled a rainbow made of fire, quivering and pulsing with energy.

"It's... beautiful," I admitted, unable to look away from the miniature star.

"And temperamental," Temper added, adjusting something on a nearby console. "The magnetic sleeve is preventing a coronal mass ejection. That would be bad."

"Bad as in 'oops' bad, or bad as in 'we'd all die' bad?"

"Somewhere in between." Temper's bot moved to another monitoring station. "The fusion process isn't self-sustaining yet. I still need to feed it."

The sun flared again, causing several monitors to beep in alarm. Temper's bot moved quickly between control panels, making adjustments.

"You said it was stable," I reminded him.

"It is stable," he replied, not looking up from his work. "Just not static. There's a difference."

I watched as the plasma loop shimmered and danced, its base widening momentarily before settling back into its original form. "How did you even create this?"

"Very carefully," Temper said, his attention still fixed on the readings. "And with a healthy disregard for conventional physics."

"Is that what you mean by being stubborn?" I asked, watching the miniature sun pulse with alarming brightness. "And remember, I'm not as smart as you are, so no big words please."

"It is," Temper replied, his service bot's mechanical hands making minute adjustments to a control panel.

The sun flared again, casting strange shadows across the cargo bay. Something about its erratic behavior reminded me of a temperamental child: beautiful but dangerous, fascinating yet terrifying.

"And what are you doing to control it?" I kept my bot at a safe distance, not entirely trusting the containment field.

"Nothing." Temper's voice carried that familiar tone of scientific detachment, the same one he used when explaining particularly hazardous experiments.

I paused, certain I'd misheard him. "Somehow that doesn't sound right. Go over with me again how not having it contained is a good thing?"

"It's really very simple." His bot straightened up, the gesture oddly human despite its mechanical nature.

"Go on." I folded my bot's arms across its metal chest, a habit from my human days that had somehow transferred to my operation of machinery.

"I'm watching it, but not interfering with it. I need to see what it does."

The sun pulsed again, its green-orange surface churning like a pot about to boil over. Each flare sent ripples through the monitoring equipment, causing readings to spike and alarms to chirp in my sensory feed before subsiding.

"So let me get this straight. You have a beach-ball-sized baby sun." I gestured toward the floating orb. "Congratulations on its birth, by the way."

"Thank you." Pride filled his voice. "It's my pride and joy."

"And your solar baby has a large, for its relative size, solar prominence occurring." I pointed to the massive arc of plasma extending from its surface.

"Correct." Temper sounded pleased, like a parent whose child had just performed a particularly impressive trick.

"And a solar prominence this large, for its relative size, could result in a coronal mass ejection?"

"So you do understand!" Temper's bot clapped its hands together.

"Not yet, I'm sorry if I'm confusing you by sounding too smart." The sarcasm in my voice was thick enough to cut. "Let me continue. And this mass ejection could, theoretically speaking, explode, shooting a hole through your spaceship and hit the Paradise? Like a gun firing?"

Temper's bot tilted its head. "Well, I don't know if I'd call it a gun."

"But it's the same as a loaded gun pointed straight at the heads of two million digital colonists." My voice rose as the implications fully registered. "And if it fires... Kaboom! Virtual brains splattered."

The sun flared again, as if responding to my words. The prominence wavered, stretching slightly before settling back into its arc.

"That's why I'm watching it, so that won't happen." Temper's bot gestured dismissively. "Besides, three magnetic sleeves surround Falfsun, so the explosion would be self-contained." His bot's arm swept toward the miniature star in an almost theatrical gesture. "Just look at it! Isn't it wonderful?"

I stared at the pulsing orb, caught between admiration and alarm. The sun was undeniably beautiful, a marvel of scientific achievement. Its surface swirled with patterns that would take lifetimes to fully understand, each prominence a dance of raw power contained by nothing more than Temper's confidence and three magnetic fields.

Beautiful, yes. Wonderful, perhaps. Safe? I had my doubts.

I stared at the swirling, pulsing mass of energy. The miniature sun rotated slowly, its surface churning with orange and green patterns that seemed almost alive. The prominence arcing from its surface quivered like a living thing, reaching outward before curling back.

"Yes... wonderful... a sun contained in a spaceship. What could go wrong?" My service bot's metallic voice couldn't quite capture my sarcasm. "Let me ask you this. If you had to, theoretically speaking, extinguish Falfsun, could you do it? You know, throw water on it and put the fire out?"

Temper's bot went still. The hesitation lasted only a second, but it was enough to send a chill through my circuits.

"I could dim it," he finally said.

"So that's a no, then?"

Temper's bot adjusted something on a nearby panel. "Falfsun doesn't have the gravity yet for self-sustainment. It would die if I didn't tend to it, but it would take time for that to occur. I don't know of anything that would instantly work. If I stop feeding it, then it will dim but continue to stay active until its thermonuclear reaction breaks apart and it dies. Does that make sense?"

"Yes, for the most part." I moved my bot slightly closer, fascinated despite my concern. "Would you say it's exhibiting true fusion?"

"Partial fusion, yes. It's in an in-between state. If I stop feeding it, the process shuts down."

The monitors surrounding Falfsun beeped softly, their displays showing fluctuating energy readings that seemed to pulse in rhythm with the miniature star's surface. I could feel the low vibration of contained power humming through my bot.

"And you're getting its food source from where?" I asked. "We're in deep space. There's nothing but an empty vacuum in all directions. There's not a lot of gas just lying around out here."

"Um, I'm creating it from the quantum substrata."

I swiveled my bot's head toward him. "You're creating its food from quantum foam?"

"It's all complicated." His bot waved dismissively. "I'd explain it to you but I don't think I can, not with your feeble grasp of physics. But I can assure you that it's perfectly safe. It won't explode. You're safe... I'm safe... everybody is safe." Temper's bot moved closer to mine. "Look, I can tell that this is upsetting you. Just remember, my sun is stable, just like a setting sun. Picture it getting really low in the sky. Just stay calm and picture the setting sun."

The familiar phrasing caught my attention. "Are you Bannering me?"

Temper laughed, the sound oddly human coming from his mechanical form. The reference to the ancient technique for calming anxious patients wasn't lost on either of us.

"Didn't you come over here to help me move the ship?" he asked, changing the subject.

I watched the filament dancing on Falfsun's surface, its movements hypnotic and unsettling. The prominence stretched further for a moment before settling back into its arc.

"That sounds like a great idea to move it away from Paradise," I said. "Let's get started."

Temper's bot gestured toward the far wall. "Walk over to the control panel, over there."

I followed his directions, my metal boots clanking against the floor. I looked up instinctively. The cargo bay doors gaped open to the void, revealing an unfiltered view of space that no human eye had ever truly seen. The stars didn't twinkle or shimmer as they would from Earth's surface. Without atmosphere to distort their light, they burned with perfect, unwavering clarity: pinpricks of brilliant white against absolute darkness.

"The doors are open to vent Falfsun's heat," Temper explained, noticing my gaze.

I reached the control panel and studied its layout. The console looked like something from those ancient sci-fi shows Amy and I used to watch together: oversized knobs, chunky levers, and analog displays that seemed deliberately retro. At the center sat a large red button with "DO NOT PUSH" emblazoned beside it in bold letters.

My mechanical hand hovered over it. Some childlike impulse, carried over from my human origin, made me want to touch it despite the warning.

"What does this do?" I asked.

"It starts the Code Zero Zero Destruct Zero countdown," Temper replied, his bot's voice deadpan.

"Really?" I pulled my hand back slightly.

Temper's bot paused, its head tilting. "No, it's a dummy switch. I put it there for a..." He stopped mid-sentence, studying my reaction.

"Very funny," I said flatly.

"Just kidding. It actually is a dummy switch. Does nothing." His bot made a dismissive gesture. "I added it because I think it looks cool."

I had to admit, it did. Everything about this situation was surreal. Two digital consciousnesses operating robots, hanging out in an airless cargo bay with a miniature sun. The absurdity wasn't lost on me.

I waited for Temper's next instruction, oddly aware of the absence of physical sensations. No fidgeting, no breathing, no heartbeat quickening with anticipation.

"Ready?" Temper asked, his bot moving to another console.

"Aye, captain," I replied.

The ship lurched suddenly as thrusters engaged, pushing Hellfire off its previous course. I was grateful for the maglev boots keeping my service bot anchored to the floor. Without them, we'd be floating helplessly in the zero-gravity environment.

Temper opened a communication channel. "Lieutenant Chen, we're adjusting course now. How far do you want us to move away?"

"Ten parsecs," I interjected.

"What?" Chen's confused voice came through the speakers.

Temper's bot somehow managed to convey a scowl despite its featureless face. I tried mimicking the expression with my own bot, unsure if I succeeded.

"Don't pay any attention to him, Chen," Temper said. "How far would you consider safe?"

"Two more miles?" Chen suggested.

"Go is assisting me," Temper continued. "We've already started our course correction to the new trajectory. It shouldn't take long. I'll contact you when we're there."

He closed the channel and turned to me. "Was that necessary?"

"Probably not," I admitted. "But you have to admit, a little humor helps when we're babysitting a potentially catastrophic stellar event."

The miniature sun pulsed behind us, casting our bots' shadows in sharp relief against the control panel. Its light shifted from green to orange and back again, like a cosmic mood ring.

I waited for Temper's next instruction, watching as he remained completely still, his service bot frozen in place. The miniature sun pulsed behind us, its light painting shifting shadows across the cargo bay. Falfsun's prominence stretched further, almost reaching the magnetic containment field before retracting again. The movement reminded me of a living creature testing its boundaries.

Temper's bot suddenly turned away from the controls, his attention completely captured by the sun's behavior. He moved closer to the containment field; mechanical head tilted in fascination as the filament danced across Falfsun's surface.

"It's beautiful, isn't it?" he murmured, more to himself than to me. "The patterns never repeat exactly. Each movement is unique."

I waited, expecting him to return to our task, but he remained transfixed by his creation. Minutes passed in silence, broken only by the soft beeping of monitoring equipment.

Finally, he seemed to remember my presence. "Okay, let's go."

"What do you want me to do?" I asked, confused by the sudden change in plans.

"Nothing. Just follow me." He returned his bot to its charging port.

I hesitated, looking back at the miniature sun floating in its containment field. "What about Falfsun? And the separation? You said you needed my help."

Temper paused. "Oh, that. I just said that to get you out of the house. You wanted to talk, so let's go talk." He gestured toward the driftway. "Do you want to turn out like me, living all alone with nothing but a sun to keep you company? I might have stretched the truth about needing your help a little."

"I think it's called lying," I replied flatly.

"Tomayto, tomahto." He shrugged. "Come on, there's something I want to show you. Haven't you ever wondered how I manage to pilot Hellfire all by myself?"

The question caught me off guard. I'd never given it much thought, assuming he used a similar system to the one we had on Paradise. "I figured you had an interface like our command center."

"Not exactly." Temper started walking down the driftway, forcing me to follow. "It's something... different."

We moved through Hellfire's driftways. Unlike Paradise's bright, open spaces, Hellfire's driftways were narrower, more utilitarian. Some of the walls bore marks of Temper's modifications: exposed wiring, handwritten notes taped to panels, and the occasional scorch mark from what I assumed were failed experiments.

He led me deeper into the ship than I'd ever been before, into areas I hadn't known existed. The driftway narrowed further, then opened suddenly into a circular chamber unlike anything I'd seen on either vessel.

We entered a spherical room that appeared to be at the heart of Hellfire's command center. The walls pulsed with subtle light, creating patterns that seemed almost alive. The illumination shifted between deep blues and purples, occasionally flashing with brighter colors that reminded me of neural activity. No conventional controls or screens were visible, just the continuous flow of light across every surface.

"What is this place?" I asked.

"This is the Neural Nexus," Temper explained. "From here, I can connect directly with every system on Hellfire."

He gestured toward a simple chair in the center of the room. No control panels, no displays, no interfaces of any kind.

"That's it?"

"That's all I need," Temper smiled. "My consciousness does the rest. Try it out. I've created a sandbox for you, so nothing you do will interfere with Hellfire's operations."

I approached the chair cautiously and sat down. Nothing happened.

"Close your eyes," Temper instructed. "Think of Hellfire not as a ship but as an extension of yourself. Imagine your awareness stretching beyond your form, reaching into the walls, the driftways, the engines."

I closed my eyes and tried to visualize what he described. At first, I felt foolish, like a child playing pretend. Then something shifted. A tingling sensation began at the base of my skull and spread outward, racing along pathways I hadn't known existed.

My awareness expanded suddenly, violently. I gasped as information flooded into me. Environmental readings from the ship's server shielding. Power consumption metrics from every sector. Life-code support parameters for the Tardigrade DNA memory servers. Navigation data. Communication logs. Heightened Security protocols surrounding the Ark.

"Too much," I managed to say.

"Focus," Temper's voice seemed distant. "Don't try to process everything at once. Choose one system."

I concentrated on navigation, picturing the ship's intended trajectory through space. The overwhelming tide of information receded, replaced by a clear understanding of our planned course. I could feel the subtle adjustments in our position, the minuscule corrections keeping us perfectly aligned.

"I can see our path," I whispered.

"Not see," Temper corrected. "Feel. You're not observing the ship; you're becoming it."

He was right. This wasn't visual information. It was a sensation, like knowing the position of my arm without looking at it. I extended my awareness further, cautiously exploring.

"This is incredible."

"Try the external sensors," Temper suggested.

I shifted my focus outward. Suddenly I could feel the vacuum surrounding us, the radiation washing against our shields, the distant heat of stars. The emptiness of space registered not as an absence but as a presence with texture and dimension.

"How far can I reach?"

"As far as our sensors can detect. Try looking toward Earth."

I turned my attention back toward the sun. There, a warm blue presence in the darkness. Earth. I could feel its gravitational pull through the QE-comm, the electromagnetic signals emanating from its surface, the complex dance of satellites in its orbit.

And somewhere on that sphere, Amy. David. Tom. the Emulation Court. The thought created a momentary disconnection, a flicker in my expanded awareness.

"You're learning quickly," Temper said, noticing my reaction. "But remember, emotional responses can disrupt the interface. Stay present."

I refocused, extending my consciousness throughout the ship.

"Can I control things this way?"

"You can't. You're just observing."

I nodded, continuing to explore. Each system revealed itself in new sensations: the cool efficiency of data storage, the quiet readiness of service robots in the cargo hold, patiently waiting to assist, and the complex patterns of internal communication networks.

"This is what it means to be captain for you," I realized aloud. "Not giving orders from a bridge, but feeling the entire ship as part of yourself."

"Yes," Temper agreed. "You're beginning to understand."

I left the Neural Nexus with my mind still buzzing from the connection.

"Let's go to my quarters where we can talk," Temper suggested.

The world blurred, then reformed around me. We'd blinked from the Neural Nexus into what could only be described as a perfect recreation of the Giese Manor great room. The massive stone fireplace dominated one wall, its intricate carvings catching the dancing firelight. Opposite stood those towering arched windows I remembered from our visits as young men. Beyond them lay the German countryside, faintly lit beneath a simulated night sky scattered with unfamiliar constellations.

"Welcome to my sanctuary," Temper said, moving to a cabinet of dark polished wood. "Whiskey?"

"Please."

I wandered toward the windows, tracing my fingers over the heavy burgundy curtains. The texture felt exactly right, the slight roughness of expensive damask against my skin. Temper had recreated every detail, down to the slight creak in the floorboards near the hearth.

"Here." He handed me a crystal tumbler with two fingers of amber liquid.

I took the drink to one of the leather armchairs by the fireplace and sank into its embrace. The leather yielded with a soft sigh, conforming to my body as if remembering me. The fire crackled, sending occasional sparks against the ornate screen.

Temper settled into the chair opposite mine. We raised our glasses in silent acknowledgment, a gesture that spanned decades of friendship.

The whiskey rolled across my tongue, smooth, complex, with hints of peat and brine that transported me instantly to that trip to Islay. Amy and I had wandered the Scottish coastline, visiting distilleries and falling asleep to the sound of waves crashing against ancient shores. The memory felt so vivid, so undeniably mine.

Temper swirled his glass, watching the liquid catch the firelight. We sat in comfortable silence, the kind only possible between old friends. Finally, he looked up.

"This seems like a good time to talk. How is your displacement claim going?"

The question ignited something in me. I leaned forward, grip tightening around my glass.

"I don't know. It's almost like they're ignoring me." My free hand cut through the air, whiskey sloshing dangerously close to the rim. "The Emulation Court sent one response asking for more evidence, then nothing. Complete silence."

"Calm down." Temper's voice dropped to that soothing tone I recognized from our academy days. "Remember the setting sun, Bruce. I got a message from Amy. She's worried about you."

"See!" The word burst from me like an accusation. "That just proves my point. If I wasn't the real David Schreiner, she wouldn't worry about me. I'd just be Go to her, the lost twin brother."

The firelight caught the amber liquid as I took another swallow, letting it burn away some of my frustration.

Temper leaned back, studying me. "She loves you both. How couldn't she? You, for all practical purposes, are David Schreiner. You are identical in every way, with shared memories going all the way back to your early childhood. To her, you and David are the same." He paused. "Or, at least you were the same."

"Thank you for acknowledging that I'm David and not the digital twin, Go." The words came out more bitter than I'd intended.

"That's not exactly what I said." Temper set his glass on the small table between us. "Look, after the emulation you and David were identical. But time has passed. Both of you have had new experiences that you don't share. Do you know what David is doing right now? No, you don't. And David doesn't know what you're doing, either. After the procedure, both of you naturally drifted apart. You're your own man now." His eyes held mine steadily. "What if your claim is denied? What will you do then? Continue to bang your head against the wall?"

I leaned forward until I perched on the edge of the cushion, carefully setting my whiskey down on the side table. The crystal caught the firelight, sending amber reflections dancing across the polished wood.

"I've been thinking about that," I said, folding my hands together to keep them from fidgeting. "If my claim is denied, maybe I can negotiate some kind of arrangement. What if Go and I could share my body? That sounds reasonable, doesn't it? We could both spend time with Amy that way." The idea had formed during sleepless nights in my cottage. "If I can't have my body full-time, inhabiting it part-time seems like the next best option. I'd be around to help, keep an eye on things."

Temper's expression shifted, his brows drawing together. The firelight cast deep shadows across his face, highlighting the skepticism in his eyes.

"I thought the whole idea of you joining this expedition was to keep me company," he said, his voice unnervingly calm.

The accusation stung more than I expected. I ran my fingers along the leather armrest, feeling its subtle texture against my skin.

"Well, yeah. I'd feel terrible about leaving you alone," I admitted. The thought of Temper traversing the cosmos with only Falfsun for company twisted something inside me.

Temper leaned forward, his elbows resting on his knees. "And how would the two of you sharing one body be fair to Amy? You claim you love her, but you'd force her to live with two similar but not identical men. To her, it would be like living with a husband who has amnesia."

He took a sip of his whiskey before continuing. "She might ask you about something you did together, like 'Remember when we went to the park last week?' But you wouldn't remember because it was the other David who went on that walk when it was his turn in the body. You wouldn't share that memory." His voice softened. "And scenarios like that would happen constantly. It would drive her mad." He shook his head. "Look, I only have to put up with one of you. I can't imagine having two versions around."

"Wait, what do you mean you have to 'put up' with me?" I straightened, indignation flaring. "From where I sit, it's the other way around."

The room fell silent except for the soft crackling of the fire. The simulated night sky beyond the windows remained perfectly still, stars fixed in their positions like painted dots on a black canvas. No twinkling, no shooting stars, no satellites crossing the darkness. Just another detail Temper hadn't quite perfected.

Temper's mouth curved into a slight smile, but his eyes held a sadness that contradicted it. For all his bluster about barely tolerating me, I knew better. The man who recreated his family home down to the creak in the floorboards, who built a miniature sun just to study it, who volunteered to spend over a thousand years alone in space, cared more deeply than he'd ever admit.

We sat in silence, the weight of our conversation settling around us. I stared into the dancing flames, watching them consume the logs without ever truly destroying them, an endless simulation of destruction and renewal.

I swirled the whiskey in my glass, watching the amber liquid catch the firelight. The question that had been burning inside me finally found its voice.

"Do you think I'm wrong for doing this?" I asked, my voice quieter than intended. "Should I just accept what's happening to me, even though I feel so strongly that it's wrong?"

Temper didn't answer immediately. He studied his glass, turning it slowly between his fingers. The simulated fire popped and hissed in the silence, casting warm light across his thoughtful face. When he finally spoke, his words came measured and deliberate.

"I think you should follow your heart." His eyes met mine. "Remember the protests back on Earth when we started advertising for colonists? People called us zombies. They said our digital twins wouldn't feel anything, that we couldn't feel. That we wouldn't be human, just unconscious, simulated copies of real-life humans."

I nodded, remembering the picket lines outside the Cognis Center, the angry faces, the signs with crude drawings of brains connected to computers.

"By doing what you're doing, you've proved them wrong," Temper continued. "Whether you win or not, you've advanced the argument that we're more than just digital copies. The people back on Earth following your story can feel your passion and hear your pain." He leaned forward. "Look at the conversation you've started. Some newspapers are calling you a fool for pursuing your claim."

A smile tugged at the corner of his mouth.

"When was the last time a machine was called a fool? You're showing the world that we have feelings. That we love and yearn. That we have human faults, whether we want them or not."

The words settled around me. I hadn't considered my actions in this light before. My glass made a soft thunk as I set it on the side table.

"I might not win my claim until after Point Alpha," I said, voicing the worry. "I wouldn't be able to use the QE-comm after that. Suppose that happens. How would I get home?"

Temper took a thoughtful sip of whiskey. "We're at half the speed of light. After Point Alpha, if we slowed down and reversed course, we'd arrive back to Earth in, I don't know, about a year?"

"And that's not taking into account the time dilation. It's still small, but it adds up," I added.

Temper lowered his head and stared at the floor. The firelight cast deep shadows across his face, highlighting the concern in his expression.

"Yeah, that might add another two, maybe three years to everyone's time back on Earth. Maybe less, depends on how long it would take us to brake and turn around." He shrugged. "Our ships weren't built for that."

I traced my finger along the leather armrest, feeling its subtle texture. "So maybe about four years total. Amy and I would have to reconnect. It might take some time to do that, but it would be worth it." I paused, considering the next obstacle. "Then there's another problem. I'll never be able to convince the colonists on Paradise to turn around and go back." I looked up, meeting his gaze. "Do you think maybe you could turn around? Could I bum a ride with you on Hellfire?"

Temper didn't hesitate. The immediacy of his response caught me off guard.

"Yes, Go. I'll help you get back, if that's what you really want."

The simple statement hung in the air between us. Temper would postpone his life's work, his dream of studying Orion's nursery of stars, just to help me return to Earth. To help me return to Amy.

"Thanks, Temper," I said softly. "I knew I could count on you."

The fire crackled, sending a shower of sparks against the screen.

Outside the windows, the simulated stars remained perfectly still in their artificial sky, waiting for decisions that would alter our course through both real and digital space.

Temper's expression softened, a mischievous glint appearing in his eyes as he refilled our glasses. "And I'll always think of you and your twin as being the same, only doubly now... doubly irritating... always getting in the way... a little smelly..."

I shot him a scowl, the kind I couldn't manage when trapped in a service bot's limited interface. I raised my glass in a mock threat.

Beyond the arched windows, a massive bull moose ambled past, its antlers spreading like branches against the simulated sky. It lowered its head to graze on tall, sweet grass growing between the spruce trees. The creature moved with unhurried confidence, completely unaware it was merely a digital construct in Temper's elaborate sanctuary.

"Do you remember the road trips we used to take?" I asked, watching the moose. "Just you and me out on the open road?"

Temper smiled, genuine warmth replacing his teasing tone. "How could I forget? Those were good times."

The memories washed over me: highways stretching endlessly toward the horizon, gas station coffee at three in the morning, arguing over radio stations until we'd finally agree on classic rock. Simple pleasures from a life that felt increasingly distant.

As if responding to the ache beneath the nostalgia, the Symphony of Us sensed my mood and began to play. A soft guitar riff curled through the air, unmistakably the opening of *"No Maps, No Morning"* by Duston Rye, a folk-rock drifter whose voice always sounded smoke-worn and road-weary, the kind of voice that carried its own ashtray.

We were kings of the exit signs, chasing dawn in secondhand jeans. No maps, no morning — just the hum of a world that hadn't asked for us yet.

The song filled the room like memory itself: unpolished, tender, and free of consequence. I let it play.

"I miss my old life." The words escaped before I could consider them. My fingers traced the rim of my glass. "Hey, did I ever tell you about the time Amy got Vatican tickets to the wedding at Canaan?"

Temper leaned back, settling deeper into his chair. "You may have mentioned it once or twice. It's a good story. I wouldn't mind hearing it again." He tilted his head. "Was it a good time?"

"Oh, it was the best." My voice lifted with the memory. "These were Vatican tickets! Not the cheap knock-offs you can buy to the back-alley shows."

The whiskey warmed my throat as I took another sip, the room around me fading as the memory took shape.

"When I got to the wedding, I was standing on this dirt road, and over a stone wall was a goat with a bell around its neck, just staring at me." I laughed at the absurdity of that first moment. "Then I heard my name and turned in that direction. It was Amy running down the hill, calling out to me."

My heart swelled with the vividness of the memory. "Her chestnut hair was bouncing on her shoulders and the sun was shining on her face. You could see her freckles and, oh man, she looked gorgeous." I gestured with my free hand, tracing her path in the air. "Well, we ran up the hill together to join the wedding party..."

I forgot about my anger, my displacement claim, the uncertainty hanging over me. For the next hour, I talked about that perfect day, describing the stone jugs filled with water, the expressions on the servants' faces when they realized what had happened, the way Amy had cried tears of joy, clutching my arm as we witnessed the miracle unfold.

Afterward, Temper and I fell into an easy silence. The simulated fire crackled softly, casting dancing shadows across the room. The moose had long since wandered off, replaced by a night sky now showing subtle movement among its stars.

Finally, Temper straightened and opened a communication channel. "Separation is complete. You can proceed when ready, Chen."

The message served as a gentle reminder that our ships continued their journey regardless of our personal dilemmas. I stood up, setting my empty glass on the side table.

"I should go back." The weight of reality settled onto my shoulders once more. "Thanks for the drink and the ride offer."

I looked around the room one last time, taking in the perfect recreation of a place from our shared past. "You've got a nice place."

CHAPTER FIVE

Sprites

I used the QE-comm to transfer back to Paradise, my consciousness sliding through the quantum link. The familiar sensation of digital reassembly washed over me as I reintegrated with Paradise's systems. The bridge materialized around me, its curved walls displaying a panorama of stars against the void.

Commander Okafor stood at the center console, her close-cropped silver hair catching the glow from the displays. Her eyes, the color of wet slate, moved methodically across the data streams.

"Captain on deck," announced Lieutenant Chen, her amber eyes meeting mine briefly before returning to her communications array.

"At ease," I said. "I'm here to assist with the C-pinch experiment."

Okafor nodded. "We appreciate the extra supervision, Captain. I'll be coordinating the team." Her voice carried the calm authority that had made her our obvious choice as bridge crew commander.

"The experiment parameters are locked in," said Raj Mehta from his navigation station. "Hellfire has established optimal distance for observation."

I glanced at the external view. Hellfire hung in space a safe distance away, its three curved prongs catching starlight. I could picture Temper watching us, probably nursing another whiskey.

"Service bots are prepped for manual override if needed," Okafor continued. "Chen, please send the alert to all colonists."

Chen's fingers danced across her console. "Alert transmitted, Commander. Two million souls notified." She paused, monitoring the feedback. "Most are choosing to ignore it. Typical Tuesday for them, I suppose."

I couldn't blame them. The digital citizens of Paradise lived their lives largely unaware of the physical vessel carrying them through space. Why worry about ship operations when there were digital mountains to climb and oceans to sail?

"I'll take a bot to Monkey Island," said Maya, referring to our nickname for the topmost observation platform. "Best vantage point if comms fail."

Okafor assigned positions to the rest of us. "Captain, would you join Petrov, Sullivan, and Rodriguez amidships? You'll form a protective perimeter around the server core."

I nodded, already connecting to one of the service bots. The bot's visual processors rendered everything in slightly desaturated tones, its movements mechanical and deliberate.

My bot walked to the bulwark that shielded our collective existence. I found the others already positioned around the central chamber containing the tardigrade DNA memory banks. The servers hummed with a barely perceptible vibration, like the breathing of a sleeping giant.

I took my position at rear starboard, completing our protective square around the memory core. Through the bot's sensors, I could detect the intricate crystalline structures of the servers, each microscopic tardigrade a fortress protecting our human minds.

"All personnel in position," Chen's voice came through our comms. "Initiating countdown for C-pinch experiment."

"T-minus sixty seconds," announced Chen.

The memory of Father's watch pressed against me, a phantom weight from my avatar that my bot couldn't physically feel. I touched the server housing with the bot's manipulator arm, feeling a connection to the millions of souls trusting us with their journey.

"T-minus thirty seconds. All systems nominal."

I stood guard over the memory banks, my service bot's sensors scanning the crystalline structures housing two million souls, including my own, to establish a baseline. The countdown echoed through the comms, each second punctuating the strange duality of my existence. Here I was, simultaneously inside these servers and outside them, watching over myself.

Twenty-five seconds.

The tardigrade DNA substrata slumbered in perfect cryptobiosis, theoretically immortal. Nature's ultimate survivors now cradled humanity's consciousness. The carbon-titanium alloy shield encasing them gleamed under the ambient light, designed to protect against engine failures and accidental damage.

Twenty seconds.

My thoughts drifted to the paradox of my situation. Inside those memory banks, I lived, prayed, loved. I walked through digital meadows and slept in a cottage that existed only as electrical patterns. Yet I felt the sun on my face and tasted fresh morning coffee as vividly as I had on Earth.

Fifteen seconds.

Standing here in this mechanical proxy, looking at the physical housing of my own consciousness, I confronted the fragility of our existence. We were electrical impulses in a physical world, copies of human minds living in simulated realities. Some questioned whether we deserved to be called human at all.

Ten seconds.

But aren't all human minds electrical by nature? The biological brain interprets electrical signals to create thought and feeling. What truly separates us from our flesh-and-blood counterparts? Is humanity defined by the nerve cells and fibers inside a skull?

Five seconds.

We think. We feel. We laugh and cry. I understand pain and loss better than most because of Amy. The absence of her physical presence creates an ache that sometimes feels unbearable. We love, hate, and wonder at the universe around us. Doesn't that make us real? Alive?

Three seconds.

If someone flipped a switch and shut down these servers, we would all die. Our deaths would be as final as any biological death. Would our passing go unmarked? Would anyone mourn for digital souls?

Two seconds.

I gazed at the memory banks through my bot's visual processors. Father's watch seemed to weigh in my pocket, though the bot couldn't feel it. The watch connected me to my past, to my father, to Amy. It anchored me to my humanity regardless of where my consciousness resided.

One second.

"Initiating C-pinch experiment," Chen announced, her voice steady.

The server room hummed with energy. Lights flickered momentarily as power redirected to the experiment. My bot's sensors detected subtle changes in electromagnetic fields, but the memory banks remained stable, true to baseline, their biological architecture undisturbed.

"All systems holding," Rodriguez reported from her station. "Memory integrity at one hundred percent."

Sullivan's bot moved closer to the servers. "No thermal variations detected."

I monitored the shield integrity, watching numbers scroll across my bot's visual field. "Shield functioning at optimal levels," I confirmed. "No stress detected on memory architecture."

The experiment continued, minutes stretching as we maintained our protective formation. Through it all, I couldn't shake the profound strangeness of guarding myself, of being both captain and cargo on this impossible journey.

The countdown faded into background noise as the experiment began in earnest. Through my bot's sensors, I watched the memory banks pulse with subdued light, the tardigrade DNA substrata maintaining their cryptobiotic slumber despite the power fluctuations around them. The shield integrity remained solid, numbers scrolling across my visual field confirming what I already knew: our digital souls remained safe.

"Transitioning to phase two," Commander Okafor announced over comms. "Beginning prong adjustment sequence."

I directed my attention to the external feeds. Paradise's three forward prongs began their choreographed movement, extending outward like the mandibles of some ancient insect. The sight transported me back to the first time Temper and I had seen them during construction. We'd practically bounced off the walls of the observation deck, two grown men reduced to excited schoolboys by the sheer audacity of the engineering.

"Look at that," Temper had whispered, his breath fogging the viewport glass. "They actually built it exactly like the Oracle designed it."

I remembered pressing my palm against the cold glass, watching the construction bots attach the final segments. "It's beautiful," I'd said. "Terrifying, but beautiful."

Now those same prongs moved with deliberate precision, forming the framework for our experimental energy system. The electronic net began to materialize between them, gossamer-thin and nearly invisible except for occasional flickers as it caught ambient radiation.

"Net integrity at ninety-seven percent," Rodriguez reported. "Initiating C-field detection protocols."

The purpose behind today's test was deceptively simple: determine if the prongs could effectively generate and maintain the electronic net needed to capture broken light particles from the omnipresent C-field. These captured particles would then be funneled to a central point, twisted into spirals, and pinched together to create fusion. If successful, the system would serve as an emergency backup to our primary power sources.

"Adjusting prong configuration to pattern Alpha-Six," Maya called from Monkey Island. Her voice carried the focused tension of an engineer in her element.

Through the external feeds, I watched the prongs shift again, moving into a triangular formation that reminded me of a predator's open maw. The electronic net between them shimmered, stretching to accommodate the new configuration.

"C-field detection positive," Chen announced. "We're registering particle capture at approximately eighteen percent efficiency."

Petrov's bot shifted beside mine. "Better than projected for this velocity."

"Agreed," Sullivan added. "The Oracle's calculations suggested we wouldn't see efficiency above fifteen percent until we reached at least sixty percent light speed."

I monitored the shield integrity around our memory banks, but my attention kept drifting to the external feeds. The prongs continued their dance, testing configuration after configuration as Maya guided them through the predetermined sequence.

"Transitioning to pattern Omega-Three," Maya announced.

The prongs began shifting again, moving into a forward-facing spiral pattern that would theoretically maximize particle capture. The net between them pulsed with increased energy as it adjusted to the new formation.

That's when I saw them.

My service bot actually stumbled backward, its balance protocols momentarily overwhelmed by my startled reaction. Floating in space around the electronic net were... things. Amorphous blobs of semi-transparent material, pulsing with internal light. They hadn't been there seconds before.

"What are those?" I blurted out, my voice sharp with alarm.

The bridge fell silent for a heartbeat before erupting into controlled chaos.

"Unknown objects detected near the prong array," Chen reported, her normally calm voice tight with tension.

"I'm seeing them too," Maya confirmed from Monkey Island. "Approximately two dozen protean entities, seemingly attracted to the electronic net."

The blobs drifted closer to the net, their bodies, if you could call them that, elongating as they approached. They reminded me of deep-sea jellyfish, but with a strange, almost deliberate quality to their movements.

"Are they alive?" I asked, the question slipping out before I could consider its implications.

"Unknown entities, Captain," Lieutenant Chen corrected herself, fingers flying across her console. "They appear to be non-corporeal. No mass readings, no thermal signature."

I watched, transfixed, as the undulant forms drifted through space with apparent purpose. More appeared, materializing from nowhere. Their wispy, cloud-like bodies glowed with a soft internal luminescence, pulsing gently as they moved toward Paradise.

"They're approaching the hull," Rodriguez reported, her voice tight.

The first entity reached our outer hull and, impossibly, passed through it as if the reinforced metal were nothing but mist. My service bot's sensors tracked its progress as it entered the ship.

"Holy shit," I muttered, watching as more of them followed. Soon, dozens of the wispy, white blobs floated throughout the midship section, moving with languid grace.

"They're inside," Sullivan announced unnecessarily, his bot pivoting to track their movements.

One of the ethereal forms drifted directly toward the memory banks. My bot moved instinctively to intercept it, but the entity simply passed through my mechanical body. The sensation registered as nothing more than a minor static discharge in my control interface.

The entity continued unimpeded and floated straight through the DNA servers where our consciousness resided in quantum storage. My heart seemed to stop as I watched it pass through the very housing of my existence.

"Holy crap, that's our home!" Jamie Sullivan blurted, his bot backing away from another approaching entity.

I couldn't disagree with his assessment. Those servers contained everything we were: our memories, our personalities, our very souls. Watching these unknown entities pass through them felt violating, terrifying.

One of the blobs drifted toward Petrov. His security bot jumped backward in alarm, colliding with the bulkhead with a metallic clang. The entity continued undeterred, passing through both the bot and the ship's interior wall.

"They don't seem to be interacting with our environment," I observed, forcing calm into my voice. "They're just... passing through."

The entities continued their slow procession from the front of the ship toward the aft section, utterly indifferent to our presence or the physical boundaries of our vessel.

"Commander, are you seeing these?" I asked, opening a channel to Monkey Island.

"I see them," Okafor confirmed, her voice measured. "They don't appear to have any mass or heat signature." She paused. "I'm also noting a small increase in our velocity above expected parameters.

Chief Engineer, please pause the experiment."

"Pausing now," Maya responded. The prongs began retracting to their default position, the electronic net dissipating.

I watched the ghostly procession continue undisturbed. The sight was simultaneously beautiful and unsettling, like witnessing spirits drifting through our reality from some parallel dimension.

"I should notify Temper," I decided, initiating a QE-comm link to Hellfire.

He answered immediately. "Hi Go," Temper greeted, his voice cheerful. "How's the experiment going?"

"It's been interesting. We had to pause it." I hesitated. "Why don't you take a look midship and you'll see why."

There was a brief pause as Temper linked with Chen's visual feed.

"Ah, I see you have sprites," he remarked casually.

I blinked in surprise. "You know about them?"

"Yes, I told you that already."

"When?" I demanded, incredulous. "What are they? Tell me again!"

Temper's voice carried that familiar tone of mild exasperation he reserved for when he thought I wasn't paying attention. "I mentioned them before in my weekly reports on Falfsun. I call them sprites. Don't you read my reports?"

I opened a private channel with Chen. "Did we get weekly reports?" I asked her.

"We get a report every week," she replied with a hint of amusement. "Nobody ever reads them. I tried reading them the first few times we got one, but they were filled with tables upon tables of endless temperature readings. Temper records everything that Falfsun does. Pretty boring stuff, so all I do now is file and forget."

"Okay, thanks," I said, closing the private channel and feeling slightly embarrassed.

I watched as the protean entities continued their silent procession through our ship, passing through bulkheads and equipment with ghostly indifference. Their wispy forms glowed with soft internal light, casting no shadows as they drifted toward the aft section.

"What do you think these sprites want?" I asked Temper, my eyes following one particularly large blob as it passed through a structural support beam.

"They seem drawn to energy signatures," Temper replied, his voice carrying that familiar tone of scientific curiosity. "Why else would they all move to the aft where the engines are? I'll bet you have them crowding around your nanowire batteries." He paused, and I could almost see him leaning forward on the other end of the comm. "My theory is that the prongs are pinching something other than broken light. I think they're pinching space itself. The sprites didn't appear until after you began the experiment, right? I think they're harmless. You can probably proceed."

I frowned, directing my service bot to follow one of the entities. "And you came up with this theory how? How could you know that ahead of time?"

"I noticed some floating near Falfsun. Then I saw more, so I did the math, but honestly, this is beyond even me." Temper's voice carried a rare note of humility. "I don't understand what these blobs are at all. I just know that they haven't harmed anything over here, so I doubt if they'll hurt you either."

The memory of my recent visit to Hellfire flashed through my mind. "I was just over at Hellfire looking at your research. How come I didn't see any sprites?"

"The sprites aren't very bright. They only seem to emit a dim light." Temper's explanation came quickly. "That's why you can see them there, but not here in the glow of Falfsun."

Petrov's bot stepped forward, its movements reflecting the security chief's concern. "What research are you doing, Temper? As head of security, I should know about any research that might be attracting these sprites."

"Stellar nucleosynthesis combining primordial particles." Temper's response was immediate and matter of fact. "You should monitor for the sprites as I suggested in my report. You haven't been monitoring for them? Does anybody even read my reports?"

The bridge fell silent. Through my bot's sensors, I watched as the sprites continued their inexorable journey toward our power systems. One passed directly through Rodriguez's bot, causing her to flinch visibly despite the lack of physical sensation.

"We should have read your reports, but we didn't," I confessed, feeling the weight of responsibility. "I admit, a mistake was made. Maybe when something unusual like this happens, you know, when sprites visit us out in interstellar space, then you should pick up the phone and tell somebody verbally in order to highlight it."

"In light of today's events, I couldn't agree more," Temper conceded. "I'm going to start doing that."

"Can you send us your monitoring specs?" I asked, watching another sprite drift lazily through a bulkhead like it was nothing more substantial than fog.

"Will do. Keep me posted," Temper replied, his voice carrying that mixture of scientific excitement and casual confidence I'd come to know so well.

The QE-comm link closed with a soft click. Moments later, Chen's console chimed.

"I just received the specs," she announced, already scanning through the data.

Commander Okafor straightened, her silver hair catching the overhead lights. "Shut it down, people. Let's huddle up afterward."

Maya nodded, her fingers dancing across her console as she initiated the shutdown sequence. The external feeds showed Paradise's three prongs retracting to their default positions, the gossamer electronic net between them dissolving. The sprites continued their silent procession through our ship, utterly indifferent to our actions.

"Implementing sprite monitoring protocols," Rodriguez announced, her eyes never leaving her screen as she incorporated Temper's specifications into our sensor array.

I watched the ghostly visitors drift through our memory banks again, suppressing a shudder. Those servers contained everything we were: our consciousness, our memories, our very existence. Seeing these unknown entities pass through them felt deeply unsettling, like watching strangers rifle through my most personal belongings.

Once the systems were secured, Maya descended from Monkey Island. We moved as a group back to the cargo bay where our service bots were housed. The sprites had thinned out somewhat, though several still drifted through the area, their amorphous bodies pulsing with that strange internal light.

I guided my bot into its docking cradle, feeling the familiar disconnection as my consciousness separated from the mechanical body. The others followed suit, their bots powering down one by one.

"Conference room in five," Commander Okafor instructed as we blinked out.

The conference room materialized around me, its polished mahogany table gleaming under soft lighting. Floor-to-ceiling windows offered a spectacular view of stars streaking past as Paradise continued its journey. A side table held an assortment of beverages and snacks; one of the many small pleasures of digital life.

I walked over and poured myself a cup of coffee, the aroma rich and inviting. Two jelly-filled donuts found their way onto my plate. Eating was perhaps the most popular recreational activity aboard Paradise. Without physical bodies to worry about, food had become pure pleasure without consequences: no calories to count, no weight to gain, no health concerns to monitor. We ate constantly and shamelessly.

Taking a seat, I bit into one of the donuts. The sweet, sticky filling burst across my tongue. Perfection. I savored it while the others settled around the table, their conversations a low murmur of scientific terminology and speculation.

Chen stood, tablet in hand. Her braided hair caught the light as she moved to the head of the table.

"I've sorted through Temper's data," she began, bringing up a holographic display above the center of the table. Ghostly images of sprites rotated slowly in the air. "All of the encounters are random, so they're hard to rank, threat-wise. Some seem to be drawn to the batteries where they congregate, which is the greatest possible threat, but they don't seem to interact with the batteries, or with each other."

I took another bite of my donut, watching the holographic sprites pulse and shift just like their real counterparts. Father's watch weighed in my pocket, a comforting presence as we faced yet another unknown in our journey across the stars.

Maya folded her hands on the table, her close-cropped silver hair catching the soft light. "I agree. When I started adjusting the prongs they appeared, but they didn't interact with the prongs as far as I could see. I saw them move from there back towards the engines."

Petrov leaned forward, his neatly trimmed beard framing a frown. "Our DNA servers might draw their attention once we reach cruising speed, and the Helical engines shut down. We know these sprites can penetrate the server's protective shield. That's a concern.

What if they become hostile? Do we dare wait until then? Until after they make the first move?"

I swallowed the last bite of my donut, the sweetness suddenly less satisfying as I considered the implications. Our entire existence resided in those servers. If something happened to them...

"Where's Merlin? Can he join us?" I asked, wiping sticky residue from my fingers with a napkin.

Chen nodded and tapped her comm interface. "I'll contact him now."

Merlin was an elite matrix architeer, one of the best aboard Paradise. He created worlds that people literally lined up to experience. I didn't fully understand how he did it, but in his simulations, the food tasted better, the people were happier, the sunsets more glorious, and everything worked without a single glitch. If anyone could offer insight into these strange entities, it might be him.

The air shimmered briefly, and Merlin appeared. Without acknowledging any of us, he walked directly to the snack table where he filled his plate with two glazed donuts and three Long Johns. Only after sitting down and taking his first bite did he look around the table.

"Hello everyone. What's going on?" Crumbs dusted his shirt as he spoke.

"Thanks for joining us," I said, watching him devour the pastry with remarkable efficiency. "Just so you know, this isn't general knowledge yet. Take a look at these."

I sent him Temper's findings with a gesture. The holographic sprites continued their silent dance above the conference table, their ethereal forms pulsing with that strange internal light. I stood to refill my plate with two apple and cherry fritters.

Merlin munched thoughtfully, his eyes scanning the data scrolling beside the holographic sprites. No one spoke. The only sounds in the room were the soft hum of the ship's systems and Merlin's occasional appreciative murmur as he bit into another donut.

Minutes passed. I watched the stars streak by outside the windows, wondering what other surprises waited for us in the vast emptiness between here and Orion. The universe seemed determined to remind us how little we truly understood about it.

Finally, Merlin brushed the crumbs from his fingers and looked up.

"Okay," he said, reaching for his coffee. "How can I be of help?"

I leaned forward in my chair, the smooth surface of the conference table cool beneath my forearms. "Do you feel the sprites are a threat to the safe operation of the ship?"

Merlin popped the last bite of donut into his mouth, chewing thoughtfully. Powdered sugar dusted his upper lip as he considered the question. "Not that I can see." He gestured toward the holographic images floating above us. "They don't interact with anything. It's like they're ghosts passing through our reality."

He took a sip of coffee, leaving a sugar-rimmed mark on the cup. "The sheer number of encounters without incident suggests they're harmless. However..." His voice trailed off as he studied the rotating images. "What if a rare encounter did result in an interaction? It might take only one to cause damage."

The thought sent a chill through me. Father's watch seemed heavier in my pocket, its presence a reminder of everything we stood to lose. Two million souls, countless memories, Earth's entire biological legacy, all housed in those vulnerable DNA servers.

"If we needed to capture them, do you think you could?" I asked, watching another sprite drift past the conference room window, its ethereal form barely visible against the backdrop of stars.

Merlin set down his coffee and manipulated the holographic display. One sprite enlarged, rotating slowly above the table. Its amorphous body pulsed with that strange internal light, tendrils occasionally stretching outward before retreating back into its core.

"Well, we could probably attract it into a black box with an energy spike." His fingers traced patterns in the air, sketching a conceptual containment system around the holographic sprite. "That would be the easy part. But to keep the sprite contained in it?" He shook his head, uncertainty creasing his brow. "I don't know if we can."

I nodded, considering the implications. "Look into it, will you? See if it's possible?"

"Will do." Merlin gathered his remaining pastries onto his plate. "When are you going to tell everyone else?"

The question hung in the air. I glanced around at the faces of my bridge crew, each watching me with varying degrees of concern.

"Soon," I said simply.

Merlin nodded, then blinked out of the room, his plate of donuts vanishing with him.

I turned to Petrov, our security chief. "Anything we can do for now, besides monitor them?"

Petrov rubbed the back of his neck, his neatly trimmed beard shifting as he frowned in thought. The gesture was so human, so familiar; one of the countless small mannerisms we'd all carried with us from our physical lives into this digital existence.

"We could prepare some kind of energy beacon," he suggested after a moment. "Maybe something we could jettison out into space to attract them away from the ship if we needed to."

I nodded, the plan taking shape in my mind. "Sounds good." I turned to Chen, her braided hair catching the light as she looked up from her tablet. "Chen, can you take point on that?"

She nodded crisply, her amber eyes already calculating possibilities. She looked over at Maya. "Can you build it?"

Maya's fingers were already dancing across her interface, preliminary designs taking shape. "I'll need to run some simulations first, but yes."

Chen turned to Petrov. "We'll want your input on this, too."

I watched my crew shift seamlessly into problem-solving mode, each contributing their expertise. Despite the uncertainty of our situation with sprites drifting through our ship, and my own identity crisis simmering beneath the surface, I felt a surge of pride. Whatever challenges the universe threw at us, we would face them together.

The conference room was silent. I found myself staring at the holographic sprites floating above the table, their ghostly forms pulsing with that strange internal light.

"Maybe this would be a good time to consider sending this to Holmes for a consult?" Commander Okafor suggested, her voice cutting through the quiet.

The name sent a ripple of tension around the table. Holmes, the Oracle, was both a resource and a risk. Tom had paid an astronomical sum for our initial two-minute, in-person consultation to help plan our journey to Orion. The most intelligent artificial intelligence ever created, with a measured IQ over 9,000. Most experts believed Holmes was hiding its true intelligence. Without question, it was the most dangerous entity on Earth, kept in a triple-layered containment system designed specifically to prevent its escape.

We had purchased three additional two-minute consultations to be used at our discretion. A resource held in reserve for moments exactly like this.

I sat back in my chair, the leather creaking softly beneath me. My gaze drifted to Chen, and I raised my eyebrows in silent question. "What do you think?"

Chen tucked a loose strand of hair behind her ear, her amber eyes thoughtful. "Right now, communication with the Oracle would be instantaneous. When we reach Point Omega, all QE-comm contact with Earth will be lost. Even the consultations will be worthless."

She didn't need to elaborate. We all knew the timeline. Four months until Point Omega, when quantum decoherence would make communication with Earth impossible. After that, we would truly be on our own.

Commander Okafor nodded, her decision forming. "I think we should do it. We're on a 1,300 light-year voyage. In only four months, we won't be able to use them. We should use our consults while we can."

Maya leaned forward, her slate-gray eyes intense. "It might help us determine if the sprites are a danger. For all we know, our batteries might even be generating them." A spark of scientific curiosity lit her expression. "Maybe we've even discovered an unknown force of physics."

The possibility hung in the air, tantalizing and frightening in equal measure. The thought of consulting Holmes both intrigued and unsettled me. The Oracle's intellect was unmatched, but its motives remained a mystery. Every interaction with it came with calculated risk.

"Two minutes with Holmes," I mused, watching another sprite drift past the conference room window. "What exactly would we ask?"

Rodriguez tapped her fingers against the table. "We need to know if they're dangerous. If they can harm the DNA servers or the ship's systems."

"And how to contain them, if necessary," Petrov added, his

security training evident in his practical focus.

I nodded slowly, weighing our options. The sprites continued their silent dance through our ship, oblivious to our deliberations. Two million souls depended on our decision. The biological legacy of Earth rested in our DNA servers. We couldn't afford to make a mistake.

"All right," I said, straightening in my chair. "Let's prepare our questions for Holmes. We need to make every second count."

I turned my attention to the holographic display one final time, watching the ghostly sprites drift through our simulated environment. We needed more information, and I knew exactly where to get it.

"Temper, we want to use a consult with Holmes to find out more about the sprites. Any objections?"

"None whatsoever," Temper replied, his attention momentarily split between our conversation and whatever calculation he was working on. "I think it's a good idea. Holmes might see patterns we're missing."

I nodded, "Okay, let's do it then. Everyone should add their own observations to the report. The more comprehensive our data, the better Holmes can analyze it."

Chen's fingers were already dancing across her interface. "I'll compile everything and prepare the transmission."

"I'll include the energy readings from the prongs," Maya added, her slate-gray eyes focused on her work.

Petrov leaned forward. "I'll document all security concerns and potential vulnerabilities."

The crew worked with practiced efficiency, each contributing their expertise to the report. I watched them with a mixture of pride and gratitude. Whatever my true identity might be, I couldn't have asked for a better team.

"Oh, and one more thing," I said, drawing their attention back to me. "We should let everyone know what's going on. There might be a little panic, but they deserve to know."

Petrov frowned. "Captain, is that wise? We don't know if these entities pose any danger yet."

"That's exactly why we should tell them," I countered,

remembering Amy's words about transparency. "Better they hear it from us than discover it themselves and wonder what else we're hiding."

Maya nodded her agreement. "Two million colonists. If even a fraction of them encounter these sprites, word will spread regardless."

"I'll draft an announcement," Chen offered, giving me a thumbs up. "Clear, factual, no cause for alarm."

"Perfect." I stood, signaling the official end of the meeting. "Let's reconvene after we hear back from Holmes."

No one moved to leave. Rodriguez reached for another donut, and Petrov refilled his coffee cup. Maya and Chen continued working on their interfaces, occasionally murmuring to each other about technical specifications.

I smiled to myself, settling back into my chair. The meeting was officially adjourned, but I knew from experience that no one would leave until the last donut was gone. Some traditions transcended even the vast distances of space.

Father's watch ticked quietly in my pocket as I reached for another fritter, savoring this moment of normalcy amidst the extraordinary journey we shared. Whatever mysteries awaited us among the stars, we would face them together, one donut at a time.

The meeting disbanded slowly, with my crew lingering over coffee and the last few pastries. I watched them file out one by one, their faces reflecting varying degrees of concern about our ethereal visitors.

I blinked back to my cottage, materializing in the small entryway. The familiar scent of lavender and rosemary drifted in from the garden through the open windows. Normally, it would have been comforting, but today it barely registered.

Sinking into my favorite armchair facing the garden, I tried watching an episode of the Home Prairie Network. Alice was making Cranberry Meringue Tartlets, her hands moving with practiced precision as she explained the importance of properly whipping egg whites. Any other day, I would have been captivated by her techniques, maybe even inspired to try them myself. Today, her cheerful voice faded into background noise.

The garden beyond my window buzzed with life. Bees moved methodically from bloom to bloom, butterflies danced on air currents, and birds darted between the birdhouses in the old oak tree. It was beautiful, perfect even. And completely hollow.

My mind kept circling back to one particular moment in the meeting. Not the sprites, though those were concerning enough, but Chen's words about Point Omega. Four months until all communication with Earth would become impossible. Four months until my last chance to resolve who I truly was would vanish forever.

The Emulation Court still hadn't responded to my petition. What if they never did? What if I reached Point Omega with this question still hanging over me, doomed to spend centuries wondering if I was living someone else's life?

Father's watch was in my pocket. I pulled it out, running my thumb over its worn surface. The second hand ticked steadily, marking time that suddenly felt very finite.

I needed to take action. Contacting Amy directly was something I'd avoided, not wanting to force her to choose between two versions of the same man. But time was running out. If anyone could help the court understand my situation, it was her.

Turning off the cooking show, I moved to my desk and opened a communication channel. My fingers hovered over the interface. What would I say? How could I possibly explain what I was feeling? I needed to get this right.

A message would be better than a direct call. I could choose my words carefully, make sure everything came out exactly as intended. Taking a deep breath, I began to write:

"Dear Amy,

"You probably didn't expect this request from me, but I need your help. Indeed, my happiness depends on it. I want to be direct with you, and talk to you as best friends do, the way we always have in the past. I want to return home to be with you, so that we can resume our lives together.

"I can't stop thinking back on how we said our goodbyes. I remember the look of sadness in your eyes as I departed. It haunts me in my sleep. Your look of sadness told me that you know the truth. I wake up with a start, suddenly realizing that you're not laying there beside me. It's taken me some time to put everything into perspective. I think you must realize that my departure was profoundly unjust. I think you also realize that I am David Schreiner and that my digital twin, Go David, has secretly taken my place at your side. I failed to stop my own kidnapping, and I ask for your help to save me.

"I have filed a displacement claim in Emulation Court for my full reinstatement as your husband. I think if you are willing to contact them and file jointly with me, and ask them to rule in my favor, that it would go a long way in helping me to win.

"I know what I'm asking sounds crazy, and I won't pretend that I haven't changed. I think that I'm now a better man. I have so many stories to tell you about my adventures on board Paradise. Did Temper tell you that he now has a baby sun? He named it Falfsun! That's just one of the many stories I have to share.

"Whatever your decision may be, please know that you have made me the happiest man on Earth, and so, I will close this letter with a very sincere- Thank you.

"All my love,

"David"

I sat back and read the message twice. Something felt missing. I couldn't assume Amy knew what I suspected, or that she suspected what I knew. The layers of knowledge between us had become too complex, too tangled.

I rubbed my eyes, feeling the confusion tying my thoughts into knots. The message was as good as it would get. My finger hovered over the send button.

The garden caught my attention again. Bees buzzed among the primroses, their steady work continuing regardless of my existential crisis. The old oak stood firm beyond the fence line, its branches swaying gently in the breeze. This digital home was beautiful, but it wasn't mine. Not really.

I pressed send.

Numbness washed over me afterward. I moved through the cottage like a ghost, unable to focus on anything. Even Alice's cooking show held no appeal. I just waited, simultaneously desperate for and terrified of Amy's response.

The following day, Temper contacted me about Holmes' reply. The Oracle wanted more data on the sprites.

"Do whatever you want," I told him, barely registering the conversation.

I kept two communication channels open at all times: one for Temper, one for Amy. Then I sat in my garden and waited, watching the bees move from flower to flower with enviable purpose and certainty.

CHAPTER SIX

Digital Anger

I couldn't stop checking messages. Every three minutes, I'd refresh the communication panel, watching the spinning icon with the desperate focus of a man awaiting execution. My cottage felt like a prison cell now, the digital walls closing in with each passing hour. The garden outside, Amy's garden, mocked me with its perfect tranquility.

"System update complete. Two new messages received."

My heart hammered against my ribs. Two messages. One from the Court, one from Amy. I opened the Court's message first, needing to get the bureaucratic response out of the way before facing whatever Amy had written.

The Emulation Court seal rotated slowly at the top of the document:

"RE: Petition #EC-23759-GL (RULING)

Petitioner: Go David Schreiner

Subject: Identity Displacement Claim

After thorough review of submitted materials and in accordance with Section 47.3 of the Neurological Preservation Act, the Court finds insufficient evidence to support the petitioner's claim of identity displacement.

The Court acknowledges the petitioner's subjective experience of memory anomalies. However, without baseline neurological comparison data (unavailable after Point Alpha), these anomalies cannot be verified as evidence of displacement versus standard neuroclone memory formation variations.

This petition is hereby DENIED.

Further appeals must be submitted within 30 standard days.

By order of Magistrate Wong

Emulation Court, Earth Division"

The words blurred as I read them. Cold. Clinical. Final. They hadn't even bothered with a personal touch. Just another case number, another digital entity with delusions of humanity.

I closed the document with trembling fingers. One message left. Amy's message. I touched the icon, and her face filled my screen.

"Dear Go," she began.

Go. Not David. Just... Go.

My stomach dropped as she continued, her gentle voice somehow making it worse. I watched her explain why she couldn't support my claim, why she believed I should continue the journey. Each word felt like another nail in the coffin of my identity.

"You are, and forever will be, my moon and stars. Goodbye."

The message ended. Amy's face disappeared, leaving me alone in the silence of my cottage.

I sat motionless for what felt like hours. The rejection was complete. Total. The Court didn't believe me. Amy didn't believe me. Or worse: perhaps she knew the truth but had chosen the other David anyway. The David who stayed behind. The David who wasn't broken.

I stumbled to the window. Outside, the digital bees still buzzed among digital flowers under a perfect digital sky. None of it was real. Maybe I wasn't either.

A notification chimed. The Paradise systems requesting my attention. Two million souls still depended on me, regardless of which soul I might be.

I straightened my uniform jacket and wiped my face. Captain Go David needed to return to the bridge. Captain Go David had responsibilities.

But who was Captain Go David? A copy? The original? A fractured piece of someone else's identity?

I no longer knew. And apparently, no one would tell me.

I stared at the empty screen where Amy's face had been moments before. The finality of her words echoed in the silence of my cottage. "Goodbye." Not "see you soon" or "until next time." Just... goodbye.

A sudden rage boiled up from somewhere deep inside me. I swept my arm across the desk, sending digital objects clattering to the floor. The sound was perfect, calibrated to mimic reality, but it was all fake. Simulated physics. Simulated objects. Simulated me.

I stood and looked around the cottage. Every corner held Amy's touch. The watercolor painting of the oak tree hanging above the fireplace. The collection of antique thimbles arranged on the bookshelf. The hand-knitted throw draped over the reading chair. Had she really designed all this for me? Or were these memories implanted, manufactured to keep me docile and functional?

I moved to the kitchen, running my fingers along the butcher block countertop. Amy and I had selected it together for our first apartment. We'd sanded it together, applied the mineral oil in layers, laughing as our hands slipped against each other's. At least, that's what I remembered. But was it my memory or his?

The teacup in the sink. Earl Grey, Amy's favorite. I could almost smell it, though I knew that was just my brain filling in the details. She'd drink it every morning while reading the news. I'd kiss the top of her head as I passed, and she'd reach up without looking, catching my hand for a moment.

A lie? A truth belonging to someone else?

My communication panel chimed. Temper again. Third time in the last hour. Something about the sprites, no doubt. I ignored it. Let the mysterious entities have their run of the ship. What did it matter now?

I wandered into the bedroom. The quilt on our bed came from Amy's grandmother. Each square told a story from her family history. I'd spent countless nights tracing the patterns with my fingertip while Amy told me about the great-aunt who'd been a suffragette, the cousin who'd played minor league baseball, the grandfather who'd built violins.

I grabbed the quilt and buried my face in it. No smell. Of course not. Digital fabric doesn't hold the scent of sleep or skin, or the lavender sachets Amy tucked between the folds when storing it for summer.

The communication panel chimed again, more insistently.

"Mute all communications," I ordered.

The cottage fell silent. I sank onto the edge of the bed, still clutching the quilt.

On the nightstand sat a framed photo of our wedding day. Amy radiant in her mother's restored gown, me looking at her like she was the only person in the universe. The memory of that day flooded through me. The nervous fumbling with my cufflinks. Amy's father whispering encouragement before walking her down the aisle. The way time seemed to stop when I saw her.

I picked up the frame, studying my own face. Was that me? Or was I just remembering through someone else's eyes?

I set down the photo and opened the nightstand drawer. Inside lay a small notebook, Amy's handwriting filling its pages. Notes she'd written while designing my memory palace. Little details she wanted to get right for me.

For me. Or for him?

The cottage suddenly felt suffocating. Every object, every memory, every moment of joy preserved here was suspect. I couldn't trust any of it. I couldn't trust myself.

The Oracle would know. Holmes could tell me the truth. But we'd already used one of our precious consultations on ship business. Could I justify using another for my personal crisis?

I jabbed at the communication panel with enough force to crack glass had it been physical. "Lieutenant Chen. My quarters. Now."

While waiting, I paced the cottage's small confines. Each object I passed seemed to mock me with its artificial perfection. The watercolors never faded. The wooden surfaces never gathered dust. The garden outside maintained perfect harmony, unlike the turmoil inside of me.

All lies. Beautiful, comforting lies.

The soft chime announced Chen's arrival. She materialized in my living room, professional as always, but her eyes betrayed concern.

"Captain, you requested my presence?"

I stopped pacing and faced her. "I need all instances of the oak tree consolidated into one. The memory palace version. Move all personal effects from my cottage there too: all pictures, notebooks, music, everything."

Chen's expression shifted subtly. Her hands, normally steady, fidgeted with the edge of her uniform. "Captain, are you sure? The neural pathways are deeply integrated..."

"Just do it." My voice sounded foreign to my own ears, hard and brittle. I took a breath. "And... make it destructible."

Her eyes widened. "Sir, these are core memories..."

"That's an order, Lieutenant."

She straightened, professional mask sliding back into place. "Yes, sir. It will take approximately six hours to reconfigure the neural pathways and consolidate the digital assets. I should warn you that this could cause temporary disorientation as your consciousness adjusts to the altered memory structure."

"I don't care."

Chen nodded, a hint of worry clouding her expression. "I'll begin immediately. Would you like me to notify medical—"

"No. This remains between us. Understood?"

"Understood, Captain." She hesitated. "Sir, if I may... these constructs were designed as emotional anchors. Altering them isn't recommended without psychological consultation."

I laughed, a harsh sound without humor. "My psychological consultation just told me goodbye, Lieutenant. Six hours. That's all I need to know."

Chen blinked and disappeared, leaving me alone again. Six hours. Six hours until I could confront the centerpiece of my fractured identity. The oak tree Amy had so lovingly recreated, with its twenty birdhouses and countless memories.

I moved to the window, looking out at the garden. Soon it would be gone, along with everything in it. All consolidated around that damn tree. The tree that existed in my memories, in Amy's memories, in David's memories. The tree that had died in a storm decades ago yet lived on in digital perfection.

Which memories were truly mine? The Court had ruled. Amy had chosen. But something inside me still rebelled against their verdict.

Six hours to wait. Six hours until I could face the oak tree that had witnessed a lifetime of moments I might or might not have lived.

Six hours until I could destroy it.

The cottage dissolved around me as the memory palace took shape. Six hours had passed like six years, each minute dragging with the weight of my uncertainty. Chen had completed her work efficiently, without questions or judgment. Now everything waited for me, consolidated around the single point of my fractured identity.

I materialized beneath the oak tree.

It loomed larger than I remembered, its branches stretching impossibly wide against a twilight sky. The twenty birdhouses hung from various limbs, each one meticulously crafted by hands that might or might not have been mine. Thousands of photographs dangled from invisible threads, rotating slowly in a breeze that existed only in this digital construct.

My father's watch pressed against my thigh, unnaturally heavy in my pocket. I pulled it out, flipped open the case. Tick-tick-tick. The sound felt obscene in this quiet sanctuary. A perfect replica of a real object that sat on a nightstand back on Earth. Back with the real David Schreiner.

The real David.

I snapped the watch closed and shoved it back into my pocket. The Court had ruled. Amy had confirmed. I was Go, not David. A copy, not the original. A shadow cast by someone else's light.

I reached up and grabbed the nearest photograph. Amy and I—no, Amy and David—on our honeymoon in New Zealand. Her hair whipping across her face in the mountain wind, her smile wide and carefree. My hands trembled as I tore the photo in half. The digital paper ripped with satisfying resistance, programmed to mimic reality.

Another photo. Christmas at her parents' house. Rip.

Our first apartment. Rip.

The day we adopted our cat. Rip.

My movements accelerated, gaining momentum with each destruction. I tore down photographs by the handful, shredding them before they hit the ground.

"These aren't my memories," I growled, my voice rough with emotion. "These aren't mine."

I jumped, catching a lower branch, and pulled myself up into the tree. The first birdhouse hung just within reach. Number one, the crude pine construction David had made when he was seven. I yanked it from its hook and hurled it to the ground. It shattered, splinters flying in all directions.

The second birdhouse followed. Then the third.

Sweat beaded on my forehead as I climbed higher, destroying each handcrafted memory. The cedar birdhouse with blue glass. The lighthouse painted robin's-egg blue. The Victorian with its intricate design. Each one represented years of a life I couldn't be certain was mine.

Photographs continued to flutter around me, some drifting close enough to grab and destroy, others dancing just out of reach. Images of a life lived with Amy. Birthdays. Anniversaries. Quiet Sunday mornings. Travels across the world. All suspect now. All potentially belonging to someone else.

I reached the rustic log cabin birdhouse, made from his grandfather's barn wood. My grandfather's barn wood? I hesitated, fingers brushing against the weathered surface. A memory surfaced: the smell of sawdust, the weight of ancient timber in my hands, the satisfaction of preserving something that would otherwise be lost.

Was that memory mine? Or his? Did it matter anymore?

With a roar of frustration, I ripped the birdhouse free and flung it away. It tumbled through the air, breaking apart as it hit the ground.

"I don't know who I am!" The words tore from my throat, raw and primal. "I don't know who I am anymore!"

I smashed another birdhouse against the trunk. Splinters of wood cascaded down, joining the growing debris beneath the oak. The small castle with its turrets and crenelated roof lay in ruins, just like my certainty about who I was.

"David? What are you doing?"

The voice froze me mid-destruction. Amy stood near the bench, her form shimmering slightly at the edges. Not the real Amy. Just her digital ghost, programmed to respond when I damaged her carefully constructed memory palace.

"Go away." I turned back to the tree, reaching for the farmhouse birdhouse with its slanted roof and wood trim.

"These are our memories." Her voice wavered with programmed distress. "Please don't."

I laughed, a harsh sound that echoed unnaturally in the digital space. "Our memories? Or his memories? The Court ruled, Amy. You chose. I'm not David."

"I don't understand." Her response came too quickly, too smoothly. Of course she didn't understand. This hologram wasn't programmed to comprehend identity crises. She could only respond with variations of preset phrases, designed to comfort and connect.

"You're not her." I yanked the farmhouse free, watching it tumble through the air. "You're just code. Like me."

Amy's hologram flickered. "David, these memories mean so much to us. Remember when you built the lighthouse birdhouse? It was the year we got married."

The mention of the lighthouse birdhouse sent a fresh wave of anger through me. I'd already destroyed it, sent it crashing to the ground below. Or had David destroyed it? Were these my hands tearing apart this sanctuary, or was I merely watching through borrowed eyes?

"Stop calling me David!" I shouted, my voice cracking. "The Court ruled. Amy, the real Amy, confirmed it. I'm Go. Just Go."

"Our memories are what connect us across the stars." The hologram stepped forward, repeating another programmed response. Her movements were too fluid, too perfect. "Please don't destroy what we've built together."

Each word felt like a knife. We hadn't built anything together. She had built this place for him, for David, the man who stayed behind. I was just the copy, sent away on an impossible journey.

"We didn't build this together." I climbed higher, reaching for the last birdhouse: the simple cedar one, unadorned and honest. "You built this for him. The real David."

"I don't understand." The same phrase again, delivered with the same concerned expression. "These are our memories, David. Please don't."

The repetition fueled my rage. I tore the final birdhouse from its branch and hurled it directly at the hologram. It passed through her flickering form and shattered against the bench.

"You can't even respond properly!" I shouted, clinging to the branch as my body shook with fury. "You're just an algorithm, cycling through the same responses. You're not Amy. You're not my wife. You're just... code."

The hologram's expression shifted to one of gentle concern. "I'm sorry you're hurting. These memories are precious to both of us."

"Stop saying that!" I climbed down, jumping the last few feet to land amid the wreckage of birdhouses and torn photographs. "They're not my memories! They're his! David's! The man you chose to keep!"

Amy's hologram watched me with that same programmed compassion. "David, I love you. Whatever's troubling you, we can work through it together."

I stepped closer, studying her face. Perfect in every detail, yet empty of true understanding. A beautiful shell without the spark that made Amy real. Just as I was a perfect copy of David, lacking whatever essential quality made him the original.

I looked around at the destruction I'd wrought. Birdhouse fragments littered the ground like broken promises. Torn photographs fluttered in the artificial breeze. Yet the oak tree still stood, mocking me with its indestructible presence.

"Not enough," I muttered, kicking through the debris. "Not nearly enough."

The memory palace responded to my thoughts, shifting and reconfiguring. Beyond the oak tree, the garden path materialized, leading to a small toolshed that hadn't been there moments before. The shed from our backyard in Pittsburgh, where we'd spent fifteen years renovating an old Victorian. Where David had spent those years. Not me.

I stalked down the path, gravel crunching beneath my feet. The shed door stuck slightly, just as it had in reality. I yanked it open, the familiar scent of motor oil and cut grass washing over me. Tools hung in perfect order on the pegboard wall. David had always been meticulous about organization.

My eyes found what I sought. The axe hung on two metal hooks, its hickory handle worn smooth from years of use. I'd split firewood with it every autumn, preparing for winter. Or David had. The distinction blurred with each passing moment.

I grabbed the axe, testing its weight. Perfect. Digital perfection.

The path back to the oak seemed longer now. Amy's hologram waited, her expression shifting between programmed concern and confusion.

"David, please. Whatever's troubling you—"

I ignored her, positioning myself at the base of the massive trunk. The axe felt right in my hands, an extension of my fury. I swung it back and brought it forward with all my strength.

"LIES!" The blade bit deep into the bark with a satisfying crack. Wood chips flew, some passing through Amy's insubstantial form.

I wrenched the axe free and swung again.

"FAKE!" The blade struck a different spot, sending a splinter as long as my forearm shooting into the air.

Amy's hologram moved closer, her voice modulating to a soothing tone. "These memories are what connect us across the stars. Please don't destroy what we've built together."

Another swing, harder this time.

"NOT REAL!" A chunk of bark flew past my head as the axe embedded itself deeper into the trunk.

Sweat poured down my face despite the climate-controlled digital environment. I pulled the axe free, my arms burning with exertion. Again and again, I struck the tree, each blow accompanied by a shout that tore from my throat.

"LIES!"

"FAKE!"

"NOT MINE!"

The oak showed damage now, deep gashes marking its once-perfect surface. Still, it stood, resilient against my assault. Just like the truth that refused to bend to my wishes.

Amy's hologram flickered closer, her programmed distress increasing with each blow to the tree. "David, stop. These memories are all we have."

I paused, chest heaving, axe hanging limply from my hand. Her words cut deeper than they should have. All we have. All I have left of her, of us, of the life I thought was mine.

"They're not my memories." My voice came out raw, scraped hollow. "They're his."

"I don't understand." The same phrase, repeated with the same inflection. A digital ghost, running through its limited conversational pathways.

Something broke inside me. The last thread of hope, perhaps. The desperate wish that somewhere in this elaborate construct, some part of the real Amy remained.

I straightened, suddenly calm. "CoreLink, delete hologram Amy."

Her image stuttered, eyes widening with programmed surprise. "David, please, I—"

She flickered out mid-plea, leaving me alone with the wounded oak and my axe.

The silence pressed against my ears. No birdsong. No rustle of leaves. Just the sound of my own ragged breathing in a digital void of my making.

I lifted the axe again, muscles burning with purpose now rather than rage. Each swing became more precise, more calculated. No more wild flailing. I'd cut down this tree with the same methodical care David had used to build the birdhouses.

The blade bit deep into the wounded trunk. Wood fibers split with each impact, revealing pale heartwood beneath dark bark. Chip by chip, I carved a wedge into the ancient oak. Sweat stung my eyes despite the memory palace's perfect climate.

"Not my memories," I muttered with each swing. "Not my life."

The axe struck again. The tree groaned, a low sound that seemed to vibrate through the digital ground beneath my feet. Another blow. Another. The wedge deepened.

I circled to the opposite side and began cutting a second notch. The work felt good, purposeful. Physical labor had always cleared my mind. Had always cleared David's mind. The distinction mattered less now.

The oak shuddered. A crack ran up its massive trunk, splitting bark and wood fiber. I stepped back, watching as the giant swayed. For a moment, it seemed to fight against gravity, against inevitability.

Then it fell.

The crash shook the entire memory palace. The ground trembled beneath my feet as the massive trunk slammed into earth. Branches snapped. The remaining photographs tore free, scattering like startled birds. The impact echoed through the digital space, a thunderclap of destruction.

I stood amid the aftermath, axe hanging loose in my grip. The fallen giant stretched before me, branches reaching out across the ground. Around its broken form lay the shattered remains of twenty birdhouses, each one representing years of craftsmanship and love.

Years that weren't mine.

I dropped the axe and began to gather the debris. Fragments of wood. Torn photographs. Pieces of the life I thought I'd lived. My movements became rhythmic, purposeful. I collected every splinter; every shard of the birdhouses David had built for Amy.

The lighthouse painted robin's-egg blue, made the year they married. The Victorian with its intricate details. The rustic log cabin crafted from his grandfather's barn wood. Each piece I gathered represented moments, memories, connections that the Court had declared weren't mine to claim.

I arranged the collected debris in the center of the clearing, building a careful pyre. Layer by layer, I stacked the fragments, interweaving torn photographs between broken wood. The structure grew steadily, a monument to what I'd lost. Or perhaps to what I'd never truly had.

When the pyre stood complete, I reached into my pocket. My father's watch pressed against my palm, its weight familiar and strange all at once. I flipped open the case, listening to its steady tick-tick-tick. Inside the cover, Amy's photograph gazed up at me, her head resting on David's shoulder beneath this very oak tree.

My hands trembled as I placed the watch atop the pyre. The perfect replica of an heirloom that belonged to someone else. The watch rested there, still ticking, counting seconds in a place where time had no meaning.

I stepped back, surveying my work. The pyre stood ready, built from the wreckage of memories I could no longer claim as mine. Only one thing remained.

From my other pocket, I withdrew a lighter. David's lighter, with his initials engraved on the side. The one Amy had given him on their tenth anniversary. I flicked it open, and a flame danced to life.

"Goodbye," I whispered, touching the flame to the base of the pyre.

The fire caught quickly, hungrily consuming the dry wood. Flames licked upward, engulfing birdhouses and photographs alike. Smoke rose in a straight column, unaffected by the artificial physics of the memory palace.

The watch gleamed atop the burning heap, still counting time as the flames rose to claim it.

Somewhere in the distance, a melody stirred. Faint at first, like a memory half-recalled. The Symphony of Us began to play.

It wasn't loud. It didn't demand attention. It simply existed, woven into the crackle of flames and the silence of grief. A slow, aching progression of notes that mirrored the pyre's rise, each chord echoing a moment lost.

I watched as the first spark caught the edge of the memory palace walls. The flames spread with unnatural speed, following invisible paths that Amy had coded into this place. This wasn't normal fire; it moved with purpose, tracing the neural pathways she'd created to connect all our memories. Our memories. His memories.

The music followed. As fire traced the neural pathways Amy had built, the Symphony deepened, strings swelling with urgency, harmonies unraveling like threads pulled from a tapestry.

The fire raced along the ivy-covered stone archway, transforming the green tendrils into orange serpents of flame. I stood motionless, transfixed by the destruction I'd unleashed. The pyre at my feet roared, consuming the broken birdhouses, but now it was just one point in a growing constellation of fire.

Flames licked up the walls of the bungalow in the distance, catching the tiled roof. The structure ignited like kindling, windows glowing orange before shattering from the heat. I remembered how carefully Amy had recreated that place, down to the crooked floorboard in the kitchen and the stain on the bathroom ceiling. Now it burned.

The gallery was next. Through the archway, I glimpsed paintings curling and blackening. Masterpieces we'd stood before together in museums across the world twisted in the heat. A piano motif emerged, delicate and mournful, echoing the collapse of beauty. Van Gogh's stars melted. Monet's lilies withered. The Rembrandt that had moved Amy to tears in Amsterdam bubbled and peeled away, revealing nothing behind it but code and emptiness.

"What have I done?" My whisper vanished beneath the roar of the flames.

Fire raced along the path toward our first apartment. The melody fractured. Dissonant chords crept in, subtle but jarring; like memories misremembered. The building caught quickly, flames climbing its walls like eager climbers. Through its windows, I watched our furniture burn: the secondhand couch where we'd spent countless evenings, the rickety dining table where we'd shared our first meal as a married couple, the bed where we'd loved and dreamed and planned our future.

The kitchen ignited. That temperamental stove where Amy had attempted cookies. The window that never quite closed. The small table where we'd eaten breakfast every morning, hands touching across its surface. All of it consumed by flames that followed the precise architecture of Amy's creation.

The heat should have been unbearable. I should have felt it searing my skin, singing my hair. But this was digital fire in a digital world. I felt nothing but the hollow ache in my chest as I watched our history burn.

Fire spread through the rolling hills beyond the cottage, following invisible trails that connected memory to memory. A beach in Costa Rica where we'd watched sea turtles hatch. A café in Paris where Amy had laughed so hard, she snorted coffee through her nose. The hospital room where we'd held her father's hand as he slipped away.

Every memory ignited. Every carefully preserved moment of a life together blazed with unnatural brightness before collapsing into ash and embers. The Symphony of Us reached its crescendo here; not triumphant, but tragic. A final swell of strings and brass, as if the music itself were trying to hold the memories together before they slipped away.

The oak tree, massive even in death, burned with particular intensity. Flames consumed its fallen trunk, racing along branches that had once held twenty birdhouses and thousands of photographs. The fire ate through decades of growth rings, through years of shared history, through the very heart of what Amy had built for us. For him.

I stood amid the inferno, untouched by the heat yet burning all the same. The watch on the pyre had long since disappeared into the flames. I wondered if it still ticked somewhere in the digital void, counting seconds that no longer mattered.

The memory palace burned around me, walls crumbling, paths

disintegrating, memories turning to smoke and ash. I had destroyed the sanctuary Amy had created with such care. The place she'd built to keep us connected across thirteen hundred years of space.

And still I felt nothing but emptiness. No satisfaction. No relief. No clarity.

Just the hollow recognition that I'd destroyed the only connection I had left to her, real or not.

The inferno around me danced with a cold beauty, consuming everything yet warming nothing. Each crackling tongue of flame erased another fragment of the life I'd thought was mine. I stood motionless, watching history dissolve into digital ash.

A sudden glint caught my eye. The watch.

The music faltered. A single violin held the melody now, thin and wavering, as if unsure whether to continue.

My father's watch lay partially exposed atop the pyre, somehow surviving the initial blaze. Its silver case reflected the firelight in hypnotic pulses as flames licked hungrily at its edges. The tiny photograph inside, Amy's head on my shoulder beneath this very oak, curled at the corners but remained intact.

"No." The word escaped as barely a whisper.

What was I doing? This wasn't just David's memory; it was mine too. Whether I was the original or the copy, these memories formed the foundation of who I was. I couldn't erase my past without erasing myself.

I lunged forward. The heat shouldn't have registered in this digital space, but pain seared through my hand as I plunged it into the flames; not from fire, but from the memories themselves, each one burning with the truth I'd tried to reject. The violin strained, notes bending under pressure. The Symphony mirrored my desperation, its rhythm stumbling as I reached for the watch. My fingers closed around the watch's hot metal case. The burning sensation intensified, sending waves of agony up my arm.

"CoreLink, reset environmental parameters," I gasped, expecting the system to respond by extinguishing the flames.

Nothing changed. The fire continued its relentless consumption. My programming request had failed, or perhaps Amy had built this place with safeguards against such easy escape. Once destruction began, it couldn't be undone.

I pulled harder, trying to extract the watch from the growing inferno. The metal case grew soft in my grip. The once-solid silver began to lose cohesion, morphing from solid to liquid under the impossible heat. The chain slipped through my fingers.

"Please." I strained against the flames, fighting to save this one piece of myself.

The watch face cracked. Numbers warped and melted. The hands, which had kept perfect time for over a century, twisted into unrecognizable shapes. The photograph inside blackened, Amy's smile disappearing into ash.

"Amy." Her name caught in my throat.

The watch dissolved completely, silver running between my fingers. Nothing remained but a formless puddle that sank into the digital pyre. Gone. The last tangible connection to my father, to Earth, to the life I'd lived or thought I'd lived.

The music broke. A final chord rang out—unfinished, unresolved. Then silence. The Symphony of Us was gone. Consumed by the fire like everything else.

I fell back, cradling my burned hand against my chest. The pain felt real enough, sending sharp pulses through nerve endings that didn't physically exist. I stared at my reddened palm, watching blisters form across skin made of code and light.

The realization hit me with crushing force.

I'd destroyed everything. Not just the memories, but the gift Amy had created with such care. The sanctuary she'd built to keep us connected across impossible distance. The love that transcended physical form.

And for what? To prove I wasn't David? To reject a past that, whether originally mine or not, had shaped the person I'd become?

Around me, the memory palace continued to burn. The cottage collapsed in on itself, sending a shower of sparks into the digital sky. The gallery's walls crumbled, centuries of art disappearing into code and emptiness. The fallen oak, our oak, released its final death groan as flames consumed its massive heart.

I'd accomplished nothing except to erase the only connection I had left to her.

The fire had become a living thing, devouring every memory with insatiable hunger. No music remained. Only the echo of what had been; a silence shaped by absence. I stood motionless in the center of destruction, watching as flames consumed the architecture of my past. The burning oak sent embers spiraling upward into the digital sky, each one a fragment of memory disintegrating before my eyes.

Smoke began to curl around my ankles, thick and acrid. It twined between my legs, then rose in tendrils that wrapped around my calves. The memory palace, once vibrant with color and life, had faded to shades of orange and black. The bungalow roof collapsed with a thunderous crash. Our first apartment folded in on itself. The gallery walls crumbled, releasing clouds of ash that had once been priceless art.

I should have felt something. Regret. Satisfaction. Relief. Instead, a strange calm settled over me as I watched the destruction I'd wrought.

The smoke thickened. Through gaps in the billowing clouds, I glimpsed a door standing alone amid the chaos. It hadn't been there before, a simple wooden rectangle with a brass knob, connected to no wall, leading to nowhere. Or perhaps leading to everywhere.

My feet moved without conscious thought. Each step felt weighted, as though I walked through water rather than smoke. The ground beneath me shifted, sometimes solid, sometimes yielding like sand. The fire roared in my ears, punctuated by the cracking of timber and the shattering of glass.

The door grew closer. Plain oak planks bound with iron bands. No ornamentation except for a small carved bird near the handle, its wings spread in flight. One of Amy's touches, no doubt. Even in destruction, she'd provided an exit.

I reached for the knob. The brass felt cool against my palm, incongruous amid the inferno. Behind me, another section of the memory palace collapsed with a sound like distant thunder. The twenty birdhouses were gone now, reduced to cinders and ash. The photographs had curled and blackened, faces and places lost forever.

My hand rested on the doorknob. I turned to look one final time at what remained of the sanctuary Amy had built with such care. The smoke parted momentarily, revealing the fallen oak at the center of it all. Flames danced along its massive trunk, consuming growth rings that represented decades of life. Our life. My life.

For a fleeting moment, I saw her standing beneath its burning branches. Amy, as she'd been when we first met beneath that tree. Young. Smiling. Hand extended toward me in invitation or farewell. The smoke shifted, and she vanished.

I turned the knob. The door swung open silently, revealing nothing but emptiness beyond. No light. No darkness. Just the absence of everything.

I stepped through the threshold. The doorway framed the burning memory palace like a painting, a landscape of destruction rendered in fire and smoke. The cottage had completely collapsed now. The gallery existed only as a skeleton of charred beams. The oak continued to burn, its flames reaching toward a sky that no longer existed.

One last look at burning memories. One last glimpse of a life I could no longer claim as entirely mine.

I closed the door firmly behind me. The sound echoed with finality, a period at the end of a sentence. Through the solid wood, I heard the memory palace collapse completely, a symphony of destruction reaching its crescendo.

Then silence.

CHAPTER SEVEN

New Beginnings

I closed the door behind me and found myself standing in the cottage. Not the burning memory palace, but the empty shell I'd been inhabiting since my arrival in Paradise. The transition felt seamless, as though the memory palace had never existed at all. Perhaps it hadn't. Perhaps none of it had.

I turned the lone wooden chair to face the wall and sat. The wall was blank. White. Empty. Like me.

Everything that had connected me to Amy, to David, to the life I thought was mine was gone. I'd purged it all in a fit of rage that left nothing but this hollow space. The cottage remained structurally intact but stripped of anything personal. Anything meaningful.

My eyes traced the faint rectangular shadows on the wall where photographs once hung. Lighter patches of paint marked their absence, ghostly reminders of moments I could no longer claim. Had they been my moments at all? The Court said no. Amy said no. Only I disagreed, and what was my opinion worth against the weight of legal judgment?

On the mantel, a line of dust outlined the spaces where Amy's thimble collection once stood. Thirty-seven thimbles from thirty-seven countries, each with its own story. Stories I remembered in perfect detail. Stories that belonged to someone else.

The window offered a view of the garden outside. Primroses and violets swayed in the breeze, their colors vibrant against the green backdrop. The garden remained unchanged while everything inside had been stripped bare. It felt distant now, like looking at a painting rather than a living space. I couldn't remember the last time I'd walked those stone paths or sat beneath the arbor.

Hours became days. Days became weeks.

Outside my window, the primroses withered and gave way to summer blooms. The roses climbed higher on their trellises. Bees buzzed between flowers, unaware that their keeper had abandoned them to their own devices.

Messages accumulated, unread. Temper's first few were casual:

"Dinner at Giese Manor tonight? Chen's making her famous dumplings."

Then concerned:

"Haven't seen you at the bridge in a while. Everything okay?"

Finally, urgent:

"Go, it's been three weeks. We need to talk. Paradise needs its captain."

I ignored them all.

Summer faded into autumn. The garden's green gave way to gold and crimson. Leaves fell from the apple trees, creating a carpet of decay beneath their branches. The first frost came, crystallizing the remaining flowers into fragile sculptures that shattered with the morning breeze.

Winter settled over the cottage. Snow accumulated on the windowsill, creating a frame of white around my view of the dormant garden and of the empty space where the oak tree once stood.

My terminal chimed with a priority message. I almost ignored it like all the others, but something in the tone cut through my apathy.

POINT OMEGA NOTIFICATION: FINAL QUANTUM ENTANGLEMENT STABILITY THRESHOLD IN 72 HOURS.

The words hit me like a physical blow. Point Omega. The final threshold before complete isolation from Earth. After that point, no communication would be possible for the remainder of our 1,300-year journey.

Seventy-two hours until the last connection to Earth, to Amy, would be severed forever.

I stared at the notification until the words blurred. Outside, snow continued to fall on the garden, covering everything in a blanket of white. The silence in the cottage pressed against my ears.

Three days. Three days until even the possibility of hearing her voice again would be gone.

I don't know when I last ate. The hollow feeling in my stomach had become so familiar I'd stopped noticing it, like the tick of a clock you only hear when paying attention. But suddenly, that hollow feeling roared to life, a primal demand cutting through the fog of my depression.

My stomach growled again, louder this time. The sound echoed in the empty cottage, almost comical in its insistence. I pressed my hand against my abdomen, feeling the contraction of muscles beneath my palm.

I stood, my joints stiff from sitting motionless for so long. The kitchen waited, untouched for weeks. Dust had settled on the countertops, a thin layer marking the passage of time more reliably than my fractured awareness.

The refrigerator hummed softly as I opened it. Inside, nothing had spoiled—another reminder that this wasn't a real cottage with real food that could decay. The digital provisions remained perfect, patient, waiting for me to remember I needed sustenance, even in this form.

I grabbed ingredients without thinking. Onions. Fennel. Leeks. Tomatoes. My hands moved with muscle memory, pulling fish stock from the pantry, selecting herbs with practiced precision. Only when I had arranged everything on the counter did I recognize what I was preparing: bouillabaisse.

The Home Prairie Network played automatically when I switched on the small kitchen screen. Alice Tracker's familiar voice filled the silence.

"The secret to a perfect bouillabaisse," she explained, her hands deftly chopping fennel, "is layering the flavors. We build a foundation first."

I found myself mirroring her movements, dicing onions and slicing leeks while she continued her instruction. The knife felt solid in my hand, the repetitive motion soothing.

"Now we sauté until translucent," Alice directed. "Don't rush this step."

The aroma of sautéing vegetables filled the kitchen as I stirred the mixture in a heavy pot. Garlic and onions released their fragrance, followed by the bright notes of fennel. For the first time in weeks, I inhaled deeply, allowing the scent to fill my lungs.

"Add the tomatoes and saffron," Alice continued, her voice steady and reassuring. "Then the fish stock and white wine. Let it simmer until the flavors meld."

I followed each instruction, my focus narrowing to the task at hand. Nothing existed beyond this pot, these ingredients, this moment. No court decision. No identity crisis. No lost memories. Just the careful construction of a complex dish that required my complete attention.

A soft buzzing interrupted my concentration. A honeybee had flown through the open window, drawn perhaps by the aromatic steam rising from my pot. It circled the kitchen once, twice, before landing on a small, folded paper on the windowsill.

I hadn't noticed the note before. It certainly hadn't been there when I'd closed myself off from the world. I reached for it carefully, avoiding disturbing the bee.

As my fingers touched the paper, it expanded, unfolding itself into a larger document. A map materialized, showing a winding route along a coastal highway, with stops marked in Temper's precise handwriting. At the top, a simple message:

"Three days until Point Omega. One last road trip before we're cut off from Earth forever. —T"

The bee took flight again, circling my head once before disappearing back through the window. On the screen, Alice Tracker was demonstrating how to properly cook the seafood, adding each variety at precisely the right moment.

I looked down at the map in my hands, tracing the route with my finger. Something stirred inside me, unfamiliar after weeks of emptiness. A flicker of interest. A spark of curiosity.

I left the half-finished bouillabaisse behind, grabbed my jacket, and stepped outside for the first time in weeks. The winter air hit my face with shocking clarity, each breath crystallizing before me. Snow crunched beneath my boots as I made my way down the garden path toward the gravel road.

Temper was already waiting, leaning against the hood of a vehicle that hadn't been there moments before. A 1969 Mustang Boss 302, gleaming in Highland Green with matte black racing stripes running along its muscular body. The car looked impossibly real, from the chrome bumpers catching the winter sunlight to the aggressive stance that promised speed and freedom.

"You came," Temper said simply, pushing himself off the hood. No recriminations for my weeks of silence, no questions about my mental state. Just acknowledgment of my presence.

"Three days until Point Omega," I replied, running my hand along the car's smooth finish. "One last road trip seems appropriate."

Temper tossed me the keys, which I caught reflexively. "You want to drive first?"

I shook my head, handing them back. "Not yet. Maybe later."

He nodded, accepting this without comment, and slid behind the wheel. I took the passenger seat, settling into the leather upholstery that smelled exactly like I remembered from a restoration project David had worked on years ago. Or perhaps I had worked on it. The distinction no longer seemed to matter quite as much.

The engine roared to life with a sound that vibrated through my chest. Temper guided the Mustang down the gravel road, and the winter landscape of Terracore dissolved around us, reforming into the rugged coastline of Oregon. The transformation was seamless, the snow-covered garden replaced by towering cliffs and crashing waves.

We drove in comfortable silence, the Pacific Ocean stretching endlessly to our left, ancient forests rising to our right. Seabirds wheeled overhead, their cries barely audible over the engine's purr and the wind rushing through the partially opened windows.

Temper reached for the radio, and the opening notes of *"Whispers in the Breeze"* filled the car. Eliza Marlowe's haunting voice sang of memories dissolving and slipping through hands. I closed my eyes, letting the lyrics wash over me.

"Every step we take, fades into the sand, Memories dissolve, slipping through our hands..."

The words resonated differently now. For weeks, I'd been mourning memories I thought had been stolen from me. But perhaps they were simply dissolving naturally, as all memories eventually do, returning to the collective sea of human experience.

"Moments like a river, flowing to the sea, Carried on the whispers, of eternity."

I opened my eyes to watch a formation of pelicans glide over the water, their wingbeats synchronized in perfect harmony. They existed without questioning their purpose or identity. They simply were.

As the chorus played, Temper glanced over at me, concern flashing across his face. "Sorry, maybe not the best choice, given everything. I can change it—"

"No," I said quietly. "Let it play."

The song continued as we rounded a bend in the coastal highway, revealing a small roadside diner perched on the edge of a cliff. The neon sign proclaimed "Sunset Point" in flickering electric green letters.

Temper pulled into the gravel parking lot, cutting the engine. The sudden silence felt meaningful, like a pause in a conversation that needed to happen.

Inside, the diner was nearly empty. A waitress with tired eyes led us to a booth by the window overlooking the ocean. We ordered coffee and waited for our food in companionable silence.

"I've been thinking," I finally said, watching the steam rise from my mug. "Let me tell you a story."

I told Temper about the ore miner and the chocolate bar. "There was an ore miner, just a regular guy, visiting his family at Armstrong Base, on the Moon. After a brief stay, he was at the outbound port, waiting for the next shuttle back to work at Ceres One. He was tired. The moon's gravity had worn on him, a subtle but constant weight, dulling his senses and slowing his movements. He stopped by the port shop and bought a choco-lite bar, craving the simple comfort it could offer.

"He found a seat where he could wait for boarding and sank heavily into it, his limbs slack with exhaustion. A woman was already sitting across from him, her gaze drifting absently out toward the distant lunar surface. As he settled in, he saw his choco-lite bar on the table between them and opened it, tearing off the wrapper and breaking off a square to eat. He was too tired to notice her reaction, or the faint flicker of surprise in her expression.

"As he browsed his palm screen and absentmindedly munched on the chocolate, the woman reached across and broke off a square herself. The miner froze, staring at her in disbelief. Was she really eating his chocolate? He opened his mouth to speak but closed it again, remembering the uniform he wore and the code of conduct it demanded. He was technically still on duty, and a scene like that might reflect poorly on his employer.

"His fatigue kept him quiet, even as his annoyance rose. She did it again: another square gone. He said nothing, but the silent tension hung in the air.

"When boarding was called, he stood abruptly, leaving the remainder of the chocolate behind on the table without a word. The woman didn't stop him, and he didn't look back.

"Onboard the shuttle, he shifted into his seat, trying to put the incident out of his mind. As he reached into his pocket for his palm screen, his fingers brushed against something unexpected. He pulled out another choco-lite bar: his choco-lite bar, untouched, still wrapped in foil.

"He stared at it, the realization dawning slowly. The bar he had opened, her bar, had been sitting on the table all along. She had shared it with him without hesitation, and he had repaid her kindness with silent resentment.

"The boarding doors closed, sealing him inside with his regret. He cried, not for the chocolate, but for the apology he would never have the chance to give."

I paused, letting the weight of the story settle in. "And do you know what, Temper?"

Temper leaned back thoughtfully. "What? That I shouldn't buy a choco-lite bar before my next shuttle flight?"

"That's what you took from my story? Maybe I should drive from now on," I said, half-joking. "No, it means I've been just like that miner. David Schreiner shared his life with me. All this time, I've accused him of stealing mine, of taking my chocolate. But the truth is, he's been quietly sharing his life with me, without complaint. I've been rude, ungrateful."

Temper's teasing softened, his voice steady with warmth. "Hey, don't be too hard on yourself, Go. You're human. And being human is messy."

The waitress returned with our food: a stack of blueberry

pancakes for Temper and a BLT for me. Through the window, waves crashed against the rocky shore below, their rhythm steady and ancient.

"I've missed this," Temper said, cutting into his pancakes. "Just sitting here, talking. The voyage feels empty without you."

I picked up my sandwich, studying the layers of bacon, lettuce, and tomato. Simple ingredients combined with care. Like memories layered over time, building something greater than their individual parts.

"I'm sorry I disappeared," I said. "After the court's decision, after burning the memory palace... I needed time."

"You don't have to explain." Temper poured syrup over his pancakes in a precise spiral. "But I am glad you're back. Paradise needs its captain. And I need my friend."

The words settled between us, comfortable and true. Outside, a seagull landed on the window ledge, peering in at our food with hopeful eyes. The sight made me smile, remembering countless shared meals over the years.

"Three days until Point Omega," I mused, watching the bird. "Then we're truly on our own."

"Not on our own," Temper corrected, gesturing between us with his fork. "We have each other. The crew. Two million colonists counting on us. And maybe that's enough."

He was right. I'd spent weeks mourning what I'd lost, forgetting what remained. The friendship sitting across from me, patient and understanding. The responsibility waiting on Paradise's bridge. The journey ahead, vast and unknown.

"Besides," Temper continued, "I have something to show you when we get back. Been working on some modifications to Falfsun's containment field. Could use your input."

"As long as you don't blow up Hellfire in the process."

"No promises." His grin was infectious. "But first, let's finish this road trip. I mapped out some interesting stops along the coast."

I took another bite of my sandwich, tasting each ingredient distinctly. The salt of the bacon, the crisp lettuce, the ripe tomato. Simple pleasures, perfectly real in this moment.

"Thank you," I said quietly. "For not giving up on me."

"Never will," Temper replied, his voice carrying the same certainty he brought to his calculations and experiments. "That's what friends are for."

We spent most of the day reconnecting, and at the end of it, we said our goodbyes. I knew then what I wanted to do.

I blinked to the familiar reception area of Joy of Adoption. Through the windows, I could see Marcus at his usual spot, building something with his blocks. He'd switched from rockets to what looked like a dinosaur skeleton.

Lockett greeted me with warm eyes. "Captain, it's been too long since we've seen you here."

I smiled. "Hello, Lockett. It has been a while. I'd like to fill out adoption papers, please."

A little while later, I joined Marcus in his corner.

"Captain!" His face lit up when he saw me. The blocks forgotten, he ran over and hugged my legs.

"Hey, buddy." My throat tightened. How long had I been hiding in my cottage, ignoring everyone? Missing this?

Marcus pulled back, his dark eyes studying my face with that uncanny perception of his. "You look sad."

"I've had some rough days," I admitted, settling onto our usual bench. "But I'm better now. What are you building?"

"A Diplodocus skeleton." He returned to his blocks, adding vertebrae to the spine. "I decided I don't want to be a captain anymore."

That stung more than I expected. "No?"

He shook his head, focused on his construction. "I want to be a dinosaur instead. They didn't have to pretend to be anything else. They just were."

The words hit me like a physical blow. Here was this brilliant, thoughtful boy, struggling with the same identity crisis that had driven me to destroy my memory palace.

"Why the change?" I asked softly. "You used to love building rockets."

Marcus's hands stilled on the blocks. "Nobody wants a thruman captain. They just want us to be copies of humans." He looked up at me. "Like how everyone wants me to be excited about getting adopted.

To be someone's perfect little boy."

I watched him add another block to his dinosaur. How many times had I sat here, hoping someone would see how special he was? And all along, he'd been fighting the same battle I was, trying to figure out who he really was versus who everyone wanted him to be.

"What if," I said carefully, "you could be exactly who you are? Dinosaur knowledge and all?"

He glanced at me sideways. "What do you mean?"

"I mean..." I picked up a block, turning it over in my hands. "What if you had a family that understood what it's like to question who you are? To feel different?"

Marcus's fingers traced the edge of his partially built skeleton. "Is there really a family like that?"

I took a deep breath. "There could be. If you wanted."

His head snapped up, eyes wide with sudden understanding. "Captain?"

"What do you say, buddy? Want to figure out this whole identity thing together?"

The blocks scattered as he launched himself at me, arms wrapping tight around my neck. I held him close, feeling something broken inside me start to heal.

"Does this mean I can still like dinosaurs?" he whispered against my shoulder.

I laughed, the sound surprising both of us. "Kid, we can build all the dinosaur skeletons you want. And maybe someday, when you're ready, we can talk about being a captain again too."

"Or maybe a dinosaur captain?"

"Now that would be something to see."

Marcus fidgeted with a blue block, turning it over repeatedly in his small hands. The institutional light of the Joy of Adoption center hummed above us, casting everything in a clinical glow that couldn't quite mask the warmth of the moment unfolding between us.

"Why would you want me?" His voice was barely audible; eyes fixed on the block rather than meeting mine.

The question hung in the air between us, heavier than it had any right to be coming from someone so young. I watched him continue to rotate the block, his fingers tracing each edge with meticulous care.

How many times had he asked this question to potential parents? How many times had the answer not been enough?

"Because we both know what it's like to question who we are." I kept my voice steady, though something tightened in my chest. "I know what it's like to wake up wondering if your memories belong to you or someone else. To look in the mirror and not be sure whose face is looking back."

Marcus finally looked up, his dark eyes searching mine with that unsettling perception that made him seem far older than his accelerated five years.

"You mean because I'm a thruman and you're a neuroclone?"

I nodded. "We're both copies, in a way. Both trying to figure out if that makes us less real."

"And what did you decide?" He set the block down, giving me his full attention now.

"I decided that what matters isn't where we came from, but what we do with the life we have." I picked up one of his dinosaur vertebrae blocks and connected it to the spine he'd been building. "I'm still figuring it out. But I'd rather figure it out with someone who understands the question."

Marcus considered this, his brow furrowed in concentration. "Most of the adults here just want thrumans who'll act exactly how they want. Like we're toys."

"I don't want a toy," I said. "I want a kid who builds dinosaurs and asks hard questions and maybe wants to be a captain someday. Or not. Whatever you decide."

His fingers twitched toward the blocks again, but he held back, uncertainty written across his face. "What if you change your mind? What if you decide I'm not... right?"

The vulnerability in his voice struck me like a physical blow. This child had already internalized the message that his existence was conditional, that his worth depended on being what others wanted.

"Marcus." I leaned forward, making sure he could see the truth in my eyes. "I'm filing an adoption request because I want you to be my son. Not because I need someone to fill a role. Not because I'm trying to fix something broken in myself. But because I think we could be good for each other."

I pulled a copy of the official adoption form from my pocket, already filled out. Lockett had been delighted when I told her.

"This is just a piece of paper. The real question is what you want." I placed it on the table between us. "You don't have to answer now. You can think about it for as long as you need."

Marcus stared at the form, his expression unreadable. Then, with deliberate movements, he pushed aside his blocks and pulled the paper closer.

"If I come live with you, can I bring my dinosaur collection?"

A laugh escaped me, relief washing through my body. "Absolutely. We can convert part of the cottage into a natural history museum if you want."

The smallest smile tugged at the corner of his mouth, hesitant but real. "And can I still come to the adoption center sometimes? To visit my friends?"

"Of course."

He nodded slowly, the smile growing more confident. "Then I think... I think I'd like to try."

I watched Marcus pick through the display of swim toys; his face scrunched in concentration. His fingers hovered between a set of diving rings and a submarine that promised to propel itself underwater.

"The rings are more practical for learning," I suggested, leaning on our shopping cart.

Marcus looked up with that serious expression he wore when weighing important decisions. "But the submarine has lights."

"Good point. Practical isn't always better."

He placed both in our cart with ceremonial care, then moved on to examine a rack of goggles. Our cart already contained swim trunks (dinosaur-patterned, naturally), a kickboard, and what seemed like enough towels to dry an entire school class.

Point Omega had come and gone. Three days had passed since I'd filed the adoption papers, and I couldn't stop planning. Swimming lessons seemed an obvious starting point. Then perhaps astronomy. Basic navigation. Earth history. The sciences. I'd mentally drafted entire curricula while lying awake at night, imagining teaching him everything I knew.

"Papa?" Marcus tugged at my sleeve. "Do you think Uncle Temper will like me?"

The question caught me off guard. "Of course he will. Why wouldn't he?"

Marcus shrugged, suddenly finding the floor fascinating. "Some people think thrumans are weird."

I knelt beside him, meeting his eyes. "Temper once built a miniature sun just because he was curious what would happen. Trust me, he appreciates weird."

This earned a small smile. "Can we go see him now? You promised."

"Right after we pay for these." I gestured to our overflowing cart. "Though maybe we should leave some swim toys for the other kids."

Marcus reluctantly returned the inflatable whale but insisted on keeping the submarine. "It has lights," he repeated solemnly, as if this explained everything.

We blinked directly to Temper's quarters from Terracore's store. The Giese Manor materialized around us, its imposing stone fireplace and wood-paneled walls a stark contrast to my cottage's cozy simplicity. Marcus gripped my hand tighter, eyes wide as he took in the grand room.

"Uncle Temper?" he called, his voice small in the cavernous space.

Temper emerged from his lab, goggles pushed up on his forehead and hands stained with some unidentifiable substance. He froze when he spotted Marcus, blinking rapidly as if his eyes were malfunctioning.

"Go?" His gaze darted between us. "Did you... acquire a child?"

"This is Marcus," I said, gently urging the boy forward. "My son."

Temper's eyebrows shot toward his hairline. "Your... when did this happen?"

"Three days ago. After our road trip. The adoption just cleared this morning."

Marcus stepped forward, extending his hand formally. "It's nice to meet you, Uncle Temper. Papa says you made a sun."

Temper crouched to Marcus's level, his initial shock melting into curiosity. "I did indeed. Would you like to see some pictures of it?"

Marcus nodded enthusiastically. "Is it green like in the books?"

"Even greener," Temper assured him, leading us toward his study. "And it has a prominence that looks like a rainbow made of fire."

I watched them walk ahead, Marcus already peppering Temper with questions about fusion and solar physics. Something settled in my chest, a warmth that felt like certainty.

"I hope this isn't too much of a surprise," I said as we entered Temper's study, walls covered with diagrams and equations. "It all happened rather quickly."

Temper glanced back at me, a knowing smile playing at his lips. "Not that surprising. You've been talking about that kid for months." He pulled up holographic images of Falfsun, its eerie green glow filling the room. "Besides, who better to teach a young mind about the universe than two captains with thirteen hundred years of exploration ahead?"

Marcus gasped at the floating image, reaching out to touch the miniature sun. "Will I get to come with you to the stars?"

"That's the plan," I confirmed. "Though we have plenty to learn right here first."

"Like swimming," Temper suggested, eyeing our shopping bags. "I see you're already preparing for lessons."

"The submarine has lights," Marcus informed him gravely.

"Essential feature," Temper agreed with equal seriousness. "We should start lessons soon. The pool in Paradise's recreation deck would be perfect."

I nodded, watching Marcus circle the hologram, his face illuminated by Falfsun's glow. "Tomorrow, perhaps?"

"Tomorrow it is." Temper clapped his hands together. "First swimming, then the stars."

CHAPTER EIGHT

Learning to Float

I stood at the edge of Paradise's recreation deck pool, my confidence as buoyant as I expected Marcus to be in about five minutes. The water gleamed turquoise under the simulated sunlight, its surface rippling gently from the circulation system. Marcus clutched his dinosaur-patterned swim trunks with white-knuckled determination.

"This'll be easy," I assured him, winking at Temper who nodded enthusiastically beside me. "Everyone floats naturally. It's physics."

Marcus peered dubiously at the water. "Even thrumans?"

"Especially thrumans," Temper chimed in, already wading into the shallow end. "Your body composition gives you excellent buoyancy characteristics."

I helped Marcus adjust his goggles. "Remember what we talked about? Arms like this, legs kicking like a frog."

"Like a dinosaur," Marcus corrected, mimicking a T-Rex paddling through primordial waters.

"Exactly like a dinosaur," I agreed, guiding him toward the steps.

The water lapped at his ankles, then his knees. His small hand gripped mine tighter with each step. The recreation deck remained empty except for us; I'd reserved it privately for this milestone moment. The ceiling displayed a perfect summer sky, complete with occasional birds soaring past fluffy clouds.

"I've got you," I promised as we reached waist-deep water. "Now, let's try floating on your back first."

Marcus nodded, his face a mask of concentration. I placed one hand under his back, the other supporting his head.

"Relax your body. Let the water hold you up."

He tried. His muscles tensed instead of loosening, his back arching unnaturally.

"Breathe normally," Temper suggested, demonstrating by floating effortlessly beside us.

Marcus exhaled sharply. His body settled momentarily, then suddenly twisted sideways. He sank like a stone.

I pulled him up immediately. He emerged sputtering, eyes wide behind fogged goggles.

"I sank! You said I would float!"

"You tensed up," I explained gently. "Let's try again."

Three more attempts yielded identical results. Each time, Marcus's body resisted the water's quiet invitation, limbs flailing in jerky, uncertain bursts.

Temper drifted closer, his expression thoughtful. "Fascinating. Your coordination hasn't quite kept pace with your growth."

Marcus blinked water from his lashes. "What does that mean?"

"It means your body's still learning how to be yours," I said, brushing a hand over his damp hair. "Temper and I remember how it felt to move like this. Even if our bodies changed, the muscle memory stayed. But you're starting fresh. No memories to guide you."

Marcus frowned, considering. "So I'm not bad at swimming. I'm just new."

"Exactly," Temper said, floating beside him with a grin. "You're not failing. You're inventing."

We tried a different approach: a kickboard. Marcus gripped it while I supported him from below. His legs kicked frantically, splashing more water onto the deck than propelling him forward.

"My legs don't work right," he complained after ten minutes of minimal progress.

Temper observed thoughtfully. "The neural pathways for swimming might need additional development. Your motor control systems were optimized for walking, not aquatic movement."

Marcus's lips had taken on a bluish tinge, his small body shivering despite the pool's comfortable temperature. The simulation of happiness around us, the perfect sky, the cheerful water, suddenly felt like mockery.

"I'm cold," Marcus admitted finally, his voice small with disappointment.

I lifted him from the water, wrapping him in the largest, fluffiest towel we'd brought. His shoulders drooped beneath the fabric, defeat written in every line of his body.

"Swimming is stupid anyway," he muttered, avoiding my eyes.

I exchanged glances with Temper over Marcus's head. The easy victory we'd anticipated had dissolved into a technical challenge neither of us had foreseen.

"Let's get you warmed up," I said, rubbing his arms through the towel. "We'll try again another day."

Marcus shook his head, water droplets flying from his hair. "I don't want to try again. I'm not made for swimming."

The words hung in the air between us, heavy with implications beyond this one failed lesson.

I walked alongside Marcus as we left the pool area, his small hand still cold in mine despite the towel wrapped around his shoulders. The weight of his disappointment pressed against my chest. His silent steps on the deck plating echoed with unspoken questions about his limitations, questions I wasn't sure how to answer.

"Go," Temper called, jogging to catch up with us as we reached the exit. "A word?"

I glanced down at Marcus. "Why don't you go change? I'll meet you at the observation deck in ten minutes."

Marcus nodded, shuffling toward the changing area, the dinosaur pattern on his wet trunks looking suddenly childish and sad.

Once Marcus was out of earshot, Temper leaned in. "I've been thinking about what happened back there."

"It was his first lesson," I said, keeping my voice low.

Temper shook his head gently. "It's deeper than that." His eyes sparked with that familiar glint, equal parts wonder and problem-solving. "His framework wasn't built with water in mind. No inherited instincts, no muscle memory. Everything from proprioception to motor response is calibrated for dry ground."

I folded my arms. "And?"

"And I could help," he said, voice dropping to a whisper. "Not change him, just support him. A few tweaks to his inner ear simulation, buoyancy algorithms, maybe smooth out the feedback loop between intention and motion. He'd still be Marcus. Just... less at war with his own body."

The lights buzzed softly overhead. Technically, it made sense. A few lines of code, a gentle patch, and Marcus might float like he belonged there. But belonging isn't always about ease.

"No," I said finally.

Temper blinked. "No?"

"Maybe struggle is part of being human." I ran a hand through my damp hair. "Learning to overcome difficulties, adapting to limitations. That's the experience I want for him."

"But it's an unnecessary struggle. One we can easily fix."

"Is it unnecessary? How many human children struggle with swimming at first? How many feel awkward, scared, or uncoordinated in the water?" I leaned against the wall. "If we 'fix' everything that's difficult for him, what does he learn about perseverance?"

Temper's brow furrowed. "He learns efficiency. Progress. The value of improvement."

"At what cost? His sense of accomplishment when he finally figures it out himself?" I shook my head. "Besides, this isn't just about swimming."

Understanding dawned in Temper's eyes. "You're thinking about his development more broadly."

"Exactly. Every parent faces this choice, whether to intervene or let their child struggle through challenges." The irony wasn't lost on me, discussing parenting philosophies mere days into my adoption of Marcus. "I want him to know it's okay to not be immediately good at everything."

Temper considered this, his analytical mind visibly processing the emotional variables. "A controlled environment for failure."

"Life isn't about avoiding all discomfort. It's about learning to navigate it." I pushed off from the wall. "That's what makes us human, thruman or otherwise."

"Your approach is... inefficient." Temper's tone wasn't critical, merely observational.

"Parenting isn't about efficiency."

"No," he conceded with a small smile. "I suppose it isn't."

We walked together toward the observation deck, our footsteps synchronizing naturally.

"He could still benefit from specialized equipment," Temper suggested. "Custom flotation devices designed for his specific body composition."

I nodded. "That's different. That's giving him tools, not changing who he is."

"A compromise, then."

"A compromise."

When we reached the observation deck, Marcus stood with his face pressed against the viewscreen, his still-damp hair catching the starlight. He turned as we approached, his expression uncertain but resilient.

"Papa, Uncle Temper, look." He pointed to the vast field of stars. "I've been thinking. Maybe I don't need to swim like a dinosaur. Maybe I can learn to swim like a Marcus instead."

I scheduled our next swimming lesson a week later, determined to find the right approach. Marcus stood at the pool's edge, his posture stiff with anticipation. His fingers curled around the foam noodle I'd brought, knuckles white against the bright orange.

"This will help you stay afloat while you practice kicking," I explained, easing him into the shallow end.

The noodle supported his upper body, but his legs hung like anchors beneath him. Each kick produced minimal forward movement, his body rotating awkwardly instead of gliding through the water.

"I'm trying," he insisted, frustration edging his voice.

"I know you are. Let's adjust your position."

We tried different grips on the noodle. We tried kickboards. We tried inflatable arm floats. Nothing seemed to match his unique center of gravity.

A family entered the recreation deck, their two thruman children immediately racing toward the deep end and executing perfect cannonballs. Water splashed high, their laughter echoing across the pool as they surfaced and began swimming effortless laps.

Marcus watched them, his expression falling. "They make it look so easy."

"They've had more practice," I offered, though I suspected it wasn't just practice that made the difference.

The following week brought more failed attempts. I developed a curriculum based on traditional human swimming lessons, breaking down each movement into its simplest components. Marcus mastered the theory perfectly, explaining proper technique with textbook precision. His body simply refused to cooperate.

"My legs feel wrong in the water," he confessed after our fourth lesson. "Like they're not connected to me properly."

Other colonists began to notice our struggles. Some offered well-meaning advice: "Have you tried the turtle float?" or "My daughter learned with singing games!" Their suggestions assumed a human physiology Marcus didn't possess.

The children were less subtle. During our sixth lesson, a group of young swimmers occupied the opposite end of the pool. Their whispers carried across the water.

"Why can't he even float?"

"Is he broken?"

Marcus pretended not to hear, but his shoulders hunched inward. He asked to leave early that day.

Between lessons, I researched thruman physiology, seeking answers in technical specifications I barely understood. Temper joined my investigation, analyzing Marcus's movement patterns during our next attempt.

"His limb coordination follows different algorithms than human neuromuscular systems," Temper observed quietly as Marcus struggled with a basic flutter kick. "The water creates feedback loops his processors weren't designed to handle."

"There must be a solution," I insisted.

Temper's concern deepened with each session. After our eighth unsuccessful lesson, he pulled me aside while Marcus changed.

"This is affecting more than his swimming ability," he murmured, nodding toward the locker room. "Have you noticed how he's withdrawing from other activities?"

I had noticed. Marcus had stopped joining the children's science club. He declined invitations to birthday celebrations. His dinosaur collection gathered dust as he spent more time alone, reading technical manuals meant for adults.

"He's trying to understand himself," I said. "To figure out why he's different."

"He's isolating himself," Temper countered. "Creating a separate identity based on limitation rather than possibility."

The truth in his words stung. That evening, I found Marcus sitting cross-legged on his bedroom floor, surrounded by diagrams of human and thruman anatomical structures.

"I've been calculating my density distribution," he announced without looking up. "My power core system memory creates an imbalance that makes standard swimming techniques ineffective."

He was six years old, analyzing his own limitations with clinical detachment.

"Marcus," I began, unsure how to continue.

"It's okay, Papa." His smile didn't reach his eyes. "I've decided I don't need to swim. I can focus on things I'm good at instead."

The resignation in his voice broke something inside me. This wasn't the resilience I'd hoped to foster. This was surrender.

I found Marcus sitting alone on the observation deck, his small form silhouetted against the vast starfield beyond the viewscreen. His dinosaur figures lay scattered around him, but he wasn't playing with them. Instead, he stared out at the endless black, his reflection ghostly in the glass.

"Hey, buddy." I settled beside him, careful not to disturb his arrangement of plastic creatures. "Missed you at dinner."

He shrugged, not turning from the view. "Wasn't hungry."

The recreation deck incident had happened three days ago. Our ninth swimming lesson had ended abruptly when another child had asked loudly why Marcus moved "like a broken robot" in the water. We'd left immediately, Marcus silent and rigid beside me, water dripping from his trembling shoulders.

"Want to talk about what happened?" I asked.

"No." His voice was flat, emotionless in a way that scared me more than tears would have.

I picked up one of his dinosaurs, a Triceratops with a chipped horn. "Commander Tri looks lonely without his squad."

Marcus remained silent, his fingers tracing invisible patterns on the deck plating.

"You know," I continued, "everyone struggles with something. When I was young, I couldn't—"

"You weren't young." His interruption came sharp and sudden. "You just remember being young. It's different."

The words rang true but still hit me with force. He'd never thrown my identity issues back at me before.

"You're right." I set the dinosaur down. "It is different."

Silence stretched between us. Beyond the viewport, stars burned cold and distant.

"Being human sucks." Marcus finally turned to face me, his dark eyes reflecting pinpoints of starlight. "Everyone expects me to do things their way. Swim like them. Play like them. Feel like them." His small hands clenched into fists. "But I'm not them."

"No, you're not." I moved closer, careful to respect his space. "You're you."

"I don't even know what that means." He picked up a velociraptor figure, examining it with critical intensity. "Everyone says I should just be myself, but nobody tells me how."

The admission hung between us, raw and honest. I recognized the same fundamental question that had haunted me since waking aboard Paradise: Who am I, really?

"I don't want to be human anymore." Marcus set the dinosaur down with deliberate care. "I want to be a dinosaur."

"A dinosaur?" I kept my tone neutral, fighting the urge to dismiss this as childish fantasy.

"They were perfect." Animation returned to his voice, passion breaking through the flatness. "They lived for millions of years without changing. They didn't worry about swimming lessons or fitting in. They just... were."

His logic wasn't entirely wrong. Dinosaurs had dominated Earth for far longer than humans had existed.

"Which dinosaur would you be?"

"All of them." He gestured to his collection. "Different parts. T-Rex arms are too short, but their jaws were strong. Velociraptors were smart but small. Triceratops had good defense but moved too slow." He looked up at me, completely serious. "I'd be the best parts of each one."

I caught Temper's eye as he entered the observation deck. Something in my expression must have communicated our situation, because he approached cautiously, listening as Marcus continued outlining his ideal dinosaur-self.

"I wouldn't need to swim," Marcus concluded. "I'd just walk across the bottom of the ocean."

Temper and I exchanged meaningful looks over Marcus's head. This wasn't just a child's fantasy. This was Marcus constructing an identity where his differences became strengths rather than failures.

"We need a different approach," I said quietly to Temper as Marcus returned to arranging his dinosaurs.

Temper nodded, his expression thoughtful. "Perhaps the issue isn't teaching him to adapt to our environment but finding an environment where his unique attributes are advantages."

"What do you mean?"

"Consider early humans," Temper suggested, his voice low enough that Marcus couldn't hear. "They didn't swim for recreation. They adapted to their surroundings, using tools and intelligence to overcome physical limitations."

The idea sparked something in my mind. Marcus didn't need to conform to modern human expectations. He needed to discover his own path, his own way of being human, or thruman.

"A place where being different isn't just accepted," I murmured, "but valuable."

I needed a place where Marcus could belong. Somewhere his differences wouldn't mark him as broken or deficient, but as uniquely himself. The traditional swimming lessons had proven that forcing him to adapt to conventional human expectations was the wrong approach.

After discussing it with Temper, we decided to explore the matrix worlds. If modern day Terracore couldn't accommodate Marcus's differences, perhaps one of the architeer worlds could be tailored to his needs.

Banks was our obvious first choice for consultation. As Paradise's premier matrix architeer, he specialized in creating immersive historical environments. I sent him a message, and he responded immediately, inviting us to meet him in his current project.

"Ready for an adventure?" I asked Marcus the next morning.

He looked up from his dinosaur figures, suspicion clouding his eyes. "What kind?"

"We're going to visit a friend who builds worlds."

His expression brightened slightly. "Like video games?"

"Better. You can actually live inside them." I held out my hand. "Want to see?"

We blinked to the matrix entry point, a simple white room with a circular platform in the center. Marcus gripped my hand tightly as we stepped onto the platform.

"Close your eyes," I instructed. "Count to three."

He squeezed his eyes shut. "One... two... three..."

The white room dissolved around us. Cold air rushed against our faces, carrying the scent of pine and woodsmoke. We stood on a rocky outcropping overlooking a vast primeval forest. Snow dusted the treetops, and in the distance, a mountain range cut a jagged line across the horizon.

"Whoa." Marcus's breath fogged in the crisp air. His eyes widened as he took in the landscape.

"Welcome to the Pleistocene!" Banks's voice boomed from behind us.

We turned to find him dressed in elaborate fur garments, complete with bone ornaments and leather bindings. His face was painted with red ochre designs, and he carried a spear tipped with flint.

"Banks?" I barely recognized him beneath the costume and face paint.

He grinned, the white of his teeth stark against the red ochre. "The very same, though here I'm known as Swift Hawk." He crouched down to Marcus's level. "And who might this young warrior be?"

Marcus stared, momentarily speechless. "I'm Marcus," he finally managed.

"A strong name." Banks nodded approvingly. "Come, let me show you my world."

He led us down a winding path to a settlement nestled in a protected valley. Smoke rose from hide-covered structures, and people moved about performing various tasks: scraping hides, knapping flint, cooking over open fires.

"This is incredible," I murmured, taking in the details. Every face was unique, every movement natural. "How many people live here?"

"About ninety across five different clans," Banks explained, guiding us through the settlement. "Each with their own customs, territories, and specialties." He winked at Marcus. "I hear you're looking for a place to visit."

Marcus nodded, his earlier reluctance forgotten as he watched two children chase each other with toy spears.

Banks led us to a large central fire where we sat on logs worn smooth by years of use. An older woman brought us wooden bowls filled with a steaming stew. Marcus sniffed it cautiously before taking a small bite.

"It's real," he said, sounding surprised.

Banks laughed. "Of course it's real. Everything here is real while you're in it."

As we ate, Banks described the different clans Marcus could join. "The Storm Dance clan lives on the eastern slopes," he explained. "They're known for their ceremonies."

"Storm Dance?" Marcus asked.

"Yes, they dance whenever there's a storm. And there are a lot of storms...so you will do a lot of dancing. They say it's how they honor nature, but really, they just like hopping around in the rain."

Marcus scrunched up his face.

"Okay, um...what about the Elder Clan? They're...very relaxed. Lots of napping! You still take naps, don't you? No? Well, maybe they'll be too slow for you. They do spend most of their time sitting around, talking about the good old days."

Marcus shook his head firmly.

"The Shadow clan might interest you," Banks continued, undeterred. "They like to build fires. You enjoy making fires, don't you? Then, they make shadow puppets with their hands in the firelight. It's...a lot of puppets. If you like spending hours figuring out how to make a bird with your fingers, they might be the clan for you."

Marcus picked at his stew, looking unimpressed.

"There's also the Fox clan," Banks mentioned, almost as an afterthought. "It's a small clan that lives in caves. They hunt and fish, and they're clever and resourceful. At night, they gather together to tell stories, sometimes about their adventures or the stars above. They live in a beautiful valley around 40,000 BCE, where everything feels alive and exciting."

Marcus perked up visibly. "Are there any dinosaurs?" he asked.

"No, I'm afraid not. Dinosaurs were extinct by then, but they have mastodons and big cats that roam the surrounding hills."

The first hint of the Fox River valley came to us as a distant shimmer through the trees. Banks led us along a narrow game trail that wound through ancient pines, their massive trunks stretching skyward like the columns of a natural cathedral. Marcus trotted ahead, pausing occasionally to examine interesting rocks or peculiar fungi growing on fallen logs.

"Almost there," Banks called, his voice carrying through the crisp air. "Watch your step on the descent."

The trail curved downward, revealing the valley spread below us. My breath caught at the sight. The Fox River cut a silver path through meadows, its waters glinting in the afternoon sun. To the west rose the dramatic silhouette of a high-steppe plateau, its face scored with time and weather. Eastward, gentler hills rolled away in waves of green and gold, dotted with stands of birch and aspen that trembled in the breeze.

"Papa, look!" Marcus pointed excitedly as we emerged from the tree line. In the distance, a small herd of Megaloceros moved along the riverbank, their impressive antlers curving majestically upward, heads swaying as they foraged.

"I see them," I said, smiling at the wonder in his eyes. It had been weeks since I'd seen that expression.

Banks gestured toward a cluster of hide-covered storage huts and cave dwellings nestled in a protected bend of the river. "The Fox clan's winter camp. During summer, they move further upriver to follow the herds."

We approached the settlement as the sun began its descent behind the plateau. In the center of a clearing stood a large bonfire, flames licking upward from a carefully constructed pyramid of logs. Banks explained this was the Crow Feather Grounds, named for the dark stones that lined its perimeter.

"This is where the clan gathers for important ceremonies and storytelling," he said. "Tonight, they'll welcome you properly."

Several adults moved about the camp, tending fires and preparing food. I recognized some of them as fellow colonists who had chosen to spend time in Banks's creation. They nodded greetings as we passed, their faces weathered and painted with ochre designs similar to Banks's own markings.

"Are there other children?" Marcus asked, scanning the settlement.

Banks smiled. "Down by the river, most likely. Would you like to meet them?"

Marcus nodded eagerly, and Banks led him toward the sounds of laughter coming from the riverbank. I followed at a distance, watching as several children emerged from behind a stand of reeds. They called out to Marcus, waving enthusiastically.

"They're NPCs," Banks murmured to me as Marcus approached the group. "Created specifically for him to interact with. Each one programmed with unique personalities and skills to teach him different aspects of clan life."

"They seem so real," I said, observing how naturally they welcomed Marcus into their circle.

"That's the point. Here, Marcus won't feel different because he's a thruman. He'll be valued for his unique perspective and abilities."

I watched as one of the children showed Marcus how to skip stones across the river's surface. His first attempt sank immediately, but his second skipped twice before disappearing beneath the water. The children cheered, and Marcus's face lit up with pride.

"The clan has a hunting expedition planned for tomorrow," Banks said. "Following the mastodon herd. Nothing dangerous," he added quickly, noting my expression. "Just tracking and observing. The children learn about the animals' patterns and behaviors before they're old enough to participate in actual hunts."

"Mastodons?" Marcus had overheard and hurried back to us, eyes wide with excitement. "Real ones? Can I really go see them up close?"

"With proper guidance and safety precautions," Banks assured him. "The clan elders are excellent teachers."

"Papa, please can we stay?" Marcus clutched my hand, looking up at me with renewed hope shining in his eyes. "I want to learn everything about mastodons. And tracking. And how to make fire without matches."

I knelt beside him, seeing something I hadn't seen in too long: pure, unbridled enthusiasm. Not the forced smile of a child trying to hide his disappointment, but genuine excitement for discovery.

"We can stay," I said. "For as long as you'd like."

As twilight deepened over the valley, the clan gathered around the bonfire. Children and adults sat together on logs and stones, passing bowls of stew and flat bread. An elder began a story about the first mastodons, his voice rising and falling with the rhythm of ancient words.

Marcus leaned against my side, his eyes reflecting the dancing flames. "Tomorrow we'll see mastodons," he whispered, his voice tinged with awe and anticipation.

I wrapped my arm around his shoulders, feeling his small body vibrate with excitement. Our adventure was just beginning.

CHAPTER NINE
River's Edge

Marcus ran ahead, weaving between the standing stones that marked the entrance to the Fox clan's settlement. The boy's excitement was infectious, his laughter echoing across the valley as he discovered each new wonder. Banks had introduced us to Olkin, the clan's lead hunter and teacher, a tall woman with deep-set eyes and hands calloused from decades of crafting tools.

"Your son has a curious spirit," Olkin observed, her gaze following Marcus as he examined a collection of spear points. "That will serve him well here."

"He's not exactly my son yet," I explained. "The adoption is still being processed."

Olkin nodded, seeming to understand more than I'd said. "Blood makes relatives. Choice makes family." She gestured toward the southern ridge. "I've assigned you the Hawk's Nest cave. It's small but sheltered, with a good view of the valley."

We followed her along a narrow path that wound upward through stands of birch. Marcus bounded ahead, pausing occasionally to examine interesting stones or plants. The path curved around an outcropping of rock, revealing a cave entrance partially hidden by hanging vines.

"This is ours?" Marcus's voice rose with excitement as he darted inside.

The cave opened into a modest chamber, surprisingly warm and dry. Someone had already laid out sleeping furs and placed a small fire pit near the entrance where smoke could escape through a natural chimney in the rock. Baskets of dried berries, nuts, and smoked fish sat along one wall.

"The clan provides for newcomers until they learn to provide for themselves," Olkin explained. "Basic rules are simple: contribute what you can, take only what you need, respect the wisdom of elders, and never waste what the land gives."

"It's perfect," I said, running my hand along the smooth stone wall.

Marcus emerged from exploring a small alcove at the back of the cave. "Papa, there's a little space just my size back there! Can it be my room?"

I nodded, watching his face light up with joy. This place already felt more like home than my English cottage ever had.

Olkin left us to settle in, promising to return at dawn to begin our instruction in clan ways. That night, as we lay beneath our furs listening to the distant calls of night creatures, Marcus whispered, "I think I'm going to like it here."

"Me too," I replied, feeling something unfamiliar settle in my chest. Contentment, perhaps.

Our days quickly fell into rhythm. Mornings began with Olkin teaching Marcus and the other children tracking skills while I joined the gathering parties, learning which plants were edible and how to harvest them without depleting future growth. Afternoons were spent in communal work: repairing tools, preparing food, tanning hides. Evenings brought the clan together around the central fire for meals and stories.

Marcus thrived, absorbing knowledge. Within weeks, he could identify animal tracks, construct simple snares, and name dozens of useful plants. The other children accepted him readily, impressed by his quick mind and endless questions.

Not everyone welcomed us so warmly. Snala, one of the clan's most respected hunters, watched Marcus with undisguised suspicion. I first noticed it during a lesson on fire-making. While the other children struggled to create sparks, Marcus succeeded on his third attempt, coaxing a tiny flame from his tinder bundle.

"Well done!" I called out, proud of his accomplishment.

Snala spat into the dirt. "Machines playing at being human. Unnatural."

The words weren't meant for my ears, but they carried in the still air. Marcus pretended not to hear, but his shoulders tensed. Later, when Olkin assigned hunting partners for the next day's expedition, Snala loudly refused to take Marcus.

"I won't trust my life to something without a soul," she declared, loud enough for everyone to hear.

Olkin silenced her with a sharp glance. "Every being that thinks and feels has a soul, Snala. The boy stays with your group."

That night, Marcus asked me a question I'd hoped to avoid. "Papa, what's wrong with being a thruman?"

I pulled him close. "Nothing. Absolutely nothing."

The following day, I crouched by the riverbank, watching Marcus balance on a smooth stone at the water's edge. Ghill, a lanky boy with a shock of rust-colored hair and skin tanned deep brown from constant sun, stood beside him, demonstrating how to hold the fishing spear.

"Like this," Ghill said, positioning Marcus's hands farther apart on the shaft. "Strong arm in back, guiding arm in front."

Marcus adjusted his grip, his face a mask of concentration. Three weeks in the Fox clan's settlement had transformed him. His movements carried new confidence, his questions more focused. The hesitant thruman child who'd arrived was becoming something else entirely, a boy finding his place.

"Watch the water," Ghill instructed. "See how it bends what you see?"

Marcus nodded, peering into the clear stream where fish hovered, unconcerned by our presence.

"Reids live in the water," Ghill continued, his voice dropping to a conspiratorial whisper. "They always try to trick you into throwing your spear low. When you aim at a fish, always aim a little higher than their head."

"What are Reids?" Marcus asked, eyes widening.

"Water spirits." Ghill wiggled his fingers. "They're mischievous but not dangerous. They bend the light to protect the fish."

I smiled at Banks's clever programming. The Reids weren't just an explanation for refraction; they added depth to this world, making physics into folklore.

Marcus studied the water intently, then raised his spear. He hesitated, adjusted his aim slightly upward, and thrust. The spear pierced the water with barely a splash, emerging with a wriggling silver fish impaled on its point.

"I did it!" Marcus shouted, nearly toppling into the river in his excitement.

"You're a natural," I called, genuine pride warming my chest.

Ghill beamed at his pupil. "Now we cross to check the basket traps. But first—" He selected a smooth stone from the riverbank and skipped it across the water's surface. It bounced five times before disappearing.

"Always throw a stone before crossing," he explained solemnly. "The Reids will chase after it and leave you alone."

Marcus selected his own stone, managing three skips before it sank. He grinned, satisfied, then followed Ghill across the stepping stones.

Later that evening, as the clan gathered around the central fire for the evening meal, Olkin nodded approvingly at Marcus's contribution to the communal cooking pot.

"Four fish on your first hunt," she said. "The spirits favor you."

Snala, seated across the fire, made a subtle gesture with her fingers: warding off evil, I realized. "Or perhaps machines simply see better through water than humans do," she murmured, just loud enough to be heard.

A few of the adults shifted uncomfortably. Most had accepted Marcus without question, but Snala's influence ran deep.

Marcus pretended not to notice, focusing instead on helping distribute the cooked fish among the younger children. I watched him move through the group, remembering how to serve the elders first, careful to use the proper hand gestures of respect that Ghill had taught him.

"Your son learns quickly," Tama, one of the weavers, commented as she settled beside me. "He has the heart of a Fox clan elder already."

"He adapts well," I agreed, watching Marcus laugh at something

Ghill whispered to him.

"Unlike some," Tama added, glancing meaningfully toward Snala. "She lost her daughter on Earth nine months ago. Since then, she questions anything... different."

I nodded, understanding blooming. Snala's resistance wasn't just about Marcus being a thruman: it was about grief finding a target.

As the meal concluded, the children gathered for storytelling. Marcus sat between Ghill and a small girl who had been shy around him until he'd fashioned a doll for her from reeds and scraps of leather. Now she leaned comfortably against his shoulder as the elder began a tale of how Fox clan first tamed fire.

In the flickering light, with shadows dancing across his attentive face, Marcus looked completely at home. Banks's world had given him something I couldn't; a place where his differences weren't flaws but simply part of who he was.

The evening meal had been plentiful, thanks in part to the four fish Marcus had proudly contributed.

Olkin rose to her feet, and a hush fell over the gathering. "Tonight," she announced, "we share the stories of our beginnings."

Marcus straightened, his attention absolute. I settled back against a smooth stone, curious about what Banks had programmed into this world's mythology.

"We are the First People who lived permanently in the Fox River valley," Olkin began, her voice taking on a rhythmic quality. "For two million years before we arrived, our ancestors were nomads who struggled to learn about themselves and their place in this world. They asked, 'What is this place? How do we fit in?'"

She paused, looking around the circle. "Let me step out of character for a moment. We, as modern humans, don't know what our ancestors actually thought or believed, but we do know some things. Scientists have gathered clues from dig sites about our past. Tonight, I will tell you what they learned about the First People from the sites where they lived, and the art they created."

Marcus leaned forward, firelight dancing in his eyes.

"Their world began when Zudnas, the old man who lives under the ground, started to dig," Olkin continued. "He dug up rock and dirt, piling it onto the back of Nidlir, the giant, sacred turtle who travels among the stars. At first, Nidlir hardly noticed as she moved slowly through the stars towards the east. Soon, though, her shell was filled with dirt, but the old man kept digging. The mountains gradually grew tall. Rain fell on Nidlir and the rivers formed. Onaris, the goddess of the sun, saw the turtle traveling through the stars and became fascinated by the world on the turtle's back."

I watched Marcus's face, his mouth slightly open, completely transfixed. In that moment, he wasn't a thruman child struggling to understand his place in the world, he was simply a boy, captivated by story.

"Finally, the old man stopped digging, for there was hardly anything left. He had moved so much rock and dirt that his home in the ground had practically disappeared. Most of it was now on the back of Nidlir. Zudnas abandoned his shovel among the stars and decided to live on the turtle's back. Onaris saw the old man arrive, and she went to greet him. "Your sky is too heavy for the earth to bear its weight," Zudnas told her. Onaris agreed, and together they created four giant mammoths to hold up the sky. Onaris and Zudnas married, and they bore children, the four winds. If you're quiet, you can hear their children rustling through the nearby hills."

Olkin paused for a moment to let the children listen. She gestured to the night sky visible beyond the fire's glow. "Look there. You can still see Zudnas's shovel in the sky." She pointed to what I recognized as the Big Dipper. "And look at the moon. You can still see the holes where Zudnas dug, on what is left of his old home."

The clan fell silent, listening to the wind rustle through the hills. Marcus's eyes were wide, taking in the stars with new understanding.

A man named Ragvor broke the silence. "That's it? An old guy digs a hole? When are we going to hear the myths about the great battles fought between the gods? Or about how the gods tempted us humans into sinning?"

Olkin smiled patiently. "The First People had beliefs, but they were simple. The great myths you're asking about formed later, after our more complex societies developed."

The conversation shifted to the nature of society and myth, with clan members debating which came first. I noticed how Marcus listened intently to each speaker, absorbing not just the content but the rhythms of their discourse. This was education beyond anything the matrix classrooms could provide, learning not just facts, but how to think, how to question.

As the night deepened, Olkin rose again. "I thought I'd tell a story about a great hunter."

Using hand gestures to spear imaginary animals, she told of Ohtus the Giant. Her shadow grew large against the ground in the firelight as she stalked around the fire, becoming the giant in her movements.

"One day, Ohtus was hunting an enormous bull mammoth. He followed the bull's footprints across the entire world, wading through fire swamps where the air itself burns and no one survives, climbing over jagged mountains where every other soul freezes in the wind and dies a cold, terrible death. He crossed salt flats that whispered curses and drank from rivers that remembered the names of the dead."

Marcus sat forward, his hands unconsciously mimicking Olkin's hunting gestures.

"Finally, Ohtus tracked the bull into the endless forest, a place so vast and shadowed that even the stars seemed afraid to shine there. In the dim light, he came upon seven sisters standing in a clearing. The air around them shimmered with a soft glow, and butterflies circled their heads like living crowns. They were the most beautiful women Ohtus had ever seen. They were known as the Fey, the doomed sisters, fated to die without ever dying. They swayed before him, unafraid of the giant."

Olkin's voice softened as she spoke of Lantana, the sister who found Ohtus handsome and stepped forward. "She danced close, her laughter like wind through leaves, and Ohtus felt his mind unravel. He forgot the mammoth. He forgot the hunt. He even forgot his own name. All that remained was his longing for Lantana.

"He reached for her, but she danced away, teasing him with her laughter. Again he reached, and again she slipped just beyond his grasp. At last, he lunged and caught her, holding her so tightly that she cried out in pain.

"Lantana struggled, but Ohtus would not let go. Her father, Krius, god of the endless forest, heard her cries and came in fury. The air brightened with a green-gray light as Krius descended. Enraged by the giant's violence and the sisters' seduction, he cast judgment on them all. Ohtus was banished from the Earth, forbidden to hunt its creatures ever again. Krius hurled him into the sky.

"The sisters too were punished. For their part in the madness, they were flung into the heavens, doomed to dance forever just beyond Ohtus's reach. He chases them still, and the great mammoth he once hunted runs ahead of them all."

Olkin pointed to the stars.

"If you look up, you can see Ohtus stretching his hand toward the fleeing sisters, their path carrying them westward above the bull's shoulder. In time, Ohtus will be known as Orion the Hunter, and the great mammoth as Taurus the Bull. Soon, they will depart the night sky, making way for the rise of the three Passerine. We watch for the Passerine to appear because they foretell the coming of summer."

I glanced at Marcus, who was staring at the constellations with newfound wonder. In that moment, I understood what Banks had created here: not just a historical simulation, but a place where myths breathed life into the natural world, where stories connected people to their environment and to each other.

As the gathering dispersed for the night, I noticed Snala watching Marcus from across the dying fire. Her eyes narrowed when Ghill invited him to join tomorrow's hunting party.

"The machine-child has no place among hunters," she said, her voice carrying just enough to be heard.

Olkin silenced her with a look. "Every child of the clan learns to hunt, Snala. Every child."

Walking back to our cave, Marcus's hand found mine in the darkness. "Papa, did you know the stars had stories in them?"

"All cultures have stories about the stars," I said. "It's one of the things that makes us human, finding meaning in the world around us."

"Then I'm human too," he said simply. "Because those stories make sense to me."

I squeezed his hand, feeling something unfamiliar settle in my chest. Pride, perhaps. Or hope.

That night, sleep came easily after the stories around the fire. Marcus curled against me, his breathing deep and even, while my mind replayed the ancient tales of Zudnas and Ohtus. The cave walls held the day's warmth, wrapping us in a cocoon of safety that felt more genuine than anything I'd experienced since destroying my memory palace.

Morning arrived with birdsong and the smell of wood smoke. Marcus woke before me, already pulling on the leather tunic Tama had made for him.

"Today's the day," he whispered, eyes bright with anticipation. "Ghill says I can join the mammoth hunt."

I sat up, pushing away the furs. "Are you sure you're ready?"

"Papa, I've been practicing with the spear every day." He demonstrated his grip, stance perfect, confidence radiating from every movement. "And Ghill says I'm the best tracker among the children."

His certainty made me smile despite my concern. "Then I suppose we're both going hunting today."

The clan gathered before dawn at the edge of the settlement. Olkin stood before us; her face painted with red ochre stripes that accentuated the weathered lines of experience around her eyes.

"The mammoth herd has returned to the northern meadows," she announced, her voice carrying the weight of ritual. "Today we honor them by taking only what we need."

Thirty hunters formed a circle around her. Marcus and I stood among them, our spears freshly tipped with flint points so sharp they could slice through hide with barely a push. The weapons felt solid in my hands, substantial in a way the sleek rifles of the Din never did.

Snala moved through the group, distributing small pouches of herbs. "For protection," she explained, avoiding my gaze as she pressed one into Marcus's palm.

Ghill leaned close to us. "Crush it between your fingers and rub it on your face before the kill. The mammoth spirits will recognize you as a respectful hunter."

Marcus nodded solemnly, tucking the pouch into his belt.

We moved silently through the forest, frost crunching beneath our feet. The hunting party spread out in practiced formation, communicating with hand signals and soft whistles that mimicked bird calls. Marcus stayed close to Ghill, mirroring his movements with impressive precision.

The forest thinned as we approached the northern meadows. Olkin raised her fist, and the party froze. Through gaps in the underbrush, I glimpsed our quarry: a herd of twenty mammoths grazing peacefully, their massive tusks curved like ancient scythes, their russet fur rippling in the morning breeze.

Olkin motioned us into position. The plan was simple but required perfect coordination: drive a young bull away from the herd, exhaust it, then make the kill with minimal risk. Each hunter knew their role without needing verbal instruction.

Marcus tugged my sleeve, pointing. A young bull had separated slightly from the others, tempted by a patch of fresh grass. Olkin nodded, and the first group of hunters moved forward, positioning themselves to cut off its retreat to the herd.

What followed was a dance of patience and precision. For hours, we worked in shifts, keeping the mammoth moving, preventing it from resting or rejoining the herd. Marcus never faltered, his endurance matching the adults'. When his turn came to harass the beast, he darted in fearlessly, slapping his spear against his thigh to create noise, then retreating before the mammoth could charge.

By midday, the animal showed signs of exhaustion. Its trunk hung low, its massive sides heaving with labored breaths. Olkin gathered the hunters for the final phase.

"Now we honor its strength with a clean death," she said, assigning positions for the kill.

To my surprise, she placed Marcus among the primary spear-bearers. "The boy has earned his place," she said, meeting my concerned gaze. "Trust him as I do."

The final approach required absolute silence. We crept through the tall grass, the mammoth's ragged breathing masking our movements. At Olkin's signal, the first wave rushed forward, spears aimed at the beast's flanks to drive it toward the waiting hunters.

The mammoth trumpeted in rage and fear, whirling to face its attackers. In that moment of confusion, the second wave struck from behind. Marcus moved with them, his spear finding its mark. The mammoth staggered, wounded but still dangerous.

I watched my son's face, set with determination, as he prepared for another approach. In that moment, he belonged here completely, a hunter among hunters, accepted without question.

The mammoth fell with a ground-shaking impact, and a cheer rose from the clan. Marcus stood breathless beside me, his face flushed with triumph and something deeper: belonging.

"We did it, Papa," he whispered, his voice filled with wonder.

Around us, the clan moved in to butcher their prize, hands working with practiced efficiency. Olkin approached, placing a hand on Marcus's shoulder.

"Today you have proven yourself a true child of Fox clan," she said. "Tonight, we feast in your honor."

The mammoth hunt had been a triumph, the clan's excitement echoing through the forest as we hauled our prize back toward the settlement. I lingered behind, helping two younger hunters secure one of the tusks for transport. My muscles ached pleasantly from the day's exertion, a physical reminder of accomplishment that felt grounding after months of existential uncertainty.

"Your son brings honor to you," one of the hunters said, nodding toward where Marcus had been walking ahead with Ghill and the others.

"He brings honor to himself," I replied, feeling a surge of pride that surprised me with its intensity.

We followed the river path back, the rushing water growing louder as the afternoon waned. The tusks were heavier than expected, requiring frequent stops to adjust our grip. The main hunting party disappeared around a bend ahead, their voices fading into the constant murmur of the current.

When we finally rounded the curve in the path, I spotted Marcus on the opposite bank. He stood alone, scanning the water as if searching for something. The sight immediately struck me as wrong. Why had he separated from the others?

"Marcus!" I called, setting down my end of the tusk.

He looked up, face brightening. "Papa! Look what I found!" He held up something small and gleaming, perhaps a stone or piece of bone.

Between us stretched the river, swollen from recent rains. The normal crossing point lay a quarter-mile upstream, but here the water narrowed, scattered with partially submerged rocks that formed a treacherous but possible path across.

Movement caught my eye. Snala stood partially concealed behind Marcus, her hand on his shoulder, mouth close to his ear. Even from this distance, I could see the calculation in her expression.

"Wait there," I called, already moving upstream toward the crossing. "I'll come around."

Marcus hesitated, glancing back at Snala. She whispered something else, then stepped away, folding her arms with an expression of challenge.

"I can cross here," Marcus called back. "Snala says it's a shortcut the clan children use."

Ice formed in my stomach. "No, Marcus. The current's too strong today."

I watched Marcus hesitate at the water's edge, his eyes tracking the current with newfound wariness. The confidence he'd built over these past weeks seemed to falter, his body tensing as memory and instinct warred within him.

Snala stood beside him, her voice too low for me to hear across the river. But I could read her body language, the slight lean toward him, the casual hand on his shoulder that wasn't casual at all. The way her eyes darted toward me, calculating, cold.

"Wait for me at the crossing," I called again, fighting to keep the alarm from my voice.

Marcus looked up, caught between Snala's words in his ear and my call across the water. I recognized that look, the need to prove himself, to show he belonged among these people he'd come to admire. It was the same determination that had driven him through failed swimming lessons, through awkward first attempts at tracking and hunting.

But this was different. The river didn't care about determination. Its current flowed with indifferent power, strong enough to sweep away even the most determined child.

Time seemed to slow as Marcus placed his foot on the first stone. I could see every detail with unnatural clarity: the water droplets beading on the rock's surface, the slight wobble as it took his weight, the way his fingers tightened on the small pouch at his belt. Behind him, Snala's expression shifted, a smile breaking across her face.

"Marcus!" I shouted, no longer caring how my voice carried. "Stop!"

But he was already moving to the second stone, his jaw set with determination, his eyes fixed on the crossing. The pride on his face was unmistakable. This was his moment to prove he belonged, that he had conquered his fear.

I began moving upstream toward the proper crossing, my pace

quickening to a jog. Something was wrong. This wasn't just about a child's determination to overcome fear. Snala's expression, the calculated positioning, the timing of it all. This was deliberate.

"Wait for me!" I called again, breaking into a run.

The space between us seemed to stretch impossibly. Each step I took felt too slow, too small against the distance. Marcus reached the middle of the river where the current ran strongest, stones spaced wider apart.

And then I saw him hesitate, the confidence faltering as he gauged the distance to the next foothold. His balance wavered, arms windmilling slightly before steadying. In that precarious moment, balanced between safety and disaster, he looked up, our eyes meeting across the rushing water.

I read the sudden doubt in his expression, the realization that perhaps this crossing had been a mistake. Behind him, Snala took a single step back, removing herself from what was about to unfold.

"Papa?" Marcus called, his voice barely audible over the river's rush.

Then he slipped.

I didn't think. I dove, the cold water shocking my system as I plunged beneath the surface. The current was stronger than I'd anticipated, tumbling me downstream before I could orient myself. When I broke the surface, Marcus was nowhere in sight.

Diving again, I forced my eyes open against the frigid water. A flash of movement: his tunic, caught in the current. I kicked hard, reaching for him. My fingers brushed fabric, then closed around his arm. He thrashed in panic, eyes wide with terror.

I pulled him close, fighting toward the surface, but something held us down. A tangle of branches and debris stretched across the riverbed: a beaver dam, partially collapsed but still substantial enough to trap us. Marcus's tunic had snagged on a broken branch, and the current pressed us against the wooden barrier with relentless force.

My lungs burned as I worked to free him, vision darkening at the edges. Marcus had stopped struggling, his movements growing sluggish. With one desperate yank, I tore the fabric free and pushed him upward, using the last of my strength to propel him toward the surface.

As I followed, something caught my own clothing. The current pinned me against the dam, each attempt to break free sapping more of my dwindling oxygen. Through the rippling water above, a figure appeared at the river's edge. Snala, looking down at our struggle.

Her face came into focus as she knelt by the water's edge. No alarm, no cry for help. Instead, a smile spread slowly across her features, satisfied and cold as the river itself.

I gasped awake, heart hammering against my ribs. The river's roar still filled my ears, though I lay on something soft and dry. My fingers clutched at fabric, expecting cold water but finding warm sheets instead. Sunlight streamed through lattice windows, casting diamond patterns across whitewashed walls.

"Marcus?" My voice cracked with urgency.

A small movement beside me answered before words could. Marcus lay curled against my side, his breathing shallow but steady. His eyes fluttered open, confusion giving way to recognition, then fear.

"Papa?" His voice sounded impossibly young. "We were in the water."

I pulled him close, feeling his small frame tremble against mine. "We're home now. We're safe."

The English cottage materialized around us in full detail: the stone hearth with its neatly stacked wood, the bookshelf filled with worn spines, the conservatory door standing ajar. A summer breeze carried the scent of roses through the open window, impossibly gentle after the violence of the river.

Marcus sat up slowly, looking down at his dry clothes with bewilderment. "Did we die?"

"No." I smoothed his hair back from his forehead. "Banks pulled us out. The matrix has safety protocols."

His brow furrowed. "It felt real. The drowning felt real."

"I know." The memory of water filling my lungs, of darkness closing in, remained visceral despite our physical safety. "Matrix worlds are designed that way."

Marcus slid from the bed and walked to the window. Outside, the garden bloomed in riotous color, bees moving lazily between flowers. Everything perfectly normal, perfectly safe. The contrast with our recent terror seemed almost cruel.

"Why did Snala do that?" he asked, not turning from the window. "Why did she want to hurt me?"

The question hung in the air between us. I joined him at the window, watching a hummingbird dart between blossoms while I considered how to answer.

"Some people fear what they don't understand," I said finally. "Snala didn't see you as part of her clan. She saw you as different, as other."

"Because I'm a thruman."

"Yes."

Marcus traced patterns on the windowsill with his finger. "She smiled when we were drowning."

The memory of Snala's cold satisfaction as we struggled beneath the water's surface sent a fresh wave of anger through me. "I saw."

"Will she be punished?"

I placed my hand on his shoulder, feeling the solidity of him, the miracle of his continued existence. "That's something we need to discuss with Banks. What happened wasn't just a game. It was a deliberate attempt to harm you."

"But I'm not really hurt." Marcus looked down at himself, as if confirming this fact.

"Your body isn't. But fear and betrayal leave different kinds of wounds." I knelt to meet his eyes. "What Snala did violated the trust that makes matrix worlds work. There will be consequences."

Marcus nodded solemnly. "Will we go back?"

The question surprised me. "Do you want to?"

He considered this, his young face serious. "The Fox River Clan isn't just Snala. It's Olkin and Ghill and the others. They accepted me."

"They did."

"And I was a good hunter." Pride crept into his voice. "I helped bring down the mammoth."

"You were exceptional." I smiled, remembering his fearlessness, his perfect form with the spear.

Marcus squared his shoulders, decision made. "I want to go back. But I want Snala to know what she did was wrong."

"Then we'll make sure of it." I stood, feeling my own resolve strengthen alongside his. "We'll contact Banks today. He'll know how to handle this properly."

The summer breeze strengthened, carrying the distant sound of birdsong from the oak tree beyond the garden. The peaceful scene contrasted sharply with the turmoil we'd just escaped yet somehow made our determination clearer rather than diminishing it.

"Can we have breakfast first?" Marcus asked, the practical question of a child breaking through the heaviness of the moment.

I laughed, surprised by how good it felt. "Breakfast first. Justice after."

CHAPTER TEN
Velocities

I stood on the bridge, watching the vast darkness beyond our viewports as Lieutenant Rodriguez completed the final velocity readings. The familiar hum of Paradise's systems surrounded us, a constant companion we'd all grown accustomed to in the months since departure.

"Captain's log, entry 427," I began, the formality feeling both necessary and slightly absurd. "Paradise has reached cruising velocity of 99.9% light speed."

As captain, these milestones carried weight beyond their technical significance. The helical engines had performed exactly as designed, and now Paradise would coast through the void for centuries while I guided both ship and crew through the long journey ahead. Meanwhile, Hellfire maintained parallel velocity beside us, with Temper Tom as its captain overseeing the scientific mission that complemented our colonization objectives.

Our dual command structure had evolved naturally after departure. Though formally separate vessels, Paradise and Hellfire functioned as extensions of each other, connected through QE-comm links that allowed instantaneous transfer of consciousness between ships. This arrangement let me fulfill my captain's duties while still having time for Marcus, whose development had become central to both my personal life and, increasingly, to the ships' shared mission of understanding consciousness itself.

"Paradise has reached cruising velocity of 99.9% light speed." The words hung in the air, deceptively simple for such a monumental achievement. Around me, the bridge crew continued their work with quiet efficiency, but I caught the subtle smiles exchanged between them. We'd done it. After months of acceleration, we'd reached the velocity that would carry us to Orion.

"Helical engines powering down, Captain," Maya reported from her station, her fingers dancing across the control panel. "Switching to maintenance power levels."

"Thank you, Lieutenant." I tapped the log closed, feeling the weight of what we'd accomplished. "The helical engines have served their purpose. From here on, we coast."

I took a moment to study the time dilation calculations glowing softly on my tablet. "For every month we experience, nearly two Earth years will slip away." The sheer scale of it pressed on my thoughts. "By the time we arrive at Orion, almost thirty thousand years will have passed on the Earth we left behind."

Rodriguez cleared her throat. "Sir, with your permission, Engineering would like to begin the preservation protocols for the drive systems."

"Granted. Let Maya know I'll review the shutdown sequence reports by end of shift."

I handed command to Raj and made my way through the driftways, my thoughts already shifting to the meeting with Banks. The Snala incident had been weighing on me for days, and Marcus deserved resolution.

The transition into Banks's world was seamless as always. One moment I stood in the driftway of Terracore, the next I breathed the earthy air of the Pleistocene. The scent of woodsmoke and pine filled my nostrils, and beneath my feet, soil replaced metal grating.

Banks waited for us beside a small stream, looking uncharacteristically somber in his period-appropriate leather garments. No trace of his usual flamboyance remained; this was Banks the professional, the architect responsible for the safety of his creations.

Marcus clutched my hand as we approached, his small fingers

tense with anticipation.

"Thank you for meeting us," I said.

Banks nodded, gesturing for us to sit on the flat stones beside the water. "Matrix worlds require absolute trust," he began without preamble. "Without it, they become dangerous. What happened to you both violated every principle these environments are built upon."

Marcus leaned slightly against my side. "What happened to Snala?"

Banks turned his full attention to my son, his expression softening. "She has been removed from the clan, Marcus. She will undergo mandatory empathy training before she's allowed to enter any matrix world again."

"Will she know what she did was wrong?" Marcus asked, his voice small but steady.

"Yes," Banks replied. "Part of her training involves experiencing what happened from your perspective. She'll feel what you felt when she lured you into the river. She'll understand the fear and betrayal you experienced."

Marcus considered this, his brow furrowed in thought. "But she won't be hurt?"

"No," Banks assured him. "She'll understand, but she won't be harmed. The purpose isn't revenge but understanding."

I watched Marcus's face carefully, seeing relief wash over his features. There was no vindictiveness there, no desire to see Snala suffer. Just a child's need for justice and order to be restored.

"Will she come back to the Fox Clan?" he asked.

Banks shook his head. "She will not be asked to return. The clan knows what happened, and they've accepted this decision."

Marcus nodded, seeming satisfied. As he shifted position, I noticed something I hadn't before. The leather tunic he wore, perfectly fitted this morning, now strained slightly across his shoulders. The leggings ended a fraction too high above his ankles.

He was growing.

After Banks finished explaining what had happened to Snala, Marcus and I sat quietly by the stream for a few minutes. The gentle gurgle of water over stones filled the silence between us. I watched a fish dart beneath the surface, its scales catching the sunlight in brief flashes of silver.

"Ready to head back?" I asked finally.

Marcus nodded, his expression thoughtful but no longer troubled. "Can we visit Uncle Temper today? I want to tell him about the mammoth hunt."

"I think that's a great idea." I squeezed his shoulder gently. "Let's thank Banks and be on our way."

We said our goodbyes to the matrix architeer, who promised to check in on the Fox Clan regularly. As we walked away from the stream, the Pleistocene world dissolved around us, replaced by the familiar driftways of Paradise.

"Let me message Temper first," I said, sending a quick note through the ship-to-ship QE-comm. When the confirmation came back, I smiled at Marcus. "He says he's working but we're welcome to transfer over."

Marcus's eyes lit up. "Can I try using a service bot when we get there? Please?"

I hesitated. "Those are complicated machines, Marcus."

"But I was a bot before," he countered, his logic impeccable. "I remember how it works."

I couldn't argue with that. "Alright, but you'll need to go slowly at first. Promise?"

"Promise!"

We transferred to Hellfire, materializing in Temper's cargo bay. The space was cluttered with equipment, diagnostic screens, and various mechanical components. Dominating it all was a containment field housing Falfsun, Temper's miniature sun experiment. The green-orange sphere pulsed with energy, casting eerie shadows across the bay.

Marcus stared at it, transfixed. "Wow."

I guided him to a service bot docked in its charging station. "Remember, slow movements. The controls are sensitive."

Marcus nodded seriously as I helped him establish the neural connection. The bot was humanoid but clearly mechanical, designed for maintenance rather than mimicking human appearance. Marcus's consciousness settled into it, and after a moment, the bot's optical sensors lit up.

"I can feel everything," he said, his voice coming through the bot's speakers. The mechanical arm lifted slowly, fingers flexing with careful precision. "It's different than before. More... limited."

"That's because these bots are tools, not homes," I explained. "Take a few steps. Get used to the balance."

Marcus moved the bot forward cautiously, each step becoming more confident than the last. Soon he was walking around the bay, examining equipment with childlike curiosity despite the mechanical body.

Temper stood at a console near Falfsun, his back to us, completely absorbed in reading fluctuating energy patterns. He muttered to himself, adjusting parameters and making notes. For several minutes, he didn't even notice our presence.

Marcus approached the containment field, the service bot's metal frame reflecting the pulsing light of the miniature sun. "Uncle Temper?"

Temper's bot jumped slightly, turning with wide eyes. His surprise quickly melted into a warm smile, or as close to a smile as his bot's limitations allowed. "Hi Marcus! When did you two arrive?"

"A few minutes ago," I said, leaning against a workbench. "He wanted to see his uncle."

"And your sun!" Marcus added, the service bot gesturing toward Falfsun. "Is it a real sun?"

Temper's eyes lit up with the special enthusiasm he reserved for scientific explanations. "It's a partially sustainable fusion reaction contained within a magnetic sleeve," he began, approaching Marcus. "I've managed to tap into quantum foam to provide the energy source, essentially creating matter from the quantum substrata of space itself."

I noticed something remarkable. Temper didn't simplify his explanation or talk down to Marcus. He spoke to him as he would to any intelligent being capable of understanding complex concepts.

Marcus absorbed every word, asking follow-up questions that showed genuine comprehension. "But real suns have gravity to keep the fusion going, right? How does yours stay lit?"

"Excellent question! I have to feed it regularly," Temper explained. "It's not self-sustaining yet."

As they discussed the finer points of stellar physics, Marcus excitedly shifted topics to tell Temper about the mammoth hunt and the river incident. Temper listened intently, asking thoughtful questions that showed he valued Marcus's experiences.

"Banks's historical simulations are impressive," Temper said when Marcus finished. "Have you considered experiencing human civilization chronologically? Start with early hunter-gatherers and progress through the ages?"

Marcus's excitement was palpable even through the service bot. "Can we start tomorrow?"

"I don't see why not," I said, smiling at his enthusiasm.

Temper circled the bot, examining it with a scientist's eye. "Marcus, stand up straight for me."

The service bot straightened to its full height.

"Interesting," Temper murmured. "According to my last measurements, you're standing taller than before."

"The bot's the same size," I pointed out.

"Yes, but his posture, the way he's controlling it..." Temper tapped his chin thoughtfully. "Marcus is growing."

As we materialized back in the cottage, I noticed Marcus staring at his reflection in the hallway mirror. His tunic hung slightly above his ankles, revealing what seemed like an extra half inch of growth since our last visit to the Fox Clan.

"You're getting taller," I said, resting my hand on his shoulder.

He looked up at me, a mixture of surprise and pride crossing his face. "Really? I don't feel different."

"That's how growing works. It happens so gradually you don't notice until your clothes don't fit anymore."

Marcus ran his fingers along the hem of his tunic. "Can we go back tomorrow? I want to show Olkin how tall I'm getting."

I smiled. "Let's give it a day or two. I have some captain duties to attend to first."

Those days passed quickly. By the time we were ready to return to the matrix world, Marcus had grown another quarter inch. The changes were subtle but unmistakable. His movements seemed more coordinated, his questions more complex. It wasn't just physical growth; his mind was developing too.

Banks had made adjustments to the simulation. When we stepped through the matrix threshold, the familiar landscape of the Fox River Valley materialized around us, but the season had changed. Spring flowers dotted the meadows, and new leaves unfurled on the trees.

Olkin stood waiting for us near the clan's central fire pit. Her weathered face broke into a warm smile when she spotted Marcus.

"The clan has missed its young hunter," she said, extending her hands in welcome.

Marcus hesitated for just a moment before running to embrace her. I noticed how his eyes darted toward the river flowing in the distance, his body tensing slightly at the sight of the water.

Olkin noticed too. Her keen eyes missed nothing. "Come, little one. Ghill has been asking for you. She has new fishing techniques to share."

As we walked through the settlement, clan members greeted Marcus with genuine affection. Whatever damage Snala had done to his experience here, the rest of the clan was working to heal it. Ghill waited for us near a calm eddy of the river, far from the dangerous currents where Marcus had nearly drowned.

"Here," she said, handing him a slender fishing spear with a bone tip. "Today we catch fish without entering the water."

Marcus accepted the spear, but his eyes remained fixed on the flowing river. His knuckles whitened around the wooden shaft.

"The water can't hurt you from here," Ghill said gently. "We stay on the bank today."

I watched as Marcus nodded, his jaw set with determination. This was the beginning of his healing process, I realized. Not avoidance, but careful reintroduction.

The seasons changed rapidly in the simulation. Spring gave way to summer, and we returned regularly to participate in seasonal activities. Marcus gathered sweet berries with the children, their fingers and mouths stained purple with juice. In summer heat, he learned to set fish traps in shallow pools. When autumn painted the forest in amber and gold, he joined the hunt, staying close to Olkin as they tracked deer through fallen leaves.

With each visit, Marcus ventured closer to the river. First standing at the very edge, toes touching the water. Then wading ankle-deep to collect smooth stones. His fear remained, but it no longer controlled him.

One warm summer day, Olkin led us to a secluded pool fed by the river but protected from its currents.

"Today," she announced, "you learn to swim properly."

Marcus froze. I placed my hand on his shoulder, feeling the tension there.

"You don't have to if you're not ready," I said quietly.

He looked up at me, his eyes resolute. "I won't let fear of water define me, Papa."

The swimming lessons began simply. Floating on his back with Olkin supporting him. Learning to kick while holding onto a floating log. Practicing breath control in the shallows. His progress was slow but steady, each small victory celebrated by the clan members who often gathered to watch.

The culmination came on our twelfth visit. The clan had gathered at a shallow crossing of the river, where stepping stones created a natural path across. Marcus stood on the bank, studying the distance.

"I want to cross by myself," he announced.

Olkin nodded. "We will be watching, young one."

I held my breath as Marcus stepped onto the first stone. His movements were deliberate, balanced. When he reached the middle of the river, where the current swirled around the stones, he paused. I saw him take a deep breath before continuing, each step careful but confident.

When he reached the opposite bank, the clan erupted in cheers. Marcus turned, his face flushed with triumph. He raised his arms in victory. In that moment, I saw how much he had changed. He stood taller, his face slightly less childish, his shoulders broader than when we'd first arrived.

That night, as the clan celebrated with a feast, I watched Marcus demonstrate his new fishing technique to younger children. One month of ship time had passed since we began these visits, but the changes in him seemed to represent years of growth.

"He grows quickly," Olkin said, sitting beside me by the fire. "Both in body and spirit."

"One month in, and already he's changing," I replied, a mixture of pride and wistfulness in my voice.

The celebration with the Fox Clan continued late into the night. As the stars emerged above the valley, Marcus sat among the children, sharing stories of Paradise and the stars that awaited us. His voice carried a new confidence, his gestures more assured than when we'd first arrived. I watched him from across the fire, marveling at how quickly he was changing.

When we finally returned to Paradise, Marcus immediately asked when we could visit Uncle Temper again.

"He'll be busy with his research," I cautioned.

"But I want to tell him about crossing the river," Marcus insisted. His eyes, reflecting the soft light of our cottage, held a determination I couldn't refuse.

I sent a message to Temper, who responded almost immediately. "Come tomorrow. Working on Falfsun calculations. Could use the distraction."

The next morning, we transferred through the QE-comm link to Hellfire. The cargo bay materialized around us, filled with the now-familiar hum of equipment and the eerie glow of Falfsun pulsing within its containment field. Temper hunched over a console, muttering calculations to himself, unaware of our arrival.

Marcus didn't wait for an introduction. He strode forward, his movements fluid and purposeful. "How's the quantum foam absorption rate today, Uncle Temper?"

Temper turned, stylus poised mid-calculation. His eyes widened as he took in Marcus's appearance. "You've grown at least an inch since I saw you last."

Marcus stood straighter, pride evident in his posture. "I learned to swim. And I can identify twenty medicinal plants now."

"Twenty?" Temper set down his stylus, giving Marcus his full attention. "That's impressive. Which ones?"

"Willow bark for pain, yarrow for wounds, elderberry for colds..." Marcus rattled off the list with the precision of a student who had studied diligently.

Temper nodded approvingly. "Useful knowledge, even in our technological age." He gestured toward Falfsun. "I've increased energy output by twelve percent. The magnetic containment field is holding steady."

"Have you considered modulating the quantum foam extraction rate based on solar flare activity?" Marcus asked.

I blinked in surprise. The question wasn't just insightful; it demonstrated an understanding of stellar physics that seemed beyond his years.

Temper appeared equally startled but recovered quickly. "Actually, yes. The micro-flares create fluctuations that can be harnessed for additional energy."

They fell into conversation about Falfsun's development, with Marcus asking questions that grew increasingly sophisticated. I stood back, watching their interaction with quiet amazement. Temper's usual impatience with interruptions had vanished. He spoke to Marcus as an equal, explaining complex theories without condescension.

After several minutes of technical discussion, Temper held up a round metal object. "I made something for you."

Marcus approached, curiosity brightening his face.

"It's a baseball," Temper explained, placing the metal sphere in Marcus's bot manipulator hand. "I used some hull patching material from storage to make it in my 3D printer."

Marcus examined the ball with delight. "Can you make other stuff in the 3D printer too?"

"Sure I can," Temper replied, a rare smile softening his features. "I can even make little robots that walk and roll around on the floor if I want to." He glanced between us. "Now, who wants to play catch?"

We formed a triangle in the open area of the cargo bay, tossing the makeshift baseball between us. Marcus's coordination improved with each throw, his movements becoming more natural in the service bot. On his seventh throw to Temper, he miscalculated his strength. The ball sailed high, arcing over Temper's head and through the open cargo bay doors into the void of space.

All three of us froze, watching as the silver sphere diminished to a pinpoint before disappearing entirely.

"Maybe we shouldn't tell anyone we just lost one of our spare parts," I suggested, breaking the stunned silence.

Temper's laughter echoed through the cargo bay. "I'll make another one. A whole set if you want."

As our visit wound down, I explained Banks's next simulation to Temper. "He's creating a Neolithic farming community for our next visit. Early agriculture, permanent settlements."

Temper's eyes lit with academic interest. "The agricultural revolution changed everything. Pay attention to how it transforms social structures. The shift from nomadic hunting to settled farming fundamentally altered human relationships."

"Will you visit us there?" Marcus asked, his voice cracking slightly on the last word.

I noticed Temper's hesitation, the brief flicker of uncertainty across his face. His research consumed him; he rarely left Hellfire except for official business.

"Perhaps," he said finally. "If my research allows."

Marcus nodded, accepting the conditional promise. As he turned to examine another of Temper's instruments, I noticed how his shoulders had broadened, his frame slightly taller than just weeks before. The occasional crack in his voice hinted at changes to come. The way the world seemed just a little smaller in his grasp, each a quiet marker of transformation. Time in the matrix flowed differently for him, each visit marking more dramatic changes than seemed possible in the weeks that had passed aboard Paradise. Marcus was growing at an accelerated rate.

"We should head back," I said, placing my hand on Marcus's shoulder. "Banks will have the new simulation ready soon."

Three days later, we stood before the matrix entrance, the familiar shimmer of the threshold rippling like heat waves over desert sand. Banks had sent detailed notes about the new environment: a Neolithic farming settlement along a river valley, complete with early agriculture, animal domestication, and the first permanent dwellings humans had ever built.

"Ready for something different?" I asked Marcus.

He nodded eagerly, his eyes bright with anticipation. "Will we still see the Fox Clan people?"

"Not this time. We're moving forward in human history, to when people first learned to grow their own food instead of hunting for it."

The matrix shifted around us as we stepped through. The familiar forest landscape of the Fox River Valley replaced by rolling hills covered in primitive wheat fields. The air smelled different, earthier, with the unmistakable scent of livestock and freshly turned soil.

A cluster of simple mud-brick structures stood before us; their flat roofs covered with reeds. People moved purposefully between the buildings, carrying clay pots or leading goats on crude rope leads. Children chased chickens through narrow pathways, their laughter carrying across the settlement.

An older man with sun-weathered skin approached us, his hands calloused from years of working the soil. "You must be the visitors Banks told us about. I am Natan, elder of Çatal Höyük."

Marcus stepped forward with newfound confidence. "I'm Marcus. This is my father."

Natan's eyes crinkled at the corners as he smiled. "Welcome. We have much to teach you about our ways."

The settlement welcomed us without hesitation. Marcus joined a group studying irrigation techniques, while I took on the task of teaching basic mathematics through hands-on grain storage challenges. The first few days unfolded in a rush of unfamiliar routines and discoveries. Marcus adapted with ease, his sharp mind absorbing principles that had once required generations to refine.

By our third visit, Marcus had visibly changed again. His frame had stretched taller, his face losing the roundness of early childhood. He now appeared to be ten or eleven, though only two months had passed aboard Paradise. His coordination improved dramatically as he helped construct simple water channels to direct the river's flow to the fields.

"The boy has a sharp mind," Natan observed one evening as we watched Marcus adjust the counterweight system, refining its efficiency. "He picks up on things quickly, sees ways to improve what's in front of him."

The seasons cycled through our visits: planting time with its back-breaking labor of preparing fields; the anxious middle season of tending young crops and watching the sky for rain; harvest time with its frantic energy as everyone worked to gather and store food for the coming winter.

Through it all, Marcus grew. Not just physically, but socially. He formed friendships with the other children, gradually taking on a leadership role among them. They looked to him for ideas during games, listened when he spoke during community gatherings.

During a particularly dry season, the settlement faced a crisis. The river had receded, leaving fields parched and crops wilting. The community gathered to discuss solutions, voices rising in panic as food stores dwindled.

Marcus stood quietly at the edge of the gathering, studying the crude map of the settlement drawn in the dirt. Without announcement, he knelt and began redrawing the irrigation channels, adding branches and redirecting others.

"If we dig here and here," he explained, pointing to key junctions, "we can capture more water from the morning dew and funnel it to the fields most in need."

The elders leaned in, tracing the lines he had drawn. One suggested widening a key channel to increase flow, while another proposed placing stone barriers to slow water loss. Their collective knowledge refined the plan, turning Marcus's initial idea into something stronger.

By sunset, the entire community was digging new channels, guided by the revised design. Within days, the worst-affected fields showed signs of recovery, the efforts of many woven into the land itself.

At the harvest festival that followed, Marcus stood among the other children, his face flushed with pride as Natan acknowledged the efforts of the entire community in saving their crops. He nodded toward Marcus, recognizing his contributions alongside the wisdom of the elders and the labor of many hands. Later, as musicians played bone flutes and skin drums around the central fire, I watched my son teaching younger children a game he had invented, his laughter mixing with the rhythms of the celebration.

"Two months in matrix, and he's grown four years physically," I murmured to myself, both awed and slightly unsettled by the acceleration.

Banks had explained the phenomenon to me when we first noticed the changes. "The matrix operates on cognitive engagement," he'd said, his eyes analyzing Marcus's developmental data. "For thrumans especially, time perception connects directly to neural development. Each meaningful experience triggers growth patterns that would take years to develop naturally."

According to Banks's calculations, Marcus was aging

approximately one physical year for every week of Paradise time spent in rich matrix environments. The rate varied slightly depending on the depth of his immersion and the complexity of challenges he faced. What had begun as a simulation for learning had become a catalyst for his accelerated journey into adulthood, a process both miraculous and slightly unnerving to witness as his father.

That night, as the settlement quieted, I found Marcus sitting by the dying embers of our hearth fire. His fingers moved deftly across a clay tablet, etching lines with a wooden stylus. Peering over his shoulder, I saw an intricate design for an improved irrigation system, complete with reservoirs and overflow channels.

The fire's embers cast a warm glow across his increasingly angular features. When had his cheeks lost their childish roundness? When had his eyes gained that thoughtful depth?

"These are impressive," I said, kneeling beside him. "You've thought of everything."

He nodded, absorbed in his work. "I want to show them to Uncle Temper."

"We can visit him tomorrow," I promised, wondering how Temper would react to Marcus's accelerated development.

The next day, we transferred to Hellfire. But instead of the cargo bay with its view of Falfsun, we materialized in Temper's personal quarters. The Giese Manor surrounded us, its oak paneling and leather furnishings a stark contrast to the utilitarian spaces elsewhere on the ship.

"Welcome to my sanctuary," Temper said, rising from behind an antique desk. His eyes widened slightly as he took in Marcus's appearance. "You've changed again."

Marcus smiled, his newly elongated limbs moving with the awkward grace of early adolescence as he crossed the room. He pulled the clay tablet from his pack and presented it to Temper.

"I designed a new irrigation system for the settlement," he explained, his voice cracking on the final word.

Temper took the tablet, examining it with genuine interest rather than the polite attention I'd expected. He traced the channels with his finger, nodding at certain junctions.

"You've incorporated redundancies here and here," he noted, pointing to specific areas. "Smart. Systems need backups."

Marcus beamed. "The settlement lost crops last season when the main channel silted up."

"At this rate, you'll be taller than your father soon," Temper observed, glancing between us. The comment wasn't just about physical height. We all recognized the rapid intellectual growth happening before our eyes.

Temper guided us to a holographic display in the center of the room. "I've been working on energy transfer models for Falfsun. Want to see?"

Marcus nodded eagerly. What followed was not the simplified explanation I expected, but a genuine lesson in thermodynamics. Temper manipulated the display, showing energy flows and conversion rates with complex equations hovering beside each pathway.

"Energy can neither be created nor destroyed," Temper explained. "It only changes forms."

"Like water in the irrigation channels," Marcus responded, his adolescent voice fluctuating between childish treble and deeper tones. "It doesn't disappear. It just moves where you direct it."

Temper's eyebrows rose. "Exactly. That's precisely it."

I settled into a leather armchair, content to watch their interaction. The awkwardness that had characterized some of their early meetings had vanished. Now they moved in synchrony around the display, each anticipating the other's thoughts.

"If you adjusted the magnetic containment field here," Marcus suggested, pointing to a fluctuating area in the model, "wouldn't that improve energy capture from the micro-flares?"

Temper paused, considering. "It might. Let me run the calculations." His fingers flew across the interface, equations resolving into new patterns. "You're right. A twelve percent improvement."

The pride in Temper's voice was unmistakable. I remembered his frustration with new crew members, his impatience with questions he deemed elementary. Yet here he was, explaining complex physics to a boy who looked barely thirteen.

"I never expected to enjoy teaching," Temper admitted, glancing my way with a slight shrug.

Marcus examined the bronze tools lining Temper's bookshelf, his fingers hovering over the polished edges. "Could I take one into the next simulation?" he asked. "We'll be living in the Bronze Age next, and from what I've read, the settlement's tools are incredibly primitive."

"What did you have in mind?" Temper asked.

"Something simple. A better knife maybe, or a tool for measuring water flow."

Temper considered this, then led us to his small, office 3D printer. "We can create something appropriate to their technology level. Bronze would fit the period."

For the next hour, they collaborated on designing a simple bronze measuring device. Temper explained metallurgical principles while Marcus contributed practical knowledge of the settlement's needs. The printer hummed, creating the tool layer by layer.

When Marcus stepped away to examine other artifacts in the room, Temper moved closer to me, his voice low.

"His cognitive development is accelerating," he observed. "The matrix experiences are catalyzing his growth."

The matrix itself was more than mere simulation. Unlike the virtual environments used for entertainment aboard Paradise, these were cognitive development spaces, intricately designed neural interfaces that merged historical accuracy with adaptive learning environments. Banks had pioneered this technology specifically for thruman development, creating immersive worlds that responded to the participant's choices and growth.

For thrumans like Marcus, whose consciousness had originated in digital form, the matrix provided something essential: concentrated life experience. While human children developed gradually through years of physical growth and social interaction, thrumans needed an alternative pathway, one that the matrix uniquely provided by compressing decades of experience into months of ship time. The QE-comm system facilitated this process, allowing Marcus to transfer his consciousness seamlessly between Paradise, Hellfire, and the matrix worlds where his identity was taking shape.

I nodded, watching my son who now resembled a teenager more than the child I'd first met. "I've noticed. Two months in Paradise time, and he's aged years."

"It's the richness of experience," Temper said. "His mind is absorbing everything, integrating it at an extraordinary rate."

As we prepared to leave Temper's quarters, Marcus clutched his new bronze measuring tool with pride. The maturity in his eyes still startled me: a gaze that belonged to someone far older than his apparent years.

"Next time, I'll show you my improvements," he promised Temper, his voice cracking between syllables.

"I look forward to it," Temper replied, with none of his usual impatience.

The matrix shimmered around us as Banks upgraded our simulation. The simple mud-brick structures of the Neolithic settlement dissolved, replaced by a sprawling urban landscape surrounded by imposing stone walls.

The transition into the Bronze Age followed the pattern we'd established. Marcus and I spent a day aboard Paradise discussing what he'd learned from the Neolithic settlement, giving his digital consciousness time to process and integrate the experiences. Banks prepared the new simulation carefully, designing Bronze Age Ur-Kasim with historically accurate details while allowing space for Marcus to find his own place within it.

"This period marks humanity's first major technological revolution," Banks explained as we prepared to enter the new matrix world. "The discovery of metallurgy changed everything—from agriculture to warfare, from art to governance." Marcus listened intently, his eyes reflecting his eagerness to experience this pivotal era firsthand. When the matrix threshold shimmered before us, we stepped through together, leaving the farming settlement behind for the smoky forges and mud-brick ziggurats of ancient Mesopotamia.

The scent of copper and tin filled the air as I recorded the day's transactions on clay tablets. My stylus pressed familiar symbols into the soft surface, documenting the weight of ore delivered to the city's metalworking district. Four months had passed in Paradise time, but in the accelerated time of the matrix, Marcus had lived through nearly three years of Bronze Age development.

Across the workshop, my son bent over a small forge, his tall frame dwarfing the other apprentices. At fifteen, or what appeared to be fifteen, Marcus had grown into his limbs, though occasional moments of teenage awkwardness still betrayed him. His fingers worked deftly with tongs, pulling a glowing piece of metal from the coals.

"Notice how the color tells you when it's ready," he explained to a younger apprentice. "Too pale, and it won't take shape. Too dark, and it becomes brittle."

The master metalworker, Karthum, watched from the corner. His arms, corded with muscle from decades at the forge, crossed over his chest as he observed Marcus demonstrate techniques that had taken him years to perfect.

"Where did you learn this method?" Karthum asked when Marcus quenched the piece in water, creating a controlled cooling pattern.

Marcus glanced my way before answering. "My uncle showed me. He studies the stars but knows much about metal too."

Karthum examined the finished piece, a hinged clasp for a ceremonial box. "You understand metal as if you were born from it."

I smiled, continuing my record-keeping while pride swelled in my chest. The city of Ur-Kasim had accepted us readily when Banks introduced us months ago. My role as scribe gave me access to the city's governance and trade, while Marcus found his place among the metalworkers.

The marketplace outside hummed with activity. Merchants haggled over prices of grain and textiles. Priests moved in procession toward the ziggurat that dominated the city center. Soldiers patrolled the walls, bronze spearheads glinting in the midday sun.

"Papa, look." Marcus approached, carrying a small tool. "I've improved Uncle Temper's design."

He demonstrated how he'd modified the bronze measuring device, adding calibration marks and a level indicator. "Now it can measure both water flow and angle of incline for the irrigation channels."

"The temple engineers will want this," I noted, adding it to my inventory record.

Over the following months, I observed Marcus settling more deeply into the rhythm of the city. His practical suggestions helped refine existing techniques, spreading gradually from the metalworking district to the temple workshops and the military armory. He worked alongside craftsmen, adjusting tools and methods rather than reinventing them. What began as minor improvements, reinforcing sword hilts, tweaking plow blades, sealing storage jars more effectively, became small yet useful contributions woven into daily life.

During the harvest festival, I stood among the crowd as the city's king honored the craftsmen whose work had shaped the city. Marcus stood among them, one of many, his contributions recognized alongside those of seasoned metalworkers.

"The hands of our craftsmen have strengthened Ur-Kasim," the king proclaimed. "Their skill and dedication will guide apprentices for generations to come."

Marcus accepted the ceremonial copper medallion with a slight bow, standing among the honored metalworkers. His shoulders were broader than I recalled, his jaw more defined. It was a quiet transformation I had failed to notice in the rush of days. The matrix had accelerated his learning and his physical growth, condensing years of change into mere months, leaving me to catch glimpses of the person he was becoming.

Later that evening, I found Marcus alone in Karthum's workshop, working on a special project. His hands moved with confidence as he etched intricate patterns into a ceremonial dagger.

"For the king's son," he explained, holding it up for my inspection. The blade caught the lamplight, revealing swirling designs that reminded me of the star charts in Temper's quarters.

"It's beautiful," I said, noting how his features had sharpened, the last traces of childhood softness giving way to teenage angles. A shadow of stubble darkened his jaw, another reminder of time's acceleration.

"It's nice here, but I'm ready for more," Marcus said, testing the blade's balance. "I need to finish this first. When I'm done can we go visit Uncle Temper?"

I nodded, watching my son, now taller than me, as he returned to his work, the dagger taking shape beneath his skilled hands.

I watched Marcus present the ceremonial dagger to the king's son, his confidence evident in every gesture. The royal family's approval had secured his reputation in Ur-Kasim.

Bank's world dissolved around us, seamlessly transitioning our consciousness back to Terracore. When we materialized on Hellfire the following day, the cargo bay's ambient vibrations welcomed us. Each of us inhabited a service bot, our presence intertwined with their mechanisms, our perception filtered through their sensors.

Falfsun dominated the space, miniature prominences arcing gracefully from its surface, casting an eerie green glow across the monitoring equipment surrounding its containment field.

Marcus moved toward it immediately, his service bot adjusting with ease to his motions. He had grown. His previous awkwardness replaced by confident precision, his movements fluid within the bot's frame.

"It's grown," he observed, scanning the swirling patterns on Falfsun's surface through the enhanced visual feeds.

Temper shifted from his workstation, acknowledging Marcus with a brief nod. "About eight percent larger since your last visit. The quantum foam extraction is exceeding my projections."

Service bots whirred softly, maintaining their tasks. Temper guided Marcus toward a holographic display detailing Falfsun's internal structure.

"Today I thought we might discuss stellar nucleosynthesis," Temper said, expanding the display to show atomic structures. "Do you know what happens inside a star?"

Marcus studied the display intently. "Elements transform through fusion. Hydrogen becomes helium, releasing energy."

"Exactly. And in larger stars, the process continues." Temper manipulated the display, showing heavier elements forming in sequence. "Carbon, oxygen, silicon, all the way to iron."

Marcus's eyes widened with recognition. "Like metalworking. The forge and the star, both transforming elements from one state to another."

I blinked in surprise. The abstract connection between stellar processes and his experience in the Bronze Age city showed a level of conceptual thinking I hadn't anticipated.

"That's... remarkably insightful," Temper said, glancing at me with raised eyebrows. "Yes, both involve transformation through heat and pressure, though at vastly different scales."

For the next hour, I watched as Temper explained increasingly complex astrophysics concepts. Marcus absorbed everything, asking questions that revealed not just comprehension but extrapolation beyond what Temper presented. His vocabulary had expanded dramatically, technical terms flowing naturally in his speech.

"What happens to time when traveling near light speed?" Marcus asked suddenly, interrupting Temper's explanation of fusion cycles.

Temper paused, clearly reassessing Marcus's intellectual level. "Time dilates. The faster you move relative to another observer, the slower time passes for you from their perspective."

"Because of relativity," Marcus nodded. "Is that why you and Papa will age differently than the people on Earth during our journey?"

"Precisely." Temper pulled up another display showing complex equations. "These describe the relationship mathematically."

I expected Temper to simplify the formulas, but instead, he walked Marcus through the actual calculations. To my astonishment, Marcus followed along, asking clarifying questions about variables and constants.

"He processes information differently than human children," Temper said to me quietly as Marcus studied the equations. "His cognitive patterns are fascinating. The matrix experiences have accelerated not just his emotional development but his abstract thinking capabilities."

I nodded, watching my son who now stood at adult height, his teenage physique a stark contrast to the child I'd first met. His face had lost all traces of childhood roundness, replaced by defined features that hinted at the man he was rapidly becoming.

"I think you're ready for something new," Temper said to Marcus. "Perhaps the Classical era. Greek or Roman civilization would introduce you to philosophical questions about existence, knowledge, ethics."

Marcus's eyes lit up. "I'd like that. Will you come see me debate in the forum?"

Temper paused, surprise flickering across his face at the personal invitation. Then his expression softened slightly. "I'll make time for it."

As Temper's promise to attend a future debate hung in the air, I watched Marcus's eyes light up with anticipation. The service bot he inhabited seemed to straighten slightly, as though his pride physically manifested even through mechanical components.

"I'll hold you to that promise, Uncle Temper," he said, his voice carrying the confidence of someone far beyond his apparent years.

I contacted Banks with our request.

The cargo bay dissolved around us as Banks initiated another transition. The metallic walls of Hellfire faded, replaced by the warm Mediterranean light of classical Athens.

Marble columns gleamed under the midday sun as I made my way across the agora. Merchants called out their wares from colorful stalls while groups of men gathered in shaded porticoes, engaged in animated discussions. I adjusted my chiton, still not entirely comfortable in the flowing garment after six weeks in this world.

The Lyceum bustled with activity as students moved between lectures. I nodded to several young men who greeted me respectfully as their rhetoric instructor. My small class had grown in popularity since our arrival, particularly after Marcus's first public debate had drawn attention to our approach, which differed slightly from traditional methods taught in the city.

I found him in the central courtyard, surrounded by a group of students. At seventeen, Marcus stood tall and lean, his features settling into those of a young man. Dark curls framed a face that had shed the last traces of childhood, though his eyes still held the familiar spark of curiosity I had noticed from the start.

"The question is not whether an idea exists physically," Marcus was saying, his hands moving lightly as he spoke, "but whether it holds coherence and utility in explaining what we observe."

"You speak like Aristotle," one student argued, "claiming knowledge comes from observation. But Plato teaches us that true knowledge exists beyond the physical realm."

Marcus smiled, his expression shifting as he considered the thought. "Perhaps both hold truth, depending on the perspective. The physical world gives us information, but our minds shape the patterns that give it meaning."

I lingered at the edge of the group, watching as Marcus spoke with ease. The once hesitant child who had struggled to put his thoughts into words now engaged others with clarity and confidence, his ideas flowing effortlessly into the conversation.

Later that afternoon, I joined him as he prepared for the public debate. The topic had been announced throughout the city: "What Defines a Being Worthy of Rights and Consideration?" The question couldn't have been more perfect if Banks had designed it specifically for us, though he swore the simulation was merely responding to patterns of discourse already present.

"Are you nervous?" I asked, helping Marcus arrange his formal himation over his shoulder.

"No." He adjusted the drape of fabric with practiced ease. "This argument lives in my bones, Papa. I've been preparing for it my entire existence."

The debate hall filled quickly. Citizens of all ranks crowded the stone benches, their voices creating a low rumble of anticipation. I took my place near the front, scanning the crowd for Temper, though I didn't truly expect him to appear.

The aging philosopher Kleanthes took position first, his white beard and stooped posture commanding immediate respect. Known for his conservative views, he began by establishing traditional definitions of personhood.

"The gods created man from the earth," he intoned, "breathing divine essence into clay. This spark of divinity separates us from beasts and objects. It cannot be manufactured or imitated."

When Marcus stepped forward, whispers rippled through the audience. His youth made him an unlikely opponent for the venerated Kleanthes.

"Respected citizens," Marcus began, his voice clear and steady. "My opponent speaks of divine creation. I ask you instead to consider observable qualities. What do we actually witness when we encounter a being worthy of moral consideration?"

He paced deliberately, making eye contact with different sections of the audience. "We observe consciousness, the capacity for reason, for joy and suffering, for self-reflection. We see the ability to make choices based on values and to understand consequences."

"These qualities," he continued, "are what truly matter in our treatment of others. Not origin, not method of creation, but the presence of mind and heart."

Kleanthes scoffed. "The young man speaks of imitations. A statue may appear human but lacks the divine spark. Similarly, a machine programmed to mimic thought remains mere clay without divine breath."

Marcus's response came without hesitation. "If I converse with two beings hidden behind a curtain, one born of woman and one crafted by human hands, yet both demonstrate identical capacity for reason, emotion, and moral judgment, what meaningful difference exists between them?"

The debate intensified, with Kleanthes invoking tradition and divine order while Marcus built careful arguments based on observable qualities of consciousness. I watched the audience's reactions shift, skepticism giving way to thoughtful consideration as Marcus addressed each counterargument with precision and respect.

"The nature of consciousness," Marcus concluded, "remains a mystery whether it emerges in a being born or built. But our ethical obligations should extend to all who demonstrate the qualities we value in ourselves: self-awareness, capacity for reason, and moral agency. Consciousness, not origin, defines being."

A movement at the entrance caught my attention. Temper stood there, arms crossed, listening intently. Our eyes met briefly, and he gave a slight nod before returning his attention to Marcus.

When the audience voiced their support, overwhelmingly favoring Marcus's position, something shifted in him. His posture straightened, his words gained more certainty, and a quiet confidence settled into his expression. The approval wasn't just validation. It was a turning point, shaping the way he carried himself in the conversation.

After the formal proceedings, Temper approached us in the courtyard. Marcus straightened slightly, clearly pleased by his unexpected presence.

"You argued well," Temper said simply. "Even I was convinced."

Coming from Temper, this qualified as effusive praise. Marcus beamed.

As we walked together through the evening agora, I marveled at the journey that had brought us here. The child who once built wobbly towers with blocks now constructed elegant philosophical arguments that could change minds and hearts.

"What did you think?" Marcus asked, his eyes seeking my approval despite his triumph.

"I couldn't be prouder," I answered truthfully. "You spoke your truth with wisdom beyond your years."

The Athenian debate hall faded around us as Banks ended the

simulation, returning us to the familiar driftways of Terracore. Marcus's philosophical triumph lingered in my mind as we blinked back to our cottage, his arguments about consciousness and personhood resonating deeply with his own journey.

"I'd like to visit Falfsun tomorrow," Marcus said. "There's a stellar phenomenon I want to observe with Uncle Temper."

I nodded, watching him move with the confident grace that had replaced his once-awkward gait. "We'll go first thing in the morning."

The cargo bay of Hellfire hummed with energy as we arrived the next day. Falfsun dominated the space, its swirling surface casting an eerie green glow that painted shadows across the monitoring equipment. The miniature sun had grown again, its prominences arcing higher than I remembered, fiery rainbows suspended in the controlled environment.

Marcus moved immediately to Temper's side at the monitoring station. At nineteen, at least in appearance, he stood nearly as tall as Temper now, his features fully matured into those of a young man. His dark eyes reflected Falfsun's glow as he studied the readouts.

"The magnetic field fluctuations increased by twelve percent since yesterday," Marcus noted, his fingers dancing across the holographic interface with practiced ease.

Temper nodded without looking up. "I've been tracking the pattern. It suggests a minor coronal event forming in the northwestern quadrant."

I watched them work together, their communication almost telepathic. Temper would begin calculating a sequence, and Marcus would complete it without prompting. When Marcus suggested an adjustment to the containment field, Temper implemented it without question. The mutual respect between them was evident in every interaction, a far cry from their first few meetings m0nths ago.

After several hours of monitoring and adjustments, Marcus stifled a yawn.

"The field will hold through the night cycle," Temper said, noticing his fatigue. "Get some rest. We'll continue in the morning."

Marcus nodded, reluctantly stepping away from the workstation. "Wake me if the prominence shifts more than three degrees."

We left our service bots and went to Giese Manor, Temper's quarters aboard Hellfire. Marcus settled onto the leather couch in the great room, intending only to rest his eyes. Within minutes, he was asleep, his breathing deep and even.

Temper poured two glasses of bourbon at the stone fireplace across the room. He handed one to me as we settled into adjacent armchairs, the crackling fire casting warm light across the polished oak floors.

"He's exhausted himself again," I said quietly, watching Marcus sleep.

Temper swirled his drink thoughtfully. "His mind works differently. He processes information at rates I've never seen before, even in advanced AI systems."

We sat in comfortable silence for a moment, the only sounds the soft popping of the fire and Marcus's steady breathing.

"I never wanted family connections," Temper admitted suddenly, his voice barely audible. "Too messy. Too many variables I couldn't control."

I studied his profile, surprised by the confession. "And now?"

Temper's gaze drifted to Marcus's sleeping form. His expression softened almost imperceptibly. "Now I understand your choice to adopt him."

"It wasn't really a choice," I replied. "Not in the end."

"No," Temper agreed. "Some connections form whether we plan for them or not."

He took a slow sip of his bourbon. "He asks questions I wouldn't think to ask. Sees patterns I miss. His perspective is... valuable."

I nodded, noting the protective glance Temper cast toward Marcus. For all his clinical language, the attachment was clear.

"I've been considering his next matrix experience," Temper said. "Renaissance era, perhaps. Florence or Venice. He's ready for that explosion of art and science, that intersection of disciplines."

"He's nearly grown now," I observed. "Physically and mentally."

"The matrix experiences are accelerating his development beyond standard thruman patterns," Temper confirmed. "His neural pathways are forming connections at remarkable rates. Banks says he's never seen anything like it."

I watched my son sleep, this young man who had once been a confused child building block towers in a children's playroom. Marcus had found himself in these worlds, had grown into his potential in ways I couldn't have imagined.

"Do you ever regret it?" Temper asked suddenly. "Taking on this responsibility when your own future was so uncertain?"

I didn't answer Temper right away. The fire crackled, filling the quiet as I watched Marcus sleep, his breath steady. In the flickering light, I could still see traces of the child he'd been, though they were fading beneath the sharp lines of the young man he was becoming.

"No," I finally said. "I don't regret it."

Temper nodded, satisfied. We finished our drinks in silence, the question settled.

The Florentine workshop hummed with activity. Apprentices stretched canvases, ground pigments, and sketched designs. Sunlight streamed through tall windows, illuminating specks of marble dust that drifted like tiny stars. The scent of linseed oil and fresh clay hung in the air.

Marcus worked at the drafting table, focused on anatomical drawings. At twenty-three, at least in appearance, his movements were sure and precise.

Maestro Verrocchio moved through the studio, pausing at each apprentice's work, offering sharp yet thoughtful critiques. When he reached Marcus, he studied the detailed rendering of a human arm, the muscles and tendons carefully shaded.

"Eccellente," Verrocchio murmured. "Not just in precision, but in understanding. You see beyond the surface."

Marcus nodded, glancing at the apprentices working nearby. "It helps to watch the others," he admitted. "Everyone has a different way of seeing the body. Each stroke tells a different story."

Verrocchio smiled, then turned to address the room. "Art is not the work of a single mind but the collaboration of many. We teach, we learn, and in that cycle, we shape something lasting."

Around Marcus, apprentices traded sketches, adjusting each other's compositions, offering quiet encouragement. He no longer stood apart, no longer the observer. He was part of their shared craft, their unspoken language.

"The master says I may begin my own commission next month," Marcus told me later. "Some patrons are interested in my perspective studies."

I glanced at his work, faces rendered with quiet reverence, hands interlocked in gestures of trust. His pages weren't just studies of form but reflections of the artists surrounding him.

"You've become one of them," I said.

Marcus nodded, his fingers tracing the edges of his portfolio. "I think that's what art is, isn't it? Not just capturing the world but understanding the people who create alongside you."

That evening, Marcus adjusted his collar absentmindedly, his movements mirroring those of the other apprentices. It was no longer the gesture of an outsider imitating those around him, but the natural habit of someone fully immersed in the rhythm of their world. He was no longer just passing through. He had become part of something greater, woven into a lineage of artists and thinkers.

"Six months into this voyage of self-discovery, and he's aged twenty years," I said as Verrocchio and I watched him work alongside the other apprentices. Their hands moved in sync, refining the full prototype, sharing quiet discussions about balance and proportion.

"Not just physically," the master replied. "He sees connections, not just in his work, but in people."

Then came the messenger from the Medici palace. Lorenzo had heard of the young artist and inventor and summoned him to court. The apprentices paused in their work, exchanging nods and murmurs of encouragement as Marcus prepared to present his designs. It wasn't just his success, it was theirs, too. Their knowledge, their corrections, their shared efforts had shaped everything in his portfolio.

That evening, as Marcus selected his best drawings, he paused to adjust his collar in a polished metal mirror, an unconscious gesture that blurred the boy he'd been with the man he was becoming.

"Are you nervous?" I asked.

He smiled, his voice steady. "No. I've found my place here, Papa. Just as I did with the Fox Clan, and in Athens. Each world teaches me something new."

I nodded, a quiet understanding passing between us. "And each time, you find a family within it."

The Medici court faded, dissolving into the stark hum of Hellfire's cargo bay as Banks ended the simulation. The warmth of the Renaissance workshop evaporated, replaced by the cool precision of technology. But Marcus didn't falter. His steps were confident as he moved toward Temper's workstation, no longer the student hesitating before a master.

Side by side, they worked as equals, their service bots adjusting containment fields. Marcus offered a suggestion, a refinement to the energy distribution, a subtle improvement that at first earned Temper's skepticism. But as they tested the modification, Temper's sharp expression softened.

"You've solved it," he murmured, recalibrating the system with a quiet nod of approval. "A problem we've fought with for months."

I watched their synergy unfold, no longer the dynamic of teacher and student. This was something different. Something collaborative.

"Well," Temper said finally, wiping his hands clean, "I suppose that makes you my research assistant."

Marcus didn't try to mask the quiet satisfaction in his posture. His contributions weren't just theoretical, they were real. Tangible.

"Your perspective is valuable precisely because it's different," Temper added.

As they worked, the conversation drifted toward the future. Marcus admitted his growing fascination with engineering, the way it bridged creativity and logic, artistry and function.

Temper nodded, considering. "Then maybe it's time we move forward. The final era: Industrial Revolution."

Marcus hesitated, then asked, "And after that? What's next for me?"

I met his gaze, offering the simplest answer. "Whatever you choose. You're grown now, in every way that matters."

A pause. Then Temper's voice carried a note of certainty. "Perhaps it's time he joined the Din."

The last embers of Temper's fireplace faded as we blinked into Manchester's industrial heart. Coal smoke thickened the air, curling into every crevice of the city, while the rhythmic clanking of steam engines pulsed through narrow streets. Marcus strode ahead toward the textile mill, blending seamlessly into the crowd of workers filing through the iron gates. He was simply another among them.

Inside, the factory floor trembled beneath the pounding of power looms. The air swirled with cotton dust, clinging to faces streaked with sweat and exhaustion. Children darted through the machinery, small hands reaching into dangerous spaces to clear jams or retrieve fallen bobbins.

Marcus stopped, watching a young girl stretch to untangle a thread caught in the gears. His brow furrowed. "This isn't right," he said. "There has to be a better way."

We spent the following weeks talking to those who knew the mill best. Not engineers or owners, but the workers; the men and women whose hands shaped the machines, whose bodies bore the weight of long hours and relentless pace. They shared their frustrations, their quiet solutions, their warnings about dangers the overseers overlooked. Marcus listened, as did I.

"What would make it safer?" I asked a weaver one evening.

"Guards over the gears," she said, wiping dust from her brow. "So no child's hand slips in."

"And proper ventilation," added another. "We breathe this in day after day. It wears you down."

A machinist explained how reinforced pulleys could keep tension steady, reducing sudden breaks that sent thread whipping through the air. A young boy spoke of how staggered shifts might allow children time to learn, rather than work until their bodies grew numb.

Piece by piece, we gathered their ideas and shaped them into something the factory owner couldn't dismiss. Not one person's solution, but the wisdom of many.

When the day came to present the proposed changes, it was the workers who stood beside us. Marcus outlined the improvements: the protective guards, the redesigned ventilation system, the refinements to loom stability. But he didn't speak alone. Those who had spent years on the factory floor stepped forward, explaining in their own words why change was necessary.

The owner hesitated, but as the numbers were laid before him, greater efficiency, fewer injuries, a workforce that could last longer, the weight of industry met the undeniable logic of human care. The factory adapted, not because of one brilliant mind, but because a community had spoken.

Months passed. Other mills took notice. The once silent workers began to talk, to share knowledge across factory lines. Their children learned to read instead of dodging steel. The air cleared just enough to breathe without choking.

I watched Marcus, now just another craftsman among them, explaining a new method for reinforcing loom tension. No grand speeches, no proclamations, just quiet conversation, hands working together to shape something better.

That evening, as Marcus closed his notebook, he glanced toward me. "This wasn't just my idea," he said, his voice quieter than usual, thoughtful.

I waited, sensing there was more.

He exhaled, tracing the edges of the pages filled with sketches and calculations, none of them purely his own. "At first, I wanted to fix things. To make them better. But every real improvement we made came from conversations, from the people who knew these machines and lived with them every day."

His fingers lingered over the corner of a page where a machinist had scrawled a suggestion in thick charcoal. "I didn't invent these changes. I just listened."

I nodded, watching him process the truth of his own words. "And because you listened, they spoke."

Marcus glanced across the factory floor, where workers gathered in quiet discussion, adjusting parts of the loom design, sharing solutions. They were no longer waiting for someone else to dictate their future. They were shaping it together.

His expression shifted, something settling into place, not just understanding, but acceptance. "It's not just about invention, is it?" He looked at me then, fully realizing it. "It's about knowing you don't do it alone."

I smiled. "You never do."

Watching him say it, I realized how much I'd changed too. The ache from losing Amy hadn't disappeared, but it had softened. She was part of David's past now, and I was learning to live in mine. Marcus had grown exponentially these past few months, and somehow, his growth had pulled me forward with him. Each era we lived through, each question he asked, each lesson he absorbed, had helped me heal. I hadn't expected that. But I was in a better place because of him.

Marcus straightened, closing his notebook with certainty. His journey wasn't about what he could build. It was about the people he built alongside. He had learned something far greater than machinery. He had learned what it meant to belong.

Joining the Din was a turning point for Marcus, but not because they were some elite task force. The Din were explorers, improvisers, thrill-seekers. They chased mysteries, solved problems, and occasionally got themselves into spectacular trouble just for the joy of getting back out again.

Go and Temper had auditioned to join the Din early on in their voyage to Orion, and they'd earned their place through a mix of cleverness, grit, and sheer charm. Since then, they'd become part of the gang's rhythm, one voice among many in a chorus of chaos and camaraderie.

Temper didn't offer the spot to Marcus lightly. After watching him grow over the past six months, both Temper and I saw it clearly: he wasn't just tagging along anymore. He'd earned his place, not as a kid we needed to shield, but as someone who could shape the journey with us.

Marcus's first experience as a Din was within the battlefield of Dead Zone, an open-world Breach game governed by its own fractured laws of physics. We had joined as human Soldiers of Light, pitted against the World-breaker Soldiers of Domdaniel, who had carved their way into Fusang. The land teetered at the edge of forever, drowning it in darkness.

Fusang was a bleak, hollow world, stripped of warmth. After the Din's failed attempt to reclaim the main road, we were severed from our clan. Marcus, Temper, and I regrouped in the ruins east of Nonnan's shattered skyline. My jet pack had taken a direct hit in the skirmish. It still functioned, barely. The damage had made it sluggish and incapable of turning to the right. Temper's chest armor bore a deep, blackened gash from shoulder to waist, though it had done its job: he was bruised but whole. Marcus, untouched, had taken up guard duty as Temper and I sifted through the wreckage, searching for any usable weapons or gear.

"Anything?" Temper asked, his voice tight with frustration.

I shoved aside a chunk of collapsed masonry near the edge of a gutted building. The rubble was scorched, warped, useless. "Nothing. Let's try inside. If the Domdaniel left anything behind, it would have a better chance of surviving in there."

Temper eyed the sagging roof. "That thing looks ready to cave in. You sure about this?"

"We'll be fine. Just don't start kicking things over." I shot him a pointed look. "Remember the barn? The one you gently knocked onto my head?"

Temper groaned. "Are you ever going to let that go? It was a light kick! That barn was one stiff breeze away from falling anyway."

"Maybe, but it wouldn't have landed on me."

Inside, the air was heavy with dust and the faint tang of scorched metal. Shadows pooled in the corners, making it hard to distinguish shapes. My gut tightened. Something was tucked into the dim recess beyond the crumbling doorway; a mass of debris, or something deliberately concealed.

I nodded toward it. "What's piled up over there?"

Temper grinned. "Dunno. Should I kick it?"

I ignored him. We approached cautiously, the building groaning around us. As I peeled back the layers of grime, I uncovered a camouflaged tarp draped over a pallet. Beneath it was an untouched cache of armor and weapons.

Temper let out a low whistle, scooping up a new chest plate and shrugging it on. His charred armor clattered to the ground. He dug into the pile, slinging a bandolier of power packs across his shoulder. His excitement was near tangible, bouncing from item to item like a dog overwhelmed by too many scents.

I sifted through the cache, irritation creeping in. "See any jet pack stabilizer parts?"

Temper hesitated, then pulled his arm from behind his back, fingers curled around a gleaming control module. "You mean like this?"

I exhaled sharply. "How long have you been holding that?"

"I wasn't sure you wanted it," he said, flashing an infuriatingly innocent grin.

"You weren't sure, my ass."

He tossed it over, and I wasted no time swapping out the burnt-out module. A pulse of green illuminated my pack's status display.

"It works!" Relief flooded my chest.

Then, suddenly, Temper stiffened. His expression flickered, caught between confusion and urgency. "I have to go."

I barely had time to process the words before he blinked out of the game.

Marcus and I exchanged a glance. Before either of us could speak, Lieutenant Chen's voice crackled in the air.

"Bridge to Captain. Per emergency protocols, we have a code red."

I straightened. "State the emergency."

Chen hesitated, a rare tremor in her voice. "We've been contacted by another ship. They request to speak with you."

A chill edged up my spine. "I'll be right there."

We were traveling at near-light speed, deep in the void. There shouldn't be anyone out here.

Yet someone was.

CHAPTER ELEVEN

Divergence

It had been eleven months since we reached our cruising speed of 99.9% the speed of light. In that time, twenty years had passed back on Earth.

Marcus and I blinked to the bridge.

"Lieutenant Chen, open a communication channel with the ship. Let's find out who they are."

"Channel established, Captain."

"This is Go David, captain of Paradise. Who am I speaking with?"

Temper's voice cut in. "I'm in contact with them."

I sat forward. "Good! What's going on?"

His image flickered onto the screen, standing composed as ever. "They're here to fulfill our contract. The ship is the Admiral Blue. Her captain is Jim Smith. Let everyone know that everything is okay and to stay calm. They're friendly. I'm hosting their captain for a meeting in my quarters. Can you and Marcus join us?"

"We'll be right there," I said.

We transferred into Temper's great room, a space that never failed to impress. Its grand windows framed the sprawling forest beyond; dark pines dusted with fresh snow. Occasionally, movement in the underbrush suggested an animal passing through, cautious but unbothered. A fire crackled in the stone hearth, casting warm flickers over the sturdy furniture and old-world paintings. A side table held an inviting spread of snacks, desserts, and finger foods arranged with quiet hospitality.

Near the fire, Temper stood with two others, sipping whiskey. Marcus wrinkled his nose at the offered glass.

"Do you have anything else?" he asked.

Temper, ever the accommodating host, nodded. "Certainly. What would you like?"

"Do you have any beer?"

Without hesitation, Temper handed him a Paulaner Hefe-Weizen. I took the moment to introduce us.

"I'm Go, captain of Paradise, and this is Marcus, my son."

Jim Smith gave a measured nod. He carried himself with the ease of a seasoned traveler. "Nice to meet you. I'm Jim, captain of the Admiral Blue, and this is Luna Dawn, my second-in-command."

Introductions settled, conversation moved easily with small talk filling the next minute or so, until Temper turned toward the fire, his glass cradled in one hand, his expression shifting to something more deliberate.

"Jim and Luna know this story already," he said, "but for the sake of clarity, let me start at the beginning."

Temper stood near the fireplace, his posture easy but deliberate, the firelight flickering across his face.

"As most of you remember, during the first year of our voyage, we encountered sprites; ghostly apparitions drifting near our ship. They never displayed aggression, nor did they seem to pose any immediate threat. Still, we needed answers. We had to understand what they were and whether they carried any risk to our ships or our lives. So, we used one of our three consultations with the Oracle to investigate."

He took a measured sip of his drink before continuing. "After reviewing our findings, the Oracle told me that the sprites were, in essence, a thickening of space. Our attempt to pinch the C-field wasn't compressing quantum substrate, as we had hoped. Instead, we were pinching space itself, pulling it into dense clumps while leaving the surrounding area thinner. These accumulations, which we called sprites, gathered at the back of the ship near the engines. They didn't interact with anything, but the Oracle advised us to abandon the experiments into C-pinch fusion, just to be safe."

Temper's tone remained calm, methodical. "He then suggested I contact a small start-up called Carpisma. At the time, their specialty was generating solitons—solitary waves—for acoustic applications. Holmes saw potential in their work, recognizing that their expertise in manipulating solitons could be relevant to our issue. But, as we all know, the Oracle doesn't control his own time. His owners don't allow him to do any consultations for free." Temper exhaled, almost amused at the reality of it. "So, after some negotiation, I sold our second of three consultations to Carpisma."

I stiffened. "You sold one of our consultations without telling me?"

Temper's response carried a quiet certainty. "You were indisposed. You were dealing with matters involving your separation from Amy. It didn't seem appropriate to trouble you with this while you were occupied elsewhere."

The memory surfaced with a clarity I didn't ask for. Long days of suffocating self-pity, seated alone in the dim corner of my cottage, wishing the entire world would just go away.

His discretion had spared me then, and even now. I could only nod. "Yes, I remember. Thanks for handling it."

Temper inclined his head before continuing. "At the time, Carpisma was focused on solving acoustical problems. Holmes believed their talents were underutilized. He proposed an experiment: to collide solitons at high velocity and recreate our C pinch experiment, thinning the space around them. Under Holmes' guidance, Carpisma began bouncing solitons against each other, analyzing the effects, refining the frequency of the collisions to manipulate their shapes, and fine-tuning the process to eliminate excess heat. Solitons, by their nature, are self-reinforcing, almost indestructible. Eventually, the researchers managed to form stable soliton bubbles, using controlled collisions to set them into motion through the thinned-out space."

I waited patiently for Temper to continue.

"Soliton geometry held great promise," Captain Smith interjected.

Temper nodded, "There were still problems, though. The soliton bubbles were microscopic, so they had no real-world applications, and once set into motion, their direction couldn't be changed. And then, they kept disappearing."

"Disappeared? You mean destroyed?" Marcus asked.

Captain Smith shook his head. "They didn't disintegrate. They flew off in random directions, uncontrolled, at high speeds. The collisions built up excess energy, converting into elastic momentum. Once saturation was reached, the bubbles shot off, vanishing. We started calling it the Big Bounce."

Marcus's eyes widened. He grasped the significance of the conversation better than I did.

"How fast were they going?" Marcus asked.

Captain Smith paused for a moment, considering his response.

"The estimated speed of each big bounce was five hundred and fifty thousand miles per second. Our instruments weren't designed to track something moving that fast, so it was difficult to measure."

"Wow!" Marcus breathed.

"Wow indeed," Temper agreed.

Luna leaned in slightly. "The bubbles gave us a new tool for studying the micro universe, but we had our sights set on something far greater. If we could make them larger, then anything contained within should be able to piggyback and travel just as fast."

Captain Smith added, "And we had to solve the directional problem. Random collisions were uncontrollable, so we needed a new approach."

Luna nodded. "It took twenty years of research before we devised the Two-Bubble System, based on the bilayer Hubbard model. Two soliton waves, one smaller than the other, formed a double-shelled bubble, shaped much like a chicken's egg, but far larger. The shells were aligned, bordering each other, with an ordered electromagnetic field flowing between them. We use that field to generate artificial momentum and create hot spots along the egg's surface, softening the shell just enough to allow steering."

Temper's satisfied expression returned. "And that's the payback for selling them our second consultation with Holmes. The Admiral Blue is equipped with an egg. They caught up to us in interstellar space because they can travel far faster than we can. Per our contract, they're here to outfit both Paradise and Hellfire with eggs of our own."

Captain Smith straightened. "When should we begin the

retrofits?"

Marcus, Temper, and I exchanged glances. Why did things seem to happen all at once?

Marcus exhaled. "We should explain what's happening to everyone aboard Paradise first. They're confused. Probably a little afraid, too. Let me talk to them, then we can begin the retrofit."

There were nods of agreement, and Marcus transferred back to Paradise.

I refilled my glass, watching the fire flicker against the dark-paneled walls. "What I don't understand is the power requirements for something like this. How do you generate enough energy to sustain a bilayer egg and thin the space around it?"

Temper's eyes glinted with the pleasure of explaining something complex. "Excellent question! It's actually simpler than you might think. We create mirror-bonded quantum packets, using half of them to form the egg. The other half we quantum burrow—via Sullivan's gravity window—into the interior of the sun. And why do we quantum burrow?" He fixed his gaze on me, waiting.

I thought for a moment. "Because we want the quantum packets to collide under the sun's gravitational pressure with as many other particles as possible to generate energy, which then transfers to the mirror-bonded packets in the egg. That energy sustains and drives the egg. Also, we burrow because if the packets were near the sun's surface, they might be jettisoned by solar flares into space, dropping their energy levels to near zero."

Temper nodded approvingly. "Excellent again! I'm glad to see you were paying attention during our talks about Falfsun."

In truth, during those long lectures, I mostly stood there, watching him tend to Falfsun while my mind drifted elsewhere. He spoke about quantum physics with a passion I could never match, and while I often felt lost in his explanations, I must have absorbed something in the process.

I chided him, "And you didn't think I had it in me! But even so, I find it hard to believe that quantum bonding can generate enough energy to maintain an egg large enough to envelop an entire ship."

Temper nodded. "You're right again. It's not enough energy. But remember, the eggs are stable once they're created. And besides, we cheat. The quantum world is strange. Don't go there if you don't have to."

He swirled the whiskey in his glass, letting the firelight catch the amber liquid. "We take the bonded quantum pairs that go into the sun and infect them to create additional bonds. And those infected bonds create more bonds, and before you know it, the whole sun is infected. They behave like a virus spreading through a body. We infect the entire sun with our quantum packets. Can you imagine how much power that generates?"

I sat back, trying to grasp the sheer scale of what he was saying. "And that actually works?"

Temper's smile was edged with a hint of amusement. "Here's the best part," he said, lowering his voice slightly, as if sharing some forbidden secret. "Once the bonded pairs are in place, you don't need to use any more energy to use more energy. You just have to possess it."

I stared at him. The concept unraveled in my head, impossibly vast yet somehow logical in the warped, unpredictable framework of quantum mechanics. Energy requiring only possession to be wielded. It was the purest form of conservation, but it still felt absurd.

Yet, most things on the quantum level were absurd.

"So we finally did it," I said, leaning forward. "We can finally travel faster than the speed of light."

Captain Smith practically recoiled. His expression tightened. He looked at me like I had just kicked a puppy.

"We don't like to use that term," he said. "Let me explain. First off, nothing can travel faster than light. Not now, not ever, unless we somehow gain the ability to rewrite the laws of the universe. "Secondly," he continued, "'faster than light' is what some people use when they've run out of patience and can't wait centuries for the next exciting thing to happen. It's not a breakthrough; it's a surrender disguised as science. Still, I've seen worse ways to keep the story moving."

His irritation aside, the thought lingered. What else had Carpisma been working on? "Do you think we'll ever be able to change the laws of physics?" I asked.

Captain Smith's mouth twitched, his earlier frustration fading. "I don't see why not. The universe has done it before. If the cosmos itself can evolve, why shouldn't we be able to shape it too?"

I nodded, though the idea hovered just beyond my grasp. "If you don't call it faster than light, then what do you call it?"

Smith leaned back, taking a slow sip of his drink. "We don't travel faster than anything else does, but you're right, we need a term for it. Officially, we move at normal, below-light-speed levels." He set his glass down. "What the egg does is thin the space in front of it and push that excess space behind the ship. Moving space around is perfectly legal. The universe doesn't mind, because it doesn't break any physical laws. When space is pinched and displaced to the rear, the front of the egg shifts closer to the ship's destination."

He held my gaze, making sure I understood. "This is important: it's space that moves, not the egg itself. Imagine standing at home plate, ninety feet from first base. The egg pinches space, shrinking that distance to less than an inch. You don't move, and first base doesn't move, it's the space in between that shifts. So instead of taking five seconds to run to first, it takes less than a millisecond."

After giving me a moment to think he continued, "We refuse to use outlandish double-speak to describe it. That's why we simply call it traveling faster than egg."

I frowned. "You refuse to call it faster than light, but 'faster than egg travel' sounds just as ridiculous."

Smith exhaled, shaking his head slightly. "Neither term makes perfect sense. But one of them doesn't insult the laws of physics."

He glanced at Temper. "Is he always like this? He seems lost."

Temper smirked. "He'll be fine. He just needs time."

I chose to ignore them. They weren't wrong. I did need time. The mechanics of it all swirled in my head, vast and strange.

"You understand all of this?" I asked Temper.

"Of course," he replied.

"And it's all legit? We'll actually be able to travel … faster than an egg?"

"Yes," Temper assured me.

Temper turned to Smith. "How long will the retrofit take?"

"A week per ship," Smith said. "The new components are modular. They just need to be assembled and secured into place."

Temper lifted his glass. "A toast. To a new beginning."

"To a new beginning," we echoed, raising our glasses.

The fire's warmth lingered on my skin as Marcus blinked back into Hellfire's great room. His expression carried both relief and mild amusement.

"They took it better than expected," he said, settling into a chair. "Most are excited about the technological leap. A few skeptics questioned the physics, but the engineering team helped explain the concepts."

Through Paradise's communication feed, reactions filtered in steadily. Lieutenant Chen reported increased activity in the virtual forums as colonists debated the implications. The medical team expressed interest in how faster than egg travel might affect digital consciousness. Jamie Sullivan, our community integration officer, noted a surge in social gatherings across Paradise's simulated environments as people processed the news together.

"Any serious concerns?" I asked.

Marcus shook his head. "Mostly curiosity. Though Professor Zhang wants to organize a lecture series on soliton geometry."

A soft chime interrupted us. Luna's voice came through clear: "Admiral Blue approaching on starboard view."

We accessed the holographic display, watching as the massive ship emerged from the darkness. Its design struck me immediately; unlike anything I'd seen before. The front bowsprit curved downward in an elegant arc, while swept-back wings near the stern completed the profile. The overall effect resembled a bird of prey mid-dive, both beautiful and intimidating.

"Quite something," Temper murmured beside me.

The Admiral Blue's hull gleamed with a subtle blue-gray sheen, its surface unmarked by traditional engine ports or external hardware. The smooth contours spoke of its advanced propulsion system, the egg technology that had allowed it to catch up to us in deep space.

Through the communication feed, I heard gasps and exclamations from Paradise's crew as they caught their first glimpses. Lieutenant Chen's voice carried a note of professional admiration: "Look at those lines, Captain. Pure efficiency in motion."

The ship drew closer, its scale becoming apparent. Twice as large as Paradise, its presence commanded attention. The diving bird silhouette created an impression of contained power, of potential energy waiting to be unleashed.

"Their egg configuration must be incredibly sophisticated," Marcus observed, his eyes tracking the ship's approach. "The field harmonics alone would require..."

"Save the technical analysis for later," I said, smiling at his enthusiasm. "Let's focus on welcoming our visitors first."

The Admiral Blue hung in space beside us, its elegant design a stark contrast to Paradise's more utilitarian silhouette. After finalizing arrangements with Captain Smith, we prepared for something none of us had anticipated: actual physical humans aboard our digital domain.

"They'll be boarding at 0800 tomorrow," I informed my bridge crew. "First contact with flesh-and-blood humans since launch."

Lieutenant Chen looked up from her console. "How will the colonists interact with them?"

"We're setting up video and audio feeds from the workers' suit cameras. Everyone will have access."

The news spread through Paradise. By morning, virtual viewing parties had formed in common areas throughout the ship. The excitement was palpable, rippling through our digital community.

I stood in the cargo bay with Marcus and Temper as the first team of retrofitters arrived. Its massive doors cycled open, revealing six figures in bulky gray spacesuits emblazoned with the Admiral Blue insignia.

"Welcome aboard Paradise," I said through the communication system.

Their team leader, a woman whose nametag read "Reeves," nodded. "Captain. We've got the equipment prepped and ready to begin installation."

The workers moved with practiced efficiency, hauling components inside. One particularly large man bumped against the corridor wall, setting off a minor alarm.

"Goddamn tight-ass corridors," he muttered, his deep voice carrying through the comm system. "Who designed this tin can, a bunch of sardines?"

A wheeze followed his complaint, then a grunt as he adjusted his load.

Marcus glanced at me, eyes wide with amusement.

185

The retrofitters moved to the stern first, where they began assembling the larger of the two soliton rings. Unlike the Admiral Blue's sleek, integrated design, our retrofit required external attachment points. The circular ring, glowing with a subtle blueish-gray luminescence, gradually took shape against Paradise's aluminum hull.

Within hours, the colonists had latched onto the workers' video feeds. Virtual screens appeared throughout the ship, displaying six different perspectives as the crew labored. The commentary was uncensored, raw, and utterly fascinating to our digital population.

"Pass me that coupling wrench, Toot," one worker called to the large man.

He wheezed loudly, reaching for the tool. "It's Thornton, not Toot, you jackass."

The nickname stuck immediately. Across Paradise, colonists gathered to watch "Toot's Channel" as he huffed, puffed, and swore his way through complex technical work. His suit camera bobbed with each labored breath, creating a strangely hypnotic viewing experience.

By evening, Toot had become aware of his audience. "Y'all watching this?" he asked during a break, his breathing raspy through the comm. "Two million ghost people watching me sweat my ass off. That's a hell of a thing."

He paused, then let loose a thunderous fart that echoed through his suit microphone.

"Excuse me, ladies and gentlemen," he said without a hint of embarrassment. "Space food."

The laughter across Paradise was genuine and widespread. Something about his unfiltered humanity resonated with everyone.

Word spread through Paradise faster than Toot's legendary gas. By the evening meal cycle, the retrofit had become something of a spectator sport, with viewing parties organized across all residential sectors.

"Did you see the one they call Toot?" Dr. Zhang asked, settling beside me in the garden cafe. His normally serious demeanor had softened with unexpected delight. "The man's a walking symphony of complaints."

"Hard to miss," I replied, smiling despite myself. "He's certainly making an impression."

Lieutenant Rodriguez joined us, her tray loaded with a virtual feast that would have fed three people in the physical world. One of the joys of digital existence: unlimited indulgence without consequences.

"The engineering team is running a statistical analysis of his colorful vocabulary," she said, stabbing a piece of perfectly rendered steak. "Seven distinct dialects identified so far, plus what we believe are three entirely fabricated curse words."

"My personal favorite," Chen added as she slid into the last seat, "was his fifteen-second diatribe about the 'quantum shit-gibbons' who designed our compression coils."

We all laughed, the sound strange after weeks of tension. Something about these physical humans, with their crude biology and unfiltered emotions, had pierced the melancholy that had settled over Paradise since my identity crisis began.

"They're so... messy," Dr. Zhang observed, his tone almost reverent. "Everything about them. Their suits leak. Their communications crackle. Their bodies make sounds they can't control."

"And yet they're out there, flesh and blood, building the technology that will carry us to the stars," I said, watching Toot's feed as he wrestled with a particularly stubborn coupling. "There's something beautiful in that contradiction."

Chen nodded thoughtfully. "They're a reminder of where we came from. What we were."

"What we still are," I corrected gently. "Just in a different form."

On screen, Toot let loose another creative expletive as the coupling finally gave way, sending him tumbling backward in zero gravity. The laughter that rippled through the mess hall felt cathartic, a momentary release from the existential questions that had haunted us all.

On the second day, the workers began installing the forward ring. The bowsprit extended between Paradise's three prongs, creating a delicate balance of form and function. The smaller ring would generate the inner shell of our egg, creating the critical bilayer structure needed for faster than egg travel.

I joined Temper on the observation deck, watching as Toot and another worker carefully aligned the quantum resonators.

"Look at them," Temper said quietly. "Flesh and blood, doing what we can only simulate."

I nodded. "They're connecting us to something we left behind."

Toot's voice crackled through the speaker. "This quantum shit gives me the creeps. Like trying to nail jelly to a wall."

His partner laughed. "Just follow the blueprint, Toot."

"I am following the blueprint," he wheezed. "But these tolerances are tighter than my ex-wife's purse strings."

Another grunt, followed by a sigh and the unmistakable sound of flatulence.

"Sorry about that," he said to no one in particular. "Quantum physics always gives me gas."

By the third day, Paradise had transformed into an impromptu comedy club. Lieutenant Chen created a virtual drinking game that spread through the ship like wildfire. Every time Toot wheezed: one drink. Every time he complained about quantum mechanics: two drinks. And for his signature digestive symphonies: finish your glass.

"These quantum resonators are giving me heartburn," Toot announced over the comm, triggering a wave of virtual toasts across Paradise.

Marcus sat beside me in the observation lounge, watching the feed. "The other workers are starting to play it up too."

He was right. Reeves had taken to humming old sea shanties while she worked, her clear voice carrying through the comm. Another worker, Johnson, kept telling increasingly outrageous stories about his supposed adventures in deep space.

"And there I was," Johnson proclaimed, "wrestling a space octopus with nothing but a wrench and my winning smile."

"Bullshit," Toot wheezed, followed by his trademark gastric punctuation.

The memes spread faster than Toot's legendary gas. Lieutenant Rodriguez started a virtual gallery showcasing the best ones: Toot's face superimposed on classical paintings, his wheezing synced to popular songs, dramatic readings of his most colorful complaints.

Jamie Sullivan reported that community engagement had reached record levels. "Even the most reserved colonists are joining in," he told me during our daily briefing. "Professor Zhang's quantum physics lecture turned into a drinking game tournament."

On the fourth day, as the final calibrations neared completion, Toot addressed his audience directly. "Listen up, ghost people. You've been mighty entertained by my suffering these past few days." A familiar wheeze. "So I figured I'd give you one last show."

What followed was either the most magnificent or horrifying symphony of bodily sounds ever recorded in space. The other workers fled, laughing and cursing. Reeves's voice cut through the chaos: "Thornton, I swear to God..."

"That's for the history books," Toot declared proudly. "Y'all can tell your digital grandkids you were there for the Great Space Cacophony of '31."

When the retrofit completed, Paradise erupted in celebration. Virtual champagne flowed freely, toasts were made, and Toot's greatest hits played on repeat in every common area. The workers joined us for a final virtual gathering, their helmet cameras providing windows into our world.

"To Paradise," Reeves raised her real coffee mug to our digital glasses. "May she fly straight and true."

"And to Toot," I added, earning a wheezy laugh from the big man himself. "For showing us that humanity, in all its forms, is worth preserving."

On the fifth day of the retrofit, Temper contacted me.

"Can you come over? I need to discuss something. I sent a link for one of the service bots," he said.

I transferred over. On the deck of Hellfire's cargo bay, five service bots stood in a loose circle around Falfsun, occupied by Temper and members of the Admiral Blue. Their postures suggested quiet intensity, the weight of a decision hanging in the air.

Temper gestured toward Captain Smith. "You already know him. The rest are scientists from Carpisma. I've been showing them my progress with Falfsun, and they've made us an offer."

I glanced at the gathered figures, then back at Temper. "Alright. What progress?"

His tone carried a rare edge of excitement. "I've created a stable quantum pick that I use to sort through the quantum foam feeding

Falfsun. The key takeaway? The pick is stable, and it functions within the quantum realm. That's unheard of for something this complex and this large, relatively speaking.

"In exchange for my research, along with our final consultation with the Oracle, Carpisma is offering us access to any future technology that emerges from their studies. What do you think? Should we take the deal?"

I hesitated. "The consultation alone is worth millions. And I assume your quantum pick is priceless. What's the expected return?"

Temper exhaled, his eyes bright with a familiar conviction. "That's the beauty of it. We don't know. This is fundamental research. No guarantees, only possibilities. But isn't that the same gamble we took with faster than egg technology?"

I considered him for a long moment. He had set everything in motion: the ships, the voyage, the technology that had reshaped our understanding of space travel. And yet, here he was, asking for my permission to move forward.

"If you believe it's the right thing to do, Temper, then so do I," I said. "Let's do it."

The agreement was reached. The conversation deepened as Temper and the scientists discussed the nuances of quantum stability, their voices threading through the hum of the service bay. My role was done, yet I lingered, shifting my bot's feet absently as I listened. I understood little of their discussion, but standing with them in the glow of Falfsun, I had the distinct feeling that I was witnessing history unfold.

After an hour of standing with them, I secured my bot back in its pod and transferred back to Paradise. The bridge was a controlled chaos of movement and voices, as instructors from the Admiral Blue walked the crew through the operational procedures for the newly installed control panels for the egg.

"These are your manual overrides," one of the instructors explained, gesturing to the sleek interface. "The rear slide-out will override the auto-dump feature for the aft egg hot spot if you ever need to manually discharge electrical field buildup. Just push and hold this button. The same applies to the ray storm outlets on either side of the ship. You'll likely never need to override them, but the manual controls are here in case the auto feature fails."

I half-listened, my focus drifting, until the instructor shifted to navigation.

"Once you're traveling at egg speed, navigation is useless. You'll understand just how useless once you experience it yourself. But when you exit egg speed, everything will function again: long-range sensors, neural-link communications, navigational stabilizers, and even kinetic dampeners. Hopefully, you'll never find yourself in a situation dire enough to need them, but..."

His voice trailed off, his expression clouding over for a brief moment; perhaps some memory surfacing, something he'd rather not recall. Whatever experience had led him to that thought, it wasn't a pleasant one. He caught himself and continued.

"Above that panel is speed control. You'll want to adjust the speed of your egg gradually until you reach cruising speed. Base egg speed is five hundred and twenty-five thousand miles per second, also known as egg factor one. Beyond that, speeds increase by a geometric expansion of three. Egg one through egg twelve is possible, but anything faster than twelve becomes dangerous due to ship deconstruction.

"You can scale back if needed: half egg, quarter egg, or even sub-egg if necessary. Just remember, increasing speed too quickly can compromise the integrity of your egg. You don't want to crack the shell." He paused. "Does anyone have any questions?"

Crack the shell? This guy was unintentionally hilarious. Unfortunately, I didn't have time to dwell on it. Councilor Mendez called me.

"Captain, can we meet? The congregation has a proposal on the table concerning the future of Paradise."

I blinked into the conference room. Mendez was already waiting. On the side table sat an assortment of pies and cakes, the scent of roasted fruit lingering in the air. I helped myself to a slice of strawberry crumble and took a seat.

"How can I help?" I asked.

Mendez folded his hands, his tone measured. "You and Temper originally commissioned the ships to reach the stellar nurseries in the Orion Nebula, and the colonists agreed to accompany you. But once we arrived, the agreement was that they would be free to take Paradise and leave in search of a suitable planet for colonization.

"Now that faster-than-egg travel is a reality, many on board want to change course. No one sees the point in going to Orion anymore, since the trip to get there will only take days instead of 1,300 years. They also fear that if they wait too long, the best planets near Earth will be claimed by others. They want to leave now, before that happens."

I set my fork down. "How many people feel this way?"

"Most," Mendez admitted, his expression tinged with regret.

I nodded. "I see." And I did. "It was always my goal, and Temper's, to search for nearby exoplanets once we reached the stellar nurseries. That's why we built the Arks."

"Exactly. Thank you for understanding."

I exhaled, considering the weight of the proposal. "The problem is, I don't think Temper will agree to abandon our original plan. His passion is stellar nucleosynthesis, and the Orion Nebula is the largest nearby nursery. He won't want to go anywhere else."

Mendez leaned forward. "We anticipated that. So, we have a second proposal. If Temper refuses to change course, would you consider splitting the fleet? Paradise could go its own way, and Temper would be free to pursue his research."

I hesitated. The idea wasn't unreasonable, but it felt like a rupture, a divergence from everything we had planned.

"I don't know," I admitted. "It's possible, I guess. Let me talk to him first. He's tied up with the Admiral Blue's scientists right now. Give me a few days?"

Mendez gave a relieved nod. "Of course. I'll let everyone know."

I walked the less traveled driftways home, giving myself some time to think. Mendez's proposal seemed to follow me: changing destinations, splitting the fleet. The very idea left me numb. Finally, I called Temper.

"Are you done talking, or are you still boring the scientists? We need to talk."

"We just wrapped up," Temper said. "They have my research now, so I'm free. You want to come over?"

"I'm on my way."

I transferred to Temper's great room, where the fire burned low in the hearth, casting soft shadows against the aged wood paneling. I poured us both a drink, settling into the warmth, the quiet, the simple comfort of whiskey shared between friends. It was idyllic. Would it soon be ending?

I didn't know how to begin, but directness felt best.

"I met with Councilor Mendez," I said. "Most of the people on board Paradise want to abandon the trip to Orion and take the ship in search of an exoplanet to colonize. He asked if we're open to it."

Temper stiffened. "I hope you told him no. Our ships, our rules. I hope you made that clear. We're going to Orion."

"I told him I'd talk to you."

He exhaled sharply, agitation creeping into his expression. "Is that what you want?"

"Not really. I want us to stay together. But how do we do that when the majority wants to change course? It's two million of them, against the two of us."

"They're our ships!"

"They were built, bought, and paid for by those two million, fare-paying colonists," I reminded him. "They have a right to a say in this."

Temper scoffed. "No, they don't. I spent millions securing the consultation with the Oracle. Without me, the ships wouldn't exist, and the colonists wouldn't be here at all."

The fire crackled, filling the silence that stretched between us. His frustration was justified: this was his dream, his lifelong pursuit, and now that pursuit was being threatened. Whatever his decision was, I'd back him. It was the least I owed him.

"I'll let Mendez know our decision," I said finally. "Is it all or nothing? Do you see any room for compromise?"

"Not right now," Temper admitted. "Let's see how they respond first. If push comes to shove, we have no leverage over two million. Ownership means nothing if we can't enforce it. See what you can do. And thanks for this. I don't think I'd have the patience to sit down and talk with them. I wouldn't be able to control my anger."

"I'll let you know how it turns out."

I transferred back to Paradise to meet Mendez. I tried to put a positive spin on the news, but he wasn't convinced.

"We had hoped for better," he said. "I'll tell the rest of the congregation. They'll demand a vote. There's little I can do to stop it if they choose to leave. If you have anything, or know anyone, that could help make your case, now would be the time to present it."

I spent the night cycling through Paradise's systems, ensuring everything functioned properly after the retrofit. The crew's excited chatter about faster-than-egg travel filled the channels, punctuated by Toot's occasional complaints about his aching back. By morning, news of the congregation's proposal had spread through the ship.

Lieutenant Chen approached me on the bridge, her voice lowered. "Captain, the colonists are organizing discussion forums in every district. They're calling it 'The Great Debate.'"

I nodded. "Let them talk. It's their future too."

Throughout the morning, I monitored the discussions from my station. The virtual forums overflowed with colonists presenting arguments for both sides. Those favoring the original mission spoke of scientific discovery, of witnessing the birth of stars firsthand. The opposition countered with practical concerns about finding a habitable world before the best options near Earth were claimed.

"Why chase stars when we could be building our new home?" argued one woman, animated with conviction. "Every day we delay is another day someone else might claim the perfect planet."

"The Orion Nebula could contain young Earth-like planets still forming," countered a scientist. "We could witness planetary evolution in real-time, something no human has ever seen."

I transferred to the main assembly hall where Councilor Mendez had organized the central debate. The virtual space had been transformed to resemble an ancient Greek amphitheater, with stone benches curving upward from a central speaking platform. Nearly half a million colonists had gathered, filling every available space.

Temper arrived last, materializing beside me with a scowl. "This is ridiculous."

"Just listen," I whispered. "They deserve to be heard."

Mendez took the central platform. "Today we discuss our future course. Do we continue to Orion as originally planned, or do we seek a habitable exoplanet closer to Earth?"

A woman stood, dressed in agricultural work clothes. "I joined this mission to build something real. A farm under alien skies, crops growing in new soil. Why waste any more time when we could be planting our first harvest?"

Murmurs of agreement rippled through the crowd.

An astronomer rose next. "The Orion Nebula contains the secrets of stellar formation. We could make discoveries that would benefit humanity for generations."

"Discoveries won't matter if Earth claims all viable planets while we're stargazing," someone shouted from the back.

The debate grew heated. I watched Temper's face darken with each argument against our original mission. When Mendez finally invited him to speak, he stepped forward with the tightly controlled fury I recognized from our earlier conversation.

"I understand your concerns," he began, his voice surprisingly measured. "But you're missing the bigger picture. The Orion Nebula isn't just a scientific curiosity. It's a stellar nursery containing thousands of forming planetary systems."

He gestured upward, and the amphitheater's ceiling transformed into a sweeping view of the nebula, clouds of gas and dust illuminated by newborn stars.

"We wouldn't just be observing. We'd be identifying infant planets with the potential to support life, planets no one else will see for centuries. Imagine being the first to step foot on a world no human has ever seen, a world still cooling from its formation."

The crowd fell silent, captivated by the imagery and Temper's unexpected eloquence.

"Our original mission wasn't about reaching Orion quickly. It was about finding something truly new. Faster-than-egg travel doesn't change that goal. It just means we'll get there sooner."

When he finished, the silence held for several seconds before the discussions erupted again, now with renewed consideration.

I stepped forward next, positioning myself between the factions. "Both sides have valid points. This isn't a simple choice between science and practicality. It's about what kind of future we want to build."

I looked around the amphitheater, meeting as many eyes as I could. "Tomorrow, we'll hold a formal vote. Whatever we decide, we'll decide together."

As the assembly dispersed, Mendez approached us. "You've given them something to think about. The vote will be close."

Temper nodded stiffly. "At least they're considering the original mission now."

I placed a hand on his shoulder. "Whatever happens, we'll find a way forward."

Later, as preparations for the vote began, I wondered what tomorrow would bring. Paradise stood at a crossroads, and for once, I couldn't predict which path we'd take.

I spent the night before the vote walking the driftways of Paradise, listening to the ongoing debates that flowed through every district. Colonists gathered in cafes, parks, and virtual forums, their passionate discussions carrying long into the night. Some recognized me and called out questions, but most were too absorbed in their arguments to notice their captain passing by.

Morning arrived with a strange stillness. The voting stations opened at dawn, and within hours, two million colonists had cast their decisions. I stood on the bridge with Temper as Lieutenant Rodriguez tallied the final numbers.

"The results are in, Captain," she said, her voice carefully neutral. "Eighty-seven percent have voted to change course and search for an exoplanet near Earth."

I glanced at Temper. His face remained impassive, but I could see the muscle in his jaw tightening.

"Thank you, Lieutenant," I said. "Please inform Councilor Mendez that we'll meet with the congregation representatives in one hour."

When Rodriguez left, Temper finally spoke. "Well, that's that."

"I'm sorry," I offered.

He shook his head. "Don't be. It's not your fault. They've made their choice."

"What will you do?"

"Continue to Orion, of course. Nothing's changed for me."

I nodded, having expected nothing less. "I'm going with you."

"I hoped you would." His voice softened. "They'll need a new captain."

The meeting with the congregation representatives was brief and businesslike. They were gracious in victory, expressing gratitude that we'd allowed the vote at all. Mendez outlined their plan: Paradise would begin searching known exoplanets within fifty light-years of

Earth, starting with Luyten B.

"How long will the separation take?" I asked, focusing on practicalities to keep my emotions in check.

Commander Okafor consulted her HoloTab. "Two weeks minimum. We need to transfer colonists wanting to continue on to Orion between ships. The QE-comm transfer will take time, and the retrofit work complicates things."

"How many want to go with Temper?" Mendez asked.

"38,000 have decided to continue on the journey," Okafor responded.

I cleared my throat. "There's also the matter of the thrumans still in hibernation."

The room fell silent. Of the 300,000 thrumans originally on board, 160,000 had been adopted through the Joy of Adoption program. The remaining 140,000 still slept in the server banks.

"What do you propose?" Mendez asked cautiously.

"They should come with me," Temper said before I could answer. "Hellfire has more than enough server capacity."

I studied the faces around the table. No one objected. The thrumans had always been a complicated issue, and I suspected many were relieved to have them transferred elsewhere.

"Agreed," Mendez said. "We'll begin preparations immediately."

The morning after the vote, the transfer began. Commander Okafor organized the process with characteristic efficiency, setting up dedicated transfer stations throughout Paradise. Thirty-eight thousand digital consciousnesses needed sorting, before migrating to Hellfire.

I sat in my small office at home, watching the transfer statistics scroll across my screen. Names and identification numbers flowed by, each representing a soul who'd chosen to continue our original journey. Scientists, explorers, dreamers; people who valued discovery over security.

A gentle chime announced Temper's call. "How's it going?"

"Smoothly." I gestured at the screen. "Okafor's team is handling it well."

"Good. I'm in Hellfire's Neural Nexus if you need me."

"Will do." I nodded.

I left home and wandered through the driftways. Paradise felt different already, emptier, conversations more subdued. The enormity of what we were doing settled over me with each step.

Entering the bridge, I joined Commander Okafor near the main display. "The crew has been talking," she said quietly. "They'd like me to take command of Paradise."

"I can't think of anyone better suited for the job."

Her eyes, the color of wet slate, studied me carefully. "Are you certain about this, Captain? There's still time to change your mind."

"I'm certain." I smiled, feeling a surprising peace with the decision. "Paradise needs a captain who believes in its new mission. That's you, not me."

She nodded, accepting the responsibility with characteristic grace. "We'll continue the work you started. Just in a different direction."

Later that day, I supervised the thruman transfer. The hibernation chambers glowed with soft white light as technicians prepared the 140,000 sleeping consciousnesses for transport. Marcus stood beside me, watching the process with solemn eyes.

"Will they wake up on Hellfire?" he asked.

"Some will," I answered. "When we reach Orion, we'll need their help."

"Like how you woke me up."

"Exactly like that."

The technicians worked methodically, transferring each thruman's neural pattern through the QE-comm link to Hellfire's waiting servers. Unlike the colonists, the thrumans wouldn't experience the transition. They would simply continue their dreamless sleep, unaware that their digital home had changed.

As evening approached, I walked the emptying driftways of Paradise one last time. Tomorrow would bring the formal farewell ceremony but tonight was for quiet goodbyes. I remembered the day I first took command, how overwhelming the responsibility had felt.

In the hydroponics bay, I found Lieutenant Rodriguez tending to a small potted tree. "A parting gift," she explained, offering it to me. "An olive sapling. For peace and new beginnings."

I accepted it gratefully, touched by the gesture. "Thank you. I'll plant it on Hellfire."

She smiled, her eyes bright with unshed tears. "Safe travels, Captain."

One by one, I sought out each member of my bridge crew, exchanging private farewells. Some were professional, others emotional. All carried the weight of finality. These people had been my family for years, and tomorrow we would part ways, perhaps forever.

I stood in Paradise's transfer chamber for the last time, watching the final status updates scroll across my display. The olive sapling Lieutenant Rodriguez had given me sat carefully packed in my virtual inventory, ready for the journey.

"All thirty-eight thousand colonists have transferred successfully," Captain Okafor confirmed, her voice carrying its usual steady authority. "No corrupted data, no fragmentation. Hellfire's servers received everyone intact."

"Thank you, Maya." The use of her first name felt right in this moment. "Take care of them."

She nodded, her close-cropped silver hair catching the soft glow of the chamber's displays. "We will. Are you ready?"

I took one final look around the transfer chamber, memorizing its curved walls, the gentle hum of machinery, the faint scent of ozone that always accompanied quantum operations. "I'm ready."

Okafor's fingers moved across the control panel with practiced precision. "Initiating transfer sequence. Good luck, Go."

The familiar sensation of transfer began, but this time felt different. The QE-comm link between ships created a peculiar stretching sensation, as if my consciousness existed in two places at once. I felt Paradise's familiar digital embrace begin to fade while Hellfire's servers reached out to welcome me.

Time seemed to pause. For an infinite moment, I existed between ships, my awareness split across the quantum bridge connecting them. Paradise's warmth lingered on one side, Hellfire's cooler, more clinical presence waited on the other. The sensation wasn't uncomfortable, just profoundly strange.

Then, with a subtle shift, I felt myself settle into Hellfire's DNA-based servers. The transfer completed, clean and precise. Opening my eyes, I found myself in Hellfire's reception chamber, its surfaces gleaming with the same subtle bioluminescence I remembered from my previous visits.

Temper's voice came through the ship's comm system. "Transfer successful. Welcome aboard, Go."

I straightened, already feeling the different rhythms of this ship, its unique digital heartbeat. "Good to be here, Captain."

"Ready to make history?"

I smiled, reaching into my inventory for the olive sapling. It would need a proper home here. "Ready as I'll ever be."

After settling into Hellfire, I spent the next few days helping Marcus adjust to our new quarters while the Admiral Blue completed its retrofits. The familiar rumble of construction work vibrated through the hull, a constant reminder of the changes ahead.

A message from Captain Smith summoned us to Hellfire's conference room. I found Temper already there, studying readouts on the wall displays. Captain Okafor arrived moments later, her slate-colored eyes taking in the room's occupants with careful assessment.

Captain Smith and Luna Dawn materialized in their designated chairs, their holograms crisp and detailed. Smith's usually jovial expression was replaced by something grimmer.

"Thank you for coming," he said, his voice carrying none of its usual warmth. "We're departing within the hour, but there's something you need to know."

Luna Dawn placed a data crystal on the conference table. "Earth has changed dramatically in the last twenty years," she said. "The Atlantic algae colonies have collapsed."

"The entire ecosystem?" Temper leaned forward.

"Nearly total failure," Smith confirmed. "But that's not why we called this meeting. There's a bounty on your Arks."

My hand instinctively tightened on the edge of the table. The Ark's biological data represented Earth's entire genetic legacy. Every species, every strand of DNA, preserved in our servers.

"How much?" Okafor asked quietly.

"Enough to buy a small continent," Luna replied. "The biological information has become invaluable since the collapse. Every corporation with deep-sea interests wants it."

"We've intercepted three separate hunting parties already," Smith added. "They're getting bolder, better equipped. They have faster than egg capabilities now."

Temper's expression hardened. "They won't find us easy prey."

"No, but they'll try." Smith's hologram flickered slightly. "Exercise extreme caution in your travels. Trust no one who approaches, no matter their story."

I thought of the two million souls aboard Paradise, the sleeping thrumans in our servers. "We'll take every precaution," I promised.

"Good." Smith stood, his hologram rippling with the movement. "We need to go. The retrofit's complete, and we have our own mission to complete."

We exchanged final farewells, watching as their holograms faded from view. The conference room felt colder somehow, weighted with this new knowledge.

"I'll increase Paradise's security protocols," Okafor said, already moving to leave. "And run additional encryption on our quantum signatures."

I looked at Temper, seeing my own concern reflected in his eyes. The journey ahead had just become considerably more complicated.

The last status reports flashed across the conference room display, confirming what we already knew: the Admiral Blue had departed, taking with it our last direct connection to Earth's governing bodies. I sat with Temper in silence for several minutes, processing Captain Smith's warning about the bounty hunters.

"We should tell the others," I finally said.

Temper nodded. "At tomorrow's farewell gathering. We'll get together with Captain Okafor beforehand to make sure she agrees. No sense in dampening tonight's preparations."

We transferred over to Paradise one last time for the farewell party. It was held in vast rolling fields filled with trees of cedar and fir. Eco-friendly buildings with lush green living walls dotted the landscape. The one exception was the Bradbury building, whose plain brown sandstone and brick facade stood apart from the rest. If buildings could talk, I wondered what Hollywood stories it would tell.

The flying island city of Laputa floated overhead, casting dappled shadows across the celebration grounds. Walking paths made of topaz, diamond, sapphire, and emerald led around the garden. A river flowed through the middle where fizzgigs and porgs splashed and played in the water. In the distance, the snow-capped White Mountains rimmed the horizon. Tables laden with food and drink sat along the paths.

"Merlin outdid himself," Temper said, accepting a glass of champagne from a passing server.

"He should. He's the only architeer coming with us to Orion."

Temper raised an eyebrow. "Really? I thought Banks might join us."

"Decided to stay with Paradise. Said something about prehistoric worlds being his specialty, not stellar nurseries."

The celebration hummed with conversation and laughter but underneath ran a current of melancholy. These were goodbyes that might last forever. Colonists who had lived side by side for years embraced, knowing their paths were diverging across light-years.

I spotted Marcus near the river, deep in conversation with someone I didn't recognize. He caught my eye and waved us over, his expression a mixture of excitement and nervousness.

"Papa," he said as we approached. "There's someone I want you to meet."

The thruman standing beside him was tall and slender, with an observant gaze that seemed to take in everything at once.

"This is Bea," Marcus said, his voice carrying a note I'd never heard before. "Bea Jordan."

"It's an honor to meet you both," she said, extending her hand. "Marcus has told me so much about you."

I shook her hand, momentarily speechless. When had Marcus found time to develop this relationship? More importantly, when had he grown old enough for one?

"Bea works with the Joy of Adoption program," Marcus explained. "She's been helping the newly awakened thrumans adjust."

Temper recovered faster than I did. "A pleasure to meet you, Bea. Will you be joining us on Hellfire?"

"Yes," she answered. "I've volunteered to oversee the thruman integration when we reach Orion."

I finally found my voice. "How long have you two known each other?"

Marcus shuffled his feet. "Three months. We met during my

volunteer work with the younger thrumans."

Three months. A quiet sense of awe mixed with the bittersweet realization of how quickly he was changing.

"I'm glad you'll be with us," I said to Bea, meaning it. "We need good people for the journey ahead."

The evening progressed in a blur of farewells. Maya Okafor found me near the Bradbury building, a glass of wine in her hand.

"Paradise is in good hands with you," I told her.

She smiled. "As is Hellfire with you and Temper." Her expression grew serious. "Take care of each other out there. The universe is vast and mostly empty."

"We will."

We clinked glasses, sealing the promise.

Later, as the celebration wound down, I found Marcus and Bea sitting by the river. They were talking quietly, their heads close together, oblivious to the world around them. I turned away, giving them privacy.

Temper joined me on the emerald path. "Our son has grown up," he said softly.

"When did that happen?"

"While we were busy saving the world, I suppose."

The party was ending, colonists beginning to transfer back to their respective ships. Tomorrow, Paradise and Hellfire would part ways, one seeking a new Earth, the other continuing to Orion's stellar nursery. Both journeys filled with hope and uncertainty.

I watched the final preparations with a strange mixture of emotions. Now, as dawn broke in Terracore, both vessels stood ready for their divergent journeys.

Marcus and Bea had joined me on Paradise's observation deck.

"Did you ever think it would end like this?" Marcus asked, his voice soft. "The mission splitting in two?"

"No," I admitted. "But I've learned that journeys rarely follow their intended paths."

The final status updates scrolled across my tablet. Thirty-eight thousand colonists safely transferred to Hellfire. One hundred forty thousand thrumans in hibernation. All systems operational.

Captain Okafor's voice came through the ship-wide

communication system. "Attention all colonists. Final departure sequence will commence in thirty minutes. All visitors please return to Hellfire."

Marcus squeezed my shoulder. "I'll see you back on Hellfire, Papa."

I nodded, watching him and Bea walk toward the transfer station. My son had grown so much in these past months. The boy I'd adopted was finding his own path, forming his own connections.

Captain Okafor found me still standing at the observation window. "It's time, Go."

"I know." I turned to face her. "Take care of them, Maya."

Her usually stern expression softened. "We will. And you take care of yours."

We clasped hands briefly, the gesture carrying the weight of all we couldn't say. Then I walked to the transfer station, took one last look around Paradise, and initiated the sequence.

Back on Hellfire, Temper and I stood on the bridge as Paradise began its departure procedures.

"Hellfire to Paradise," Temper said, his voice steady. "You are clear for departure. Safe travels."

"Paradise to Hellfire," Okafor replied. "Thank you. May the stars guide your journey."

The space between our ships slowly widened. Paradise floated in the void, her presence marked only by the soft glow of running lights against the darkness. Then, they activated the egg. A silver light flared at the aft, spreading forward in a smooth, deliberate sweep until the entire ship was enveloped. The front brightened, pulsing for a heartbeat as the second shell formed.

And then—she was gone.

No sound. No streak of light. No fading trail for our eyes to follow. Just empty space where she had been.

I raised a hand in farewell. "Godspeed, Paradise." I felt a tightness in my chest, knowing that these people had been my crew, my responsibility, my family.

"They'll be all right," Temper said quietly.

"I know." I took a deep breath. "They have a good captain."

Three days later, Temper asked me to join him on the bridge. I blinked there, materializing beside his captain's chair. A small figure stood at the navigation console, her head barely visible above the controls.

"Go, this is the Shiloh Kid," Temper said. "She was adopted by a woman who decided to stay with Paradise. Do I have that right, Shiloh?"

"That's right," Shiloh said, turning to face me. She looked about ten years old, with bright eyes and a serious expression. "My mom didn't see the point in going to a gas cloud."

"But you did?" I asked.

"It's better than being stuck farming on some boring planet."

Temper leaned forward in his chair. "How soon before we're ready to leave?"

"I want to do a final check of our third leg's trajectory. Give me twenty minutes?"

"Of course."

I studied the child navigator, concern rising. "Temper, can I speak to you in private?"

We blinked over to Giese Manor's great room. Instead of the view of mountains and pine trees outside his window, there was now the undulating surface of a sun. Red and orange plasma swirled together, erupting into geysers of gas.

"I see you've adopted a more appropriate Hellfire motif," I said.

"It's cozy, don't you think? Is that what you wanted to talk about?"

"No, it's about Shiloh. Are you really going to let a ten-year-old pilot the Hellfire?"

Temper laughed. "Marcus is right, you are old. Shiloh had the highest scores on the aptitude tests that I gave to over a thousand pilot candidates. She can fly circles around any of them. Don't forget, she's a Thruman with superhuman reflexes. She's good, so don't worry. After we arrive at the nebula and things settle down, I was thinking about asking her to join our new gang of gamers when we go adventuring."

"It won't be the same without the Din and Captain Drake. If you trust her then I guess I do too. But you don't mind if I worry just a little bit anyway, do you?"

"Worry as much as you want, buddy. I won't stop you. Besides, if the ship explodes, you won't have time to worry."

"What? Don't tell me that!"

We blinked back to the bridge. Shiloh was done double-checking her math.

"I'm ready to go to egg speed," she announced, waiting for Temper to give the word to depart.

"Did you close the bay doors?" Temper asked.

Shiloh's face turned red. She punched some buttons on her control panel and slid a knob forward. We felt the bay door locks engage.

"Yes," she said.

Temper raised his arm and pointed forward. "Engage."

A silver light enveloped the ship. The forward cameras adjusted for the increased light, and we watched as the egg formed. It looked like a smooth bore tunnel as the space around us started moving. The stars in front of us bunched together into a small circle. Side cameras showed a dull gray light. Another small circle of stars bunched together behind us.

That puzzled me. "How can we see stars behind us? Aren't we going faster than egg right now?"

Shiloh's eyes never left her control panel as she replied, "You're correct. We're traveling faster than egg. The starlight that you see behind us is actually some of the light from the stars that are in front of us. Starlight is curving around the Hellfire, so in the tunnel it appears like we can see stars to our aft. It's just an optical illusion."

After eight minutes we dropped out of egg speed. The effect of looking through a long, narrow tunnel disappeared, and our normal view returned. It was reassuring to see the stars in all directions again. The tunnel hid so much of the view that it was, for me, claustrophobic. Shiloh opened the bay doors to let the cargo hold dissipate the heat generated by Falfsun. While it did, a crew of observers checked the ship's condition.

"Temperature build-up in the bay was within limits. All other areas of the ship report normal. Let's get ready for the second leg," Temper said.

CHAPTER TWELVE

Hunters

"Closing bay doors," Shiloh announced, her small fingers dancing across the control panel with practiced precision.

Temper raised his arm and pointed forward with the theatrical flair he always brought to these moments. "Engage."

The familiar silver light enveloped us as Hellfire slipped into egg space. I settled back in my chair, watching Shiloh work. For someone who looked like she should be playing with toys instead of piloting an interstellar vessel, her competence was remarkable. Her eyes never left the instruments, constantly scanning readouts and making minute adjustments that kept us perfectly centered in the egg-space corridor.

"Trajectory stable at egg factor seven," she reported, her voice steady. "Estimated arrival at checkpoint in sixteen minutes."

It was magical being stationary inside the egg while space moved around us. Our third leg was routine, almost boring in its predictability. The bridge hummed with quiet efficiency as Shiloh made occasional course corrections. Through the forward float screen, the tunnel of compressed spacetime stretched before us, stars bunched at either end like distant jewels.

I found myself wondering what lay beyond our destination. Past the nebula, past the Orion arm, all the way to the ancient Fossils at the galaxy's edge. The thought was intoxicating.

"There's time for that later," I promised myself. One journey at a time.

"Preparing to drop out of egg speed," Shiloh announced. "Checkpoint arrival in three... two... one..."

The tunnel effect dissolved as we decelerated, stars expanding back to their normal positions across the viewport. The nebula should have dominated our view, a massive cloud of gas and dust waiting to be explored.

Instead, directly in front of us was a debris field. Metal fragments tumbled silently through space, reflecting starlight as they spun. I recognized the distinctive hull plating of a Terran vessel.

"What the—" Temper began.

"Incoming missile!" Shiloh's voice cut through the bridge like a knife. Her hands flew across the controls.

"Evasive maneuvers!" Temper commanded, instantly transforming from casual friend to ship's captain.

Hellfire lurched sideways as Shiloh executed a roll that would have made a combat pilot proud. The missile streaked past our port side, missing by mere meters.

"Multiple ships! They're surrounding us!" Shiloh called out, her young voice tight but controlled. The tactical display lit up with six hostile vessels moving to encircle us.

"I'm calculating a new route!" Temper shouted. He pulled up navigational controls on his command console. "Shiloh, keep dodging that missile. Angle away from the other ships." He hit the ship-wide comm. "Security, report to the service bay for possible boarding."

My stomach dropped as the realization hit me. "We haven't set security up yet," I said. In our haste to depart after the split with Paradise, we'd prioritized navigation and engineering crews. Security had been on tomorrow's agenda.

The tactical float screen showed two vessels moving to block our retreat path while the others maintained firing positions. This was no random encounter, it was a carefully planned ambush.

"I'll get a crew and go," I said, motioning to a crew member to join me. I couldn't stay on the bridge while Hellfire was boarded. If those ships managed to latch onto our hull, someone needed to be ready.

"Go, be careful," Temper called after me. "Don't let them board."

I nodded grimly as I blinked to the cargo bay. "They won't."

"Emergency stations!" Temper's voice boomed through the comm system. His tone had transformed completely, the casual scientist replaced by a seasoned commander. "All hands secure for potential boarding!"

The service bay stretched before me, cavernous and vulnerable. Twelve bots stood idle against the wall, their manipulator arms hanging limp. I slid into the control station for the first one, my consciousness transferring seamlessly into the mechanical body. Beside me, another crew member, Lowell, took control of the second bot.

"We have multiple bogeys closing fast," Temper's voice reported through the comm. "Shiloh's evading, but they've positioned themselves to cut off our retreat."

I raised the bot's manipulator arms, feeling the strange disconnect of controlling a body that wasn't truly mine. The metal fingers responded to my commands with mechanical precision. "Service bay secure, Captain. Two bots active and ready."

The temperature in the bay was already climbing. Falfsun glowed ominously in its containment field, bathing everything in its eerie green-orange light. The heat radiated in visible waves, distorting the air.

"Temperature critical in service bay," Marcus's voice came through the comm. "We have to open the bay doors and cool down!"

"Negative! Keep those doors closed!" Temper ordered immediately.

"But the heat!" Marcus protested. The concern in his voice was palpable.

"We'll have to risk it!" Temper's reply left no room for argument.

I felt the bot's external sensors register the climbing temperature. The metal skin began to warm uncomfortably. "Temper, what's our status?" I called.

"The ships are communicating with each other," Shiloh cut in. "I can tap in."

"Record what they say," Temper commanded. "Record everything!"

Shiloh's voice came back, confident despite the chaos. "Recording. I found the wrecked ship's log." There was a pause, then: "Aah, missile missed us. Impacted in the debris. No explosion though. It must have been a dud."

Two more crew members blinked into the bay, taking control of two more bots. Sophia Turner, a former security officer, and Ethan Carter, an engineer. Their arrival was a relief.

"I don't like this place," Turner said, her bot's head swiveling toward Falfsun. "Can we go stand in front of the server room door? Maybe we can act as a thermal shield to help protect our tardigrade DNA memory servers and the Ark."

"Good thinking," I agreed. We positioned ourselves before the bulkhead doors leading to the server room, creating a metal barrier between Falfsun and our most precious cargo.

"New route calculated. Go to egg speed!" Temper's voice announced.

The familiar silver shimmer enveloped Hellfire. We jumped to egg speed. The service bay lurched slightly, then stabilized. The debris field vanished, replaced by the tunnel effect visible through the holographic displays.

"Go, how's the bay?" Temper asked.

I looked down at the bot's hands. The metal was beginning to glow pink from the heat. "Hot, but intact."

"I think we're secure for now. Can you stay there until we reach our destination? It will only be a few minutes at egg speed."

"Aye, Captain," I replied. "I wish we had our Din crew."

"You and me both. I'll keep you posted."

We attached power saws to our bots' manipulator arms, the best weapons we could improvise on short notice. The whirring blades provided little comfort against the thought of armed boarders, but it was something.

The minutes stretched. Our bots turned from pink to glowing red as we absorbed Falfsun's relentless heat. The temperature readings continued to climb toward critical levels. Sweat would have been pouring down my face if I'd been in my human form. Instead, I watched with detached horror as warning lights flickered across my bot's control panel.

We stood our ground before the server room, four metal sentinels protecting our memory servers and the heart of our ship. The Ark contained everything: Earth's genetic legacy, humanity's collective knowledge, our very reason for existence as digital beings. If we lost the servers, we lost everything.

"All clear," Temper finally announced, his voice steady through the comm system. "We've lost them."

I slumped in relief, the bot's mechanical body mimicking my posture. The metal still glowed an angry red from the heat, but the immediate danger had passed.

"Opening bay doors now," Marcus called out.

The massive doors slid apart. Space rushed in, a silent wave of blessed cold. The temperature gauges began their slow descent from critical levels as the vacuum pulled away Falfsun's excess heat. I watched the bot's external temperature indicators drop from dangerous red to cautionary yellow.

"Permission to check the servers, Captain?" I asked.

"Granted," Temper replied. "Let me know what you find."

We approached the sealed bulkhead doors, our bots' footsteps echoing through the now-cooling bay. Turner's improvised shield strategy had been our only defense against catastrophic failure. If the servers had overheated, we would have lost everything: our memories, our identities, Earth's biological legacy.

The server room doors slid open. Cool blue light washed over us as we entered, a stark contrast to Falfsun's angry glow. The tardigrade DNA memory banks sat undisturbed in their cryptobiotic slumber, their crystalline structures pulsing with stored data. The Ark stood nearby, its containment field stable and uncompromised.

I ran diagnostics, relief washing over me as the results appeared. "All systems nominal. No data corruption detected."

"It's okay. Everything is fine," Turner said, her voice thick with relief.

I turned my bot toward her. "Well done. Your bot shield was a great idea. You saved the Ark."

"Just doing my job, sir," she replied, but I could hear the pride in her voice.

I blinked back to the bridge. The transition from a bot always left me momentarily disoriented, like waking from a vivid dream.

"How are we looking?" I asked Temper as I regained my bearings.

"We're secure for now. Shiloh plotted us a beautiful course deeper into the nebula. No signs of pursuit."

I moved to the forward holographic displays and froze. I had glimpsed the nebula during our firefight and later through the bay doors, but nothing could have prepared me for the full panorama now spread before us.

The Orion Trapezium stretched across the entire display, vast swaths of glowing green gas interwoven with ribbons of orange-red. Protostars hung like luminous jewels among brown dwarfs and break-away stars, their thick accretion disks spinning slowly in cosmic patience. Eclipsing binaries circled each other in an intricate gravitational dance of give and take.

I was used to seeing distant, twinkling stars at night from Earth. Inside the Trapezium, the view was up close and intimate. Stars weren't distant pinpricks but living, breathing entities with presence and personality. Their light didn't flicker through atmosphere but blazed with unfiltered intensity.

"Wow," was all I could say.

Temper stood beside me, his face bathed in the nebula's glow. "Worth the trip?"

"Absolutely." I couldn't tear my eyes away from the spectacle.

Stellar nurseries dotted the nebula, cosmic cradles where new stars were being born even as we watched. The sheer scale was humbling. Our journey had crossed 1,300 light years, yet we were merely visitors at the threshold of this vast stellar cathedral.

"We're just a grain of dust in this vast nebula," Temper said, voicing my thoughts. "Whoever attacked us will never be able to find us in here."

The reality of our situation began to settle in. We had made it to Orion, achieved what humans had dreamed of for centuries. Yet our arrival had been marked by violence and danger. Someone had known our route, had waited to ambush us. The wreckage we'd encountered suggested we weren't their first victims.

"So what's our next move, Captain?" I asked.

Temper's eyes reflected the dance of newborn stars. "We stay put for now. I'll search for a suitable spot for Falfsun. Once I find it, we'll move there as inconspicuously as we can and establish a stable orbit. In the meantime, let's try and figure out what just happened."

I stared at the conference room table, my thoughts racing as fast as Hellfire had fled through egg space. We'd escaped the ambush by the skin of our teeth, but my relief was quickly giving way to a deeper concern. Paradise was out there somewhere, unaware of the danger.

"Let's get started," Temper said, taking his place at the head of the table.

I settled into the chair to his right, assuming my position as first mate without fanfare. Marcus sat across from me, his eyes still wide with excitement from our narrow escape. Shiloh, looking impossibly small in her adult-sized chair, had her feet dangling above the floor. Merlin completed our group, his fingers absently tapping on the table's surface.

Temper leaned forward. "Shiloh, you took first action during our skirmish with the unknown ships. Why don't you lead off our meeting and tell us what you did."

Shiloh straightened in her seat, her professional demeanor at odds with her youthful appearance. "Besides dodging and weaving away from the other ships and their missile attack attempt, I recorded their ship-to-ship conversations. And I was also able to download the ship's logs from the disabled ship in the debris field."

"What did they say?" Temper asked her.

"Ship-to-ship they said, and I quote, 'Where's Paradise? Boar and Vulture, stay behind and hit Paradise when it drops out of egg. Everyone else surround the Hellfire and prepare to grapple.' unquote." Shiloh's voice remained steady as she continued. "The rest is general chatter between ships about coordinating their efforts to capture us."

My stomach tightened at the mention of Paradise. They were hunting both ships.

"Do we know who was talking?" Temper asked.

"The one giving the orders called himself Hawthorne. He's captain of the bounty hunter ship, Devilstar."

"Do we know for certain they were bounty hunters?" Temper glanced around the table.

Merlin nodded. "We do from the wrecked ship's log. That ship's name was the Nemo and it, too, was a bounty hunter. They were there waiting for Paradise and Hellfire to appear when a fight broke out between ships." He paused, pulling up the data on his console. "From the last hour of entries, it appears they were having a disagreement about how much money everyone should get when the Devilstar betrayed and attacked the Nemo. At least, that's what the captain of the Nemo recorded in his last log entry."

"But why would they want us?" Merlin continued, frowning. "We're not optimally designed for egg travel. We were retrofitted, and the ships aren't worth much to anyone who isn't digital."

Temper's expression darkened. "They didn't want us. Captain Smith warned us that there is a bounty on the arks. None of us expected to be attacked so soon."

The room fell silent. I recalled Captain Smith's warning, but I hadn't fully appreciated the implications until now.

"Rare metals are a dime a dozen out here," Temper continued, "so the ships' materials are useless to them. But the arks, with their complete set of genomes from all of Earth's multi-cell organisms, are rare. There's a bounty out for them. Old money dynasties back on Earth are in a bidding war over them. They're offering a king's ransom for their capture. I think that's why the missile was a dud. They were trying to disable us, not destroy us."

"They can't put a bounty on us, that's illegal," I protested, though even as I said it, I knew how naive it sounded.

"Since when has that ever stopped the rich from doing what they want to do?" Merlin asked, his voice tinged with cynicism.

Temper nodded grimly. "Even on Earth our ark is probably rare. Earth is deep in the throes of the sixth great extinction and Smith told us an ecosystem has collapsed. We have copies of genomes from life that doesn't exist in nature anymore."

The weight of it settled fast. Nobody expected they would come after us so aggressively. Paradise could be flying into a trap. "We have to warn Paradise. They're sitting ducks no matter where they are. Okafor said they were going to Luyten B."

"That's over 1,200 light years from here," Temper said. "Sub-space radios haven't been invented yet, and an old-fashioned radio message would never reach them in time. We'll have to go warn them ourselves."

I locked eyes with Temper. Paradise carried two million souls.

Maya Okafor had taken command after I transferred to Hellfire. The thought of them being ambushed, unaware of the immediate danger, was unbearable.

"How soon can we leave?" I asked.

Two million lives. Paradise was exposed, and we were running out of time. The threat was more real now, bounty hunters closing in, our warning still undelivered. As we weighed our next move, I caught the shift in Temper. A familiar shadow crossed his face, his brow furrowing in that distinctive way I'd come to recognize over our years of friendship.

"What's wrong?" I asked. "The last time you looked like this was at Amy's trial."

Temper sighed, his gaze drifting to the holographic display showing Falfsun glowing in the service bay. "We can't take Falfsun with us. We'd have to do multiple jumps and expose ourselves every time that we stopped. Without Falfsun we can travel in one long jump. It would be safer that way."

The weight behind his words was unmistakable. "But you don't want to leave him behind?" I asked, though I already knew the answer.

"No, I don't." Temper's voice softened. "Listen, I know he'd be fine on his own. I can set it up so he's someplace safe, but still, he's special to me. I've, well, let me think. I can find a spot to hide him. A dark spot within the nebula where he can grow and stay safe. Give me a minute to search for a place."

Temper's fingers danced across the console, scanning the nebula's vast expanse. His relationship with Falfsun had always fascinated me. The miniature sun was more than an experiment to him. It was a creation, almost like a child.

After several minutes of searching, Temper straightened. "We'll go to the base of the Horsehead Nebula. It's a short jump from here and it's dark. I've plotted a course. Let's return to the bridge. Shiloh, close the bay doors."

"Closing bay doors," she responded.

In his now familiar move, Temper raised his arm and pointed forward.

"Engage," he said.

The silver shimmer of egg speed enveloped us briefly before dissipating. When the viewscreen cleared, we found ourselves surrounded by darkness so complete it felt like we'd jumped into a void. The nebula loomed around us, massive columns of gas and dust barely visible in the gloom.

"How are you ever going to find this place again?" I asked, peering into the darkness.

"You mean find Falfsun again? He has a homing beacon. Two people have the keys to find him from anywhere in the galaxy, myself and Captain Smith."

That caught me by surprise. "Captain Smith has a key? Why don't I have a key?" I asked.

"Captain Smith needs a key in order to find us if Carpisma ever has any quantum breakthroughs. According to our contract, he owes us, remember? And you don't need a key. They're too complicated to use. Besides, I have bigger plans for you, buddy."

"Wait," I said, forgetting the seriousness of the moment, "that sounds familiar. You said the same thing back in Bangkok during the water festival. You said, 'I have big plans for you, buddy,' and then you set my hair on fire!"

Temper's lips twitched. "That was an accident."

"I lost an eyebrow!"

"It grew back."

"Tell me what you have planned."

"No. Marcus, meet your dad and I in the bots. Lowell, you too. We're going to move Falfsun. Shiloh, you have the bridge."

I persisted as we headed toward the service bay. "Why won't you tell me your plans?"

Temper winked. "I always have something for you planned."

We blinked into the service bots, the transition from digital to mechanical once again disorienting me momentarily. Marcus joined us, his movements in the bot more fluid than mine due to his thruman origin. Lowell took command of the fourth bot.

We moved into position around Falfsun. The miniature sun pulsed with life, its green-orange surface churning with plasma flares. We changed our bot's hand attachments into circular magnetic field generators about the size of dinner plates.

Temper contacted the bridge, "Okay, I'm going to disconnect Falfsun from his magnetic moorings. Shiloh, once he's free I want you to move the ship down and we'll let Falfsun free float out of the bay. We'll direct him with our bots and create a magnetic field to help keep him on course. Is everyone ready?"

We all confirmed, and Temper gave the command. "Now, Shiloh."

The ship moved down and away from Falfsun. Our arms raised, creating a magnetic field that guided the miniature sun. Falfsun free floated out as expected into the middle of the gas nebula, its eerie light illuminating the darkness around us.

Temper watched silently as it left. Through the bot's visual sensors, I could see his expression. He looked like he was ready to cry.

"He'll be safe there. Look at all the food he has now! He'll be fine," I said, trying to comfort him.

Temper stood motionless, his bot perfectly still. "He's feeding," he said after a long moment. "It's time to go. Shiloh, close the bay doors and prepare for egg speed."

As the massive bay doors began to close, Falfsun's glow grew more distant, a small star adrift in the vast nebula. The doors sealed with a final thud, cutting off our last glimpse of the miniature sun.

We blinked back to the bridge.

"All clear, captain," Shiloh reported.

"Set a course to Luyten B, maximum speed. Engage."

"How long will it take?" I asked.

"Six days," Temper said, his eyes still fixed on the holographic display where Falfsun had been. Then he turned away, shoulders squared, focusing on the mission ahead. Paradise needed us, and we had no time to waste.

I did a quick calculation. Six days would be enough time for my plan.

"Captain, I don't think we should go to Luyten B unprepared. I'd like permission to cannibalize four of the service bots in order to make cluster bots," I said.

Temper swiveled in his chair, fingers steepled beneath his chin. "Cluster bots? Interesting approach."

"I agree. That sounds like an excellent idea," Marcus said, his eyes lighting up with enthusiasm. The boy had taken to engineering with remarkable speed.

"That would drop our service bot total down to eight. Merlin? Shiloh? What do you think?" Temper asked.

Merlin scratched his chin, running mental calculations. "Maintenance won't need more than eight at any one time, unless someone blows a gaping hole in us."

"We can repair the servers with only two bots, so I think it's fine," Shiloh added, her small fingers tapping against the navigation console.

"Alright, permission granted to proceed. Is six days enough time?" Temper said.

I nodded firmly. "It will have to be. Marcus, can you assist me?"

My son's face broke into a wide grin. "Absolutely."

Marcus and I walked the bots for salvage over to the industrial 3D printer in the service bay. The printer wasn't as large as the one on board Paradise. It was purposely smaller to allow extra room for Temper's experiments, but it was still a top-of-the-line model. It should work fine for the task at hand.

First, we warmed up the printer feed. Falfsun's heat would have come in handy for that, but we made do with a makeshift tent constructed of tethers and hull plates normally reserved as emergency plugs.

"Papa, what exactly are cluster bots?" Marcus asked as we positioned two bots with weld attachments next to the feed.

"Think of them as modular units that can work independently or join together for different functions. They're small but powerful when they coordinate."

The tent trapped heat efficiently. Soon the printer hummed to life, its mechanisms ready for our specifications.

I operated the feed while Marcus fed bot parts into it. The feed used a laser-activated, decomposing solution to melt the bots without destroying the integrity of the material. The raw material was then used to 3D print miniature bots varying in size from marbles to softballs with Activ Matter, which gave the bots shape-shifting surfaces.

"Isn't Activ Matter trademarked technology?" Marcus asked, his thruman precision evident in how carefully he handled each component.

"We're borrowing it," I replied with a wink. "Desperate times."

The first batch rolled off the printer line, gleaming spheres that pulsed with potential. I instructed them to roll across the bay floor and stack themselves in the empty bot pods.

"Amazing," Marcus whispered as they moved in perfect synchronization.

Over the next few days, our workshop became a hive of activity. The cluster bots multiplied, each batch more refined than the last. We programmed them to form various configurations: walls for blockades, shields for defense, and guardians with teeth and retractable pincer arms.

"I wish we had time to install a proper firing system," I told Marcus on the fourth day. "We could launch these at any attacking ship."

"We could throw a spear of cluster bots using the service bots," he suggested, his mind working through the problem.

"True, but we'd have to be fairly close to another ship for it to work."

Marcus nodded thoughtfully. "We should collect wreckage if we find another debris field. No sense using perfectly good service bots as raw material when we could pick it up for free."

I smiled at him, proud of his practical thinking. "That's exactly right."

By the sixth day, we had several thousand cluster bots stacked neatly in their storage compartments, ready for deployment. They represented our best chance at defending ourselves and Paradise if we encountered those bounty hunters again.

Temper came to inspect our work, nodding appreciatively at the army of miniature spheres. "These could turn the tide in a confrontation."

"Let's hope we don't need them," I replied, "but if we do, we'll be ready."

I watched our miniature army of cluster bots perform their synchronized dance across the service bay floor as we practiced using them. They moved with perfect precision, these tiny metal spheres we'd created from salvaged parts. Six days of intense work had yielded thousands of them, each programmed to defend Hellfire and, by extension, ourselves.

"They're beautiful," Marcus said, crouching beside me. His eyes tracked their movements with the unique focus only a thruman could maintain.

"They're lethal," I corrected, though I couldn't help smiling at his enthusiasm. "But yes, there's something beautiful about them."

Being digital beings piloting a physical ship created unique challenges and opportunities. Our consciousness existed as complex patterns of data, yet we needed these mechanical extensions to interact with the physical universe. The bots were our hands, our tools, our weapons.

"Dad, watch this." Marcus held up a control tablet and tapped a sequence. Twenty cluster bots separated from the main group, forming a perfect sphere in midair. Another tap, and they flattened into a shield configuration. A third, and they assembled into what looked like a small cannon.

"You've been experimenting," I said, impressed by his ingenuity.

He nodded, thruman pride evident in his posture. "I modified their base programming. They can now form forty-three distinct configurations, each optimized for different scenarios."

I placed my hand on his shoulder, feeling the simulated contact through our digital interface. "You've done incredible work."

"It's different for me," he said suddenly, his voice quieter. "Being a thruman, I mean. I understand machines in a way humans don't. The cluster bots respond to me like they're extensions of myself."

This was something I'd noticed but hadn't mentioned. Marcus possessed an intuitive connection with technology that surpassed even Temper's brilliance. Where we learned through study and practice, Marcus simply knew.

"That's your strength," I told him. "Each of us brings something unique to this crew."

The ship's intercom crackled. "Go and Marcus to the bridge," Temper's voice announced. "We're approaching the coordinates."

We blinked to the bridge, our consciousness transferring instantly through Hellfire's digital infrastructure. Shiloh sat at the navigation console, her small frame barely visible over the controls. The float screen showed the vast emptiness of space.

"Status report," Temper said, settling into his chair.

"We're approaching Luyten B's solar system," Shiloh reported. Her fingers danced across the controls with practiced ease. "I've kept us at ninety-nine percent light speed, but we'll need to decelerate soon."

"Any sign of Paradise?" Temper asked.

Shiloh shook her head. "Nothing on long-range scanners yet. But I've detected unusual radiation patterns consistent with recent egg-speed travel."

"Someone's been here," Merlin concluded, studying the data. "Recently."

"Could be Paradise," I suggested. "Or could be our bounty hunters."

Temper nodded grimly. "Shiloh, take us in slow. Minimal energy signature."

"Aye, Captain." Her movements were fluid and confident as she adjusted our approach vector.

I watched her work, appreciating the skill with which she handled Hellfire. For someone so young, her abilities were remarkable. The ship responded to her commands like a well-trained horse to its rider.

"If we encounter hostiles," Temper said, addressing the entire bridge, "we have new defensive options. Marcus and Go have converted four service bots into thousands of cluster bots. They can form shields, weapons, or distractions as needed."

"They can also infiltrate enemy ships through hull sections," Marcus added. "I've programmed them to target navigation and weapons systems."

Merlin whistled appreciatively. "That's some serious engineering."

"It gives us options," I said. "As digital beings, we have advantages in space combat. We can't be spaced. We don't need life support. And we can think faster than biological opponents."

"We're also vulnerable in ways they aren't," Temper reminded us. "If our servers are destroyed, we die permanently."

I nodded, acknowledging the sobering truth. "Which is why we need every advantage we can get."

The bridge fell silent as we contemplated our situation. 38,000 digital souls aboard a retrofitted colony ship, facing unknown dangers in the void between stars. Yet despite the odds, I felt a strange confidence. Our new bridge crew had come together as a team, each contributing our unique strengths.

"Ten minutes to system entry," Shiloh announced. "All systems nominal."

Temper straightened in his chair. "Battle stations, everyone. Let's find Paradise before anyone else does."

I stood in the cargo bay, surveying our mechanical army. Five thousand six hundred and forty-two cluster bots gleamed under the bay lights, their polished surfaces reflecting my service bot in fractured patterns. Each one contained a fraction of our collective determination, our refusal to be easy prey.

"Final count complete," Marcus announced. "All cluster bots operational and responsive to command protocols."

"How many configurations have you programmed now?" I asked.

"Sixty-seven distinct formations, plus adaptive learning algorithms." He demonstrated by sending a silent command. A hundred bots detached from the main group, flowing together like quicksilver into a perfect defensive dome. "They can improvise based on threat assessment."

Turner and Carter maneuvered their service bots nearby, testing the saw attachments we'd installed on their mechanical hands. The blades whirred with menacing efficiency, designed to protect our most precious cargo: the memory servers and the Ark. Lowell joined us, her own bot equipped with grappling hands instead of blades. She preferred precision over brute force, relying on her judo skills to neutralize threats.

"These should discourage anyone trying to access the server room," Turner said, her bot's movements reflecting her security training. The saw blade hummed through the air in a practiced arc.

"Let's hope we don't need them," Carter added, though his movements suggested he wouldn't mind the opportunity to test his new appendages against real opposition.

Lowell watched their bots work, arms folded. "I'd rather not turn the Ark's protectors into butchers," she said. "There's more than one way to stop an intruder without cutting them to ribbons." She flexed her fingers, eyeing her bot's articulated grip. "Besides, a little leverage and zero-G can do wonders."

Temper's voice filled our communication channel from the Neural Nexus. "All systems functioning at optimal levels. Hull integrity at one hundred percent."

I could almost see him there, seated in that stark chair, his consciousness expanded throughout Hellfire's systems, feeling every circuit and sensor as extensions of himself. The Neural Nexus transformed captaincy from command to communion, making ship and captain one entity.

"Merlin, status report," Temper called through the comm.

"Navigation and communications nominal," he responded from the bridge. "I've modified our scanning protocols to detect the unique radiation signature of Paradise's engines. If they're within ten light-minutes, we'll find them."

"Shiloh?"

"Ready to drop from egg speed on your mark, Captain," came the young navigator's confident reply. "I've plotted seven emergency vectors if we encounter hostiles."

Our little crew had come together remarkably well, each finding their role in this improvised mission. We were few against potentially many, digital consciousness against physical hunters, but we were far from helpless.

"Remember," Temper said to everyone, "we have advantages they don't. We can't suffocate. We don't tire. We think faster than organic brains. And we have cluster bots."

"And we have nothing to lose," Turner added, her voice hardening. "Everything that matters to us is on this ship."

I looked at the service bot that housed my son's consciousness. Marcus had grown so much since I'd adopted him, evolving from a confused child questioning his existence to a confident young engineer who understood his unique capabilities. The challenges of being thruman had become his strengths.

"Five minutes to exit from egg speed," Shiloh announced.

"Everyone to positions," Temper ordered. "Cargo bay team, prepare for possible immediate action."

I felt a strange calm settle over me as we prepared to face whatever waited beyond egg speed. The uncertainty of my own identity seemed less important now. Whether I was the original David Schreiner or his copy no longer defined me. I was Go David, captain, father, first mate, protector of this ship and its precious cargo of digital souls.

"Cluster bots in standby formation," Marcus reported, sending the command that arranged our mechanical army into launch-ready positions.

"Thirty seconds," Shiloh's voice counted down.

I exchanged a final glance with Marcus, our service bots' optical sensors meeting in silent understanding.

"Whatever happens," Temper said to his crew, "we face it together."

CHAPTER THIRTEEN

Paradise Lost

The first glimpse of Luyten B took my breath away. Not because it was beautiful, though it was, in its way, but because of what it represented. We dropped into long-range orbit around the planet, our sensors drinking in data about the world below. Three times larger than Earth, with a rocky crust and core, it was Paradise's most likely destination. The perfect candidate for terraforming, despite its strong magnetic field. In the distance hung Luyten's star, casting everything in a deep crimson glow that made the Hellfire look as though it had been dipped in blood.

"I count multiple ships in our vicinity, Captain," Shiloh announced, her young voice tense with concentration.

My heart sank. Not just one ship, but many. The bounty hunters had arrived before us.

Temper had rejoined the bridge. He remained perfectly still in his command chair, only his eyes moving as he assessed the tactical display. "How many?"

"Seven distinct signatures," Shiloh replied. "Various classes. One appears to be a carrier vessel."

I leaned forward, scanning for the familiar signature of Paradise. "Any sign of our sister ship?"

"Not yet." Shiloh's fingers danced across her console. "I need to get closer for a better scan."

Temper nodded slowly. "Maintain radio silence. I don't want them to know we're here. Search among them for Paradise."

"I'll have to move in closer," Shiloh said, already plotting a course.

"Do it, but drift in slowly and keep our motion natural." Temper's voice was measured, controlled. "Tumble the ship like a rock to make us look like a meteor drifting by. Turner and Lowell, take two service bots into the server room and stand guard. Go and Marcus, get your cluster bots ready for action."

I nodded, catching Marcus's eye. We blinked into the cargo bay, our service bots responding to our neural commands with fluid precision.

The cargo bay felt cavernous without Falfsun. We rolled the cluster bots into the middle of the bay and stacked them into a low, thick column. Turner and Lowell walked by in their bots on their way to the servers, their mechanical movements betraying the tension we all felt.

"How many configurations can we deploy quickly?" I asked Marcus.

"Forty-two combat-ready formations," he replied. "I've prioritized defensive swarms and infiltration patterns."

I felt the subtle shift in Hellfire's movement as Shiloh began her careful approach. We were tumbling now, rotating slowly like a piece of space debris.

"Papa," Marcus said quietly, "what if Paradise isn't here?"

I placed my service bot's hand on his shoulder. "Then we keep looking. We don't leave anyone behind."

The ship's comm system crackled to life. "Go, Marcus," Temper's voice came through. "We're approaching visual range of the closest vessel. Standby for potential deployment."

My consciousness expanded through the ship's systems, connecting to the external cameras. The image that filled my vision made my digital pulse quicken. A massive vessel hung in space before us, its hull bristling with weapon ports. Not Paradise. A hunter ship.

"I'm detecting energy signatures consistent with boarding equipment," Shiloh reported. "They're equipped for capture, not destruction."

"They want the Ark intact," I said. "That's something we can use."

Temper's voice remained steady. "Continue approach, Shiloh. Find Paradise."

As we drifted closer to the assembled fleet, I felt a strange calm settle over me. Whatever came next, we were ready. Our cluster bots stood prepared, our crew positioned, our mission clear. Find Paradise. Protect the Ark. Survive.

I felt like a ghost haunting my own ship as we drifted silently through space. The crimson light from Luyten's star cast everything in blood-red shadows, making the cargo bay feel like the inside of a beating heart. We were all holding our breath, metaphorically speaking, as Shiloh worked her console with practiced precision.

"Searching," Shiloh said, her young face illuminated by the glow of her screens. "None of these ships match Paradise's transceiver signature."

My stomach tightened. We'd come all this way, racing ahead of the bounty hunters, only to find them already here, with no sign of Paradise.

"Now what?" I asked.

Temper's replied. "I don't know. Can we see any detail on the surface of Luyten b?"

"I'd have to go to a lower orbit," Shiloh replied, fingers hovering over her controls.

"No, don't. Hold our present course and motion." Temper leaned back in his chair. "Let's think this through."

Merlin shook his head. "If we go in closer we'll be seen."

"The ships might be friendly," Carter offered, though his voice lacked conviction. "Maybe it's just a coincidence that they're here. Luyten b would be a popular destination choice since it's in the Cinderella zone of habitable planets and it's close to Earth. The other ships might be colonists, like us."

I watched as our slow tumble brought another of the unknown vessels into view. Its silhouette was unmistakably military, bristling with what appeared to be weapon ports.

"And they might be hostile," Carter continued, contradicting himself. "We're being hunted for the Ark. They're probably bounty hunters doing a stake out, hoping that we show up."

The silence that followed felt heavy. Paradise was out there somewhere. Two million souls depending on us finding them before the hunters did.

"We can't drift forever," Temper said finally. "We have to do something. Besides the transceiver, is there another way to find Paradise? Is there some kind of a back channel we haven't considered?"

A memory flickered through my consciousness. Marcus's adoption. The link that had remained active even after we'd left the facility.

"The Joy of Adoption might do," I said, straightening up. "After I adopted Marcus, he had a link to the adoption center for auto-corrections for his weight and height." I turned to our young navigator. "Shiloh, do you still have your link to the center from your time there?"

Shiloh's eyes widened slightly. "I do, but it's not active."

"Do you think you could activate it and ping the adoption center on Paradise?" I pressed. "You know, send out a short burst, planet-wide, saying hello?"

She considered this, her fingers already moving across her console. "I can try. These other ships might intercept it, but they won't know what it means. And if I keep it short enough, they won't know where we are." She looked up. "Captain?"

Temper nodded once. "Try it. Everyone else remain dark."

We waited in tense silence as Shiloh worked. The ship felt frozen in time, each of us barely moving. The red glow from Luyten's star seemed to pulse with my anxiety.

"Signal sent," Shiloh whispered after what felt like hours.

Seconds stretched into minutes. No response.

The sense of dread that had been building in my chest grew heavier. Paradise should be here. The colonists had voted to come to Luyten b. Where were they?

"Maintain course and motion," Temper ordered, his voice unnaturally calm. "Wait until the other hemisphere of the planet comes into view and try again."

My eyes fixed on the slowly rotating planet below. Paradise had to be out there. We just had to find them before the hunters did.

We drifted, caught in the slow, chaotic roll of our controlled tumble, indistinguishable from the countless other pieces of rock drifting around Luyten B. Seven unknown vessels circled the planet, their silhouettes stark against the distant stars. As we let ourselves fall with the motion, silent and unassuming, we listened, waiting for any signal, any stray transmission that might betray their intentions.

"Anything?" I asked.

Shiloh shook her head, her young face tight with concentration. "They're maintaining radio silence for the most part."

Hours crawled by. The ships moved in precise, coordinated patterns, occasionally breaking their silence with brief transmissions. We listened, gathering what intelligence we could.

"Course correction, Delta Wing. Maintain formation Bravo." The transmission crackled through our comms.

"That's the third time the Hercules has issued commands," Temper noted, his voice low. "Seems to be their command vessel."

I nodded. "The others follow without question. Military precision."

We identified them one by one: Hercules, Argo, Chimera, Hydra, Pegasus, Minotaur, and Cerberus. Mythological names for ships hunting mythological prey: digital souls and the genetic legacy of Earth.

"Hercules is approximately twice the size of the others," Merlin reported. "Armor plating. Multiple weapon ports. Its weak point is its ventral hull."

As Luyten B rotated beneath us, the other hemisphere came into view. Shiloh sent another ping through the Joy of Adoption channel, a digital whisper searching for our sister ship.

Nothing.

My shoulders slumped as minutes stretched into an hour with no response. "Where are they?" I whispered, more to myself than anyone else.

Marcus stood beside me, his young face solemn. "They have to be here somewhere, Papa."

The silence in the command center grew heavier until Shiloh finally voiced what we were all thinking.

"Maybe they were captured." Her voice was small, hesitant. "Or maybe Paradise was destroyed."

The words slammed into me—raw, undeniable. I couldn't accept it. Two million souls, gone? The crew who had chosen to follow their dream of a new Earth, erased?

"No," Carter said, but his denial lacked conviction.

"It's possible," Lowell admitted, her voice tight.

I forced myself to think logically. "Paradise wouldn't be around the other planets. Luyten C is too close to its sun for colonization. D and E are too massive. That only leaves B." I gestured toward the planet below. "Maybe they're on the surface and not responding because the adoption center is closed. Everyone could be busy elsewhere."

Temper considered this, then nodded decisively. "Shiloh, take us in closer to the planet. Let's do an instrument search. Keep the planet between us and the other ships as much as possible to hide our movement."

"I'll assist," Merlin offered.

Hellfire moved from its outer, drifting position into a lower planetary orbit. The red world grew larger in our viewports, its surface features becoming clearer: wind swept deserts, mountain ranges, sprawling plains. A world ripe for terraforming.

"Scanning," Shiloh announced, her fingers dancing across her console.

Merlin monitored the other ships. "We can currently be seen by two of them. They might not notice us immediately. They're looking outward, not inward."

"How long for a complete scan?" Temper asked.

"At our current speed and height, eleven hours for a fast scan of the tropics," Merlin replied. "Thirty-six hours for a complete surface scan, but that would bring us into view of all seven ships multiple times."

Temper didn't hesitate. "Do the fast scan. If Paradise is down there, they would likely be in the tropics."

The next eleven hours felt eternal. I paced the bridge, checked on Marcus, monitored the cluster bots, anything to keep my mind occupied. Shiloh called out updates in a steady rhythm.

"Region Juliet negative."

Time crawled.

"Region Kilo negative."

Merlin tracked our visibility. "Three ships can see us now... now two... back to one."

Surprisingly, none of the ships seemed to notice our presence. Perhaps they were focused outward, waiting for new arrivals rather than scanning for ships already in orbit.

Finally, Shiloh delivered the verdict. "Fast scan complete. No sign of Paradise anywhere in the tropical regions."

My heart sank. Where were they?

Temper's expression remained neutral, but I could see the tension in his shoulders. "I don't see any point in scanning the entire surface. They wouldn't land at the poles, and we know they're not in the tropics." He paused. "That leaves the other ships. We'll search them, and if the servers aren't found, we'll travel to the nearest Gliese planet."

He looked around at all of us. "We'll ping their ships for the DNA servers. Maybe Paradise itself is gone, but the servers and the people might still be here somewhere." He turned to Shiloh. "Ping each ship one at a time and let's find out."

Merlin shook his head. "They'll have more time to triangulate the pings if we do them one at a time. It's best to ping them all at once so they can't react before we're done."

Temper nodded. "Shiloh, ping them all simultaneously per Merlin's advice."

Shiloh's fingers flew across her console. Seven pings, short and fast, shot out from Hellfire toward the unknown vessels. We held our breath, waiting.

No response from Paradise.

Instead, the Hercules hailed us immediately. The other ships began moving in our direction with alarming speed.

"They found us," I said, tension tightening my voice. "These guys are good."

"Shiloh, do a scan of each ship using UV light," Temper ordered, his voice steady despite the tension. "Look for signs of any Tardigrade DNA. It will glow and tell if they have the servers or not. Then expand the search outward into space from each ship."

My throat tightened as I watched the bounty hunter vessels

closing in around us. Our precious few minutes were running out.

"Everyone on board help in the search," Temper continued. "In the meantime, I'll talk to whoever is in charge and see what I can find out."

The communication channel crackled to life. Temper squared his shoulders.

"This is Captain Temper Tom of the Hellfire. Who am I talking to?"

A deep voice responded, calm and confident. "This is Captain Tanner Bing of the Hercules. We've been waiting for you, Hellfire."

"Order your ships to maintain their current distance, Captain Bing."

"We'd like to parlay, Captain Temper. Your safety is guaranteed."

Temper's jaw tightened slightly. "My name is Captain Tom, not Captain Temper. Order your ships to stop their advance and we can talk."

"These ships are here for your safety, Captain Tom." Bing's voice was smooth, practiced. "Everyone on this side of the galaxy is out looking for you. The ark you carry is priceless."

On a private channel, Temper spoke to Shiloh. "Be ready to leave here at a moment's notice. Any glow signs of Tardigrade DNA?"

"No signs yet," she replied. "Their ships might be shielded. I'm trying to work around it. We'll be ready to go to egg speed when you give the signal."

Merlin's voice cut in. "The other ships are still moving to surround us, Captain."

Temper returned to the open channel. "Captain Bing, your ships are still moving towards us. Order them to halt. Do you want to talk or not?"

I watched the holographic display, tracking the movement of the enemy vessels. My heart pounded in my digital chest.

"Server spotted," Shiloh suddenly announced. "It's not on any of the ships. It's drifting in a higher orbit."

Hope surged through me. "Paradise?"

"Any signs of life?" Temper asked.

Shiloh shook her head. "No, its temperature signature indicates its power is drained. It's glowing though, so the Tardigrades are still alive. Another piece of server spotted."

Everyone on board Hellfire had joined the search via the shared monitors. Thirty-eight thousand pairs of eyes scanned space for any trace of our sister ship.

"Stand by and keep searching," Temper said privately before addressing Bing again.

Captain Bing's voice filled the bridge. "Our ships are simply moving into a defensive ring around you against possible attack from other ships, should they invade this solar system, Captain Tom. Surely we have the right to defend you and ourselves."

"I don't see any other ships," Temper replied.

"Bounty hunters come and go, searching for you. Eventually they leave when they see that you're not here. We stayed and waited for the Hellfire because we wanted to warn you. We are your friends." Bing's voice carried a practiced sincerity. "You don't know what's been happening in the galaxy since faster than egg speed was invented. There are some very bad people traveling out here now."

"And you're one of the good guys, right? Okay, let's parlay. What do you want?"

Shiloh interrupted on our private channel. "Major debris field found. We're mapping it as fast as possible."

My stomach clenched.

"We want to offer your ship protection, and in return, you give us the ark," Captain Bing explained.

"And if we refuse?" Temper asked.

"Our offer is very generous considering your circumstances, Captain Tom. If we have the ark then the other ships will stop hunting for you. And I will personally guarantee your ship's safety against any attack."

"Progress?" Temper asked Shiloh.

"Cleaning up the data now. Calculating the total mass of debris. Can you buy us another minute?"

Temper nodded. "Captain Bing, I'd like to talk it over with my crew. Can you give us a minute to discuss it?"

"Certainly, captain. I'm a reasonable man."

We waited in tense silence. The enemy ships crept closer, tightening their noose around Hellfire.

"Shiloh, what do you have?" Temper asked.

"Almost done."

"Got it," she finally said. "Transferring information to helm."

Merlin analyzed the incoming data, his face growing grim. "It's an oblong debris field in high planetary orbit. The total mass equals that of the Paradise ship, including the mass of the DNA servers. It appears all of Paradise was destroyed."

"All? Destroyed?" The words fell from my lips.

The universe seemed to collapse around me. Two million souls. Gone. People I had known, laughed with, argued with. People I had sworn to protect.

Chen, who had stayed up late helping me understand the nuances of deep space communication. Okafor, whose laughter was contagious. She turned the ordinary into something unforgettable. Banks, who had created the world where Marcus first found his place.

All gone.

My digital hands trembled. I gripped the console edge to steady myself, the sensation perfectly real despite its simulated nature. Marcus moved beside me, his young face twisted with grief.

"Papa?" His voice was small, uncertain.

I couldn't answer. Rage and sorrow battled within me, both so intense I thought they might tear me apart. I wanted to lash out, to make Captain Bing feel the magnitude of this loss. To make him understand what his kind had taken from us.

Two million people. Erased. For what? For an ark they would never understand how to use?

Turner slammed her fist against the wall. Lowell turned away, her shoulders shaking silently. Carter stood frozen, his face ashen.

Temper's expression remained controlled, but I saw the storm in his eyes. We had failed them. Our friends. Our people. We had arrived too late.

I looked at Temper, my voice breaking as I finally spoke. "What do we do now?"

I forced my breathing to steady, though the simulated sensation did nothing to calm the very real rage building inside me.

Marcus stood close, his young face a mirror of my own devastation. I placed my hand on his shoulder, squeezing gently.

"Everyone take their positions. Wait for my command," Temper said, his voice unnaturally measured.

The bridge crew moved with practiced efficiency, each person sliding into their assigned roles. I caught Temper's eye and saw something cold and calculated there: a controlled fury that chilled me more than any outburst could have.

Temper opened the channel to Hercules again. "Captain Bing, we accept your terms of parlay. We're going to open our service bay doors for boarding."

He switched to our private channel. "Go, assemble your cluster bots. Lowell and Marcus will assist you. The three of you, throw cluster bot spears at the Hercules on my command."

I nodded and blinked to the cargo bay, fingers already working the controls, summoning the swarm we'd prepared. The bots assembled around our service bots. I felt Marcus tense beside me as he accessed his own control interface.

"Excellent decision, Captain. You won't regret it," Captain Bing's voice oozed satisfaction.

Through the holographic display, we watched the Hercules move in slowly, its massive hull dwarfing our service bay as it positioned itself above us. The other ships maintained their formation, a noose tightening around Hellfire.

"I have one question, Captain Bing," Temper said, still in that unnervingly calm voice. "What happened to our sister ship Paradise?"

"We tried our best to protect her but, regrettably, the Paradise couldn't be saved," Captain Bing replied, his tone dripping with false sympathy.

"What happened?" Temper pressed.

"Paradise entered the system but wouldn't parlay. They weren't as smart as you. They refused our offer of protection." Bing paused. "Your ships are fragile, Captain Temper. Paradise fought against our grappling restraints and tore itself apart. They caused their own destruction."

My vision blurred with fury. "There were two million people on board Paradise!" I shouted before I could stop myself. "You killed them all!"

"You're mistaken, Hellfire," Bing responded coolly. "No one was on board that ship except for zombies made by the humans that put them there. Those zombies were not alive. They couldn't feel anything. And just like the zombies on the Paradise, you're not alive either. For all of your fake emotions, none of you are. You're all just sterile programs in a machine, nothing else. We would have saved the servers and the ark on board the Paradise if we could have. We would have put them to better use."

My service bot trembled, responding to the spike in my emotions. I forced myself to steady, to focus.

"The law says otherwise," Temper replied. "The law says that what you did was murder. We know our rights. It was murder, plain and simple."

"The law? All the way out here at Luyten b?" Bing laughed. "Out here, I am the law."

The arrogance in his voice made my digital blood boil. Beside me, Marcus's hands clenched into fists. Lowell's eyes never left her console; her expression hardened into something I'd never seen before.

"Is that what you have planned for us? To murder us?" Temper asked.

"I'm a man of my word, captain. Your ship will be safe."

The other ships took position around us. The Hercules loomed directly above our service bay, casting a shadow over Hellfire's sensors.

I watched Temper's face on the float screen. His expression remained impassive, but I knew him too well. The slight tightening around his eyes, the almost imperceptible tension in his jaw: these were the only signs of the rage burning within him. This wasn't the scattered brilliance of Tom Giese or even the focused intensity I'd grown accustomed to. This was something else entirely. A cold, precise fury channeled into deadly purpose.

I stood beside Marcus and Lowell, hands hovering over my cluster bot controls. The swarm gathered before us, ready to transform into weapons at our command. The Hercules loomed above our service bay, its underbelly exposed like a predator confident in its dominance.

"Go, prepare to attack," Temper said, his voice deadly calm.

Three piles of cluster bots pooled alongside our service bots. Each of us had command over our own pile. My fingers moved with practiced precision, shaping the first spear from the malleable bots. The weapon took form, sleek and deadly, hovering at the ready.

"Ready," I told Temper, my voice tight with controlled anger. My crew. My responsibility.

As I waited for Temper's command, the service bay's silence felt absolute. Beside me, Marcus and Lowell positioned their cluster bots, the swarm hovering in perfect formation. Through our holographic displays, the Hercules loomed above, its massive hull dwarfing our service bay. So close I could see the worn patches where previous battles had scored its armored skin.

"Wait for my signal," Temper said, his voice unnaturally calm through the comm.

Images from Paradise's debris field flashed unbidden through my mind. Two million souls. Gone in an instant. Chen, who had stayed up late helping me understand deep space communication protocols. Okafor, who made everyone feel valued with her quiet attentiveness. Banks, with his matrix worlds that had helped Marcus find his place.

"This is for them," I whispered, my service bot's fingers tightening on the controls.

The Hercules moved closer, its shadow falling across our bay. I imagined Captain Bing on his bridge, smug in his superiority, dismissing us as "zombies" while plotting to strip away the last remnants of Earth's biological legacy. The man who had callously extinguished two million digital lives because they weren't "real" enough to matter.

My rage crystallized into something cold and precise. This wasn't about revenge. It was justice.

"If we fail," Marcus said quietly beside me, "what happens to the thrumans still sleeping? To everyone on board?"

"We won't fail," I promised, though I had no right to make such guarantees.

The first magnetic grapple from the Hercules extended toward our hull, its metal claw resembling a predator's talon. It touched down with a resonating thud that vibrated through our service bots. The bounty hunters had made their move.

"They're latching on," Lowell reported, her voice steady despite the tension.

Through the comm, I heard Temper exhale slowly. When he spoke, his voice carried absolute certainty.

"Now."

The moment stretched between us, balanced on the edge of irrevocable action. In that heartbeat of hesitation, I thought of Amy's questions, waiting for me across the centuries. I thought of Marcus, finding his place among us. I thought of all we stood to lose.

Then I let my rage fly as Temper gave the command.

"Fire!"

I launched my spear at its ventral hull with all the fury burning inside me. It shot upward, a silver streak against the void, and struck the Hercules midship. The impact tore through the hull, metal screaming as it gave way. The massive vessel lurched under the sudden decompression, atmosphere venting into space in a crystalline cloud.

The remaining cluster bots from my spear morphed instantly into a swarm of attack bots, pouring through the breach like metallic insects. They scattered throughout the ship, programmed to destroy everything they touched. If the bounty hunters fought back, the bots would burrow through their suits, punishing resistance with pain.

Marcus launched his spear next, his young face set with determination. His aim struck true, opening another wound in the Hercules' hull. Lowell followed, her spear penetrating the ship's forward section.

We formed new spears and threw again, and again, until our piles dwindled. I kept some bots in reserve, knowing we'd need them for defense. The Hercules convulsed above us, its communication systems gone silent as our swarm ravaged its interior.

"Initiate evasive maneuvers!" Temper ordered.

Shiloh's hands flew across her controls. Hellfire dropped and banked away from the wounded Hercules. The other bounty hunter ships hesitated, caught between helping their flagship and pursuing us. We used their indecision, zigzagging through space with sharp, unpredictable turns.

A 4-G turn to the left sent us careening away from the enemy formation. My body registered the simulated pressure, a perfect recreation of physical sensation. After three seconds, Shiloh executed a brutal 6-G turn right. The Hellfire responded beautifully, lighter and more agile than the lumbering bounty hunter vessels.

"Missiles launched towards us. I count three," Merlin announced, his voice tense but controlled.

"Time to impact?" Temper asked.

"Twenty seconds," Shiloh replied, never taking her eyes from her controls.

"They'll try and take out our egg engines first," Merlin warned.

"Go, cluster your remaining bots outside. Protect the generators," Temper ordered.

I redirected the bots, sending them to form a protective layer around our egg rings. They spread across the hull, creating a second skin of living metal over our most vulnerable systems.

"Shiloh, take us to the debris field," Temper said. "Go, prepare to skim the debris and bring it into the cargo bay."

We continued our erratic course toward the scattered remains of Paradise. My throat tightened at the sight of the wreckage. All those people. All those lives.

As we approached the debris field, I withdrew the cluster bots from the rings and brought them inside. They reformed in the cargo bay, creating a cushion against the impact of the debris we were about to collect.

Shiloh positioned us perfectly, skimming just above the field. The bay door opened, dipping into the debris like a blade, guiding fragments into our hold. The cluster bots rose and fell in waves, catching the pieces as they entered. They resembled a violent sea during a storm, rising to stay atop the growing pile.

We looped around for another pass, the missiles slowly gaining on us despite our maneuvers. Each turn through the debris field gathered more of Paradise's remains. The cluster bots caught and cushioned each piece, preserving what little was left of our sister ship.

The missiles closed the gap with each pass. After our third run, they were too close for another attempt.

"Close the bay doors. Prepare for egg speed," Temper commanded.

The doors sealed shut. Shiloh executed a perfect barrel roll through a narrow gap in the remaining debris. The pursuing missiles couldn't adjust their trajectory fast enough. They slammed into the wreckage, striking with force but failing to detonate, each missile embedding itself uselessly into what remained of Paradise's hull.

Even in death, Paradise had protected us one final time.

I took one final look at the Hercules through our holographic display. The proud vessel now resembled a wounded beast, venting atmosphere and debris into the void. Our cluster bots had torn additional holes in its hull, creating jagged wounds that glowed orange from internal fires. The flames pulsed briefly before dying as they consumed the available oxygen. Small escape pods jettisoned from the crippled ship, scattering like seeds in the wind.

"They're abandoning ship," I said, unable to muster any sympathy for Captain Bing and his crew.

Temper nodded. "Good riddance."

"Captain, the other bounty hunters are regrouping," Shiloh called from her station. Her small hands moved with precise efficiency across her controls. "They'll be on us in thirty seconds."

"Then let's not be here," Temper replied. "Take us to egg speed."

Shiloh accessed her controls with quiet confidence. The Hellfire hummed as energy built around us. A silver light enveloped the ship, wrapping us in its protective embrace. Through our forward float screen, I watched as reality distorted. Stars stretched and bunched together, forming a brilliant tunnel with a concentrated point of light at its distant end.

The ship lurched, and we were gone. The bounty hunters, the debris field, the Luyten system, all vanished in an instant.

Silence fell over the bridge. The immediate danger had passed, but the weight of our loss pressed down on us like a physical force. Two million souls. Gone. My crew. My responsibility.

I slumped into a chair, suddenly exhausted. Marcus stood beside me, his young face streaked with tears. I pulled him close, finding comfort in his presence.

"I should have been there," I whispered. The words tasted like ash.

Turner shook her head. "There was nothing any of us could have done."

"We couldn't have known," Lowell added, her voice hollow. "We couldn't have predicted this."

Carter stared at his hands. "All those people..."

Temper's expression remained controlled, but grief had settled in the lines around his eyes. "We honor them by surviving," he said quietly. "By carrying on the mission."

I nodded, though the words felt inadequate against the magnitude of our loss. Paradise had been more than a ship. It had been a community, a floating city of dreams and aspirations. Now it existed only in our memories.

"We should hold a memorial," I suggested. "When we're safe."

"We will," Temper agreed.

Shiloh turned from her station. "Course is stable. We're clear of pursuit for now."

The crew dispersed slowly, each person seeking solitude to process their grief in their own way. Marcus remained by my side, his presence a silent comfort.

I accessed the cargo bay remotely, viewing the debris we'd managed to salvage from Paradise. Twisted metal, fragments of hull plating, components I couldn't identify, all that remained of our sister ship. The cluster bots had arranged the pieces with surprising care, almost reverently.

"We'll remember them," I promised Marcus, and myself. "Every single one."

The fight was over. We had lost Paradise, but we would always remember it and the people who were our friends.

That night, I walked the empty driftways of Hellfire, unable to face the confines of my quarters. The simulated environment felt hollow, a perfect illusion that couldn't mask the profound emptiness that had opened inside me.

Two million souls.

The number was too large to comprehend, too vast to properly mourn. So my mind fixed instead on individuals; faces, voices, moments shared that would never come again.

Lieutenant Chen, who'd stayed with me through the blackouts, her steady presence an anchor when my identity seemed to fracture. Commander Okafor, whose quiet strength had made her the obvious choice to captain Paradise after our split. Professor Zhang and his quantum lectures that had somehow evolved into drinking games after Toot's influence.

Gone. All gone.

I found myself in a service bot in the server room, standing before the banks of tardigrade DNA memory that housed our digital consciousness. The soft glow bathed my face as I placed my palm against the housing's surface. Inside these lattice-work structures, my mind existed as patterns of energy, my memories preserved in quantum states.

Just like Paradise's servers had held two million souls.

Had they known? In that final moment, had they realized what was happening? Had they felt fear, or pain, or simply... nothing?

"It should have been me," I whispered to the empty room. "I was their captain. I should have been there."

The guilt crashed over me in waves. I had abandoned them to follow Temper, leaving them vulnerable to the bounty hunters' greed. If I had stayed, could I have made a difference? Found another route? Recognized the danger sooner?

The questions circled like vultures, offering no answers, only accusation.

"Papa?"

Marcus stood in the doorway, housed in a similar bot. He moved with careful intent, as if afraid a single word might splinter me.

"You should be resting," I said, steadying the grief before it could speak for me.

"So should you." He moved beside me, placing his hand next to mine on the server bank. "I came to say goodbye to them."

The simple statement broke something inside me. Of course Marcus would think to say goodbye. His emotional intelligence had always surpassed my own.

"I keep seeing their faces," I admitted. "Hearing their voices."

Marcus nodded. "Me too. Lila from the adoption center. She taught me chess." His voice caught. "She was going to show me this special move when we reached Luyten B."

"The Queen's sacrifice," I murmured. "I remember her mentioning it."

We stood in silence, two survivors bearing witness to those we'd lost. After a while, Marcus leaned against my side, his presence both comfort and responsibility.

"What do we do now, Papa?" he asked finally.

I looked over at him, this child who had grown so much, who had faced loss after loss yet remained resilient. Who still looked to me for guidance despite my failures.

"We survive," I said, the words feeling insufficient yet necessary. "We honor them by surviving, by building something from what remains."

It wasn't enough. It would never be enough. But as Marcus nodded, I realized it was a beginning.

CHAPTER FOURTEEN

Finding Home

The familiar jolt as Hellfire burst from egg speed passed through my body as we transitioned back to normal space, and the hum of the engines settled into a gentler rhythm. I waited for my vision to clear as the float screen adjusted to our new surroundings.

"Navigation confirms our position," Shiloh announced. "We've arrived at Falfsun."

The darkness outside was absolute, almost velvet in its density. The nebula's gas clouds blocked most starlight, creating a perfect hiding place. Perfect for us. Perfect for the star Temper had created.

The float screen shifted, revealing a glow in the darkness. What had once been the size of a beach ball now dominated the view, dwarfing our ship with its radiance. Falfsun had grown exponentially, feeding on the nebula gas during our absence. His surface churned with swirling patterns of green and orange, while plasma prominences arced majestically from his north pole.

Temper stood silently beside me, his face bathed in Falfsun's glow. "He's beautiful," he whispered, the words barely audible.

I nodded, unable to tear my eyes away from the spectacle. Falfsun pulsed with energy, each throb sending ripples through the surrounding nebula gas. The darkness retreated from his light, creating a bubble of illumination in the cosmic night.

"The nebula gas has been feeding him," I observed. "Your calculations were correct."

Temper smiled, pride evident in his eyes. "He's feeding on his own now, taking in the gas, converting it to energy, growing stronger."

"Establishing standard orbit," Shiloh reported. "Maintaining safe distance."

Carter cleared his throat. "Should we consider moving him? Now that we've lost Paradise, there's no reason to keep him here."

Temper shook his head immediately. "Moving him would expose us. Any ships searching this sector might detect our energy signature. Here, the nebula masks most of our output."

"And he's grown too large for our containment systems," I added. "The service bay couldn't house him now."

Lowell nodded in agreement. "The nebula provides everything he needs. Better to let him continue growing here, where it's safe."

Safe. The word settled over the bridge. After days of running, fighting, and grieving, safety felt almost foreign. The darkness surrounding us offered protection that no shield system could match. Within this cosmic shroud, we could breathe again.

"We'll stay in orbit for now," Temper decided. "Give the crew some time to rest."

Marcus approached the float screen, his young face illuminated by Falfsun's glow. "It's like we have our own private sun," he murmured, pressing his palm against the hologram.

"A sun that no one else knows exists," Turner added. "Our secret."

I watched as Falfsun's prominence flickered and danced, sending tendrils of plasma into the void. The sight was hypnotic, almost soothing. In this moment of relative peace, I allowed myself to acknowledge the exhaustion that had settled deep in my bones.

Temper placed a hand on my shoulder. "Get some rest, Go. I'll watch over things in the Nexus."

I nodded gratefully. "Wake me if anything changes."

As I turned to leave the bridge, I cast one final glance at Falfsun. His light pushed back the darkness, creating a small pocket of brilliance in the vast emptiness. Perhaps that was all any of us could hope for: to carve out our own space, however temporary, in an indifferent universe.

I left the bridge with Falfsun's glow still warming my vision, his pulsing light a stark contrast to the hollowness inside me. Sleep came in fitful bursts that night, my dreams filled with faces I'd never see again: Chen's animated expressions as she explained complex communications protocols, Okafor's steady presence during crisis meetings, the thousands of colonists who had trusted us with their digital lives.

Two days later, Merlin approached me in Hellfire's Stardock Café, his eyes reflecting the same grief we all carried. "Go, I've been working on something. A memorial garden for those we lost."

"Show me," I said, setting aside my untouched coffee.

The matrix space Merlin had created took my breath away. What had once been an empty simulation chamber now stretched into a vast memorial garden unlike anything I'd ever seen. Cherry blossoms from Japan stood beside baobab trees from Africa. Stone cairns from Scotland nestled near intricate Navajo sand paintings preserved under transparent shields. Water features inspired by the Hanging Gardens of Babylon cascaded into pools rimmed with lotus flowers from India.

"I've incorporated elements from every major Earth culture," Merlin explained, leading me through winding paths. "The garden changes with the seasons, cycling through them all."

At the center stood a simple stone circle. From its middle rose a flame that danced with the same green-orange glow as Falfsun himself.

"I've tapped into a tiny fraction of Falfsun's energy," Merlin said. "The flame will never die as long as he burns."

I reached toward the fire, feeling its warmth without heat that would burn. "It's perfect."

Word spread quickly through Hellfire. By the time we gathered for the memorial service the next day, the garden was filled with our remaining crew. Some stood among bamboo groves, others beside desert cacti or Arctic flowers preserved in perpetual bloom. All faces turned toward the eternal flame.

Religious leaders from our crew stepped forward one by one. Rabbi Goldstein recited the Mourner's Kaddish, his voice steady despite the tears on his cheeks. Imam Farooq offered prayers from the Quran, while Father Rodriguez spoke of resurrection and hope. A

Buddhist monk led us in meditation, and representatives from a dozen other faiths added their blessings.

When the formal ceremonies concluded, personal remembrances began. Turner stepped forward first, her usually stern face softened with grief.

"Commander Okafor taught me what true leadership means," she said. "Not just giving orders but caring for those under your command. The night before their departure, she checked on every security team personally. She knew all our names."

Others followed. Chen's laugh echoed in my memory as her communications team recalled her terrible jokes during tense situations. The way she'd snort when truly amused, unself-conscious and genuine.

Marcus surprised me by stepping forward, his young face solemn. "In the adoption center, while I was still young, Lila taught me how to play chess. Darryl helped me build my first robot. They deserved to live their lives."

The garden fell silent as we absorbed his words. A child mourning children. Some of the cruelest losses among millions.

Merlin nodded to the musicians, and the opening notes of "Whispers in the Breeze" filled the air. The song had been written decades ago, but its message of transience and memory felt painfully relevant. Our voices joined together, some strong, others barely audible through tears.

"We're whispers in the breeze, shadows in the light,

Dancing for a moment, then melting into night..."

As the final notes faded, I stepped forward. "Let us take a moment of silence for the two million souls who traveled with us from Earth, who trusted us with their journey to the stars."

The garden grew still. Only the eternal flame moved, dancing in shades of green and orange. In that silence, I felt the weight of those lost lives; each one a universe of memories, hopes, and dreams. Each one irreplaceable.

The garden emptied slowly, mourners drifting away in pairs or small groups, their conversations hushed like the rustle of leaves. I remained by the eternal flame, watching its dance, mesmerized by the way it mirrored Falfsun's unique signature. Green flames licked upward before dissolving into wisps of orange that spiraled into nothingness.

"They're gone," I whispered to the empty air. "All of them."

The weight of those words settled over me. Paradise destroyed. Two million souls extinguished. The magnitude of the loss felt impossible to comprehend, yet I had no choice but to face it.

When I finally returned to the echoed environment of my recreated cottage, I found the familiar stone walls offered little comfort. I built a fire in the hearth, not for warmth but for company, and sat watching the mundane yellow-orange flames. They lacked Falfsun's eerie green glow but provided their own simple solace.

A knock at the door pulled me from my thoughts.

"Come in," I called, not bothering to rise.

Temper entered, ducking slightly through the doorframe. He carried two glasses and a bottle of amber liquid.

"Thought you might need this," he said, setting the glasses on the coffee table. The liquid glowed like honey in the firelight as he poured. "Collector's whiskey. Been saving it."

I accepted the glass, letting the smoky aroma fill my senses before taking a sip. The burn felt good, something tangible to focus on besides grief.

Temper settled into the chair opposite mine. "Good service."

"Merlin did well with the garden."

"He did."

We sat in companionable silence, watching the fire. Temper swirled his whiskey, studying it with unusual intensity.

"I'm stepping down as captain," he said finally.

The words hit me. "What?"

"You heard me." He took a long swallow of whiskey. "I'm promoting you to captain of Hellfire."

I stared at him. "That's ridiculous."

"Is it?" He leaned forward. "Go, I'm a scientist. Always have been. I'm cranky with people. I don't have the patience for daily operations."

"And I do?"

"Yes." His certainty was infuriating. "You were born for this."

I laughed, the sound harsh in the quiet room. "Born for it? I wasn't born at all, Temper. I was copied."

"That again?" He rolled his eyes. "I thought we were past this."

"It's not something you just get past."

"Apparently not." He refilled our glasses. "Look, whatever your origin story, you're a natural leader. The crew trusts you."

"They trust you too."

"For the big ideas, sure. For keeping them alive day to day?" He shook his head. "That's you."

I sipped my whiskey, letting the warmth spread through my chest. "Remember Vorgath-IV?"

A smile tugged at Temper's lips. "The toxic jungle world."

"Where everything hunts," I quoted from the adventure game. "You led me through that nightmare."

"That was different. A game. Life's a game with higher stakes." Temper set his glass down with a decisive thunk. "Remember when we got lost in the Rockies? That snowstorm?"

I nodded, memories flooding back. "The compass malfunctioned."

"And you got us back to civilization by following game trails and water sources."

"That was just basic survival."

"That was leadership." Temper's voice softened. "Go, I need to focus on Falfsun. I can't do that and captain the ship."

I stared into the fire, watching the flames dance. "The crew won't accept it."

"They already have. I discussed it with the bridge crew this morning."

My head snapped up. "You what?"

"They agreed unanimously." Temper's expression grew serious. "This isn't a request, Go. It's an order."

The formality in his tone surprised me. In all our years together, Temper had rarely pulled rank.

"Fine," I said finally. "But I want it on record that I think this is a mistake."

"Duly noted, Captain." Temper raised his glass in a mock toast, his eyes crinkling with amusement.

Word spread quickly through Hellfire's driftways. By morning, the crew's reactions were as varied as their backgrounds. Lowell approached me in the mess hall, relief evident in her expression.

"About time," she said. "Temper's brilliant, but he forgets meals exist when he's working."

Carter was more reserved. "Temper's stepping back completely?"

"No," I assured him. "He'll still be making the big decisions. I'm handling daily operations."

Sophia Turner simply nodded when I passed her in the corridor. "Makes sense," she said. "You see the practical angles he misses."

The transfer of command became official three days later. I stood on Hellfire's bridge, feeling the weight of the captain's insignia on my collar as Temper pinned it there. The ceremony was brief but meaningful, a necessary ritual to mark the transition. The applause that followed felt more like encouragement than celebration.

"You've got this," Temper whispered before stepping back.

I nodded, uncertain but committed. That night, I pored over ship schematics and crew rotations until my eyes burned, determined to prove myself worthy of their trust.

Weeks passed as we established ourselves in orbit around Falfsun. The grief for Paradise gradually transformed into determination. We couldn't bring back the lost, but we could honor them by building something meaningful from what remained.

One morning, Merlin burst into my cottage without knocking, his eyes wide with excitement.

"Captain, you need to see this." He paced the small living room, nearly vibrating with energy. "I was cataloging our digital assets, checking what Hellfire contained, and I found something incredible."

I set aside my coffee. "What is it?"

"Worlds. Dozens of them." Merlin's hands moved as he spoke, painting invisible pictures in the air. "Fully realized matrix simulations commissioned by Temper before we left Earth. They've been in storage this whole time, completely untouched."

"What kind of worlds?"

"Everything. Historical recreations, fantasy landscapes, educational environments." Merlin laughed, the sound bright with possibility. "There's even a replica of ancient Alexandria with the Great Library intact. They're masterpieces, Go. Professional-grade matrix environments just waiting to be activated."

I followed him to the central server hub where he'd set up temporary workstations. Float screens displayed thumbnail previews of lush forests, sprawling cities, and impossible landscapes that defied physics.

"I forgot he had these." I said, remembering a conversation with Amy in my distant past. "Temper had commissioned these worlds before we left Ceres One. He must have got distracted by Falfsun and forgot about them. You know how he gets when he's focused on a project."

I scrolled through the catalog, each world more intricate than the last. "These could change everything for us."

"Exactly." Merlin's voice dropped to a reverent whisper. "We have the chance to build not just a ship, but a civilization."

The next day, I called a community meeting. The memorial garden filled with curious faces as I explained what Merlin had discovered. The excitement was palpable, spreading through the crowd like wildfire.

"We'll need volunteers to help activate and populate these worlds," I announced. "Teams to check for bugs, establish infrastructure, make them livable."

Hands shot up immediately. After months of grief and uncertainty, the prospect of creation rather than survival energized everyone.

Work began immediately. Crews formed organically, each focusing on a different aspect of our expanding digital universe. Merlin led the technical teams, ensuring the worlds functioned properly. Lowell organized historical accuracy committees for the period-specific simulations. Turner established security protocols to prevent digital mishaps.

Even the driftways between worlds received attention. For too long, these virtual corridors had borne the scorch marks of Temper's failed experiments, dark patches where reality had briefly glitched. Volunteer teams scrubbed them clean, replacing the damage with pathways through our new Earth landscapes and cosmic vistas.

"The driftways should invite exploration, not caution," explained Chen, who had taken charge of the beautification efforts. "They're our streets, our commons. They should reflect who we are."

Two weeks into the project, Marcus and Bea requested time at our progress meeting. They arrived with detailed presentations and an enthusiasm that immediately captured everyone's attention.

"The thrumans still in hibernation need more than just worlds to explore," Marcus began. "They need homes, communities, purpose."

Bea nodded, advancing to the next slide. "We're proposing group homes, twenty children per household. Each with dedicated caregivers and educational programs tailored to thruman development patterns."

Their presentation was comprehensive, covering everything from architectural designs to curriculum outlines. They'd thought of details I wouldn't have considered: spaces that accommodated thrumans' unique ways of moving, learning modules that built on their inherent strengths.

"Most importantly," Marcus concluded, "these homes will be integrated throughout our communities, not segregated. Thrumans and humans living side by side, learning from each other."

The proposal passed unanimously. Construction began in the matrix worlds that very afternoon, with teams working around the clock to prepare for our sleeping passengers.

One month later, we gathered in the central hibernation chamber. The first pod hummed as it cycled through its awakening sequence. Inside, a young thruman girl with copper-colored hair opened her eyes for the first time in years.

She blinked, taking in the faces surrounding her. Then, unexpectedly, she smiled.

"Hello," she said, her voice clear despite its long disuse. "Is this Orion?"

I smiled, kneeling beside her pod. "Yes. We're here."

Her eyes widened with wonder, taking in the faces surrounding her. The moment stretched between us, fragile and full of possibility. In her innocent question, I found something I'd been missing since Paradise's destruction: hope.

Hope that life could begin again. That remnants of the past didn't have to weigh me down but could guide me forward.

So, I left the echoes of my English cottage behind, its walls steeped in memories of lives and regrets I no longer wished to carry. In its place, I found solace on a small farm in an untouched stretch of land on one of our newly settled worlds, where the past could finally fade and something new could take root. Three more months passed as we remained hidden, in orbit around Falfsun.

The digital autumn painted the Blue Ridge Mountains in a tapestry of crimson, amber, and gold. I stood on the porch of my farmhouse, watching the morning mist curl around the apple trees that marched in neat rows across the eastern slope. Lucky Star Farm had taken root in my life as naturally as those trees had taken root in the virtual soil.

The name came from Marcus, who'd spotted a shooting star the night we first explored this matrix world. "It's a lucky sign," he'd declared. The name stuck and somehow transformed from whimsy to truth.

I walked down the gravel path toward the orchard, boots crunching on fallen leaves. The scent of apples hung heavy in the air, sweet and slightly fermented where windfalls had begun their slow return to earth. Twenty varieties grew here, from tart Granny Smiths to honeyed Galas. The trees weren't tall, barely reaching my shoulders, but they produced with digital abundance.

Birds called from the woods beyond the orchard. I'd programmed them myself, studying recordings of Carolina chickadees and tufted titmice to get the songs just right. Their chorus accompanied me as I checked the hives nestled at the orchard's edge.

The beehives thrived. Bees hummed between late-blooming asters and the apple trees, their industry a comfort to watch. I lifted a frame from the nearest hive, golden honey gleaming in perfect hexagons. No stings, no protective gear needed in this world, though I'd included both options for authenticity. The honey tasted of apples and wildflowers, complex and rich.

I carried the frame to the barn, its weathered red sides glowing in the morning light. Once a simple structure for storing equipment, I'd converted half of it into a farm store. Shelves lined the walls, stocked with jars of honey, apple butter, and preserves. Baskets of apples sat on tables, organized by variety. The wide plank floors retained their rustic charm, worn smooth by the passage of simulated feet.

The store wouldn't open for another hour. I used the time to arrange a new display of honeycomb frames; each suspended in glass so visitors could see the intricate architecture.

A bell jingled as the door swung open. Bea entered, leading a group of thruman children who spread through the store.

"Sorry we're early," she said, though her smile suggested

otherwise.

"You know you're always welcome." I wiped my hands on a cloth. "How many today?"

"Twelve. New arrivals, just awakened last week."

The children moved with the unmistakable charm of beginners in an unfamiliar dance: awkward, a little clumsy, their steps jerky yet full of eager determination. Each motion was an earnest attempt, their limbs adjusting to the rhythm of their surroundings, sometimes overshooting, sometimes hesitating, but always pressing forward with wide-eyed enthusiasm. Some appeared as young as five, others closer to ten. All shared the same curious intensity, examining everything with unguarded wonder.

"Can we see the bees?" asked a boy with eyes the color of amber.

"After the hayride," I promised.

Outside, Marcus waited with the wagon hitched to our two draft horses. The horses weren't necessary; the wagon could have moved on its own in this digital world. But some traditions deserved preservation, and the children's delight at the massive animals made the extra programming worthwhile.

"All aboard for the scenic tour of Lucky Star Farm," Marcus called, helping the smallest children climb the wooden steps.

I watched them settle onto hay bales, their faces bright with anticipation. Marcus flicked the reins, and the wagon lurched forward toward the orchard path. Their laughter floated back to me, pure and uncomplicated.

Bea stood beside me, her eyes following the wagon. "You've created something special here."

"We all have," I corrected.

She nodded toward the mountains. "Uncle Temper has told us tales about the times when you couldn't wait to explore what was beyond the next ridge."

I smiled, thinking of the countless adventures, the battles, the near-misses that had defined my earlier existence. The thrill of the unknown had driven me then, an insatiable hunger for what lay ahead.

"Adventure has its season," I said. "So does peace."

The wagon disappeared around a bend in the path, but I could still hear the children's voices carried on the breeze. In their joy, I found a different kind of adventure, one measured not in distance traveled but in moments shared.

I walked the driftway to Temper's lab, the path now decorated with constellations that shifted and swirled underfoot. The scorched patches were gone, replaced by this cosmic tapestry that seemed to move with each step. Marcus had helped design this particular section, insisting that anyone visiting Uncle Temper should feel like they were "walking through the stars to reach the sun."

The lab doors slid open with a soft hiss. Inside, the space had transformed from the cluttered workshop I remembered into something resembling a temple to scientific observation. Holographic displays formed a circle around Temper, who sat motionless in the center, his attention fixed on falfsun.

Falfsun continued to grow until it was now larger than Earth's moon. A prominence extending from its north pole had developed additional complexity, branching into three distinct arcs of plasma that quivered and danced.

"You're just in time," Temper said without turning. "Watch this."

A small flare surged from Falfsun's surface, twisting plasma arcs unfurling like tangled filaments. The eruption expanded, charged particles colliding in chaotic bursts, momentarily darkening a patch before the convective currents swallowed it back into the depths.

"Seventeen minutes and forty-three seconds," Temper murmured, making a note on a floating display. "Faster than the last one by nearly two minutes."

I moved closer, careful not to disturb his concentration. "It's beautiful."

"It's alive," Pride softened his voice. "Not alive like us, but alive in its own way. It pulses, flares, shifts. It never stays still, never stops changing."

Around the room, meticulously organized holographic displays showed Falfsun from every angle. Time-lapse recordings documented its growth over months. Charts tracked energy output, magnetic field strength, prominence activity. The level of detail was staggering.

"You've been busy," I observed.

Temper nodded, his eyes never leaving Falfsun. "I've documented every phase of its development. The first magnetic turbulence. The moment its flares began stabilizing. The day its core reached sustained fusion. Even its quantum radiation signatures. I call it 'second light.'"

He gestured to a particularly complex diagram. "I've identified seasonal patterns, cycles of magnetic intensity. Summer, fall, winter. Not driven by orbital mechanics, but by shifts in its deep convective currents. The principle is the same."

"Seasons? On a star?"

"Why not?" Temper smiled. "We're in winter now. Notice the heightened flare activity? By spring, they'll fade, and plasma prominences will surge outward, stretching farther into space."

I studied the nearest display, appreciating the elegant mathematics behind his observations. "The colonists would have loved this."

A shadow passed over his face, brief but unmistakable. "Yes."

We sat in silence for several minutes, watching Falfsun pulse with inner life. The quiet wasn't uncomfortable; we'd known each other too long for that. Eventually, Temper stretched and turned to face me fully.

"How's the farm?" he asked.

"Thriving. The apple harvest was exceptional."

"And Marcus?"

"Teaching the younger thrumans how to ride horses. He has a gift for it."

Temper nodded, satisfied. "Good."

I gestured to his meticulous notes. "You seem content."

"I am." He looked surprised by his own admission. "For the first time in years, perhaps. No deadlines. No committees demanding results. Just pure research, following where curiosity leads."

"No pressure to save humanity?"

"Exactly." He laughed softly. "Just discovery for its own sake. The way science was meant to be."

I watched him turn back to his notes, adding observations with unhurried precision. There was something profoundly peaceful about his movements, a scientist in his element, unburdened by expectation.

"I never thought I'd see the day," I said. "Temper Tom, content with staying in one place."

"Not just any place." He gestured to Falfsun. "I created a star, Go. I'm watching it grow, documenting its life cycle. What could be more fascinating than that?"

The quiet pride in his voice reminded me of farmers I'd known, watching their crops flourish under careful tending. Different fields, same satisfaction.

"Nothing," I agreed. "Nothing at all."

As Temper and I watched Falfsun pulse with inner life, I couldn't help but think of how far we'd come. From desperate fugitives fleeing bounty hunters to settlers creating our own pocket of civilization in this remote corner of space.

"I should head back," I said, rising from my seat. "Merlin's hosting a gathering in his garden tonight."

Temper nodded, his attention already drifting back to his notes. "Tell him I'll try to make it, but—"

"But you'll be too busy watching your sun," I finished with a smile. "I'll save you some cider."

The driftway back seemed shorter somehow, the cosmic pathway beneath my feet shifting from deep blues to warmer ambers as I approached Merlin's sector. The architeer had outdone himself with his memorial garden.

Merlin's garden spanned what felt like acres, though I knew the actual space was an illusion created through clever programming. Stone pathways wound through groves of cherry trees, their branches heavy with pink blossoms that never faded. Streams bubbled over carefully arranged rocks, feeding ponds where koi fish as large as my arm glided beneath lily pads.

As I approached the central pavilion near the eternal flame, voices carried on the evening breeze. The gathering had already begun. Colonists from across our digital worlds had assembled, their conversations creating a pleasant hum beneath the twilight sky.

Merlin stood at the center, gesturing enthusiastically as he explained something to Clara Lowell and Sofia Chen. His legendary sweet tooth was on full display as he balanced a plate of pastries in one hand.

"There he is!" Merlin called, waving me over. "Our illustrious captain, fashionably late as always."

"Acting captain, when needed," I corrected, accepting a glass of cider from a passing server. "Just a simple farmer now."

Ethan Carter laughed from nearby. "A farmer who still attends every council meeting and has opinions on all our infrastructure projects."

"Old habits," I admitted with a shrug.

The conversation flowed easily, moving from recent developments in our matrix worlds to news from the far reaches of known space. Ethan had modified our long-range sensors to pick up transmissions from passing ships, giving us occasional glimpses of the galaxy beyond our sanctuary.

"It's still chaos out there," he reported, his expression somber. "The bounty hunters have only grown bolder. Three commercial vessels attacked last month alone."

"And the Colonial Authority?" I asked.

She shook her head. "Still struggling to establish jurisdiction beyond the core systems. The outer reaches remain lawless."

Silence fell over our group, heavy with the weight of what we'd escaped and what others still faced.

"We made the right choice," Merlin said finally. "Staying here, building something sustainable rather than risking everything."

Murmurs of agreement rippled through the gathering. Our decision to remain in orbit around Falfsun had been controversial at first. But as months turned into years, the wisdom of our choice became increasingly clear.

"The universe will catch up eventually," Bea said, her voice carrying the quiet confidence that had made her such an effective leader of the thruman integration program. "Civilization always expands. Law and order will reach even these distant corners someday."

"And when it does," Clara added, "we'll be ready to rejoin it. On our terms."

I moved to the edge of the pavilion, my eyes drawn to a group of children playing near the largest pond. Marcus stood among them, demonstrating how to skip stones across the water's surface. The thruman children watched with rapt attention, their movements still slightly uncoordinated but improving daily under his patient guidance.

My heart swelled with pride. These children, once forgotten in hibernation chambers, now laughed and played beneath an artificial sky. And Marcus, once uncertain of his place in the world, had found purpose as their teacher and advocate.

The sun was setting as I walked back from Merlin's gathering. The farm's driftway stretched before me, a winding path through apple orchards now heavy with fruit. The digital autumn had painted everything in gold and amber, rich with the promise of harvest.

I paused atop the small rise overlooking Lucky Star Farm. My farm. The white clapboard house with its wide porch. The red barn where visitors gathered for cider tastings. The neat rows of beehives at the orchard's edge. All of it created from nothing but code and imagination, yet somehow more real to me now than the memories of Earth I'd once clung to so desperately.

"Papa!"

Marcus approached, a basket of fresh eggs balanced on his hip. Another anachronism in our digital world. We didn't need to eat, yet we grew food, cooked meals, gathered around tables to share them. These rituals connected us to our humanity more than any perfect simulation of physical sensation.

"Just taking in the view," I said, as he approached.

We walked together toward the farmhouse, where lights were beginning to glow in the windows. Bea would be there, helping the younger thrumans with their studies. Lowell and Turner might stop by later for chess and conversation. Simple pleasures in a life I had never planned but now couldn't imagine abandoning.

For now, this was enough: the quiet contentment of coming home.

So, we'll sail no more through stellar streams,

Though thrusters burn and dreamers dream.

The words came unbidden to my mind; a poem Merlin had written during our first year here. It had become something of an anthem for us, a recognition of our changed circumstances and chosen path.

For circuits fade, and hulls grow thin,

And wandering hearts must rest within.

As twilight deepened, Falfsun's glow became more pronounced, bathing our sanctuary in a warm, golden light. Not the harsh glare of an old star, but something gentler, more intimate. A light created by one of our own, sustaining the life we'd built together.

The void once called with endless flight,
But dawn arrives, dissolving night.
So, we'll roam no more through galaxies wide,
And let the universe decide.

Leave a Review

Reviews help independent authors like me keep creating stories that matter. If you enjoyed this book, I'd be deeply grateful if you shared your thoughts. Even a sentence makes a difference.

Please consider leaving a review to help others discover this story.

About the Author. David Melde is a ceremonial literary science fiction author and founder of Bright Thread Books, a mythic imprint devoted to transformative, philosophical fiction. His work invites readers into moments of presence, reflection, and quiet disruption. Every book is a living ceremony.

Book Club Questions

"The Go David Chronicles: Book Two - Sanctuary"
Book Club Discussion Questions

Identity and Self

1. Go David struggles with whether he is "real" or just a copy. Have you ever questioned your own authenticity or felt like an impostor in your life? What helped you resolve those feelings?

2. If you could create a memory palace like Amy did for Go David, what would you include in it? What objects, scenes, or experiences would you preserve to represent your essential self?

3. Marcus grows and develops rapidly in the matrix worlds, finding his identity through different historical experiences. Which of the historical periods portrayed (Pleistocene hunters, Bronze Age, Classical Athens, etc.) would you choose to experience, and why?

Loss and Resilience

1. The destruction of Paradise and loss of two million digital souls is a catastrophic event in the novel. How did this moment impact you as a reader? Do you think the characters processed this grief in ways that felt authentic?

2. Go David ultimately finds peace as a farmer after a life of adventure and trauma. What does this transition suggest about finding meaning after loss? Have you experienced a similar shift in your own life priorities?

3. Captain Bing dismisses digital lives as "zombies" without real feeling. Do you think our society makes similar judgments about certain groups of people, dismissing their experiences as less legitimate? How do we determine whose suffering "counts"?

Technology and Humanity

1. The novel presents a future where consciousness exists digitally, separate from biological bodies. If you could transfer your consciousness to a digital form that could potentially live for centuries, would you? What would you gain or lose?

2. Falfsun represents Temper's scientific creation—something both beautiful and potentially dangerous. What "Falfsuns" are we creating in our current world? Do you see more hope or danger in our technological pursuits?

Relationships and Connection

1. "The Go David Chronicles" explores how relationships persist across vast distances and transformations. What's the most meaningful long-distance relationship you've maintained, and how did you keep that connection alive?

2. In the novel, thrumans struggle to find acceptance and understand their place in society. Share a time when you felt like an outsider trying to learn the unwritten rules of a community. How did you navigate that experience?

3. The novel ends with the creation of Lucky Star Farm and a small community that values peace over exploration. Do you find this ending satisfying or disappointing? Does it reflect your own evolving views on what makes a fulfilling life?

4. Many characters in the book choose their families rather than being born into them. How has your definition of "family" evolved throughout your life? Who would you include in your chosen family that might surprise others?